The Fall

Martin Lee

Preface

Michael O'Neill
March 1998

On February 14th, 1942, Michael O'Neill died.

Now, here he was sitting in the back of a cab, twisting a faded purple scarf around his liver-spotted hands. He saw the eyes of the cabby staring at him in the rear view mirror.

'You ah, you not from here, is it?'

'No.' The finality of the answer seemed to have no effect on the taxi driver.

'Not from here, from where?'

'Good question.' He knew he shouldn't have come. Better to have spent the day in the cool of the hotel, resting. He stared out of the window and watched the buildings of Singapore blur past. An occasional engraved sign caught his eye, the shape of its Chinese characters strangely familiar to him. The roar of a container truck reverberated through the small blue taxi but he took no notice. Everything about this place had changed from before. None of it was the same.

His gaze dropped to the wrinkled, liver-spotted hands holding the purple scarf. It was all so long ago, when he had been young and not so free.

The driver's eyes appeared again in the rear view mirror, followed by the voice. 'You ah, famous or not? Seen your picture in *The Straits Times* this morning, didn't I?'

'Did you?'

'*Diiiiiiiid.*' The taxi driver dragged out the word in a long, singsong exclamation of certainty. 'You actor, right?'

'Right.' Michael wished the man would leave him alone.

'You playing the old man, the mad one, right?'

'Yes, King Lear, the mad one.' He looked out of the window once more, hoping the taxi driver would eventually shut up.

'Wah! Newspaper said you naked in front of all those people, true or not?'

Michael sighed. He was used to these sorts of questions, even in London. Slowly he explained, as he had done in countless interviews across the world. 'In the scene on the heath, Lear loses his mind so it seemed obvious to me he should lose his clothes as well.' It was a well-practiced answer. 'Not in Singapore, though. I will be keeping my clothes on here. Quite a few school children at the performance might be shocked to see an old man's todger.'

'What?'

Michael thought about explaining but he was too tired and too hot and too old. 'Nothing, nothing, just an English phrase.'

The taxi driver seemed happy with the answer. 'You ah, got friend here or not?'

'Yes, I've got friends here.' For the first time Michael O'Neill turned and faced his interrogator. 'They've been here a long time.'

Quietly, he reached out to touch the wreath lying on the plastic seat beside him.

'Nearly there. Road works, building new racecourse. Always jams. Singapore a lovely place when it's finished.' The taxi driver laughed loudly at his own joke. He had told it a thousand times before and it always got a good response from his passengers. This time though, an awkward silence filled the cab until he asked, 'You ah, been in films, right?'

'A few.'

'Saw you on TV, in the war movie. You damn fierce in it.'

As he was talking, the taxi driver suddenly accelerated to a stop in the outside lane and, without indicating, swung sharply right across the oncoming traffic.

The wreath fell on the floor. Michael O'Neill looked down at it, the dead flowers waiting to celebrate the dead. 'You can stop here.'

'But car park is at top of hill.'

'It's okay. I'll walk.'

The taxi driver reached over to his meter and pointed to the amount, $21.30. Michael O'Neill gave him $25.

'You want me to wait? Damn hard to get cab here.'

'No. No, thank you. I don't know how long I'll be.' Without saying goodbye to his new friend, Michael folded the scarf neatly and picked up the wreath from the floor.

The heat hit him like a blast from an open oven as he stepped out of the cab. He stopped there for a moment, feeling every pore in his body open and release every drop of water he had ever drunk. Feeling the heat, hearing the smells, tasting the bitterness in his mouth.

The taxi driver took an age searching for the exact change, waiting for the magic words – 'keep it'. They never came. Michael O'Neill was already walking away. Behind him, he heard the taxi driver put the cab into reverse with a crunch of ragged gears. He took one last glance back and then began to slowly inch his way upwards. The rounded hunch of his back leaning into the slope, caressing it like a snail caresses the ground.

The hill was not very high. The slope of the path was gentle. In his youth, he would not have even noticed. But now, now it was different. These days, being on stage was so exhausting. Each night leaving him drained of everything but the desire to rest his head and sleep. Thank God, his eyes were all right. The rest of him may be going but his eyes still saw everything clearly.

Up above, the concrete memorial dominating the cemetery had become closer and grown bigger. He stopped. 'There's no rush. Take your time. They'll wait. They've always waited,' he said to nobody but himself.

He listened to the odd mixture of sounds that surrounded him. To his left, the banging and hammering of construction. On the wind, he heard the shouts of some strange language. Fragments of sound, fragments of words blown away from mouth and ears and carried, barely heard, past him and down into the valley, never to be heard again.

To his right, the valley ran gently down to the road. A few lonely birds, the smell of grass, the low drone of traffic going nowhere.

He walked upwards, with every step getting nearer to the past. The sun beat down as it had always beaten down. The wind gave a few feeble puffs from the hearth of the earth. The sparse trees barely threw a shadow across his path.

And then he saw them. Long white rows of teeth sticking out of the ground. Each one represented a man he might have known, a friend he might have drunk with, a human being that was no longer human and had no sense of his own being.

They lay in neat rows, aligned as if by the hand of God to cover the broad summit of the hill. Above them towered a giant wing, its columns carved with name upon name of men who had once lived and, perhaps, still lived on, in someone's memory, somewhere.

He looked up in the sky and remembered the planes diving to machine gun him. He heard the whine of the shells. He felt the earth shake with every explosion. He smelt the cordite, the oil, the burning and death in the air. It had been so long ago but for him, at this moment in time, it could have been yesterday. Every sight, sound and smell as clear as words on a script or the lines of a play.

After a short search, he found them lying side by side in the middle of the cemetery. These men who had once breathed the same air as he did and felt the same pain. He sat down opposite their gravestones and rested his weary bones.

BOOK TWO   He realised then he had buried the memories for far too long. It was time to tell the real story of what happened on that hazy February day in 1942. The day he died.

BOOK ONE

Chapter 1

Richard Longhurst.

October 1938.

The country sort of crept up on us. One minute it was a long grey smear hovering above the horizon. Next, it was a thicker, blacker line like a stroke from a piece of Chinese calligraphy. Then, it had a definite green tinge, with an irregular fringed top.

As this was happening, as we were getting closer to this foreign shore, everyone around me was quiet. Eddie, Reg Dwyer, even Serjeant Shelley, all just stared at the approaching coastline.

'Do you want one?' Eddie offered me one of his Capstans. I shook my head.

I looked across at the others, all of them gazing toward the land, all of them with faces marked by the sun, all of them dressed in their tropical khaki, empire soldiers for life.

I leant out over the gang rail and saw the whole scene repeated on the other decks. Along the side of the ship, their legs and bodies pressed hard to the wooden rail, were row upon row upon row of young men. I looked up and behind me, only to see the same anxious staring faces. For once, the desperate need to make a joke had been forgotten.

Even the officers seemed to have been infected by the men's mood. Their jovial, public school boy jests replaced by a stillness unusual for them.

A thick, clogging, waft of cigarette smoke filled my nostrils and mouth. I heard Eddie cough and I watched as the dead Capstan made a perfect swallow dive into the dark waters of the sea.

I squinted my eyes to see the shore better. Its green was greener now and I could clearly see stands of thick forest on the edge of a palm-fringe beach. I say beach, but it was more like a grey concrete dust than golden sand. It wasn't like the pictures I'd seen at all. Not the colours anyway. The water wasn't a vivid aquamarine blue. The beach wasn't a golden yellow. The trees weren't a rich tropical green. All I could see was a slash of dark, muddy brown sea, a stroke of grey beach and an ebbing, fading, mist-laden green, rising to no great height.

'Is this it?' I said, louder than I meant to. 'Is this really Malaya?'

The rest stayed silent.

'Give us a fag, Eddie.'

'You just said you didn't want one.'

'Well, now I do. Go on, give us one.' I often spoke like this with Eddie. He expected it from his little brother, though I was about three inches taller than he was.

I took the Capstan, lit my cigarette and inhaled deeply, feeling the tobacco reach into the depths of my lungs. I blew the smoke out and watched as it danced in the rays of the sun.

The sharp acrid taste took me back to the time when we were training in York. A horrible place that camp was. But the town was lovely; old fashioned narrow streets, friendly people who didn't mind squaddies, great beer, and the Minster. How I loved the Minster. On my days off, I would go and sit there, listening to the songs of the choir as the sound rose to the rafters, echoed off the stone pillars, and escaped out of the pale red of the rose window.

I'm not religious at all, but, on those days, when the singing was so beautiful, God would have had to have been a hard-hearted bastard not to listen.

I met a lovely girl there too. Emily her name was. She worked at the chocolate factory so she always had a rich, ravishing smell about her. After we made love once on the settee in her mum and dad's parlour, I remember burying my face in her hair and wallowing in the thick, sweet-bitter aroma of chocolate that clung to every strand.

Of course, I had to leave York when we were told to join the regiment in Southampton. I didn't have time to say goodbye before I left. Well, I suppose I did have time but there was no point really. She was a nice girl. Much too nice for me.

I heard cheering all around me. Suddenly, I wasn't in York smelling the scent of chocolate in her hair and on her skin any more, but I was here on the ship.

We were much closer to the shore now. I could see houses regularly spaced along the coast facing the sea.

The lads were cheering at an old tramp steamer, which was sailing between the shore and us. An old man was hanging out his washing on a line across the stern. A young child with a round, shaven head was

9

waving and smiling at us, his eyes a crease and his nose flat against his face. He looked like a football had been stuck on a pair of child's shoulders.

'Hey mate, fancy doing my washing while you're at it,' shouted a broad Manchester voice from above me. The men laughed. The man ignored them, going about his work as if we didn't exist.

The harbour around us was full of activity. Bumboats, dredgers, coastal steamers, tankers, fishermen, junks, all the ships of the world, jockeying for position in the narrow strait. Of course, we took precedence. Everyone else seemed to be trying to get out of our way.

I could see the city now in the distance. Its grey blur shrouded in an even greyer blanket of haze.

Then I smelt it. A cloying, clinging smell, full of rotting vegetables, fruit, charcoal, car exhaust, fish, more fish, more shit and, above all, full of humanity. That's people, not kindness. Full of these putrid smells of man: a delicious blend of sweat, hard work, sorrow, despair, duty and sacrifice, mixed with just a smidgeon of joy. Not much, mind you. Don't want to spoil the aroma with too much joy. That wouldn't be right, would it?

The docks were in sight now and docks were the same the world over. Ships gushed black smoke out of charred funnels. Derricks and cranes like nurses, carefully feeding their cargo to the voracious mouth that was the hold. Endless rows of warehouses with piles of goods, chattels, and bales from all over the world. The rattle of chains, the constant chug of compressors, the steady whirr of winding gears.

And, surrounding it all, what seemed like endless nests of ants, all pulling, tugging and scurrying together to feed the ships.

I wiped the sweat dripping from my face onto my uniform. It was as if someone had turned a tap on in my body and decided it would constantly ooze liquid from every pore.

With all the other lads, I cheered and cheered and cheered as we finally docked in the centre of the city.

In Singapore, I melted away to become nothing. But I wasn't to know that. Not yet, anyway.

Chapter 2

Reg Dwyer
Block 15, Tanglin Barracks, Singapore
24th October 1938
My dearest Marjorie,
Well, we're here. We spent nearly four weeks on that boat. I'll be glad if I never see one again. There really was no room to sleep or eat. Me and the other lads of the battalion had to make do as best we could. You can imagine the pong as we were all crammed beneath the decks. Tommy Larkin didn't wash himself or his socks for the whole time. Mucky bugger!

Anyway, we arrived in Singapore on Tuesday. It smells here as well. And the docks, you should have seen them. Full of coolies, those are the local labourers, carrying sacks on their back without a care in the world.

It's hot here too. Every day the sun beats down. The lads and me just sweat and sweat and sweat. We don't have to do anything at all, sitting here and writing to you is bringing me out in a flood.

The barracks are pretty nice. There's me and fifteen others from our section in one block. I've got a locker for my stuff and the bed is pretty comfortable. We've even got electric fans. But they don't seem to help much, they just move the warm air around a bit more. We don't need a blanket to sleep at night, it's far too hot!

Anyway, enough of me. How are you, dear? Not letting your mother get you down too much I hope. How are Tommy and Evelyn? You tell Tommy from me he's to be a good boy when he goes to school. He's not to fight or throw his tantrums. They must be both getting taller now. I would love to see them.

And Baby Grace, is she being good? Not keeping you up at night, I hope.

I spoke to Captain Moriarty on the boat. They do have married quarters here and even some for privates. But it would be easier if I made corporal.

So that's what I'm doing at the moment, dear. Keeping my head down, putting lots of spit and polish in. As soon as we all settle in, I'll put in a request for married quarters. Captain Moriarty says with a bit of luck and a clean record, I'll be able to get them.

Some of the officers' wives and children came out on the boat. It was really hard to look at them and think of you and the kids.

I miss you so much but I'm sure we'll be together soon. I hope you can bear living in Singapore, it's so hot. The kids would love it though. They could run around naked in the jungle all day long.

Anyway, I must go now. I keep your picture beside my bed and I'm always thinking of you.

Your husband,

Reg

Chapter 3

Richard Longhurst

So many people. As far as the eye could see there were heads, all intent on going about their business. Some were shopping, some carrying two heavy loads balanced across their shoulders on a bamboo stick. Some walking their children in the late afternoon sunlight. Some shouting their strange wares from the stalls lining the street. Some just standing, watching and waiting.

We'd decided one Sunday afternoon to go down to Chinatown for a lark. And here we were, in the middle of all these people.

It was Eddie who spoke first. He'd been looking around at the houses that snuggled up closely to Telok Ayer Street. 'You know, somewhere in these,' he pointed down the long street lined with a myriad of garishly painted windows. 'Somewhere in there, someone, somewhere, is fucking. I mean it stands to reason. There's so many of them out here, there must be some of them still inside making some more. I mean it stands to reason, don't it?'

The others laughed. There was a sort of logic to it though. A sort of Eddie logic that reduced life to its basics.

Amidst all this humanity, I spotted an old temple set back from the street.

I moved away from the lads and stepped over the entrance and into the first courtyard. Around me, women struggled to get past. But none of them paid me any attention. As I walked into the courtyard, the smell of thousands of burning joss sticks assaulted my nose, reminding me here was the East, here was something foreign I neither understood nor needed to understand.

I stepped forward past a group of worshippers into the open courtyard. Ahead of me lay the main building of the temple. Behind me, I could hear the sound of laughter as the rest of the lads arrived.

'Jesus H. Christ, what a fucking pong.'

'Smells like your socks, Reg.'

'Nah, more like his grundies. You know Reg never washes them.'

'I do, too. At least once a month. Whether they need it or not.'

I crossed the courtyard, trying to move away from the lads behind me. I entered the main body of the temple. The garish altar, covered in a long-faded gold cloth, weighed down by a host of smoke-stained red Gods, dominated the rear walls.

In front of the main God – an evil looking bugger with fierce glowing eyes, dark tattered hair and a streak of some dark gooey substance on his face – old women were bowing down, mumbling some incantation to themselves.

The air was stained with smoke from the joss sticks of the worshippers and from six huge cylindrical temples of incense that looked like immense mosquito coils. They were suspended from the ceiling and their smoke fought with the rays of the sun to create dancing motes in front of my eyes.

For a moment, I wasn't certain whether this was heaven or hell.

Around me, the mumbles of the worshippers merged to form one long drone of sound. A hypnotic sound like an infernal choir.

I picked up a bundle of joss sticks and watched the women as they approached the altar.

I imitated them as they dipped the ends of their handfuls of sticks into the flame and, clasping their hands together as if in prayer, they swayed backwards and forwards, chanting in their strange tongue.

I'm not sure what happened next. One minute I was standing watching these old women, the next I was with them on my knees in front of their smoke-eyed God.

I don't know how I got there, kneeling before the garish altar. But all that filled me were the wild eyes of the God. His mouth twisted into a sardonic smile. His cheeks red with anger. His eyes glaring down at me. Knowing all my sins, aware of all my faults, conscious of exactly who I was and who I wasn't.

Still the old ladies droned on around me, ignoring me completely as if having an English soldier praying in their temple was the most normal thing on earth.

It was then I heard the sniggers.

'Well done, Lanky lad, say a few prayers for me.'

'While you're there, see if he'll send me a big, dirty woman tonight. Something I can really get my teeth into.'

I got up, my face red with embarrassment and pushed past them, their laughter ringing in my ears.

I ran out past the joss sticks, past the old worshippers, through the ornate gates and back into the real world.

And there, I stood with my hands on my knees, panting as if I'd just run ten miles, the sweat dripping off my nose to melt soundlessly into the red dust of the street.

Chapter 4

Eddie Longhurst

God, I love the bleeding army.

Who else would pay you to sit around in the sun all day long?

Now don't get me wrong, I'm not a waster. Never have been. But working down the pit or slaving over some fucking machine in some god-awful factory is not my idea of a life.

The army is, though. Joining up was the best decision I ever made. Training was a piece of piss. I don't know why those bastards moaned about it all the time.

You know the army's all about having pride in yourself. Pride in your body. Pride in your uniform. Pride in the regiment. Pride in yourself. I understand that sort of pride. It's not what you find in Civvy Street at all. How can you have pride in the dirty arse-end of a back-to-back, washing hanging on the line and smoke spilling from the chimneys around it? I remember me mam used to complain that half the bloody time the washing was dirtier after it had been on the line than before.

How can you have pride in standing on the corner of a street all day doing nothing but smoking a fag and burying your hands deeper in your pockets?

How can you have pride in yourself when you have to go down to the dole office each week, only to be told by some four-eyed shit behind the counter to fuck off back to the slums where you belong?

The answer is you can't.

You know I never understood what life was about until I joined the regiment. It's about discipline. Because that's what the army teaches you. Discipline.

You get things done but you do them in a certain way. You don't have to think much because someone tells you what to do. And you know where you belong. For once in your life, you belong to something much bigger than yourself. You fit in, you have a role in life.

Of course, you have to follow their rules and their ways of doing things but that's easy. As long as you do it without question, you're a 'Tad', a member of the regiment.

As long as you play by the rules then they look after you. At Tanglin Barracks, we get four square meals a day – none of that Chinese muck our Richard likes – there's the canteen, a few beers, a laugh with your mates, cinemas, football, a few fags and something to believe in.

What more could anyone want?

It still doesn't stop the bastards moaning though. They'd moan if someone gave them thousands of pounds and said go fuck all the girls in the world. They'd complain they were too tired, and they didn't want to do it, or it was always the fucking army giving orders.

Stupid bastards.

I love the army. I love being an Empire soldier, I love the regiment. End of fucking story.

*

Reg Dwyer

Block 15, Tanglin Barracks, Singapore
2 December, 1938
My dearest wife,
Well, we've been here for over a month now and I'm still sweating. It's as if someone pours a bucket of water over me the minute I wake up. As you can guess, it's really hard to keep our uniforms dry and clean. We're lucky though we have a Dhobi man who comes every day to do the laundry. We have to pay him, mind, but it's not that expensive, and it stops us all being told off by the NCOs for being scruffy.

Talking of NCOs, my platoon leader for 13 Platoon is Serjeant Shelley. He's going to try and help me with the application. That's for married quarters so you and the children can come and join me here. I put the application in last week to Captain Moriarty. You should have seen the number of forms I had to fill in. They asked for your maiden name, your mum's maiden name and lots of others. I made most of it up. For the life of me, I couldn't remember. Well, you don't, do you? I then had to write a letter saying why I thought I deserved married quarters. I wanted to write, 'because I'm stuck out here defending the Empire far away from my wife and kids'. But Richard, he's one of the lads, said that's not what they wanted to hear. So he helped me write it. Hard it was, full of big words I didn't rightly understand but Captain Moriarty said it was well written and the best letter he'd ever seen. It was all about improving regimental efficiency and the family giving a solid foundation for a soldier to avoid the inequities of the Orient. Whatever that means.

Anyway, Captain Moriarty has passed it on to Major Tudor, the company commander. If he likes it, it will go to the Battalion Adjutant and the CO for approval.

As I'm writing this, I'm crossing my fingers, dearest heart, and praying every night and day we can be together again.

The mail seems to be slow out here but I finally got your letter. You tell that David Endersby to leave the allotment alone. It's nothing to do with him. Get Harry to look after it for the time being until I come back. That allotment has got the best drainage in all of Stockport. No wonder bloody David Endersby and his bloody leeks want it. Make sure you tell him now.

I hope my mum is better. She should look after herself more during the cold winter nights. The flu can be real bad for someone her age. Has Harry really started stepping out with Rita Henderson? That must have caused some gossip up and down the street. My brother seeing hoity-toity Rita Henderson. Good on him. I hope she doesn't treat him bad though. Harry can be a bit soft where women are concerned. I suppose it runs in the family.

Give my love to Tommy, Evelyn and Grace and tell Tommy he's not to play football with his new school shoes. Does he think they grow on trees?

I've sent you and the kids some Christmas presents from Singapore. For you, I've got this lovely embroidered kimono from a Japanese store in Middle Road. It's sort of like a nightgown but you're not to wear it until I come home. I want to be the first to see you in it. For Tommy I've got a model of a rickshaw. That's the little cabin on wheels we use to go around town.

Me and the lads have to bargain with the rickshaw Johnny every time we use one , but it's fun. We don't bargain too hard, though. The buggers are always so thin and scrawny. Bit like a whippet really. I'm always feeling sorry for them.

Lastly, for Evelyn, I've got a pair of the red Chinese slippers the women wear out here. I hope they are the right size. I know what a proper little madam she is.

Anyway, dearest heart, I've got to go now. The lads are calling me. We're going to the cinema tonight. I'll tell you all about it in my next letter.

Look after yourself. I miss you and the children so much but I know we'll be together soon.

Your husband

Reg

P.S. Don't let David Endersby anywhere near my allotment, understand!

*

Eddie Longhurst

I can see that bastard from the Gordons set himself.

The inside of his boot is swinging back to curve around the ball like a boyfriend puts his arm around a girl in the movies.

But I've already dived. The bastard doesn't know it yet but I can read his mind, I know what he's up to, the glory he's seeking, the perfection of a ball curved into the top left-hand corner.

I've read his mind and I know he's one of those glory boys.

I've already dived, my body arched, my right hand thrown up in the air.

I'm still watching, mind. I can see the laces coming toward me. Their bright orangeness a flash of colour against the spinning brown of the leather.

Keep watching Eddie son, keep looking. Reach a little more, push your body through the air, extend that right arm.

I feel the heavy, damp leather hit my palm. I twist my head and watch the ball curve elegantly three inches wide of the left-hand post.

Now the landing, feel the ground, see the ground come close. *Hrumpfff.* Always that loss of air, that thump of body against ground as I return to earth.

I hear 'Great save Eddie lad, great save,' and 'Well done, chaps,' and 'Come on the Tads' and 'Get intae heem, Heelanders,' from the touchline.

I milk the applause, bask in the congratulations, getting up quickly to show I'm not hurt. Taking time to wipe away a lump of mud stuck to my knee. Active now, watching the game, ready for action.

'Magic Eddie,' says Harrington, our centre-half.

'How come he had so much fuckin' time eh?' I shouted in his ear. You can't let the bastards relax. Keep in their faces. Let them know who's boss.

The corner comes in. Easy. No problem. I'm up in the air, nobody's challenging, catch it and bring it down to my chest, look around. Big Liddle, there he is, all on his own, their centre-half slowly galloping back like the big old Scots carthorse he is. Two bounces then a big boot up field.

We've only been in Singapore for a month or so and already in our first match. The Jocks have been here a while already and seem to have the pace of the place much better than us. The bloody heat is a killer. Just trying to breathe takes all my breath away. Fuck it. Just concentrate. Watch the ball, follow its movements, don't let your head wander.

Breathe, lad. Get your breath back. We're one-nil up. Can't be long now to the end. I look at the rows of lads along the touchline. The Tads on my left and the Jocks on my right. Got to keep them apart. The Jocks are mad with their razors. Only small cunts mind, but I wouldn't like to meet one on a dark night in a back alley off Anson Road.

That pillock Liddle has fucked it up royally. They're coming back now down the left. Their winger's got a good left foot. Out to the edge of the six-yard box. Get the angle right, you never know when that bugger will let one fly.

It's a one-two. Bastard's through. Out, out quick Eddie, narrow the angle. Harrington's coming across, the little Scots winger dummies him, but Harrington, the big, clumsy twat clatters into his legs, bringing him tumbling to the ground.

100 Jock voices seem to roar in unison, 'Foockin ell, ref, penaldy.' On cue, Serjeant Major Whatmough whistles and his arm points to the spot. The Jocks roar. The Tads groan. Harrington holds his head. You won't have a bleedin head left to hold when I get hold of you mate.

The Scots winger gets up and they throw him the ball. The little cunt is feeling his leg but he still wants to take it.

Right mate. It's just me and you now. I bang my boots on the rusty goalpost, knocking the clumps of mud from between my studs. I look for the midpoint of my line and stand there. He's placing the ball on the spot now.

I'm staring at him, drilling my eyes into the back of that ginger head. I'm inside that brain, kicking the fucking shit out of it and him. I move a little to my left, encouraging him to shoot to my right. Easier for me to get down on that side.

I check my balance, slowly shifting my weight from one leg to the next. I'm still staring at the bastard. He's back at the beginning of his run up now. Not looking at me. Can't look in my eyes, the dickhead. Come on, just one look. Take them, hold them.

He glances first to my left, then to my right, deciding where he should put it.

My mind is shouting 'To my right bastard, can't you see, there's more room. Even a dopey cunt like you can see.'

Then I see his eyes glance directly at me. I've got him, I've got the bastard. Hold him, Eddie lad, you've got him now. Bastard's fucked and he knows it.

All that's left is me and him. Nothing else exists. Not the referee, not my team, not the bastards on the touchline. There's just me and him. And I've got him. He knows it, too.

I see a furtive glance to my right. That's where he's going to go, exactly where I want it.

I crouch lower, ready to spring like a cat, ready to milk the applause with the save.

He starts his run-up. Coming towards me now. I've still got his eyes, though, still holding him like dog gripping a bitch on heat..

He's close to the ball now, I see the little turn of his body, I see his left foot open to caress the ball into my right hand corner.

I dive.

I dive.

I dive.

Watching still watching.

I land.

I land.

I land.

I hear the cheers erupt round the ground. I see our players' heads go down. I see the ginger Jock turn with his hands in the air, milking the congratulations of his teammates.

I look behind me. Nestling in the corner in the other side of the net is this little brown lump of shit, still with its bright orange laces.

I hear the referee blow for the end of the game. 1-1. Would you fuckin' believe it? Held to a draw by a bunch of rabid Scots dwarves.

Would you fuckin' believe it? The answer's no, twathead.

Neither would I.

*

Reg Dwyer

Block 15, Tanglin Barracks, Singapore

12th January, 1939

My dearest wife,

Happy New Year. I hope you didn't get too tipsy with the next-door neighbours. You know what you're like when you're a wee bit tipsy, hah, hah.

We're all settled in pretty well here, the lads and me. They're a happy bunch. Richard and Eddie Longhurst are brothers. But as different as chalk and cheese. Richard's a quiet chap, hardly says anything but you can see he's a thinker. Eddie's the opposite. Always moving about, full of energy. He's on the battalion's football team. We're doing quite well this year. Then, there's Tommy Larkin. He's from Accrington. A young lad still wet behind the ears and a bit slow like Henry from no. 12. He's all there but slow on the uptake.

Joe Silcock, Terry Teale, Ray Lloyd and Fred Mytholmroyd all hang around together. We never see them apart. The four stooges we call them, after those American comedians nobody likes.

There was another lad, Ted Hunt, but he got malaria real bad. He's in the camp hospital now and there's talk about him being sent back to Blighty.

He was in a real bad way but I'd try to get malaria as well if it meant we could be together again. They give us these pills, quinine they are. We're supposed to take them because it stops malaria. But they taste real bad. Ted could never stomach them. He was forever throwing up. That's why he ended up in hospital. Lucky bugger though, if he can get back to England.

I realise I haven't told you much about the camp. It's real big. There's a cinema, canteen, shops and laundry, even an hospital. It's like a small town. If we didn't want to go into the city, we would never have to.

Everything's here. There's even a golf course reserved for officers. Silly game anyway, not like football.

I read in The Straits Times United had lost 2 – 1 to Everton. They're near the bottom of the table again. I hope they don't go down to the second division. I'd never be able to show my face in the street if they did.

Anyway, you can see I'm keeping up with the news. We get it pretty quickly out here. The local paper even prints the football scores on Monday. And there's always the Radio. Eddie Longhurst got one from somewhere (no questions asked, no lies told) for our barracks. So now we can listen to George Robey and the latest tunes from the BBC.

Sometimes I think you're listening to the same programme as I am. Except it's breakfast in England and teatime here. When I think like that, I miss you so much and want to hold you tight, like we did at Belle Vue when we were courting. Do you remember?

Anyway, mustn't be too sad. We'll be together soon, I know. I had to rewrite the letter. Major Tudor said it wasn't quite right to hand it to the Adjutant. So I did. Couldn't see the difference myself but he said it was all a matter of tone. It wasn't pleading enough I think for him. It's done now. I hope you and the kids can come here soon. I miss you all so much.

I went out with the lads last week. We saw Gracie Fields and Victor McLaglen at the Alhambra in 'We're going to be rich'. That Gracie Fields can sing like a nightingale. And to think she used to be a mill girl from Rochdale. There's hope for all of us yet. May be we can all be rich soon, hah, hah.

The others went to the cafe for a drink but I went back to the barracks. They can meet girls there but you don't have to worry about me. There's only room in my heart for one girl and that's my own Marjorie.

You tell Tommy he must do his schoolwork real well. Not to be like his dad, a slacker at school. That way he can get a proper job and not be another poor bloody squaddie like me.

Well, lights out has been called, love, so I've got to go. Keep yourself well and never mind what Mrs Dempsey says. She's just another know-all who knows nowt.

Your husband,

Reg

Chapter 5

Richard Longhurst

'Sure, is this 13 Platoon?'

The speaker had popped his head around the door without knocking.

Most of us were asleep on our beds. It was siesta time after all, and we'd had a particularly heavy morning of it at the parade ground.

I lifted my head from the pillow.

'Your man said this was 13 Platoon's digs.'

I saw a round, florid face with sparkling green eyes and thin shallow lips, a mass of unruly ginger curls, sitting on top of his head like a nest of orange springs.

'*Grumph*,' I said as I blinked the sleep from my eyes.

'I'll take that as a yes.' The body followed the face through the open door. He must have been over six foot tall and well-built. A good-looking man if ever I saw one. 'Michael O'Neill is pleased to be meeting you.'

He stuck his hand in my face. Without thinking, I shook it.

'I'm to replace Ted Hunt in the platoon. Shame about your fellow, isn't it? Only goes to show you've got to take your little green pills or the big mosquito gets you. Where's my bunk?'

He looked straight at me. I'd been listening but not listening, if you know what I mean, to the sound of his voice. A wonderful, soft, mellow sound like a country day with cows in the field and the soft doze of a sleepy afternoon. The voice was Irish of that there was no mistake. I'd been listening to it, not hearing the words.

'I'm sorry?' was the only thing I could think to say.

'Why, what've you done?' He laughed once. And then laughed again when he saw the incomprehension on my face. 'Just my little joke. You like the craic, do you?'

'Like the what?'

'The craic. The fun. The joke. A happy time between mates. A bit of a laugh.'

'Yes, sure. I think.'

'Well, that's all well and good. I don't want to be saddled with a boring bunch of farts now, do I? Is this mine?'

He dumped his kit on the best bunk in the barracks, facing the door and directly under the fan.

'No, that one's taken. It's Eddie's.'

'Well, I'm sure your man won't mind. He's not sleeping on it right now.' O'Neill shifted his kit off the bed and jumped on it, boots and all. 'Not bad, not bad. A man could get used to this very easily.'

He then placed his arms behind his head and nodded off in the speed it takes a baby to go to sleep.

I lay awake waiting for the inevitable explosion. I could hear the others in the bunks, pretending to be asleep, waiting for Eddie to return from football training.

We didn't have long to wait. I heard the door open. Eddie stood there, still panting from his exercise, dripping sweat onto the wooden floor of the barracks.

He walked over to his bed and saw a body lying on top of it, asleep.

For a moment, he was confused. He looked around him as if worried he had come into the wrong barracks by accident.

He checked out the beds and recognised me, Larkin, Dwyer and Teale.

Then he looked back at his bunk counting along from the end of the row. I could see his mind working as the realisation hit him.

It was like Goldilocks and the Three Bears. Yes, this was his bunk and yes, someone was sleeping there. Someone he didn't know and it wasn't him.

At that moment, O'Neill woke up, blinked his eyes once and said, 'Good morning to you. You must be Eddie. I hope you don't mind but I've taken your bunk. You see I need the fan directly above me. I suffer terribly from the heat.'

He pointed at the fan whirring above his head. Eddie looked up at it, then down at O'Neill.

He seemed to be counting to three and then he erupted. Grabbing the edge of the bed, he tipped it over, throwing O'Neill over the side.

He then picked up the kitbag and whirling it around his body, tossed it to the far corner of the barracks where it landed on the sleeping Larkin.

'What's up? What's happening,' shouted Larkin, awoken rudely from his dream of being Greta Garbo's passionate Manchester lover.

25

By now, O'Neill was getting to his feet. Eddie didn't say anything. He just snarled in pain and went for him. Like a bull, he charged, grabbing him by the throat and pinning him against the wall.

O'Neill's arms and legs waved feebly like a puppet no longer controlled by its master.

We could hear him choke as Eddie punched his hand deeper and deeper into O'Neill's throat, pushing him back against the concrete wall of the barracks.

None of us moved. None of us said anything.

O'Neill choked once more, his arms and legs swinging ineffectively.

'Let him go, Longhurst.'

Eddie pushed O'Neill harder into the concrete.

'LET HIM GO. LONGHURST.' It was Serjeant Shelley, the voice even Eddie had to obey.

He let drop to the floor.

O'Neill flopped forward onto his knees, his chest heaving as he grabbed for precious air.

'Tenshun!' someone shouted.

We all leapt out of our bunks and stood to attention in our underpants.

Only O'Neill remained panting on the floor, unable to move.

Shelley strutted into the room, looking at us all balefully.

He walked up to Longhurst and whispered in his ear. 'You're on a charge, you stupid bugger.'

He then looked down at the kneeling O'Neill, still gasping for air like a fish out of water.

'And so are you, O'Neill. Right, the rest of you can do ten laps around the parade ground. O'Neill and Longhurst come with me.'

He marched out, followed by Eddie and, reluctantly, by a gasping O'Neill. 'Sure, I'll be seeing you later lads,' was the last thing the Irishman said before he stepped out on the long march down to the Guardhouse.

'Right then lads, you heard Serjeant Shelley. Ten laps around the parade ground.' That was the ever-such-a-goody-two-shoes Reg Dwyer.

'You haven't got your stripes yet, Reg.'

'But he's trying for them, aren't you? How far is your tongue up Shelley's arse?'

'Brushing the inside of his teeth, isn't he? You notice how he always puts a toothpick on the end of his tongue these days. All the better to clean it with Serjeant.'

'Right, that's enough, let's be having you.'

And we all trooped out like the good little troops we were.

*

Eddie Longhurst

Whilst all other bastards are sleeping, I'm out here on the field doing football training.

We're led by the battalion PT Instructor, Serjeant O'Connor, and a right sadistic bastard he is too.

He's got us running relays at the moment on the football pitch.

It looks easy, but in this heat, it's a fucking killer. All you have to do is run around the pitch, alternatively jogging and sprinting as you hit each line. So starting at the far corner post, you jog until the half-way line, then sprint to the next corner post, jog across to the penalty box and sprint behind the goal and on, and on, and on.

This continues on until the bastard thinks you've had enough. Which is usually next Tuesday or until you're so fucking knackered you can't breathe, whichever comes first.

All the other lads moan about it but I don't. I love to feel my body getting stronger. There's a real sense of pride as you realise these muscles that used to be so weak and puny, now have real size and definition.

No bastard pushes me around anymore. No fucker messes with Eddie Longhurst. Not anymore.

But there's another reason why I love training. It's a time I can dream. After about ten minutes of running, the sweat is pouring off me but I'm no longer thinking about running, that sort of happens of its own accord like breathing.

Instead, my head's gone back to the last shag I had, reliving every soddin' moment of it. Or I'm back in Manchester as a kid playing on the Dodgem at Belle Vue. Or I'm beating hell out of O'Neill, enjoying every punch to his nose, every kick in the teeth, and every Irish moan coming from that stupid soddin' Mick.

I'm in a world of my own when I'm running. I'm not me, Eddie Longhurst, any more. I'm someone else. I don't know who I am, I'm just not me.

I hear O'Connor's voice, telling us to stop. But I want to keep on going. I haven't finished this dream yet. Don't stop now, you bastard, don't stop now.

*

Richard Longhurst

'Come on. Larkin, you're pretty enough.'

Larkin was still grooming himself in the only mirror, one of the prize possessions of Block 15. He combed his hair once again and ran a touch of Brylcreem through the ends. But he could do nothing about the red acne that stained both cheeks

'Let's be having you.' This was Eddie, smart as usual. 'Time to celebrate. Only a another bloody draw against the Engineers but we'll do better next time.'

There was me, Teale, Reg, Eddie and Larkin going on a big lads night out. Our first since we had arrived in Singapore.

We all piled out of the Barracks, all of us as smart as tailors' dummies in our best uniforms. But before we had walked ten yards down the hill, we were already sweating.

Then out past the duty Serjeant at the Guard House, 'Gate closed at 2:00am lads. Make sure you're back before then.'

'Yes, Serjeant,' we chorused back to him.

A waiting taxi. Sod the expense, let's grab it.

'Take us to Lavender Street.'

'Where ah?'

'Lav-en-der Street,' mouthed Reg slowly, as if he were talking to a moron.

'Oh la-VEN-dah Street.'

'That's right.'

'Sure la-VEN-dah Street. Three dollar.' The taxi driver held up four fingers.

'Bugger off. It's only two dollars,' argued Eddie.

'Saturday night. Three dollar.' Again, the taxi driver held up four fingers.

'Let's not hang around. The girls will be waiting,' said Reg.

'Ok. Ok. Three dollar. But only if you drive quick, OK?'

The taxi driver smiled, 'Sure thing.'

They all piled into the Austin 7. Its springs moaned at the arrival of five sex-starved squaddies from Manchester.

Only the taxi driver seemed happy at the result. He started the engine still with a smile on his face, released his hand brake with a resounding crash and forced the gear into its correct position.

We were off.

'Do you think it'll be horizontal?' asked Reg to nobody in particular.

'What will be horizontal?'

'You know…that.'

'You know…what?'

'The thing…the woman's thing. You know…that.'

'Well, tonight's the night, we're gonna find out, isn't it?'

'I heard they like doing it upside down.' This was Larkin.

'Upside down?'

'Yea, you know, with the woman on top and the man beneath.'

'Jesus, that'd be different,' said Reg. 'How'd you get Bobby in?'

'Bobby?' they all chorused.

'You know, your todger, your willy.'

'Why do you call it Bobby?'

'Because it's short for Robert.'

'And?'

'And nothing. It's short for Robert.'

'Just fucking short, that's all,' grunted Eddie.

The conversation lapsed into silence. There wasn't much else that could be said.

The taxi driver found something though. 'You, ah not from here, is it?'

'No, from Manchester mate. Best fucking city in the world. Manchester is. See this,' Eddie pointed to the fleur de lys on the breast pocket of his shirt. 'That's the symbol of the Manchester Regiment. Best fucking regiment in the whole wide world.'

'Oh,' said the taxi driver meaningfully. 'You just got here then, is it?'

'Yes, mate, five weeks ago.'

The car went round a roundabout at speed, they all leant into each other. The taxi driver honked his horn and a rickshaw driver jumped out of the way, mouthing a long stream of unintelligible obscenities at the departing blue smoke of the taxi's exhaust.

'I show you No. 1 club on La-VEN-dah Street. Best girls in town. No problem.'

'Sounds right up our street, mate. Right up Lavender Street, hey,' Eddie elbowed the taxi-driver to join in the joke. He gave us a weak giggle and concentrated on the heavy task of driving.

After, twenty minutes of crashing gears, swearing and the roar of a tired engine, he stopped with a moan of brakes. The taxi driver pointed to a large sign above a purple-lit door. It said 'Lady Club.'

'See. Best club in town. Lot of good girls. Good girls who get better when bad.' Now he laughed at his own joke and nudged Eddie in the ribs.

Eddie stared at him.

'OK. You give me the three dollar. No tip.' Eddie handed over the money.

'Well lads,' he said, 'what the fuck are we waiting for?'

We piled out of the taxi and stood outside the front door of the nightclub. The place seemed quiet. Too quiet.

'It's fucking shut.'

'No, it isn't, you tosspot, Larkin. It's just quiet.'

'It doesn't look like the best place in town.'

'D'ye think the taxi driver has done us in?' asked Reg.

'I'll fucking do him in if he has,' answered Eddie, staring viciously in the direction of the departing blue exhaust.

'Well, we ain't gonna find out by standing here. Come on Manchesters.' I pushed through the purple-lit door of The Lady Bar.

It was the first time we went there, but it certainly wasn't going to be the last. I waved two bead curtains aside and walked through another orange painted doorway.

A small, very pale Chinese woman rose to greet us like Stanley greeted Livingstone. 'The Manchesters, I presume.'

'You bet your life, lady,' said Eddie over his shoulder.

'No, but I'll bet yours, soldier. Come this way.'

She spoke with a perfect English accent. In fact, she spoke more like one of the officers than anything else. We went through yet another doorway and finally we were in the back.

It wasn't much to look at. A long L-shaped Mahogany bar on the left, behind which sat a surly Chinese barman who was at the moment investigating his ears with his pinky nail.

Next to the bar were a few scattered tables on which stood a pile of beer mats and what looked like a votive candle. The sort people light at church when they want to send a prayer to God. Though why God should listen to prayers simply because someone has lit a tiny candle was beyond me.

Behind the tables was a small stage with one solitary microphone. All the walls were painted bright orange and the only other colour in the bar was a slash of bright red velvet curtain, guarding the stage like a sleeping beefeater.

The bar was empty of customers. It looked naked.

'Have we come to the right place?' whispered Reg in my ear.

'The girls will be along shortly gentlemen. Until then, what can I get you to drink? Beer ok?'

We nodded like the naughty children we were.

'Tigers, Ah Fai, for our guests.'

With these words, the mama-san departed. I found out later her name was Judy, she'd been born and educated in Guildford, and her father was once a rich merchant, who had lost everything in one mad card game in 1935.

She didn't regret anything though. 'Yuen fen,' she called it in Chinese. She believed that was her fate, so she lived her life expecting to lose. Of course, she was never disappointed.

The drinks arrived at our table courtesy of the unsmiling Ah Fai.

'Let's do a runner. This place is a dead as a donkey's donger.'

'Hold your fucking horses, Reg. Madam said she was going to get the girls, so let's wait and see, huh. The beer won't hurt us anyway.'

'Lanky, you make a toast, you're the one with the words.'

I thought for a moment before saying, 'To us, may we always be the best of mates and worst of enemies.'

'I'll drink to that,' said Larkin.

The glasses rose as one and clicked together, making a noise that resounded with all the clarity of a bell.

'It's got no bloody taste,' shouted Reg, staring disappointedly at his Tiger.

'I like it, refreshing, it is,' said Larkin.

'Piss,' said Eddie.

'Good stuff. Like German beer,' said Teale.

'When were you in Germany?'

'I went over for one of the summer camps. For the B.U.F.'

'You were a Fascist?'

'Aye, founder member in Manchester, I were. Met Mr. Mosley a few times I did. Shook his hand. Great speaker that man. Great speaker.'

'We nearly went to war with those buggers last summer.'

'Aye, I hope we don't. Jews will be behind it if we do. You mark my words.'

'Don't be a stupid tosser, Teale—'

But before he could finish, the mama-san, Judy, had arrived back with a line of girls trailing behind her.

They peeled off like dutiful chorus girls and sat next to each of us. One per squaddie.

'Ey up lads, meat pies have come,' shouted Eddie gleefully.

I looked up and saw this angelic face looking down at me.

I stood up and pulled out a chair for her to sit down.

She couldn't have been more than five feet tall, with a short pageboy haircut, the smallest mouth and the brightest sparkling eyes I'd ever seen. She was wearing a creamy flowered cheongsam, which was cut up to the top of her hip to reveal the outside of her thigh. But she didn't look sexy. On the contrary, she looked demure, innocent almost.

'You buy drink, ok?' were her first words.

'Sure, what would you like?'

'Whiskey water.'

I waved at Ah Fai, who suddenly managed to avoid my eye, looking everywhere; at the walls, at the labels on the Gin bottles, at his fingernail, finding them all terribly more interesting than my waving arm.

'Ah Fai.' The voice of Judy cut clear across the bar. 'And let's have some music.'

Slowly, Ah Fai rose from his stool and went to an ancient Rediffusion radio that sat at the end of the bar. He turned it on, the light flared, followed ten seconds later by the crackle of static.

Ah Fai fiddled with it for a while in a bored, disinterested manner before Joe Loss and his orchestra filled the room with 'Please be kind.'

I turned back to the girl. Her tiny foot was tapping to the music.

'What's your name?'

'Mona.'

'Mona what?'

'Mona Lot.'

'What?'

'Mona Lot.'

'Really?'

'No. Just a joke. Soldier taught me. Real name. Mona Lim. But he said I should be called Mona Lot. Dunno why.'

She was silent as Ah Fai put down a shot-glass full of dark-coloured liquid in front of her.

I knew this was tea but we all maintained the fiction it was whisky water. You see the girls made money by encouraging the squaddies to buy them drinks. The more they drank, the more money they made. Simple economics really.

I saw Ah Fai was now serving the other girls with their dark-coloured liquids as well. The lads looked happy. Eddie already has his arm around a long-haired dark girl with luscious, brown lips.

Reg was sitting demurely, not even looking or talking with his girl.

Larkin was talking non-stop. I watched as the girl stifled a yawn with a red cotton handkerchief.

And Teale was already tickling his girl, making her squeal for mercy.

'What's your name?'

I was brought back to earth by Mona's question.

'Richard, but they often call me Lanky. That's my brother, Eddie.'

She stared at Eddie, one arm around the dark girl's shoulder, the other already holding her hand.

'Don't look like you. You sure brothers?'

It was my turn to look at Eddie. 'I suppose you're right. We don't look very much alike at all. But we're brothers. Our mam says so.'

'Our what?'

'Mother.'

'Oh your mother.' At this, she went quiet and looked down at the table. Ah Fai was there again, putting another round of beers in front of us.

'Get it down your neck, Richard,' shouted Eddie above the sound of 'Blue Skies are round the corner'.

'But I'm still on this one.'

'Get it down your neck, son.'

Then Teale's girl got up and led him to the area in front of the stage. They danced, or rather shuffled around vaguely in time to the music.

They were soon joined by Eddie and his girl, and Larkin and his. While they danced, Larkin was quiet to the obvious relief of his girl.

Myself and Mona watched, until I asked her, 'This soldier, was he your boyfriend?'

'Not boyfriend, just friend. His name Wilf.' She said this like Wolf and immediately the image of a savage beast ravishing the poor sweet innocence of Mona jumped into my mind. 'Wolf good man. He non-umbian Fus lear.' Her mouth fought prettily with the words, eating them like one would eat a bagful of marbles. 'He left now, gone home.'

'Yes, we replaced them. The Manchester Regiment. The Royal Northumberland Fusiliers have gone to India on the same boat we came in. *The Empress*.'

'I went to dock to say goodbye to Wolf. I cry. Him good man. He writes me.'

We both sat in silence again. Another set of beers was delivered to the table by the ever-diligent Ah Fai.

'You buy me drink?'

'Let me guess, whiskey water?'

'How you know?'

'I'm a mind reader.'

'A what?'

'It doesn't matter. I mean I see what people are thinking. Like now, you're thinking about Wilf.'

'No.'

'So what are you thinking about?'

'Money.'

Silence again.

'You funny.'

'Is that funny, ha ha or funny peculiar?'

'What?'

'Funny.' I mimed a laugh. 'Or funny.' I mimed someone who was crazy.

She sat back and looked at me, those sharp eyes staring straight at me. 'No, just funny,' she finally answered.

The bar was filling up now. At a couple of tables sat men dressed in civilian clothes also with a chorus of girls.

Behind the bar, Ah Fai had been replaced by an equally unsmiling gentleman dressed in the same uniform of black trousers, white shirt and black bow tie. It was as if God had made thousands of Ah Fais, all from the same mould.

There were more couples dancing now. All of them shuffling together to the music from the radio. None of them able to move more than a few inches before they bumped into the elbows, arms or legs of a neighbour.

At the door, the mama-san stood guard, occasionally looking at her customers with the jaundiced eye of a recently cuckolded husband.

Eddie came back to the table holding the hand of his girl. He picked up one of the glasses of beer and downed it in one.

'Mother's milk,' he said, wiping his mouth. He looked directly at me, 'Not dancing, Richard?'

'No, not yet. Maybe later.'

'Well, see you later. Come on, doll.' He dragged his girl back to the dance floor. I watched her eyes go up into her head with that bored 'Oh no, not this again look'.

Mona noticed it as well.

'Her feet tired.'

Eddie dragged her away to the dance floor, put his arm around her, and pulled her to him. She tried to pull away, but he pulled her in even tighter.

The rest of the evening passed in a bit of a blur. I remember Eddie dancing. Him holding Mona and dancing. More glasses of Tiger. More shots of dark-coloured liquid. Eddie's hand on his girl's breast. Her smile. Mona's hand on his knee. Teale being slapped. Falling down. Getting up. Eddie vanishing. Reg kissing his girl. Teale vanishing. Me and Mona. Me and Mona.

Then we were outside the bar and I was being sick in the gutter. A deep, deep gutter that separated the front of the shop houses from the road.

Mona watched me as my heart leapt once again out of my mouth to land somewhere around my boots. And in her eyes a softness, a sadness I hadn't seen in the others.

She waved down a trishaw and told it to take me back to the camp. Slowly I climbed in the back and slumped across the leather-covered seat. The trishaw rider began peddling for all his might.

I looked back over my shoulder. She was still watching me leave. She waved and I tried to wave too before falling back into the rickshaw.

I was to go back to the Lady Bar many, many times when I was in Singapore. But I never saw Mona again.

On another visit, I asked Judy, the mama-san, where she was. 'She's gone back,' was the answer. There were no more details and I was always too afraid to ask.

Over the years, there were many other girls like Mona. Many other girls for whom I bought glasses of coloured water. Many other girls who wore thin cotton cheongsams. Many other girls who danced, talked and sang with me.

But I would always remember Mona.

You always remember the first.

Chapter 6

Michael O'Neill

Rain, rain go away, come again another day. Fat chance of that. I was standing at the door of our barracks, leaning against the pillar, looking at the lake that was the parade ground.

An hour ago, it had been as dry as a bone, blue skies, singing birds, whistling crickets and all that shite.

Now all you could see was water. It never rains but it pours in Singapore.

Of course, I had to be caught in it, didn't I. Coming back from a visit to the medical officer. Good man, shame that he didn't give me anything for my bad back. But I'm sure with a little encouragement I'll be able to get a few days off, excused duties.

Anyway, coming back to the barracks I was like a ghost, trying to sneak past Shelley without him knowing.

I'd gone the long way back. Round the back of the officers' mess, across the golf course and through the football changing rooms.

I could see some of the officers out there playing golf. Jesus, your men must be stupid to hit a wee small ball into a wee small hole and enjoy it. Well, they are officers that's all I can say. Noel Coward put it best when he sang 'only mad dogs and Englishmen go out in the midday sun'. Sure, your man got that right, didn't he? Even if he were a roaring pillow biter.

I'd strolled past the football changing rooms, when didn't the heavens open up. I was soaked to me skin within three seconds. Drowned like a dead rat I was. I started to run but it only gets you wetter. So I stood still, there in the middle of the parade ground.

Jesus, it felt lovely. Like having a warm shower in the freshest, clearest water you'd ever felt.

I remember the water barrel at home. We didn't go in for bathrooms or any of that palaver where I was dragged up in Mayo. Just a water barrel next to the house. You stripped to the waist and poured the water all over your body.

The bloody stuff was always cold mind you. In summer, it woke you up something lovely on a warm shimmering morning. But in winter, it was a different sack of potatoes. Jesus, ye had to break the ice on top before you could even get the stuff out.

But my ma always made me wash every morning. She said 'no son of mine is going out smelling like a tinker.' I always thought tinkers smelt alright and one day I even made the mistake of telling her. 'Ye heathen. Ye lazy, good for nothing heathen,' was her only reply as she boxed my ears. Then she started crying. She wouldn't let me comfort her either. Just kept shrugging me off and telling me to get to work.

So I stood there like a stupid banjax and asked her if she was thinking about my da.

She hit me one slap across the face. 'Never mention his name to me again. The man was a dreamer who upped and left us without a by your leave.'

That wasn't exactly true, but even an eejit like me knew that this was not the time to tell her.

I never did find out why she cried. When you're young like that, you never really know. Truth is when you're old you never really know either.

Anyway, standing in the middle of the parade ground under the tropical rain reminded me of my mum's tears.

Jesus, I miss her. And my pals. And Ireland.

One day, I'll have to get out of here and go back. As a hero mind, and rich to boot. I couldn't go back otherwise.

I threw the end of the fag in the gutter and watched it being strangled by the surging waters and racing down the hill.

I mustn't think of Ireland. Not when it rains, I mustn't.

*

Reg Dwyer
Block 15, Tanglin Barracks, Singapore
March 10th, 1939
My dearest Marjorie,

Sorry, I haven't written for so long but we've been so busy recently, I haven't had time to think, let alone write.

Last week, we celebrated Ladysmith Day. It meant we had to troop the colours in front of General Bond, the G.O.C. Lord. For about a month before that they had us tramping up and down, and marching here, marching there, and marching bloody everywhere. My feet hurt, my shoulders are sore and my back aches. I hope I never see another parade ground for the rest of my life.

It all went very well through. And you would have been proud of us. We all looked so smart and the colours were so beautiful. It made me proud to be a Tad. Even the General said we were as good a body of men as he'd ever seen. So there. Stick that up your pipe and smoke it, as George Formby says.

I'm glad it's all over though. And so are the lads. Remember the one I told you about who got Malaria. His name was Ted Hunt. Well, he got it real bad and passed away last week. So, he will be going back to England but not in the way he wanted. All the lads take their quinine now even if it does make them sick.

Life goes on as usual. We get up about six; have breakfast at 7:00 am. It's just getting light then. It's the best part of the day. When it's cool and there's the lovely smell of washing in the air. I always love it. Like Stockport on a summer's morning, if you know what I mean. I know you've asked me to describe what I do and my life in the letters, but you know I've no way with words, dearest heart. I always know what I want to say but it never really goes down on the paper. I hope you understand.

Anyway, after breakfast we do our work like drill or training or looking after the camp.

In the afternoon, we have a nap for a couple of hours. All the Europeans in Singapore have a rest then. It avoids being in the heat of the day. The Asiatics don't though. Different sort of blood I suppose. Later I might look after my uniform but mostly that's done by the Dhobi men. Then it's time to head down to the canteen for my tea and maybe listen to the radio for a while. I'm afraid it's all very boring dear.

We don't see the officers much. They always seem to be playing golf or in the officers' mess. The NCOs really look after us. Serjeant Shelley is my platoon Serjeant. We get on well. I hope he'll put me up for promotion soon. Because, if I get the promotion, it will be easier to get married quarters. My application is with the CO now and, as soon as he signs it, then we'll be alright. But Serjeant Shelley says we may be changing CO soon and so it's difficult for the old CO to promise something he won't be able to deliver.

I think I understand, but then it means we'll have to wait a bit longer before we're together. I don't know if I can last much longer, I miss you so much.

Thank God, all that stuff with Hitler and the Germans has been sorted out. I knew it would. No one wants to go to war anymore, do they? Not after the last little lot anyway.

The lads are all well and we've been going down to the town together. It helps beat the boredom. One day we went past one of the temples and watched the local Chinese praying with their joss sticks and banging their head on the floor in front of these statues. It was very strange. And the colours, the brightest reds you've ever seen, all over the place. It was packed as well. Full of people praying or sitting having a chat. It wasn't quiet like our local church and I didn't see a priest anywhere. Seems like they don't need them to speak to their Gods.

Richard, Eddie's brother, took a bunch of incense sticks, and kneeled in front of the statues, praying like the old women. It was really funny. This tall white man and these old, Chinese women. Just like something from George Formby. We were laughing our heads off. Then, I saw Richard's face as he turned round and he were deadly serious. Sometimes, I wonder about Richard. Far too bright for his boots, I think.

It seems Harry and Rita have really hit it off then! Well I told you our Harry was a good sort. Far too good for her. When are they announcing the happy day? August would be best. I always think August weddings are beautiful. Shame we got married in December. But we couldn't wait, could we?

Lord, I do miss you and the kids. I don't know why I joined the army anymore. I just know I want to be with you. You help me understand things. Without you, I always feel lost, like a little boy, like Tommy. Some days I feel like running away, getting on a boat and going straight back to England. But I know they'd catch me and then we'd never be together again. I've got to be patient and trust the regiment to bring us together. I know they will soon.

Please look after yourself. I haven't received any more letters from you since I got the first one, so please write soon.

Give my love to Tommy, Evelyn and Grace. I'm glad they liked the Christmas presents even if they did arrive late.

Remember to save your kimono until I get home. I want to be the first to see you in it.

Your husband

Reg

Chapter 7

Eddie Longhurst

We got a right bollocking after the loss against the Royal Artillery. O'Connor was waiting for us back in the changing rooms. He had his arms crossed over his chest. He stood there waiting for us to troop in. Our heads down, our studs clattering on the teak floor.

'Well, a right load of bollix youse is,' he started straight away in his broad scouse accent. There weren't many scousers in the Manchester Regiment but O'Connor was one of them. God only knows why.

'I've seen more aggression in the Neil Street Nancy Boys. What were you trying to do Broad, tickle the ball off them? You're a load of bollix youse is, a load of bollix.' He stared across at Ted Harrington, our centre-half. 'Remember what you're supposed to do? When the ball's in the air, you jump up and hit it with this.' He pointed to his head. 'It's calling heading the ball. You load of stupid bleeders are slower than Harpo Marx. Why didn't you do it, Harrington?'

'I dunno, Serjeant.'

'I dunno Serjeant,' he mimed in a powder puff voice. 'I'll give you I don't fucking know.'

He started walking around, his hands on his hips, shaking his head and muttering under his breath. 'Losing to the fucking Gunners. I'll never look the Battery Serjeant in the face again.'

Then he seemed to come to a decision. 'Right, get changed and get out of my fucking sight. Youse lot are gonna have extra training all next week. It'll teach you to lose to the bleeding Gunners.'

He stormed out of the changing hut, slamming the door behind him.

And here I am, running round the pitch again. I don't mind through because it means I can go back into my memories and have a think.

It's really the only time I do it. Thinking that is. Now take our Richard, he seems to spend his life doing it. Thinks far too bloody much, if you ask me.

He's always got his nose buried in a book. Whilst the rest of us are sleeping, or doing something useful like football training, our Richard is stuck into another bloody novel.

Last week I got back early and found him writing notes about one of them.

I whipped the book off his head and read the title, 'Homage to Cata-Cata-Cata-to-na – by George Orwell. What's it about Richard. Any fucking in it?'

He answered in that bored, cocky, know–all voice of his, without looking up from his writing. 'It's about this man who goes off to fight in Spain during the Civil War.'

'So he's a squaddie, like us.'

'Sort of, except he's fighting for the Republicans against Franco's army.'

'Another bleedin' leftie.' I threw the book back down on his bed, 'but he lost in the end, didn't he. A regular army is always going to beat a load of wallies anytime.'

For the first time, he looked up from his writing. 'Yes, he lost in the end but he says it was because they fought amongst themselves. They beat themselves. They weren't beaten by Franco.'

'That's as maybe. But a regular army is always going to beat a bunch of civvies any day. It's all about discipline and training see.'

'But the Republicans were doing really well in the first year of the war. It was only when Hitler and Mussolini came to Franco's help with men and machines they started to lose ground. That and when they started to kill each other.'

'Well, I still say the regulars would have won in the end. Stands to reason, dunnit.'

Richard looked at me, opened his mouth as if to continue the argument then thought better of it and returned to his writing.

I got the better of my clever clogs brother that time, didn't I? All you have to do is use common sense with these clever bastards, works every time. They never have an answer.

'Right, youse lot, give me 50 sit-ups.'

We all stopped running and dropped to the floor. 1-2-3-4-5. I counted in my head, as I bent my body up to touch my outstretched legs. 6-7-8-9-10.

You know, there's too much attention put on cleverness. Take our Richard. He's bloody clever, God knows where he gets it from, but he ain't got an ounce of street smarts.

11-12-13-14-15.

I remember a night at Anson Road in the Green Papaya. Now, we don't really go in that bar, it being sort of unofficially reserved for the Loyals.

Anyway, Richard were there, with the rest of us, having a few beers and checking out the talent. He'd been approached by this lovely Eurasian piece of crumpet. Gagging for a seeing to she was. Richard, though, was being his usual shy self, hardly able to get a few words out to say hello to her.

He's getting on right well with her he is. She even starts to tickle him right there in the bar. Now our Richard is real ticklish and this girl had obviously worked out this were his soft spot. He's wriggling away like only Richard can and the girl is laughing at the sheer pleasure of it. Really enjoying herself she was.

41-42-43-44-45.

I'd noticed this corporal in the Loyals looking at us right strange. I'd thought it were because we were in his local. But then this girl laughed even louder and I looked across at the corporal to see him turning bright purple.

46-47-48-49-50.

Quick as a flash, he's across our table, grabbing the girl's arm and dragging her away. And Richard is just sitting there, watching him do it. Well, I picked up the nearest bottle and smashed it over his fucking head didn't I? Can't have dickheads like that taking liberties with our women. We'd never hear the last of it.

Well to cut a long story short. All hell let loose. Right good scrap it was too. Best I've had for a long while. We were lucky to get out of there with only a few bruises to show for it.

And you know all Richard had to say was, 'Why'd you hit him? He could have had the girl for all I care.'

I was lying on my back now, staring at the blue sky above me, my chest heaving with exertion of the sit-ups, my body flooding with sweat. 'Why did you hit him?' That's our Richard for you. Always asking the most stupid bloody questions.

'Right you lot, five minutes of jumping jacks.'

There were groans from the rest of the lads but I'm up for them. I love this, I really do.

Reginald Dwyer
Block 15, Tanglin Barracks, Singapore
3rd May 1939
My dearest wife,

It was wonderful to hear from you. I'm glad Tommy likes school so much. He'll be our professor I'm sure, and show those knobs what for. Harry and Rita Henderson announcing their wedding in August was a real shock. I was only joking when I wrote to you a couple of letters ago, August weddings are the best. It's all a bit of a rush, isn't it? She isn't in the family way is she? I wouldn't put it past her to lead our Harry down the garden path to lead him up to the altar. If you know what I mean.

I know it was Evelyn's fourth birthday last week and I didn't send her anything. Tell her Daddy is real sorry. But, everything is so expensive here love, and after they've given you your money there's not much left for me. I don't mind, you and the kids always come first in my book. But it does make it hard to enjoy those treats like buying the kids something for their birthday or having an extra jar of beer of a night. I'm lucky though the single lads often treat me. They say 'Have one on me, Dad' so I do. Thank you very much. Great lads all of them.

Don't listen to that old tart, Mrs. Lloyd. She's just trying to get your back up. Eastern women do nothing for me. You're the only one who is always in my heart, dearest heart, you know that.

In my next letter, I might have some good news. I can't say anything yet because you know how superstitious I am. But I'm touching my lucky penny at the moment and holding on to the table. I hope it'll happen because it will be great for both of us.

Eddie Longhurst is playing a blinder for the battalion at the moment. The way he leaps around the goal like a monkey. With a bit of luck he will make all us Tads right proud.

It was good to hear Harry put that David Endersby in his place. Cheeky bugger. Pardon my French. Trying to take over the allotment without so much as by your leave. I'd have loved to have seen his face when Harry produced the transfer paper from the council. Harry always was the smart one of the family. But I know he can't be bothered to grow anything. Ask Uncle Dennis if he'll take it over. He'll get a right good crop of marrows and leeks. But remind him if he wants his peas, they'll only grow at the far end where I've put the trellis.

So, dearest heart, I hope I'll have news for you soon. (You know what about). Give my love to Tommy, Evelyn and young Grace. And give yourself a special hug from me.

Your husband

Reg

*

Richard Longhurst

'No, no, no, you bloody bunch of useless wankers. Like this, watch me.'

Serjeant Shelley then proceeded to show us exactly how to present arms in the new marching style.

This was a big event for us. A new army march past to be carried out for the first time in Singapore by the Manchesters.

Before, the army had always trooped its colours on the King's Birthday by marching in fours. Now somebody on the General Staff had decided it would look more dignified if we marched past in threes.

I couldn't see the difference myself. But for us poor bloody squaddies it meant a lot of spit and polish, and time spent under the baking sun out there in the parade ground.

We'd spent two years learning how to go smoothly from our parade ground formation into the march in fours past the reviewing stand. Changing into a parade in threes meant the timings were all different; the way we marched was different and even the present arms was different.

All because some bloody idiot thought it looked more dignified.

One good thing came of it though. The officers were out there with us because the captain of the guard had to rehearse as well. They were not well chuffed I'll tell you.

But that's the army for you, a mixture of lunacy, sadism, bullying and toffs.

I remember when we were training in York, we had this old fart of a Serjeant who thought because he had fought on the Somme, he had the God-given right to make life hell for all the recruits and me in particular.

One day, we were told to run an obstacle course that had buried wire, brick walls, balance beams, crawl-throughs, and a deep mud and shit filled hole at the end.

46

Now, ever since I was child, I've always been afraid of jumping across holes and streams. I don't know why. It must have been something that had happened to me. My mam would never tell me about it, but I have this scar on my chin, which, for the life of me, I can't remember how or when I got it. I know it's a stupid thing to be frightened of, but I am and I can't help it.

This bastard Serjeant knew I hated the last swing across the hole. He always made me start the obstacle course first so everyone could see me suffer as I tried to cross it.

'Right then, you shower of shit. We're going to do the Somme again. This time there ain't no Jerries waiting for you, there ain't no bleeding whiz-bangs going over your head and there ain't no pansy officers after you with their Webleys to encourage you forward with a little bit of lead. No, today ladies, you've just got me, Serjeant Harrison, your best friend, who's gonna help you go through this like a dose of senna pod.'

Then, the crafty bugger paused for a few seconds, rubbed his mangy chin and said, 'Of course, if any of you lot can't finish, then you'll all be cleaning out the latrines. There won't be no sweet trips into town to get your hole on Friday. Right my lovelies, is that clear?'

He looked up as he always did, selecting his victim, waiting for signs of weakness. 'Right then, Longhurst, you go first. The others will follow at ten-second intervals.'

He looked straight at me, but it was my brother who stepped forward.

'Yes, Serjeant.'

'No, not you, shithouse. Him, the tall one, Lanky Longhurst.' There were a few laughs from behind me that Eddie silenced with a withering look.

'Lanky, you can start.'

I picked up my rifle and crouched in a running position. Up ahead, I could see the course and, in the distance, the mud hole which I would have to swing across. It was there waiting for me.

Then I heard the bastard blow his whistle and next second I was off running. It was as if I didn't control my body any more. The bastard did with his bleeding whistle. He blows. I run. End of story.

I felt the pack banging against my back, got to tighten those straps another half-inch. Still too loose.

Then, I was at the first obstacle. Get down, keep your head low, hug the earth. Then get the elbows, wrists and knees working to push myself under the wire.

Behind me, I heard the whistle blow again. I heard my brother scream as if he were charging. I don't know about the rest of them but it put the fear of God in me.

Elbows, wrists and knees still going well. The wire's a piece of cake. I don't know why the old farts go on about the wire, as if it was some devil that will always haunt them.

I can see daylight now. Keep those elbows and knees working, Richard lad, don't get up too early. Might snag the pack.

Well clear now. I'm up on my knees running like Jesse Owens except I'm white, I'm carrying a sixty-pound pack and a rifle, and I'm travelling about ten times slower. Never mind, it's the thought that counts, isn't it Jesse?

Across the beam. Dead easy. Look straight ahead, not at your feet. No problem.

Still running, I do a quick check up. Ankles and knees all right. Chest heaving a bit but I'll survive. Arms starting to hurt from the rifle. Kidneys getting a pounding from the pack. Got to tighten those straps.

I'm up over the wall now. Another piece of cake. Sometimes, it helps to be built like a streak of piss.

I look up and I can see the hanging rope now in the distance. And the hole. And the dark, turgid mud filling it to the brim. I can see it waiting for me.

I look behind. The rest of the lads are running now, all stretched out in a long line with Harrison shouting at Tommy Larkins for getting his pack caught on the wire. 'On the Somme, you'd be dead now. And all of your mates would be dead. All of them full of holes like a fucking colander, all because you're a stupid lump of shit. What are you?'

I didn't hear the answer but I could guess it. Eddie was right behind me now, running with his usual easy stride, as if he weren't carrying anything.

I kept my head down, extended the rifle, and charged at the scarecrow of straw standing in front of me.

Thrust, turn, pull out, and charge again. I went through the drill in my head. Thrust, turn, pull out, charge. Now, for the last straw–filled corpse.

'Put some life in it Lanky. You're killing someone, not asking them to foxtrot.'

I screamed louder to please him.

'Louder man, don't scream like a namby–pamby girl. You're a Tad, a Manchester lad, not a bleeding girl guide.'

Suddenly, Eddie was beside me. He wasn't out of breath or anything. Just running along at a gentle lope that seemed to eat up the yards.

He looked across as he passed me. 'Keep your head down and jump. Don't think about it. Just jump. Watch me.'

He slung the rifle across his shoulder and picked up the pace. Without stopping, he jumped at the rope, holding on to it with both hands. The force of his momentum took him swinging through the air, over the hole, and onto the other side, landing sweetly on both feet facing me.

I saw his smile. A real Eddie smile that always said, 'See, I told you. A piece of piss.'

I could feel Harrison getting closer. The others were passing me now, all going for the ropes.

It was now or never.

I ran as hard as I could. The pack and the rifle banging my back with an irregular rhythm. 'Don't look up, don't look up,' it said.

I looked up.

The rope lay in front of me, but I wasn't running any more. I was standing there. I could hear Eddie and the others encouraging me to jump. I even took hold of the rope and held it with both my hands. At least, I think I did.

I looked up at the sky. Grey, cloudy. I heard a voice in my head. It was in Harrison's bastard voice. 'I knew you couldn't do it,' he whispered in my ear, 'they're going to hate you.'

I let go of the rope and turned to face Harrison.

'Lanky here has bottled out. So it looks like you lovely ladies are going to be cleaning the bogs this weekend. Tough shit, isn't it? If any one of you would like me to give your women a good time, I'd be more than happy to oblige.'

'Serjeant, it's my fault not theirs.'

'What's that, Lanky? Did you say something? Well, what is the world is coming to when this pile of shite decides he should speak?' He strutted around the muddy hole dramatically, then he stopped as if thinking,

'Well Lanky, you haven't finished yet. You've still got to get to the other side.'

I started to walk around the hole.

'Oh no lad, it's mined there.' I took another step. 'And there. In fact, it's mined all around this bloody place. No lad, the only way is to go through it all.'

I looked down at the hole. It was full to the brim with dark oozing mud. Here and there, I could see bits of rotten vegetables, potato peelings, and bones. My nostrils were filled with the sweet smell of shit and decay.

'Well, off you go lad. We haven't got all day.' He blew his whistle.

I looked at the shit. It looked at me. And I stepped into it up to my waist.

'You bloody idiot, Larkin.' Shelley was bellowing again.

I was brought back to the heat of Singapore by the Serjeant's voice.

'No, no. You're not in a straight line. I've seen more life in a piece of wood. You, Larkin, yes, you, next time your arm swings higher than 90 degrees I'm gonna chop it off, you understand me lad.'

He stared at Larkin until the squaddie was forced to look down at his boots. 'Right then, let's do it one more time. Remember to count three before you peel off into the next line. That's all you have to do, count 3. Not 2. Not 4. Just 1-2-3. Even you can do that, Larkin.'

The band started up again playing 'The Jolly Twister.' The CSM, Shelley in this case, led the way, followed by the first line of three. All went well until it came to Larkin who must have marched off early and not with the beat.

Suddenly the whole line was a mess. Men tripped each other up, rifles clattered to the ground, muffled grunts and swearing erupted from the ranks.

Shelley silenced the music with an imperious wave of his arm. 'Right, you shower of shit, we're gonna be here from now until next Wednesday. And we're gonna stay here 24 hours a day until we get this right. Understand? There'll be no food, no little trips to Lavender Street, and no beer until you do get it right. I'm not having D Company being the laughing stock of this regiment. What are you laughing at, Larkin?'

Larkin suddenly woke up. 'Nothing, Serjeant.'

'Well, wipe the smile off your face or I'll wipe it off for you. Right, once more by the right, shoulder arms.' His order barked across the white parade ground.

The sun beat relentlessly down.

The band played on.

And we marched on and on.

Chapter 8

Reginald Dwyer
Block 15, Tanglin Barracks, Singapore
June 15th, 1939
My dearest wife,

It was lovely to get your letter finally. Proper brightened up my day it did. And it were a real long letter, you know how to put the words together when you get going, don't you Margie?

Now let me try and answer it. Of course, it's alright for you to go out dancing once in a while down at the Hippodrome. I've told you not to listen to that Mrs. Lloyd. If she didn't gossip, her knickers would fall down. I've got a lot of stories I've heard about her and her gang as well. So, don't worry, you go dancing with the girls, if you want. I know life must be as boring for you without me as it is for me without you.

All the preparations are going ahead for Harry's wedding on the eighth are they? I'm sorry I can't be there but I'll remember to go into town and send him a telegram wishing him well for the night, as it were. At least the best man will have something to read out. The aunties will be pleased as well. A telegram from Singapore they'll say, well I never ooh, aah. I can hear them now, dearest heart, and their arms across their bosoms sitting with their half pints of Mackeson. I do wish he would be careful of Rita and her family though. They think they are too good for us I know. But our Harry's better than all of them put together.

Life goes on as normal here. We don't seem to do much at all. The heat takes a terrible toll so most of the time we sleep in the afternoon. There's always the dhobiwallahs and the rest of them to clean up after us and to look after our kit. The only lads who don't use them are the ones who are too mean or stingy with their money. I've organised my own little brigade, so if boots need polishing or a piece of kit needs mending, I get it from the lads and give it to the dhobiwallahs. Of course, I take my share of the money. It's only fair isn't it. There's no flies on Reginald Dwyer, let me tell you. Well, there are really. The whole place is full of flies. When you and the kids come over, we'll have to make sure we've got mosquito nets and all of the rest of the stuff to protect you. Talking of that, a tiny bird whispered in my ear the other day, so I'm going to have some news for you, but mum's the word for now.

Got to go to eat, Margie, at the canteen. Give my love to the kids. I saw the picture you sent of Grace. Lord, she's a big, bonny baby isn't she? You must be feeding her too much! Don't you worry your head about all the talk of war. It's not going to happen. Who could want another Great War? It goes without saying Mr. Chamberlain wouldn't be that stupid. Remember last year at Munich. I'm sure they'll all sort it out again.

Anyway, those politicians never really matter to the likes of us, do they? Give a big hug to Tommy and Evelyn and baby Grace from their dad out here in Singapore.

Your husband,

Reg

*

Richard Longhurst

I don't know when it was that Eddie and I started to drift apart. I mean we were never what you call close. Even back in Manchester there was always something that separated us, never allowing us to be real brothers.

I remember the old witch next door. Mrs. Hargreaves her name was. An old bag who used to spend hours kneeling on the pavement scrubbing her front step so as she could watch the comings and goings of her neighbours. Eddie and myself used to wait until she had finished and had taken her scrubbing brush, pumice stone and bucket back inside to her kitchen. Then we'd run through any of the shit or puddles in the street, making sure our shoes were mucky. A few quick stamps from both of us and her step was like any other in the street; nice and dirty once more.

Anyway, the cunning old bag must have realised what was going on. One day, she climbed ever so slowly up from her knees, picked up her brushes and bucket and went back into her house. Eddie and I saw our chance. We ran down to her house, stepping in as much crap and as many puddles as we could. Then, before we got to her door, Eddie noticed a large pile of dog shit in the gutter. He ran over to it and jumped up high in the air, landing in the middle of the turd with a loud splat. Well, you should have seen it, dog shit exploding everywhere like a bloody water bomb. Then we both went to the step and did our little dance, our own special soft-shoe shuffle.

But the crafty old bitch had been waiting for us, hadn't she? All I remember is being lifted up by these powerful forearms, made strong by years of scrubbing and polishing.

'Oh, it's you two wee shites is it? I wondered who'd been messing up my step. Wee, bastards.'

Eddie was by now struggling and trying to punch and kick her. I was lying still in her arms.

'Right then lads off ye come.'

She dragged us off to our house, Eddie still struggling to get out of the grip of the powerful forearms.

'Keep still ye wee shite or I'll give you a clip round the ear hole. You two, nothing but trouble. You especially,' she said, staring at Eddie, 'you're gonna be no good. Like I told Mrs. Arkwright from number 23, her with the bad legs, when a woman takes up with a man while the husband's away, nothing good will ever come of it.' She let go of me and gave Eddie a slap across the face. 'And I were right.'

The old cow marched both of us up the street to our door. Mam was in of course, and gave us a right belting. Me and Eddie both sent to bed without our supper.

Lying there, I tried to understand what Mrs. Hargreaves meant. Eddie was mumbling to himself all night. 'I'm gonna get the old bitch. I'm gonna get the old bitch.' On and on and on, like a priest mumbling his prayers. He never did though. She died not long after. Scrubbing her step one day, she just dropped down dead. Eddie's only comment was 'Good riddance to bad rubbish.'

A few years later at school, we were so different even the teachers started saying it to us.

'I don't know what to do with your brother, Longhurst. Great at sports but hopeless at everything else. And you, probably the best pupil in the school, too. Definitely not two peas in a pod, you two. Definitely not.'

You see, I had done well at school. I loved History, finding out about all the kings and queens and what happened to them. Eddie on the other hand, had been kept back a year. So even though he was two years older than me, he was only one year above me. Eddie was cock-of-the school though. Great at football and would stand no shit from nobody. He wasn't a bully though, not yet anyway, but most of the other kids were wary of him. Didn't like to get on his bad side, just in case. Me? I basked in the reflected glory. So I never had any problems at all, even though I was already shooting out of my trousers and was as thin as a rake. Mam could never get trousers to fit me. Seemed like every time she bought a pair, my body would decide to shoot up again so they were always too short.

'Hard lines,' she used to say, 'You're going to have to fly at half-mast for the rest of the year. Trousers don't grow on trees.'

That's where I got the name 'Lanky' from. That and the fact that we were from Lancashire. And the surname Longhurst of course. Mustn't forget that either.

So school wasn't Eddie's world. I loved it though. Books were where I could lose myself. You see, in a book there's a whole new world waiting to be discovered. Where words form pictures in your mind. For a few hours, you can become someone else.

When I was fourteen though I had to leave, just like Eddie. The step-dad was on the dole again, sitting all day in the house moping. And when he wasn't doing that, he was down the pub getting drunk.

By then of course, I knew myself and Eddie were different. We never spoke about it. Couldn't really, what with our mam always around. But we both knew. Strange thing is, it made Eddie try even harder to be my brother, a real brother.

Even after we left school he would look after me. Sharing his fags, making sure I didn't get into trouble with the other lads. One day, he even bought me my first pint. I was standing outside the Crown on Duke Street, hanging around with the other kids. There was nothing to do, certainly no jobs to go to.

Then Eddie came out with a pint in his hand and a packet of pork scratchings. 'Here, get these down your neck,' he said handing them to me. I sipped the brown liquid in the pot. 'Pint of best mild that is. Puts hairs on your chest.' Then, he went back inside the pub.

Well, I didn't want to let him down but the stuff didn't taste great so I gave most of it to the other kids. I ate the pork scratchings though. They were the best part of it.

A couple of years later there was the fight with the step-dad. I could have stayed of course. I think Mam would have liked me to. But I couldn't leave Eddie, not after all those years. I couldn't leave him, could I?

Eddie Longhurst

Proudest day of my life today.

I got called into Shelley's office about 9.30. All the others had gone for their cup of tea and bacon sandwich. I was a bit pissed off when Shelley asked me to go with him to his office. I like my tea and bacon in the morning. Best part of the army is the food. At least, there always is food, not like bleeding Manchester.

Sometimes, we used to go into the pantry and there was nothing there except a bit of stale bread. Mum was down the pub with her fancy man, this was before they got married, and myself and Richard were about eight and ten years old. Fuck, was I hungry all the time then. We used to go down to the shop on the corner and nick some sweets to keep us going. No, let's tell the truth. I did the nicking. Richard sort of pretended to nick stuff but he never did. I always shared with him what I got, didn't I? Well, he was my brother.

Anyway, in I marched to Shelley's office, expecting another bollocking for something I'd done. I looked across and there was Lieutenant Whitehead. Well, you hardly ever see the officers down our end of the woods. But, quick as a flash, I snapped him my smartest salute. The toffs like that sort of crap, don't they?

'At ease,' he said. I looked hard and I heard the sound but I didn't see his lips move. I waited, maybe I hadn't heard him right.

'I said at ease.' Again, I heard the words. Again the lips didn't move. Nevertheless, I went to the 'at ease' – hands behind my back, shoulders squared, legs exactly 11 inches apart.

'Well...,' he looked down at the piece of paper in front of him, 'Well...Longhurst. Serjeant Shelley has been giving me reports of your progress as a soldier. You've been doing very well in the Battalion's football team, although personally, I can't see why we don't have a rugger team. Much better game.'

'None of the men know how to play it sir,' said Serjeant Shelley.

Lt. Whitehead just sniffed. 'Well, maybe they should learn, Shelley. Sorts out the men from the boys does rugger. At my prep school, we played it all through winter. I don't know what schools teach anymore.' He looked back down at the file lying in front of him. 'Well, Longhurst, Shelley here wants to promote you to corporal. What do you say?'

I thought for a moment. Me a bloody corporal. 'Thank you very much sir.'

'Don't thank me corporal, thank Serjeant Shelley here. It's his choice, nothing to do with me. Although, if you should let us down......,'

He left the threat hanging there. 'Don't worry, I won't let Serjeant Shelley down. Or you,' I added to keep the twat happy.

'Good, jolly good show.' He picked up his swagger stick, pulled his Sam Browne down and walked out of the office. 'Carry on, Serjeant Shelley,' he said on his way out.

Shelley turned to me. 'Listen, Longhurst. I've put you up for this and I can pull you down. Get me?'

'Yes, Serjeant.'

'Go and get your breakfast. You can tell the lads yourself.'

'Thank you Serjeant.'

Would you fucking believe it. Me a fucking corporal. I'll make Serjeant next, like Shelley. Would you fucking believe it?

Chapter 9

Reg Dwyer
Block 15, Tanglin Barracks, Singapore
August 23rd, 1939
My dearest wife,
From what you wrote, the wedding sounded like a real knees up. Fancy Mr. Harris from down the street being able to play the piano so well. I would never have believed it. After all, he just works at the hat factory, tying the ribbon around the crown. Well it goes to show you. Still waters run deep, as my mum used to say.

Shame about the to-do at the end of the night. Tell Rita not to worry about it too much. I'm sure it didn't really spoil her wedding. They were just letting off steam. Too much to drink and men say lots of stupid stuff. I bet you were surprised to hear she had been walking out with Joe Suggs though. Funny two grown men fighting over nothing. I would have loved to have been there.

That was a real long letter you sent to me last time. Lord, it must have taken you years to write. I'll try and answer your questions one by one but first let me tell you my good news.

Your loving husband is now a lance corporal. That's right, I were promoted last week. Aren't you pleased? Serjeant Shelley had whispered in my ear a couple of months ago but I was sworn to secrecy. And you know how superstitious I am. I knew if I told you it was never going to happen. I hate to jinx everything. Anyway, it means a bit more money for you, which I'm sure you'll be pleased about. But even better, it means I'm now an NCO. They have their own married quarters and there's far more for them than for privates. Serjeant Shelley says there are at least three houses empty at the minute. As soon as the new CO arrives my application should go straight through. I have to do it all again though, because there are different forms for NCOs. Lord what the army would do without its forms in triplicate, I don't know.

Eddie Longhurst, remember me telling you about him, well he was made corporal at the same time. So the lads gave us a party last week to celebrate. I got a little drunk. It won't happen again though it were just that once.

I was sorry to hear Mum was ill again. She's getting old now but she still wants to scrub that step of hers every day. It's not as if it ain't clean enough already. She's probably better now, but tell her to look after herself and take a small glass of whiskey every night before she goes to bed to take the chill off her chest.

Uncle Dennis has started on the allotment has he? That's great, I don't mind if he puts his pigeons down there, a heap of pigeon droppings won't hurt the soil. May even help it. Tell him no, I've never tried runner beans on it. But, I'm sure they'll probably do quite well near the peas.

You're not to worry about Tommy at school. It's natural he should get into a few fights with the other kids. They're only trying to work out who is boss. Kids that age are forever falling in and out of friends. So don't worry, at least he can stick up for himself. It's always good to learn early.

I think that answers most of your letter, dearest heart. But, you can write though. Fair had me blushing some of the things you put down on paper. Let's just say, I feel exactly the same way too. I miss you and the kids so much. But now I've been promoted, I'm sure we'll be together again soon.

Oh and about all the news in the papers about Hitler, don't worry. It's only that Churchill mouthing off. He always was a little toe-rag. Look what he did to the miners. They'll sort it out again like last time. Nobody wants to go to war again, least of all the Germans. Churchill and his lot are war-mongers. You ignore it all and just make sure the kids are well looked after. Trust you me, they'll all sit down together and talk it through. Who wants to go to war over bloody Poland!

Anyway, I've got to go now. We're going down to one of the cafes tonight for a drink and then to the cinema to see George Formby in 'It's in the Air.' I'm sure it'll be funny. Next week we've got a big football game against the Gordon Highlanders. Eddie's playing and I hope we beat the mad Scots.

So, good night, dearest heart. I miss you and the kids but I know it won't be for long now. I know we'll be together soon.

Your husband

Reg

Reg Dwyer

We were all clustered around O'Neill's radio. By all, I mean the usual crowd of lads sharing Barrack 15. Eddie was cleaning his nails with a knife. O'Neill was lounging on his back, staring into space as he does. What the hell he has to think about God only knows. Terry Teale was reading the *Daily Sketch* from two weeks ago, somebody must have nicked it from the Officers' Mess. Then there was Tommy Larkin, the biggest waste of oxygen this side of Stockport, he lay on his bed farting. It was a normal, long, boring Sunday night in Singapore.

I looked at the fan turning slowly above me. What a bloody waste. All it did was to disturb the already muggy air. Margie would hate nights like this.

It was another bloody Sunday, a day of rest and all that. Most of us were resting our hangovers. Bad night, the night before. Saturday always was down the Lady Bar. We must have poured gallons of Tiger down our throats.

It was Lanky who came rushing in around five o'clock to tell us to switch on the radio right now.

Most of us told him to shut up. But Lanky insisted as he always did. They were playing really boring music – some sort of classical stuff – sounded more like a funeral march to me.

Larkin even checked the paper. 'It's supposed to be Greg Farrell and his Orchestra. They've got Dinah Lane as their singer. Bit of a cracker she is, and she can sing. Voice like a turtle dove she has.'

'Don't you mean a nightingale?' said Lanky, always the clever one.

'She's a great bird whatever she is,' answered Larkin.

Then the announcer broke in. 'Now, here is an important announcement from her Majesty's Government.'

'Well, who else it would be fucking from,' added Larkin. We all told him to shut up.

'This morning the British Ambassador in Berlin handed the German Government a final note stating that, unless we heard from them by 11 o'clock that they were prepared at once to withdraw their troops from Poland, a state of war would exist between us.'

'Fuck me,' said Larkin.

'SShhhhhhhhhhh,' was the response from a platoon of throats.

'I have to tell you that no such undertaking has been received and consequently this country is now at war with Germany.'

'Now may God bless you all. May he defend the right. It is the evil things that we shall be fighting against – brute force, bad faith, injustice, oppression and persecution – and against them I am sure that the right will prevail.'

You could have cut the silence with a knife. Finally, Larkin spoke, 'Does this mean we're at war again. Fighting like.'

It was Eddie who put him straight. 'That's right, Larkin me old son. Finally gonna see some fuckin' action we are.'

'But I didn't sign on to fight. Just to be a soldier. No fighting. They said nothing about fighting.'

'God, are you stupid or what? This is the army, course we're gonna be fighting. That's what we're paid to do. Take orders, fight and die.'

'They said nothing about dying when I signed on. Nothing about that at all.'

'Will you both shut up?' It was Lanky who spoke. First time I ever heard him raise his voice. I think it was the last as well.

'Well, it looks like they'll send all us home now,' I said.

Everyone nodded.

'Margie and the kids would have loved it out here. Well, there you go, back to Blighty for us.'

'I don't want to fight,' said Larkin.

Eddie suddenly launched himself at Larkin, showering punches, kicks and elbows all over him.

Larkin just covered himself up. We all ran to pull Eddie off. It wasn't easy mind. Eddie was built like a brick shit house. Took four of us to drag him off Larkin.

'You'll fight Larkin, don't worry,' he said, jumping in the air, 'you'll fight or I'll kill you myself.'

Larkin was silent. Smart bugger. I wouldn't cross Eddie Longhurst if I were him.

'Fuck it. If we're going to leave Singapore, we'd better get some leg over time in before we do. Who's off down the Pussy Cat with me.' Eddie looked around, challenging us all not to go.

We all raised our hands. As I said, it didn't pay to cross Eddie.

*

Michael O' Neill.

'Oh Michael, you know how I feel about you.'

'Yes, Scarlett, I know you're madly, crazily in love with me but frankly, my dear, I don't give a damn.'

I cupped her small breast in my hand and slowly lowered my head to her waiting red-nosed nipple.

'Don't, Michael, it's not fair to my sister.'

'I know she loves me too but she'll have to marry Ashley.' I lowered my head to nuzzle her breasts again, gently biting the round soft nipple with my teeth.

'Hands off cocks, hands on socks. Look lively, you shower of shit. You've heard the news, let's get a move on.'

I opened my eyes. It wasn't Scarlett O'Hara standing over me with her long auburn hair and those green eyes that shone like the leaves of a shamrock, but Serjeant Shelley with a sneer on his lips, and eyes that stared like pissholes in the snow.

'What are you smiling about O'Neill? Get your arse out of there.'

He picked up the edge of my mattress and heaved me out of bed to lie naked as a newborn babe on the floor.

'Sure it's a terrible thing to shake a sleeping man like that, Serjeant. Me poor heart's pounding with the fright.'

'Shut the fuck up, O'Neill. I want to see you and the rest of the platoon outside in full battle gear in five minutes.'

The spalpeen strode out, and without a by your leave.

'Well, Scarlett, I'll have to be leaving you for a while my dear. A man's got to do what a man's got to do.'

'Hurry up O'Neill. We'll all get it in the neck if we're not ready. We're at war now.'

'Yes, Reg my boy, me head's at war, me feet are at war, but I'm not sure if the rest of me has decided to join in yet.'

'You were well gone last night.'

'Aye, it was a great night. A night when the throat was well oiled, the craic was good and life took a rosy hue. Ah that Rosey, she sure has a lovely hue.' I shook my head trying to remove the cobwebs the fucking spider had spun in it. 'But I must remember only to drink that Tiger in even numbers. My old da used to say 'Michael, my boy, take it from someone who knows. Only drink in even numbers. Them odd numbers are bad for you. Certain to get a bad head and piles if you drink in the odd numbers.'

'Piles of what, da?' I ask.

'Piles, son, just piles. Enigmatic he was, my da. He even died enigmatically.'

'Get your bleeding clothes on O'Neill. We don't have all day,' said Richard.

'Yes sir, Private Longhurst 9634518, sir.' I attempted to salute him but only served to hit myself above the eye.

Well, time to do as the good Serjeant says. I throw on my shirt and shorts. Nearly miss. Comb hair. God, you're a handsome son-of-a-gun. Errol Flynn has nothing on you. 'Yes, but he has got Maureen O'Sullivan,' said a voice in my head. 'Not for long, not for long,' I say. I looked at the mirror. Socks on. Boots to follow. Great shine Reg, you'll always do me proud. Grab my kit. Nicely packed Reg. You're going to make someone a lovely wife one day.

Fasten the webbing, one last look in the mirror. Comb your hair, you mucky pup. Put the cap on careful now, boy, don't want to mess your hair.

One last look in the mirror. 'God, you're handsome.' Pick up my kit and saunter out. The others are still running around like blue-arsed flies trying to get their lives organised. Poor bastards, they never get it right.

Shelley is waiting outside, looking at his watch.

I walk over to him, place my kit bag down on the ground in regulation position, snap my head to attention and salute.

'Top of the morning to you, Serjeant.'

'Fuck off, O'Neill.'

'Now that's not a very friendly greeting on this beautiful September morning in the sunny island of Singapore to the first member of the platoon out on parade, is it Serjeant?'

'Fuck off O'Neill.' He marched off to the barracks.

'Ah, I see, that English word has so many meanings, Serjeant. Now which of the versions am I meant to be understanding myself?' It was wasted though. The bastard was already bellowing in the barracks.

'Get a fuckin' move on. Anyone who isn't out at parade in thirty seconds is on a charge.'

Shelley stepped back as they all piled out of the barracks, Richard and Eddie Longhurst, Reg Dwyer, Tommy Larkin and the rest, all in their khakis and carrying their battle kit.

We lined up in parade ground formation. Arm's length apart, kit in front of us, waiting for inspection.

Shelley stood at the end of the line, his hand on his hips, his uniform perfectly ironed, starched and creased.

He moved in front of me, adjusted my solar topee so it was off my eyes.

'You're not Baden Powell, O'Neill. This is how you wear your topee. Open you bag.' I pulled open the regulation knot of the regulation army kit bag and revealed, (thank goodness, crossing myself and saying three Hail Marys) that Old Reg had done me proud. It looked smarter than the Galway point to point.

'Very good, O'Neill,' I heard him say. Bastard begrudged me every single letter of every single word.

He carried on moving down the line making comments, occasionally grunting. Then he got to poor Tommy Larkin. The poor man was already shaking.

'Sorry Serjeant, I...,'

'No talking on parade, Larkin.' Shelley took one step back and looked Larkin up and down. Not once. Not twice. But again and again.

'Jesus, all fucking mighty...'

'Serjeant?'

'You're on a charge Larkin. Talking on parade.' He walked closer to Larkin until his face was only inches away from the poor little shite. 'You're not a soldier Larkin. You're not a man. You're a cockroach. One of those black shiny things I crush under the heel of my boot. What are you?'

Larkin was going to answer but Shelley put his finger to his lips to indicate silence.

'You're not going to be in my platoon much longer, Larkin. You're going to discover the toilets, or the kitchen, or maybe the laundry is in dire need of your services. SO FUCK OFF OUT OF HERE.'

There was a small cough to my left.

'If you will excuse me, Serjeant, I have to make a short statement to the men.'

It was Lieutenant Whitehead, our platoon commander and a sorrier looking weak-kneed Englishman you wouldn't find this side of heaven or hell. His uniform was immaculate of course, but somehow he always looked wrong. When you saw those knobbly knees sticking out from them horrendously wide shorts, you couldn't help but think God had an immense sense of humour where the English were concerned. That's probably why they were such a sour race. God always playing little jokes on them.

And God always had to have more than one laugh. To those knees he had added a tiny mustache above a thin-lipped mouth. You know the type, it looked like two caterpillars had joined hands and danced a wee reel on the man's lip. Above the caterpillars were a pair of horn-rimmed spectacles sitting on his nose like a squirrel on a cow's arse.

This Englishman was going to lead us to war. Jesus, Mary and Joseph, save our souls, because I'm sure nobody else will.

'Stand at ease men,' Lt. Whitehead announced in his tired, oh-so-well-bred, public school drawl. 'As you may have heard yesterday on the radio, the Germans have refused to stop their attacks on plucky Poland, so Mr. Chamberlain has been forced to declare, um, a war, on that said country.'

Oh, you stupid shit. We do understand the King's English even if it is a heathen language, fouled by millions of English throats for years. Not like the liquid tones of Ireland. I miss the sweet sound of Mairead O'Connor when she sang her love songs in the Gaelic. It was enough to make a nun want to ravish the pope.

'Well men, it's going to be a jolly little scrap. It probably won't affect us out here in Singapore, but we mustn't let the home team down, what?'

He looked around for agreement from the men. I kept my face blank. I wasn't going to give the shite the time of day.

'Today, we're going to our war positions at Changi. Let's put on a good show. Remember we're Manchester and Empire soldiers. Carry on, Serjeant Shelley.'

With that sterling finale to his speech, I watched him put his topee on, ship his swagger stick under the arm and slouch off toward the officers' mess.

After about five paces, he stopped and turned around. 'I say, Serjeant, I knew there was something else. We haven't got enough lorries so we've hired some Chinese ones. They should be coming soon. Make sure the men get all they need from the QM. You know, rifles, socks those sort of things.'

'How long are we going to be at our position, sir?'

'You know I never thought to ask. That's a very interesting question, Serjeant. Ask the RSM, he'll probably know.'

'Yes sir.'

'Carry on, Serjeant Shelley.' With a wave of his wooden swagger stick, Lt. Whitehead resumed his stroll back to the waiting eggs, bacon and coffee of the officers' mess.

'Jesus, Mary and Joseph, save us from eejits.'

'What was that, O'Neill?'

'Nothing, Serjeant, just clearing my throat. Dry as a drover's dog, it is.'

'Remember, O'Neill, they may be idiots. But they are officer idiots. And they are our idiots. Is that clear?'

'Yes, Serjeant, clear as mud.'

He looked at me, deciding whether to kick my head in, put me on a charge or simply allow it to pass.

Luckily for me the third option won. But I could see it was a close run thing. I'm going to have to be watching my mouth with our Serjeant Shelley. 'But where's the fun in that,' said the voice in my head, 'you be keeping your mouth shut from now on.' I realised I had spoken out loud, but Shelley was miles away, going through Larkin's kit.

'This is a disgrace Larkin…Longhurst.'

'Yes Serjeant,' both of them chimed in at the same time.

'Help Larkin sort out his mess, will you, Eddie.'

'Yes, Serjeant.'

He stood up and stepped back from the platoon, 'Right lads, we've got a busy day ahead of us. Larkin, Longhurst E. and Dwyer, you three go to the QM and get the gear. Murphy and Teale come with me to the armoury for the Vickers. The rest of you ensure that we're ready to go as soon as the lorries arrive.'

'Yes, Serjeant,' came a chorus of voices including my own. Then another voice, separate from the others, could be heard squeaking across the parade ground. 'But what about breakfast, Serjeant.' It was Larkin, the poor, stupid eejit.

Shelley walked up to him and stuck his face two inches away from Larkin's. 'What about breakfast Serjeant,' he mimicked the man's high-pitched whine. Then his face changed, becoming redder and redder. 'WE'RE AT WAR SONNY DIDN'T YOU HEAR. WE'RE AT FUCKING WAR.' Spit gathered at the edges of his mouth. A few drops landed on Larkin's face and uniform. I could see his fingers trembling, itching to go to his face to wipe it off. But he didn't. He let the spittle sit there on his cheek like a single tear.

Shelley walked back to his position in front of us. 'The rest of you will eat breakfast after we have requisitioned all the stores. You, Larkin, will ensure the barracks' washrooms and toilets are spotless before we leave today. Is that clear?'

'Yes Serjeant,' chorused us all like a happy flock of sheep.

'Well, Larkin?'

'Yes, Serjeant.'

'Right, jump to it. And don't fuck around. Those lorries could arrive any minute now.'

That the trucks didn't arrive till near eleven o'clock wasn't his fault of course. As he said himself, he could have 'built the fucking things himself' in the time they had been waiting. Smart way to go to war that, Serjeant Shelley. But it was his next line that really got me going.

'Well, we've got the trucks but the bleeding Chinese drivers have pissed off, saying it's not their job to drive us all the way to Changi. So, can any of you lot drive?'

I couldn't help myself. I sort of half giggled and half swallowed a giggle all at the same time. Eddie Longhurst looked at me with eyes that threatened severe violence.

'Come on, one of you must know how to drive a truck.'

Then Eddie Longhurst spoke up. 'O'Neill knows how to drive, don't you, O'Neill?'

The bastard. The shite-arsed bastard. Didn't they ever tell him nobody volunteers for nothing in the army?

'Well, O'Neill, do you?'

'Well, Serjeant, it's like this...' My mind was galloping like a thoroughbred over the jumps at the Curragh '... I've driven a little bit, it was a long time ago. And I'm sure the trucks are different in Ireland.'

'They still have four tyres and a steering wheel, don't they?'

'That they do, Serjeant,' says I enjoying his joke.

'Well, then, it's settled. Come with me and we'll drive the truck up here.'

I marched off behind the Serjeant, throwing my best evil eye at Eddie Longhurst. Got to be careful though, the bastard would break every bone in the poor body if he had the chance. Even worse, the bastard knew it. He smiled back at me. Well, I'll bide me time but we'll get even, Corporal Longhurst 96341547.

I was still cursing my luck when we got to the truck park. There they were, eight Chinese trucks. Fords I think. The sort of truck that carried cargo from the docks. Open topped at the back so lads can get a tan I thought, laughing to myself.

Along the side were large Chinese characters with a small English translation beneath them. 'Ah Hing Transportation'.

'What are you waiting for O'Neill, we haven't got all day.'

'Serjeant, can you start her for me.' I got in the cab and handed Shelley the starting handle. Again I could see him weighing up the options in his mind, whether to tell me to do it my fucking self. Again though, he just took the handle, went round the front of the truck and put it into the starter.

It was time to have some fun with the bastard. I pushed the clutch in and put the truck in gear.

'Ready, sarge.'

'It's Serjeant to you, O'Neill.'

'Yes, Serjeant.'

I watched as he bent over, arse in the air, and gave the starter a heave.

Nothing.

He took off his topee and wiped the sweat from his forehead. Bending down once again, he took the starter handle in the grip of his massive paws and gave it an almighty heave that would have started all the trucks in heaven.

The engine coughed and died.

'Are you sure everything is ok with this bloody truck?'

I pretended to check the dash board. 'It looks ok here, sarge.'

'That's Serjeant to you, O'Neill. I won't tell you again.'

'Yes… Serjeant.'

He bent down once more, this time spitting between his hands and rubbing them furiously. With a fierce grunt, he then grabbed the starting handle in both paws and gave it two almighty swings.

Still nothing. Not even a cough or a splutter.

Sweat was pouring off the poor bastard now. I almost felt sorry for him. The sweat was dribbling down his nose and onto the front of his starched, pressed, and oh-so-neatly creased uniform. Beneath his arms, huge, dark, liquid semi-circles had appeared, becoming larger by the minute as he stood beneath the boiling noonday sun.

I started whistling 'Too darn hot', luckily the bastard wouldn't know Cole Porter from his elbow. He stood there wiping his face in the sun. 'Are you sure the truck's ready to start?'

'Yes, Serjeant,' said I in the most innocent voice I could muster.

I must have overdone it as I usually do, because quick as a flash he said, 'Here, let me have a look.' He comes round to the cab before I can take the truck out of gear and pull the choke out.

He's there looking over my shoulder. I can see his eyes going over the gears, taking in the gauges, checking the knobs. 'It looks ok to me.'

'See, I told you, Serjeant. One more go should do it.'

He walks around to the front of the truck again, I push the clutch in and disengage the gears. Then, as he goes through his strongman routine: checking his sleeves are rolled up properly, stretching his muscles, spitting between his palms and finally grabbing the starting handle with his two immense paws, I slowly ease the choke out. Not too much now or the bugger will flood the engine and then I'll be badgered.

He bends down, sticking his arse in the air. All I can see in front of me is this immense arse jerking up and down like a dog on heat. Jaysus, that's what a woman sees. What an ugly sight. How do the poor things put up with a sight like that? Even more, how do they actually look at it?

His arse gave this immense heave and the engine coughs into life, running as sweetly as Mrs. Healey's cows. Shelley gave me this huge boyish grin.

'See, all you have to do is put your back into it, Serjeant,' said I.

The grin vanishes from his face. I always go too far. It's the story of my life. Always push it just that little bit too much. 'Aye, but where's the craic if you don't try,' says the voice in my head.

I didn't answer him. There was no point. The bugger was always right anyway.

Shelley got in the truck next to me. 'Get a move on, O'Neill.'

I put the clutch in, eased the truck into gear, eased the clutch out and the engine put-putter-putterred and died.

Silence.

Shelley looks across at me. I shrug my shoulders. Now is not the time to say a word, nor is it the time to make a joke.

For once. I use my head and kept quiet. Shelley gets out of the truck, waddles round the front and starts going through his strongman act again. He bends down in front of the truck and is about to give the starting handle an almighty heave. When my mouth seems to open of its own accord.

'Really put your back into it this time, Serjeant,' says I.

I could see his body tense, his arse gives this tiny twitch of irritation and I think I've gone too far this time.

But all he does is give the starting handle a violent twist like he's screwing my head off.

The engine kicks into life. He gets into the cab next to me. 'Get a fucking move on.'

'It's the double de-clutching Serjeant. I'm sure I'll get it right this time.'

I put the truck in gear, remembering to double de-clutch and then slowly ease it out, depressing the accelerator with my right foot.

The truck moves forward. Jaysus, we're moving. I've never driven one of these before but I used to watch my Uncle Sylv do it on his truck. It looked simple then and begod so it is.

We roar up the hill towards the barracks, going at least five miles an hour.

'Have you ever driven one of these before?'

'Yes, Serjeant,' says I.

'Couldn't we go a bit faster?'

'That we could Serjeant.' I put the truck into second, easing the clutch out. There was a frightening sound of screeching, grinding metal like a whole orchestra of violins on heat. The truck picked up speed. I ignored the sound.

'Are you sure it wasn't a horse and cart?'

'No, Serjeant, it had a few more horsepower than that. I used to drive fish from Galway to Knock in Mayo.'

'Wouldn't it have been easier to drive a truck?' says Shelley, laughing at his own joke.

'Very funny, Serjeant,' I deadpan. 'We did it twice a week. Me and my Uncle Sylv. You see Knock's a pilgrimage place and a lot of the pilgrims will give up their meat and potatoes when they're waiting at the shrine, especially on Fridays.'

'The shrine.'

'To our Blessed Virgin Mary. The blessed virgin appeared in Knock in 1889. She was seen as a vision by these people high on the side of a wall in the centre of the church itself.'

'They'd just come from the pub, had they?'

'Serjeant, how could you say such a thing about the Blessed Virgin Mary?' I crossed myself quickly. This ignorant blaspheming English heathen wasn't going to put my mortal soul in peril.

'Anyway, enough of your Catholic crap. Go left here.' So I swung left. A little too sharply maybe, because I went over the white stones and across the edge of the colonel's flowerbed.

'Fucking hell,' says Shelley, looking behind him at the damage.

I slow down to stop and he shouts in my ear, 'Just drive, drive, and get out of here.'

I accelerate away from the scene of the crime. Shelley is frantically checking if anyone has seen us. We turn right toward our barracks.

'You'll be the death of me yet. O'Neill.'

'Well, if I am, I'll pray for your soul, Serjeant, that I will.'

We accelerate to a stop in front of the barracks and I remember to keep the engine running. Sure, I don't think Serjeant Shelley would let me out of the cab alive if it died.

Shelley hops out and immediately orders the men to load up the truck and get in the back.

I take it out of gear, proudly sitting up front as the poor squaddies have to load all the stuff.

'Hurry up, get a move on, put your bleeding backs into it,' I hear Shelley shouting. I chuckle to myself. Ach, it's not a bad life really. But you've got to take your fun seriously. Especially when you're surrounded by a poor set of fools like I am.

Chapter 10

Eddie Longhurst

One day I'm going to put O'Neill in hospital. That's not a threat, it's a promise. I'll enjoy the crunch of my fist against his nose. The beauty of it. The sheer fucking pleasure of it.

Sometimes, I lie in bed at night conscious of my body, conscious of the power of it. I'm fit. Fit as a butcher's dog me. Bastards like O'Neill don't understand what it's like to feel a strength inside you ready to burst out of your ribs. They don't know what it's like to feel your muscles beneath the skin. To be aware of all that strength, waiting to be unleashed right smack into the middle of O'Neill's grinning paddy face.

One day. One fuckin' day.

But here I am, shifting all this gear with a load of soft buggers who are about as much use as tits on a camel. I take hold of the Vickers – cradling it like a baby. I carry it to the truck where Reg and Larkin are waiting. Now's the time to show them. I roll the Vickers up my chest until it's resting across the top of my shoulders. Now Eddie lad, breathe, breathe, then I drop my knees, pushing up with my arms. The Vickers starts to go above my head then stops. The bastard isn't going to beat me though. I grit my teeth, stick out my chin and push the Vickers above my head and onto its mounting at the back of the truck.

Then I go back for the ammo boxes. I take hold of two of them. Use your legs lad, get them to do all the heavy lifting. Up we go. Hold it. Hold it. Now start moving toward the truck. The legs do a little wobble but that's only to be expected. Keep going, keep breathing. I get to the truck. Reg and Larkin are looking at me like I was the last piece of black pudding on the plate. I push the boxes up to my chest and heave them onto the floor of the truck.

Done. Dusted. Fucking shown 'em, haven't I?

Reg and Larkin take hold of an end each and move one of the boxes to the front of the cabin.

'Sure, you're going to break your back doing that Eddie,' says O'Neill, looking out of the window of the cab.

I imagine my fist slamming into that grinning face. I could feel my cock getting hard at the thought of it. Is this what Joe Louis feels when he knocks a man down, I thought. And then I imagined the pleasure of hitting O'Neill. The shock of the punch jarring my elbow, then the spreading of his nose. The blood, the crunch of bone. Him falling, falling, me standing over his bloody body as it lies beneath me.

I turn back and begin loading the ammo.

One day, O'Neill. One day.

*

Reginald Dwyer

'Sit up here with me Reg, sure it will be a lot more comfortable than sitting in the back with your arse out in the sun.'

It was O'Neill, of course. I looked over my shoulder and saw Shelley supervising the last of the loading. The others were already sitting on the wooden planks at the rear of the lorry.

'Will you get a move on or will I be after waiting until the cows come home.'

I looked at the others sitting on these wooden planks. Then I looked at the comfortable seat in the cab next to O'Neill. It was no contest really.

'Will you hurry up and move your arse. We'll be leaving right now.'

I looked at Shelley again. Bollocks, he can only ask me to get in the back. What's the harm of trying? Nothing ventured, nothing gained, Margie always says.

I ran around the front of the truck and was about to put my bum on the comfortable leather seat in front when O'Neill stopped me.

'Ah, before you get in, Reg, be a good man and give the engine a start, will ye?'

He held out the starting handle to me. I should have known. There's always a catch with O'Neill. I took hold of the handle, went round the front of the truck and did the business.

'Sure, what a fine starter you are, Reg Dwyer. I think you've found your vocation in life.'

The engine was throbbing nicely. I stepped up into the shade of the cab, easing my bum into the soft leather of the passenger seat.

Then I saw Shelley glaring at me. 'What are you doing, Dwyer? Making ourselves comfortable are we?'

My mouth flapped a few times like a goldfish out of its bowl.

'I don't know the way to Changi, Serjeant, so Dwyer here has kindly offered to be my guide.'

'You know the way to the DP at Batu Pahat do you, Dwyer?'

I didn't know what to say. My mouth flapped a few more times.

'Dwyer's been out swimming there with his lady friends, haven't you Reg?'

O'Neill nudged me in the ribs. So without thinking out came a strangled 'Yes' from my lips.

I could see Shelley's mind working overtime. He glanced quickly at his watch.

'But if you want to sit here Serjeant. We'll get Dwyer here to sit in the back with the lads.'

'No, no. We're late already. He'd better guide us there. O'Neill, get a move on, we haven't got all day.'

'Yes, sarge.'

Shelley adjusted his uniform and then hopped up the side of the truck and into the back.

'Bloody hell O'Neill. What did you say that for? I've never been there in my life. Much less with any lady friends. If our Margie hears about...,'

'Shut your cackling. Sure it's easy. We just follow the way the taxis go down to Lavender Street, and then you'll work out the direction using this.'

He pulled out a map he'd found under the seat with a loud 'ta da'.

I grabbed it off him and gave it the once over. 'But it's in Chinese.'

'I know, Reg, but the roads are the bloody same, aren't they?'

'What are you waiting for O'Neill? Get a bloody move on,' shouted Shelley from the back of the truck.

'Yes, Serjeant, doing one last once over, Serjeant, before we get this beast on the road.' Then he turned to me. 'Reg, you work out the map while I get this old donkey moving.'

Bloody O'Neill. Always shooting his mouth off. Shelley will have my guts for garters. If he ever finds out. I could lose my stripe. I COULD LOSE MY STRIPE. 'You're always being taken advantage of Reginald Dwyer. Why don't you stand up for yourself? Show those army people what you're really made of.' I always kept quiet when Margie went on at me. If I spoke it only made her angrier. I never seemed to say the right thing. Words weren't my strength. They were always there in my head, don't get me wrong, but somehow or other, they never seemed to come out of my mouth.

It was always later I thought what I should have said. But later was always too late. It always was. No point in saying it then. Margie would only get angrier and then she'd make me sleep out in the shed again.

My son, Tommy, found me out there once. Lying all curled up on the floor, an old woollen blanket around my shoulders, my head resting on my tool bag and my teeth chattering like Fred Astaire's shoes. It were bloody November you see and we'd had a big fight about something or other, money probably. It was usually money.

'What you doing there, Dad?' says my boy looking down at me.

I opened one eye and saw him standing over me, all ready and dressed for school. I stretched, yawned and had my first fart of the day.

'Dad,' whined my son, 'what do you say?'

'Excuse me for having broken wind.' Margie taught them all the words to say if they farted. I always thought it were stupid, kids fart, adults fart. Better to let it out than keep it in.

But Margie thought differently. 'We're going to teach our children manners, Reginald Dwyer, so when they go up in the world, they'll remember how to behave proper.'

I farted again, following up with a quick 'Excuse me for having broken wind,' before Tommy could say another word.

He did speak anyway though, 'Dad I asked you what you were doing out here?'

He had a funny way of talking. All proper like. He didn't drop his aitches like the rest of us. I used to like the way he spoke. Made me feel right about the way me and Margie had brought him up. But sometimes, just sometimes, his voice really made me feel small. Like he wasn't from me at all but from somebody or somewhere else.

Now was one of those times. 'It's alright Son, your dad was checking the floor of the shed to see if it's strong enough to last the winter.'

'Oh that's alright then,' he said opening the door of the shed to go back home, 'because Mum says she's not angry with you anymore and will you come in right now to eat your breakfast.'

He ran down the garden path between my carrots and onions.

I farted once more. A long warm summer of a fart and said under my breath 'Excuse me for having broken wind.'

But that was a long time ago, back in Stockport, before I had lost my job, before I had joined the army, and before we had been sent out to Singapore. God, I miss Margie and the kids so much.

'Reg, Reg, we're going round Orchard Circus. I'll go down Bras Basah Road and turn left at the Union Jack Club onto Victoria Street. How are you with the map?'

'What?'

'How's the map? The thing with pretty colours and streets and all manners of things on your knees.'

I heard a tremendous grinding of gears, followed by a loud squeal of brakes.

O'Neill turned back to me, 'Your man drives like an eejit.'

I looked where we had been and a cab driver was shaking his fist at us. I closed my eyes, I couldn't keep them open any more. We were racing within inches of the parked cars at the side of the street. Mothers with children saw us coming, took hold of their kids' hands and took one step backwards from the pavement.

Even the rickshaw drivers, normally fearless as they searched for customers, agreed to give the mad Irishman with the flaming red hair room on the road.

'Don't you love the feeling of the open road stretched before you, Reg?'

I opened my eyes. A particularly foolhardy pedestrian had decided to cross at the red light in front of us. He got halfway across, realised the truck coming toward him wasn't going to stop, panicked, jumped right, then left before diving back into the gutter.

'Jaysus, don't you love a quiet afternoon drive.'

I looked at the map. I couldn't work out which was the right way up, never mind where we were, where we were going, and how we were going to get there.

There was a screeching of brakes, a crash of gears, and a whine of tyres as we took a sharp left. I saw the Union Jack Club flash past on my right in a blur of white and green.

There was a bang on the roof. Suddenly Shelley's disembodied face appeared at the top right of the cab. 'Slow down, O'Neill. You'll get us all killed.'

'But Serjeant, you said to get a move on.'

'Slow down … now.'

There was more screeching of brakes and crashing of gears. Shelley's shoulders and head appeared once again fleetingly before jerking back into the rear of the truck.

'Jesus, Mary and Joseph. The bloody army. Never know what they want. One minute it's hurry up. The next it's slow down. They'll be the death of me yet.'

O'Neill carried on muttering to himself in some Mick language I couldn't understand.

The map now lay on the floor of the truck beneath my feet. It's no bloody use. I'll never be able to find the way there. O'Neill's done for me this time. No more stripe for Reginald Dwyer. You've had your chips mate. Margie will kill me if she ever finds out. 'You stand up for yourself Reginald Dwyer.' I can hear her voice ringing in my ears. 'You stand up for yourself.' But I can't Margie love, I can't. It's not in my nature. The way I see it there are men who are thugs. Men like Shelley or Eddie Longhurst. Men who are selfish like Richard Longhurst or O'Neill. And there are the rest of us. Men like me. The followers who just muddle along and get by. And you know, I don't want to be a thug and I don't want to be selfish. I want to be me, Reginald Dwyer, who just gets by.

I lean forward to pick the map up from the floor of the cab when O'Neill suddenly lets out a huge whoop, and brakes. I jerk forward, kissing the dashboard with my forehead. I could feel the lump coming up straight away. A large round egg being laid beneath the skin. 'Steady on, O'Neill, you nearly killed me then.'

'Oh shush your silly noise me darling, Reginald, I've solved all your problems.'

'What?'

'I've solved all your problems. We can get to Changi really easy now. We'll just follow that.' I followed his pointing finger to a large, dusty green and yellow thing roaring away from us in a plume of blue smoke.

'It's a bus,' I said.

'That it is, Reginald, you observant fellow. But even better, it's a bus that's going to Changi.'

I looked at the small handwritten sign perched in the back window of the bus, 'No 11 Changi Village. 'You're right it is, O'Neill, the bloody thing's going all the way.' Saved by a single decker bus. Margie will be pleased. Not that I'll tell her, mind. That would be taking honesty a little too far.

O'Neill pushed the pedal down to the floor and we roared after the rapidly departing plume of smoke.

Around me, the grey shop houses flashed past. Here and there I could pick out a few details: A Japanese department store with its gaily-painted banners. A coffee shop with its wooden tables behind which sat a few pasty-faced customers. A strange store with what looked like paper houses hanging from string on its balcony. And always, always, people bustling here and there, carefully avoiding the heat of the sun, scurrying from shade to shade along the sheltered pavement.

I looked across at O'Neill, nonchalantly lighting his cigarette, holding the steering wheel with a combination of his knee and his left elbow.

'Jesus, O'Neill, be careful.'

'Don't take the Lord's name in vain, Reg.' He looked up at the sky. 'Forgive him dear God, for the heathen knows not of what he says.'

'But you're forever saying Jesus, Mary and Joseph.'

'Sure it's different. When I say it, I'm calling on the Almighty for his patience to help me understand the ignorant pagan heathens I'm surrounded by.' He crossed himself quickly, once again taking his hands off the wheel.

'Jesus, will you stop doing that.'

'You're a nervous old ditherer you are Reginald Dwyer. Driving one of these is as easy as sucking eggs.'

He overtook the stopping bus and accelerated past it, bumping on down the road.

'What are you doing now, for god's sake. The bus is back there.'

'Jesus, Mary and Joseph, Reginald Dwyer, will you not have faith in your own Michael O'Neill? Have I ever let you down before?'

He looked across at me with those piecing green eyes. I kept silent.

'Tell me, have I ever let you or yours down?'

'No,' I squeaked. I had to. The bastard kept on looking at me. I had to get his eyes back on the road.

'That's right. Now, this is Changi Road see. And even a heathen man of little faith like your own dear self, would be able to work out Changi Road probably leads all the way to Changi. Am I not right?'

'Yes... I mean no.'

'Ah, Reginald Dwyer, you'll be the end of me yet with your lack of faith. Errol Flynn said the same in *Captain Blood*. There, that was a film for you. He really buckled his swash in that one.'

I kept my mouth shut like Reg Dwyer always did. One day though, one day, I would know what to say and what to do.

One day.

*

Richard Longhurst

I was standing here, leaning on the cabin of the truck as all the others sat on the floor behind me. I could feel the warm breeze ruffle my hair and creep into my topee. We must have been near the sea. I could smell the sharp salty freshness of the air mixed with the mellow, oily sweat of the engine.

The landscape had changed now. Gone were the long rows of shop houses, crowding each other in a desperate attempt to claim frontage on the street. Gone were the long lines of washing hanging on bamboo poles. Gone were the crowds of every race under the sun.

Instead, I could see large ornate houses set back from the road. The gardens with summer yellow flowers. Each house was brightly coloured: a livid green, a bright, cheery blue and even, on my left, a loud salmon pink looking like it was suffering from a very bad case of sunburn.

The road itself had changed now. The surface was less tarmacadam and more dust. The ditches on either side held a long stagnant pool of mosquitoes and a few drops of water. And the occasional coconut tree, its large, mop-like head gracefully arching over the road, stood on sentry duty, saluting the passing vehicles in the breeze.

I looked behind at the others sitting in the truck. My brother, Eddie, as stiff-backed as ever. Next to him, Sergeant Shelley was re-reading the orders and looking worriedly down the road. Larkin was next on the bench, his uniform mis-buttoned and mis-shaped. I liked Larkin but he was such a waste of a human body. Further along Teale and Lloyd were sharing a woodbine. Thick as thieves those two, no wonder so much stuff went missing around the camp.

I looked across the top of the lorry's cabin. Up ahead an old Indian was driving his bullock cart loaded with coconuts toward us. I will never forget his face. A jovial, happy dark man with a bright grey dot of ash between his eyes.

I heard O'Neill wrestle the truck into gear and accelerate. I looked ahead. The man, the bullock cart and bullock were closer now. Getting closer every second.

The noise from the truck increased, the cabin rattled in its mooring. I heard Larkin shout and watched as the breeze blew Larkin's topee off his head and rattled down to the rear of the truck. Grumbling, Larkin lurched after it, tripping over knees and legs and tarpaulins and equipment as he scrambled after his hat. Sergeant Shelley shouted something at Larkin but his words were snatched away by the wind.

Eddie stared down at the wooden floor of the truck. He had taken off his topee and lain it on the bench beside him, forcing Teale and everybody else to move along. His short curly hair flowed back from his large forehead, his eyes mad with excitement and his mouth set in a fierce grin, the way a child sets its mouth when it wants something it knows it can't have.

I turned back and stared down the road. The old Indian man had seen us now. He had looked up from the backside of his cow and caught the truck coming straight toward him. But there was no fear, no sharp movement to the side of the road. Just a look at the truck.

I heard O'Neill honking the horn violently. Then the truck seemed to go even faster, as if spurred on by the sound of the horn.

Still the old Indian stared at the truck.

Still O'Neill drove on. Again, he hammered the horn. Two loud squeaks of pain came from the truck. The bullock looked up now, saw the charging truck and turned to the left to escape, managing only to block the road.

It was too late to do anything now. I think I shouted something but I'm not certain. O'Neill wouldn't have heard, though.

We ploughed straight into the bullock, catching it squarely across the shoulders. The cart was sent upward and backwards. I saw a fleeting glimpse of a bundle of rags sailing through the air as if someone was throwing a sheet from a window. Coconuts flew past the truck and bounced on down the road.

We were past now. And O'Neill was stopping.

I pushed past the others and jumped down from the truck, running back to the body lying by the side of the road behind us.

I remember the sound of my boots on the road. I remember the sound of the wind in the coconut trees. I remember there was one bird calling somewhere on my left. I remember it all, every small detail.

The bundle of rags was lying about ten yards from his cart. A small stream of blood oozed from his head. His body lay at a strange angle, the arm bent back on itself as if trying to scratch an incredibly annoying itch.

The smile was still there, though. And the grey dot of ash on his forehead. But the eyes were as dead as a fish lying on a marble slab; yet this once had been a man and now he was lying in the middle of the road.

Over to my right, half hanging in the ditch, the bullock's leg gave one violent twist as if to kick his master awake. Then it too lay still as the night.

O'Neill was beside me now, looking down at the body.

'Sure, there was nothing I could do. Your man turned straight in front of me. There was nothing I could do.'

I said nothing. There was nothing to say any more.

Shelley and the rest of the lads stood beside O'Neill.

'There was nothing I could do, Serjeant. He turned into the path of the truck. I couldn't get out of the way, though I tried. And I did try, Serjeant. But there was nothing I could do.'

Shelley stood there immobile. The three stripes on his arm shining brightly in the sun.

'Don't worry, O'Neill. I saw it all,' he said quietly. 'The old man underestimated the speed of the truck even though you were only doing 35. He tried to turn right to get on that path.' He pointed to a small track that led off to a grove of coconut trees. 'He turned straight into the truck. You could do nothing about it. That's what happened, isn't it O'Neill?'

O'Neill was shaking but gave a quick nod of his ginger head.

Shelley stared at me directly now. 'Isn't that what happened, Longhurst?'

I didn't know what to say. I looked down at the bundle of rags at my feet. And, for the life of me, I couldn't help but think of his wife, his kids and his life, oozing from his head.

'Isn't that what happened, Lance Corporal Dwyer?'

Reg looked down at the body at his feet. He looked at me, then at O'Neill and finally back to Shelley.

'I suppose so, Serjeant.'

'You suppose so or you know so, Lance Corporal Dwyer?'

Reg looked down at the body once more, the bundle of rags lying at his feet. I watched as the air seemed to leave his chest. He nodded just once. 'Yes, Serjeant, that's what happened.'

The rest of the lads were standing around us. 'Well, this one has had its chips,' said Teale, pointing to the white cow.

'Done its last moo.' This time it was Eddie, prodding the cow with his foot.

The other lads laughed.

'I'd love a bit of sirloin.'

'You'd love any one's loins.'

The jokes went on around me. I just looked down at the rags at my feet.

I glanced across at O'Neill. He was also looking at the body. A small smile crossed his lips, his eyes blazed fierce green and he whispered a few quiet words.

He noticed me watching him. I caught the full glare of the eyes, framed by that shock of orange hair.

It wasn't O'Neill. It was somebody else. Somebody I didn't know any more.

*

Reg Dwyer

I couldn't say anything else, could I? Not with Shelley looking at me. And you have to stick up for your mates, don't you? That's what the army is all about, sticking together, looking after each other. Being a mate.

I looked down at the old Indian man lying there on the road. I noticed one of his shoes had come off. It lay a few inches from the man, its sole facing toward me, the brown upper resting in the dust of the road. Then I saw the foot. Its heel was cracked with age and the nails were thick and rough with dirt. Strange how the sole was a different colour than the rest of the skin. I looked up at the man's face. Brown skin, brown face, an unshaven chin dotted with sprouting white hair. Eyes dead. No life there anymore.

I've only seen one other dead person. This was in the funeral home back in Stockport. My Uncle Fred had died and for some reason Margie had asked me to go and check on him. It sounds stupid doesn't it? Go and check on a dead person. He wasn't going anywhere. But I went anyway. Best to keep Margie happy about stuff like that. Myself and my brother-in-law went together to keep each other company I suppose. Well we got into the funeral home and this bloke in a black suit with a face like yesterday's washing showed us into this cold and dark room. There was Uncle Fred lying in his coffin, hands crossed in front of his privates, wearing a shirt and tie. I never did understand why would they dress him in a shirt and tie like he was going to a funeral? Well, I guess he was.

Jackie, my brother-in-law, took two bottles of Mackeson's out of his jacket and gave me one. I felt the dark liquid ooze down my throat. It felt great at that moment to have a beer and know I was alive, not lying in some coffin wearing a bloody suit and tie.

I saw Jackie lift his beer bottle up towards the coffin. 'Cheers, Fred lad. The beer's from your crates in the shed. You know, the ones you always kept hidden from me. Anyway, thanks for the drink. It's the first one I've ever had on you.'

He then drained the rest of the beer and put the empty bottle down next to the coffin. 'Come on Reg, let's drink the rest of this tight bastard's beer. He ain't gonna need it now.'

I looked back at Fred lying in his coffin, cold as the corpse he was, and went off and got drunk. Margie gave me hell for it the next day and I think I spent the next couple of days in the shed, but it was worth it. I'd proved I was alive.

Not like this bloke though. I looked down at the feet with their light soles. For the life of me, I couldn't stand it anymore. I picked up the shoe, lifted the dead man's leg and wrestled it onto the foot. I let it drop back to the dusty road and pulled his clothes down to cover the leg.

There, all brown now.

'Dwyer, get over here. We are going to the camp.' It was Shelley shouting as usual.

I ran to join the others in the back of the truck. I wasn't going to sit up front with O'Neill any more.

Shelley was barking orders. 'O'Neill, take this lot to the camp and then drive back here. Me and Longhurst will wait here until the police come. What are you waiting for? Get a move on…,'

I heard a muted 'Yes Serjeant' from O'Neill. The truck's engine roared and we started to move forward. I tried not to, but I couldn't help looking at the body lying in the road.

I don't ever want to be like that, lying in a road, dead.

Let me die in my bed please Lord, let me die in my bed.

Chapter 11

Richard Longhurst

O'Neill changed after the accident.

I don't mean in a physical sense at all, but there was no doubt he was different. At first, I just put it down to him feeling sorry for the man he killed. The taking of human life being wrong and all that.

But it soon became obvious to me it wasn't sadness, regret or guilt at all. It was something different. It was as if he had discovered something new about himself after killing the old man. Something he had never known and was surprised to discover.

And I wasn't the only one who noticed it. Even Tommy Larkin, usually obsessed with his stomach and how many shits he'd had that day, remarked on it.

We were putting up Lt. Whitehead's tent at the DP, me and Larkin. Suddenly, he stopped what he was doing. 'O'Neill's gone a bit doolally, hasn't he?' He mimed his fingers pointing to his temple and twisting. 'Reminds me of my Auntie Vi he does, after she ate the cat.'

Luckily, the thought of food made him change tack before I could hear any more.

'When are we going to eat? I haven't had any snap since last night. Cleaning the bloody toilets I was, while you were stuffing your face with bacon, eggs and beans. God, I'd kill for a plate of eggs right now. You know how I like them. Sunny side up with the white well cooked and the yolk still soft and sunny. So when you dip your bread in it, the egg oozes over the white. My mum cooked a great egg. Magic it was.'

I'd switched off by now. You couldn't waste your life listening to Larkin talk about his mum or food, otherwise you'd become a raving idiot like him.

I hammered in the last tent peg on my side and stood up to look at my handiwork.

Of course, Larkin had cocked up his side. I went round, pulling out all his pegs, stretching the grey lines taut and then hammering them back in, one by one.

'You're bloody hopeless, you are Larkin.'

'Don't get like Shelley, Lanky. I have to take it from him all bloody day long, I don't have to bloody take it from you, too.'

We began moving Lieutenant Whitehead's kit in from the back of the Headquarters truck. An extra soft camp bed, sheets and pillows, a table that folded out to the length of our dining table at home, two folding chairs like the ones you see Hollywood directors sitting on, a gramophone with a pile of records, most of which I'd never heard of, a large mosquito net, his kit bag, spare uniforms, three pairs of shiny boots non-army issue, a pump lamp and a portable wine box.

'God, I think the bastard's brought half of Robinson's with him. Look, this desk set still has a bloody label on it, $32. Fuckin' hell, that's more than a month's bloody wages for a couple of pens and a bit of wood. If he'd have asked, I'd have made it for him myself. I did it for my mam once.'

I woke up as he was saying the last line. Then I made the mistake of asking him a question.

'Did what?'

'Made a desk set. Have you got bloody cloth ears?' He pushed his glasses back up his nose in that peculiar way he always did. Then he launched into another long monologue. Paul Muni with a Manchester accent, that was him. Not the looks mind you. In the looks department, he had been born from whippets; a thin, callow face with red-pimpled cheekbones that stood out like Mae West's bust. All dominated by his ill-fitting moon-shaped glasses constantly slipping from the bridge of his nose like a dog pulling at its leash.

'It was lovely too. I found a bit of wood on the tip. Oak it were. Some stupid bugger must have thrown it away. Polished it myself. I wasn't working then so I had lots of time. Just been laid off from the milk round. I could never remember who got what, when or where. That was, of course, when I could remember to get up.'

'Yeah, a milkman that can't get up in the morning. Could be a problem.'

'That wasn't why I got sacked. Nah, they were okay about that. It was the hoss that did me in.'

'The hoss?' I asked stupidly.

Instead of answering, Larkin looked at me through the bottle bottoms of his glasses. 'Sometimes Lanky, I don't think you're from Manchester at all. And all that crap about you and Eddie being brothers. Well, you don't fool me, you're as different as two peas in a pod.'

'Well, we are. Got it?'

He nervously pushed his glasses back onto the bridge of his nose. 'No offence meant, Lanky, it were a joke, ok?'

'Just remember, ok?' I imitated his whiny voice.

'Yeah, no offence meant. Anyway, I got sacked because of the hoss. The nag didn't like me. I used to tell it to go one way, it went the other. I tried to feed it, it refused to eat. I think it complained to the boss one day and I was sacked.'

'The hoss complained to the boss?'

'I'm sure it did. The boss came up to me one day. As cool as a cucumber he says, 'The hoss and you aren't getting on. Now, I can get milkmen any day of the week but I can't get a hoss like that down the Labour.' So I was out on my arse. As I was taking off my apron and walking to the office to punch up my card, I heard the hoss give a loud whinny. It was like the bastard were saying 'Fuck off, dick head and don't come back.' I got the bastard back though, didn't I.'

'What do you mean?'

At this, Larkin leant in closer as if telling me a secret. 'Nipped back later than night didn't I. Put some ball-bearings in his feed. I pity the poor bugger sitting behind that when it farted.' With a self-satisfied look on his face, Larkin pushed his glasses back up his nose and smiled his wonderfully cross-eyed smile.

We had finished putting all the furniture in the tent by then. Lieutenant Whitehead was walking toward us through the debris of the semi-prepared camp.

'Watch out, bollock brains is coming,' said Larkin.

Lieutenant Whitehead looked inside the erected tent. The bastard must have been watching us all the time, waiting for us to finish.

'Well done, men, well done,' he said it with a peculiar accent, somehow managing to produce the words without moving either of his lips. Like the ventriloquist I saw once at the Empire, except we were the bloody dummies.

'You'll be as snug as a bug in a rug here sir.'

Lieutenant Whitehead looked at Larkin with all the disdain of someone who has discovered something exceedingly smelly attached to the sole of his shoe.

'Yes, quite, Larkin. You two report back to Serjeant Shelley. I'm sure he's got something for you to do. Ask my batman to come and unpack my kit.'

'Yes sir,' we chorused, saluting him with all the smartness we could fake. Well you have to keep up appearances, even for a wally like him.

We turned and marched away from the tent toward the rest of the platoon. We hadn't gone far before Larkin grabbed my arm. 'I'm gasping for a fag, Lanky, let's skive off for half an hour.'

I looked around me. We were in the middle of a clearing in a rubber estate about the size of a football field. It sloped away down to a fringe of coconut palms at the bottom. Beyond the fringe of trees was a short, rough stretch of lallang then the beach itself. The other three sides of our camp were surrounded by rubber trees marching away into the distance in those long, geometric lines.

Lieutenant Whitehead's tent lay at the bottom of the slope about 50 yards away from the tents of 13 and 15 Platoon. It had a wonderful view through the coconut trees to the rolling waves of the South China Sea.

I took Larkin's arm and dashed off into the fringe of coconut trees. Now we were out of view, walking through the lallang bordering the beach. Larkin dropped down beside one of the coconut trees, its grey rubber bark stretching above him like an elephant's trunk.

I sat down beside him, producing from my pocket two flattened Capstans.

The first drag of the day was wonderful, as the thick blue smoke grabbed hold of my lungs and strolled into them both like a copper with a truncheon. I coughed, twice. 'I needed that.'

For once, Larkin was quiet. The sun over on my right was deciding whether or not to go to bed, the moon deciding whether it was its turn to rise. I could see the gentle grey waves of the ocean quietly lapping the shore as a dog laps from a bowl of water. The sound lulled me into a sense of wonderful peace I hadn't known for a long, long time.

Then Larkin spoke. It was too much to expect him to keep quiet. He would never understand the beauty of a moment, the stillness of peace. He would always speak, to wake the dead.

'My mam loves coconuts.'

I kept quiet.

'I remember winning one at Belle Vue fair. Big thing it was. A right bugger to open though. We had to take the axe to it. Split it open and all, all this water ran out. We threw that away but we ate the white stuff. "Just like a coconut macaroon without the macaroon" she said.'

I was on my back now staring up at the clouds, stained through the feathery fronds of the coconut tree.

'Lanky?'

'Yeah.'

'Why'd you join the army? I mean you're smarter than the rest of us put together. You don't need to be here, not like us.'

'It's a long story.'

'Go on, I'm listening.'

'I wanted to live life and see the world.'

'No really, why did you join up?'

'It was Eddie really, he decided. After our dad died, Mam married again, Eric his name was. I don't know why she married him. No job and no chance of getting one. Eddie, me, and him didn't get on. One day Eddie said 'Get your coat on, we're going out.' Just like that, we went down to the recruiting office and said we're going to sign up. The strange thing was, I was accepted immediately. At first, the Serjeant wasn't going to accept Eddie. Said he wasn't right. He had to get our mam to fill in a form. She would have said no, so I filled it in, signing her name on the bottom. The Serjeant took one look at it and saw what we'd done. 'You lads must be desperate,' he said. He gave us some money and told us to be at Victoria Station next Monday at 9:30 sharp.

'That Monday morning, we sneaked out of the house without telling anyone. I remember Eddie waking me up at 5:30, all dressed and ready. That's it really.'

'But you've spoken to your mam since haven't you?'

'Oh yeah, we sent her a card from York telling her what we'd done. She wrote back saying we were bloody fools but she never came after us. I think she was glad really. Glad to get rid of us, I mean.'

'What are you two likely lads doing here?'

It was Shelley's voice. I sat up immediately, throwing away my fag. Larkin nearly jumped out of his shoes, his glasses flying off his head into the sand.

'It's alright boys. Sure you don't have to get up on my behalf.' We both looked behind us to see O'Neill emerging from behind the tree.

'You bastard, O'Neill, I nearly died a death. Look my heart's beating faster than Tommy Dorsey's drummer.'

'Oh Larkin, don't be such an old woman. Has no one ever told you, you look lovely when you're angry?'

'Fuck off, O'Neill. Give us another fag, Lanky.'

'Ah, that wonderful English gift for the repartee again. My Larkin, you could fill the Dublin Odeon with your wit. Have you ever thought of becoming a comedian?'

'Fuck off, O'Neill.'

'There it is again, the quick response cutting me to the quick with its incisive wit.'

'Leave him alone, O'Neill. What are you doing here? I thought you'd be with the others setting up the camp.'

'Well that's an interesting thought. But I'm sure that the camp can set itself up perfectly well without my help. And without yours either I see.'

He sat down beside us. 'Shift that there carcass of yours Larkin. I've seen more life in a corpse.'

'Up yours, O'Neill.'

'If wit were shit you'd be constipated, Larkin. Give me one of your wonderful smokes, Richard, my lungs are dying for a drag.'

I handed him a squashed cigarette, catching for one second his eyes as he took it. They had wildness in them I had never seen before. It was like they were pushing themselves out of his skull, forcing their way from his sockets. The whitest whites I had ever seen. The pupils, a rich, vibrant emerald green like two gems burning out in the white embers of a fire.

I watched the blue smoke rise toward the sky as he exhaled.

It was Larkin who spoke. 'Shame about that man, wasn't it? Old feller and all, probably got a wife and kids. Not a nice way to die.'

O'Neill was silent for a while, sucking at the glowing ember of his cigarette. Then he spoke soft as the breeze, 'There's no nice way to die, Larkin. The Lord Giveth and the Lord taketh away.'

Then, he was silent. We expected O'Neill to make a joke, take the piss out of this poor ignorant Englishman.

But he didn't, he just stared at his cigarette, clutched tightly in the fingers of his right hand.

'It's time to go back, Shelley will be missing us.' It was me that spoke but I didn't recognise my voice. It came out high and nervous, like it had never broken.

'Yeah, got to get back, said Larkin, throwing his dead cigarette into the lallang and getting to his feet.

'Are you coming, O'Neill?'

He carried on staring at his cigarette. I repeated the question. He slowly turned his head toward me and looked up. 'No, you lads go on, there's nothing back there for me.' He took a long drag at his cigarette. 'I understand now what your man meant. "A terrible beauty is born."'

I shrugged my shoulders and walked off to the camp, leaving him behind, still staring at his cigarette.

'He's gone fucking bonkers. Doolally, round the fucking bend.'

'Keep your mouth shut Larkin and don't mention it to anyone, least of all Shelley. Got it?'

'But he's off his fucking rocker.'

'Keep your mouth shut.'

We walked back to the platoon and were immediately greeted by Shelley.

'Where have you two been?'

'Helping Lieutenant Whitehead as you told us, Serjeant,' said Larkin. I had the sense to keep my mouth shut.

'That's strange because I went across to Lieutenant Whitehead's tent ten minutes ago. You two were nowhere to be seen.'

Now, Larkin had the sense to keep quiet.

'Fasten your top button Larkin, you're improperly dressed. And go and help dig the latrines. Some hard work will teach you two not to skive off again.'

I always find a joy in latrine digging. I know it's bloody strange but I'm not lying. There's this wonderful sense of focus; nothing else to do except dig this shit box down to six feet, fill it with lime and earth and cover the holes with the thunder boxes.

We helped the lads build two latrines. One for the officers and one for the men. Both served the same function though; a box over a hole in the ground where you had a shit. The only real difference is we divided the officer's latrines into cubicles by using coconut palms, the men's we left open.

There was always something funny about seeing this long row of hairy white arses sitting together. Sometimes, there would be a queue.

'Get a move on Harry. I'm dying for a dump.'

'Hold your horses, you can't hurry this you know.'

'Hurry, you could have cooked and eaten a meal by the time it takes you to crap.'

'I've got slow bowels.'

'Slow bowels is it? More like a slow fuckin' arse.'

Toilet humor I think it's called. And, we seem to possess more of it than anything else. Put it down to coming from Manchester. You always get toilet humour from a shit city.

We'd just about finished when Shelley called us over to get some grub and a cup of tea.

'I could eat a horse,' was Larkin's only comment.

It was one of the best meals I had ever eaten in my life. The bread was stale, the beef tough, the beans tasteless, but it tasted wonderful when washed down by a hot cup of tea, sitting there in the coconut grove.

God, I miss my mum's tea. She'd leave it on the stove all day long till you could stand a spoon in it. Thick, rich bitter tea, there's nothing like it to remind me of home and Manchester except rain perhaps. That always does it as well.

Nobody said much. A few farts here, few grunts there, a few moans everywhere. But nothing of any real substance.

Funny, though, I didn't see O'Neill. He had come back not long after us, but hadn't come out for his grub. Shelley didn't seem to worry about his absence. As if he had given him permission to be away from us. Maybe he did, or maybe he just didn't care. You can never tell with Shelley. 'You lot have got a busy day ahead tomorrow so get your heads down early tonight. No fucking around in the tents. Lights out at 10:00. Guard duty in two watches. 10 to 2 am and 2 am to 6 am. Teale and Larkin take the first watch. The two Longhursts take the second. Any questions? Right then, it's 8:00 o'clock now. You're free till 10:00.'

'Why is it always me?'

'Sorry, Larkin, did you say something?'

'No n-n-n-nothing, Serjeant, nothing.'

'Well say nothing more quietly, lad.' With that word of advice, he spun on his heels and marched off toward the Serjeant's quarters. Marching like he'd got a broom handle stuck up his arse.

'It's always fuckin' me.'

'You should stop larking around Tommy,' said Teale. 'Ho, fucking ho, dick head,' was Larkin's only response.

As we lay back enjoying a smoke after the meal, I thought about taking O'Neill some food. I went over to the remains of the side of beef. There wasn't much left, a few bones and a bit of a gristle. There's nothing like a bunch of hungry squaddies for stripping a carcass. Except maybe a pack of hyenas but even then, I think the squaddies would win out.

I put what was left on a plate and started to walk over to his tent. I had just reached the latrines when I saw him leave his tent and walk towards the beach.

He moved slowly, mechanically, like someone walking in their sleep.

He passed in front of me, ignoring me completely, as if I weren't there at all. His eyes were wide open though. Wide open to God knows what.

I followed him about fifteen yards behind.

To my right, Lt. Whitehead was loudly playing Elgar's "Nimrod" on his gramophone, over and over again, the melody filling the night.

I loved the soaring wave of music rolling towards me, but once you've heard it ten times you become sick of it. It always reminded me of York Minster though and the red, red light of the rose window.

O'Neill was walking through the lallang now. I could see it tearing and cutting his legs but he didn't seem to mind and he certainly didn't slow down.

I called after him a few times but he didn't hear me. Or pretended he didn't hear me.

And then a strange thing happened. As he reached the beach, an electrical storm lit up the shore.

The colours were beautiful. Reds, Greens, electric blues and sudden awful flashes of light that filled the sky with a brilliant radiance.

But the strange thing was there was no sound. No thunder claps. No crashes. No explosions of noise.

Only the sound of Elgar on the wind.

O'Neill just stood there, his body sharply silhouetted against the grey sea and the even greyer sky.

Then, he began to move. At first, I thought he was starting to turn around and go back. But all he did was raise his arms.

It was then the wind began. I know you'll think I'm stupid or superstitious or O'Neill had got to me with his mumbo-jumbo. But as he lifted his arms the wind began. A violent ghostly wind that forced me to step back as if it had pushed me firmly on my shoulders.

My cap flew off and crazily sailed against the body of the coconut tree and on back to camp. The sand stung my eyes, almost blinding me.

Still O'Neill stood there unmoved by the wind, his arms raised to the light in the sky.

The rain followed soon after. No ordinary rain but huge gobbets of water that drenched me to the skin within seconds. I stared through the rain, the light and the wind at the one figure who was unmoved by all of this.

O'Neill. Still standing there his arms raised to the heavens, as if he were asking for mercy.

*

Eddie Longhurst

It was that bloody Mick idiot O'Neill again. We had to drag him away from the beach, kicking and screaming. And you know what he was shouting? For the life of me, I can't believe the bastard.

He was shouting, 'The Lord giveth and the Lord taketh away.'

Stupid pillock. I mean he's just a dumb Mick from the bog who wouldn't know his arse from his elbow. Me, I would have given him a good kicking, thrown him in the hole and fucking thrown away the key.

But Shelley always goes by the rules. So me and that dopey bugger Dwyer had to drag him off the beach, through the lallang and back to his tent.

I'll tell you I was so pissed off with the bastard. I was ready to give him a good kicking in the tent. Bring him back to his senses and show him he can't treat his mates like shit. After all, me and Dwyer should have been enjoying a few quiet beers before lights out. But instead we were soaked through, dirty and torn to fuck ourselves.

Bastard O'Neill.

But Shelley wouldn't have it. I got one little dig in though before Shelley stopped me. Lovely it was, just on that soft part of the back above his kidneys. I'm sure the bastard felt it. As least his ribs did. But he didn't flinch. Didn't even cry once. Just sat there, mumbling away to himself about light and God and power and all that bullshit.

Mind you, I never put O'Neill down for one of those religious nutters. A mad Mick maybe. But not a God squadder, not him. Liked the tarts too much didn't he. And a drink. Like all Micks, he loved his pint.

Well, there's no telling where some people end up.

Shelley tried to speak to him but O'Neill wouldn't even listen, just kept mumbling. Finally Shelley stands above him and shouts, 'Private O'Neill, this is a direct order. Stand to attention now.'

Scared the shit out of me it did. Shelley's voice and his face I mean. I nearly jumped to attention myself.

But O'Neill just sat there. Then he stopped mumbling, took one deep breath and, as if speaking to a child, he said, 'You can do nothing to me, Shelley. I'm above all this.'

Well, you could have knocked me down with a feather. His hair streaming wet, his uniform covered in shit, his legs and arms cut to ribbons, he's sitting in the middle of this muddy puddle and he says 'he's above all this.'

I nearly shat myself I were laughing that much. Shelley didn't laugh though. He just stared down at O'Neill. 'You're on a charge son. Willfully disobeying a direct order. That's at least a month in the glasshouse, if the provost marshal's feeling in a happy mood.'

O'Neill didn't react, he just whispered, 'I'm above all this,' and went back to his mumbling.

Shelley looked straight at me and Dwyer. 'Both of you guard this lump of shit until we get back to camp. If he comes to any harm or gets away, you two will be running so fast to the guardhouse your feet won't touch the ground, is that clear?'

'Yes, Serjeant,' we both answered.

'I'm above all this,' said O'Neill from the ground.

It was the last thing I heard him say that night.

*

With the compliments of Serjeant Percy B. Shelley.
Report of Deployment: 4th September 1939 to 10th September 1939.

Sir,

Orders received on morning of 4th September 1939 to proceed to 'D' company semi-deployment position (DP) in Changi sub sector.

Deployment proceeded as planned employing the requisitioned Chinese trucks supplied by Transportation Command.

One truck driven by Pte. O'Neill 9522467 with acting Lance Corporal Dwyer commanding was unfortunately involved in an accident with a native bullock cart. Both the native driver and the bullock were fatally injured.

Inspector Dean of the Straits Settlement Police investigated the incident immediately afterwards. He found no blame could be attached to either Pte. O'Neill or acting Lance Corporal Dwyer, as the native driver had underestimated the speed of the truck as he was making a left turn to an estate.

I attached a copy of the police report from Inspector Dean for your perusal.

This unfortunate incident slightly slowed the deployment of 13 Platoon at the Changi sub sector but nonetheless all troops were in position and in camp by 20:00 hours on the evening of the 4th.

*

5th September

As per instruction, a reconnaissance of the beach frontage of 'D' company was undertaken by Major Tudor, CSM Hoar, myself and the other platoon serjeants.

However, due to the arrival of a 'Sumatra' late on the evening of the 4th, the reconnaissance was abandoned until the 6th. The 'Sumatra' produced high winds and torrential rain, blowing down the rubber trees surrounding the position and severely damaging the tents and stores of 'D' company.

The rest of the 5th being given to moving our tents onto higher ground. Due to the hard clay soil of the rubber estate in which our camp was deployed, it had become awash from the constant downpour.

Lt. Whitehead decided that 13 and 15 Platoon should move to higher ground at the rear of the DP at 16:30 hours.

This was effected by 22:00 hours on the evening of the 5th.

*

6th September

Reconnaissance of the beaches in front of 'D' company was once again abandoned by Major Tudor. This was due to the inclement weather and the refusal of the landowner to allow us to cross his land.

The troops were employed throughout the day in a rigorous regime of calisthenics supervised by Major Tudor and led by myself.

In addition, all equipment was checked for faults and breakdowns. Five out of six Lyon lights were found to be inoperable due to faulty storage. In addition four of the six generators were malfunctioning. All non-usable equipment has been returned to the battalion engineering section for repair.

*

7th September
Orders received at 11:00 hours to return to camp due to continuing inclement weather.

All equipment was salvaged and accounted for. However, much was found to be inoperable. A full inventory is appended for your approval.

Deployment from the position achieved successfully and by 16:00 hours, 13, 14 and 15 Platoon all returned to Tanglin camp.

*

Other matters:
As much of the company's equipment was destroyed by the 'Sumatra', urgently request the QM and myself issue new equipment based on my appended list.

Discipline:
Pte. Larkin 9516471 charged with slovenliness.
Pte. Teale 9726548 charged with being asleep whilst on guard duty.
Pte. O'Neill 9522467 changed with gross insubordination and dereliction of duty.

All three men will face the battalion provost marshal.
I remain sir, you faithful and obedient servant.
Signed Percy B. Shelley Sjt.
The Manchester Regiment
Tanglin Barracks

BOOK TWO

Chapter 12

Reg Dwyer
Block 15, Tanglin Barracks, Singapore
30th September, 1939
My darling heart,
So it's started then. You know, I never thought it would come to this. After all, I always believed everybody had their fill of it in the Great War. Uncle Harry and Uncle Fred dying on the Somme and Dad getting a lungful of gas. He was never the same again was Dad. Every October, when winter came on, he used to cough up this horrible green stuff from the bottom of his lungs. I remember as kids we were always frightened of Dad when he was coughing. He was like a great big breathless bear.

Anyway, I suppose they know what they are doing, Chamberlain and the rest of them. Herr Hitler has to be put in his place somehow or other. With a bit of luck, he'll realise his mistake and it will all be over by Christmas.

Tell our Harry not to be stupid. He's just got married so he's not to go enlisting. They'll call him if they need him. He's got a wife to look after now. It'll be funny calling Rita Hendricks, sister. Her with her posh voice and all that.

The kids must look strange in their gas masks but you should make certain they know how to use them. Also, make sure they know where the bomb shelters are. You can never be too careful with the bloody Germans. Remember what Uncle Tom used to say before he caught it on the Somme.

Life here continues on as if nothing has really happened. On the first few days XXXXXXXXXXXXXXXXXXXXXXXXX
XXXXXXXXXXXXXXXXXXXXXXXXXXXXXXXXXXXXXXXXXXXXXX
XXXXXXXXXXXXXXXXXXXXXXXXXXXXXXXXXXXXXXXXXXXXXX
XXXXXXXXXXXXXXXXXXXXXXXXXXXXXXXXXXXXXXXXXXXXXX
XXXXXXXXXXXXXXXXXXXXXXXXXXXXXXXXXXXX but that's all there was really. We went back to barracks and back to the old routine.

We can read all about what's happening though. The Straits Times is full of it. Poor old Poland seems to be getting a right battering. They are a tough lot though the Poles, I'm sure they'll pull through.

We've got a new CO who's just arrived. Colonel Holmes he is. A proper Tad in that he's been with the regiment for years. He even won the Military Cross during the Great War. All the lads respect him. Major Tudor says it's too early though to bother him about you and the kids coming to live out here. But I will go and see him soon.

Tell Tommy, Evelyn and Grace to be good and you look after yourself now.

Your husband

Reg

Censored by Lt. Whitehead

*

Richard Longhurst

'Fuckin' wogs. We're doing all this for a bunch of fuckin' wogs. What's the point of owning the fucking empire if we do all the bleedin' work. Answer me that hey?'

It was Eddie who was speaking and all this was pitching a row of tents, digging latrines and erecting wash houses for the 4/19 Hyderabads who were going to be camped on the lower football fields of Tanglin Barracks.

'I mean, it's not right is it? Us doing all the work and those bastards sitting on the ship waiting for us to finish.'

He wiped the sweat from his bare-chested body with an old towel. I don't know why he bothered because ten seconds later new beads of sweat appeared all over his chest and shoulders.

'I wouldn't mind but where are we going to play football now with all those Indian buggers on our pitch?'

'There's still two other pitches at the top of the camp, isn't there Eddie?' This was Larkin who was concentrating on hammering in a tent peg and only succeeding at hammering his own fingers.

I watched Eddie weigh his own hammer in his hand and throw it straight at Larkin. It whistled past his ear landing with a deep thud in the soft earth behind him.

'Hey, you could have killed me.'

'Watch your fuckin' mouth or I won't miss next time, got it?'

Larkin didn't answer, merely looking down at his tent peg and pretending to concentrate on the job at hand.

'Come along ladies, we haven't got all day. The wogs will be getting here at 16:00 hours. We have to be finished by then.' It was Shelley, chivvying us along to get the job done.

'It's not easy, this, Serjeant,' whined Larkin.

'Well, let me make it easier for you Larkin.' He paused for dramatic effect like he always did. A right bloody actor was our Serjeant Shelley, I could learn a lot from him. 'If you're not finished by 15:00 hours, I'll make you clean the shithouses for these wogs for the next month. Now doesn't that make the job easier?'

I could see Larkin counting on his fingers. 'But that's three o'clock Serjeant.'

'I can see you've been getting lessons on reading the time again, Larkin. Which one of you lot has been teaching him?' He looked around at us all in mock anger. Like I said, a right bloody actor is our Shelley. 'Time you got a bloody move on then, isn't it?'

'Yes, Serjeant,' moaned Larkin, attacking his tent peg with even more fervour.

'And the rest of you will be helping him clean the khazis too unless you finish in time.'

There's nothing like a threat to motivate a bunch of squaddies. That's the army for you. Collective responsibility, collective punishment. I suppose they think it builds esprit de corps and all that tosh. But all I think it breeds is collective fear. How can you have a lot of soldiers all shitting themselves with fear whenever they see a pip or a stripe. What use are they to anyone? The fear doesn't stop with us though. It goes right up through the ranks. I can see Major Tudor covering his arse with the Colonel. And I'm sure the CO does exactly the same with General Bond. And so on, onwards and upwards until you reach the end of the line, wherever that is.

The army breeds incompetence through fear. They'll never change though because there's no easier way to motivate a bunch of squaddies. We skive. They threaten. We work. They relax. We skive. They threaten. It's the one thing that has kept the British army going for the last 400 years. That and poverty of course.

It's the eternal struggle between the squaddie and his Army. Nobody ever wins. There are no battles, no set-pieces, just a long series of inconclusive skirmishes. And it goes on and on and on. God, I'm sick of it all.

Anyway, I'm beginning to sound like one of those actors who jump up on an old wagon and do skits on the streets of Manchester.

To Larkin's relief, we finished building the tents well within time and we marched back to our barracks, with official permission, to skive for the rest of the afternoon.

Most of the lads played cards. Reg Dwyer got stuck into a long letter to his wife. Me, I read. *The History of the World* by H.G. Wells. I know what you're thinking. What's a squaddie doing reading a book like that? Well, I've already had enough stick about it from the lads. But I don't care.

I think coming to Singapore opened my eyes to the world. Now I want to understand it better. Why had it got into this position? Why the Jews are fighting the Arabs? How the Empire was created? How did 20000 Englishmen, Irish, Welsh and Scots from a small island off the coast of Europe control the lives of 200 million Asians? Why the Romans, Greeks, 1066 and all that?

I know I'm not like the rest of the lads; happy with a few beers, a game of cards and their hole every Saturday night. And I feel it more and more every day of my life.

Even me and Eddie are drifting apart now. I don't think he understands me and I can't be bothered talking about football, women or the army with him. Blood's thicker than water, but we're not as close as we used to be.

About six o'clock, I got bored with old H.G. Wells. His eternal optimism can be really depressing. Man isn't getting better and better all the time. Just look at Adolf Hitler and you know that isn't true. Silly tosser. He finally got to me, so I decided to go for a walk down to the football field.

The Hyderabads were already there. A huge bustle of activity filled the field. Brown faces everywhere carrying stores, lugging equipment or simply doing what soldiers do best: absolutely nothing.

On my left, there were about six black faces topped with khaki turbans, sitting around the entrance to one of the tents we'd put up. They looked like six pints of Holts sitting on a table.

Poor bastards, I hope they checked those guide ropes because the first breath of wind that comes along is going to blow their shelter all the way to the Green Cat Club.

One of the black boys saw me looking at him. He smiled, a big white smile illuminating his face like a lighthouse in a dark, stormy sea. Next minute, he was up on his feet gesturing for me to join them.

I looked over my shoulder. Did he mean me? There was nobody behind me. It must be me. He waved his arm again. The others, seated at his feet, were also waving.

What the hell. I walked toward them and said 'Hello'.

This greeting was met with a round of laughter and a long stream of words like water running over stones. There seemed a lot of 'r's and 'u's. Lovely sound though. I could listen to it for ages.

The one who had gestured to me first, sat down and haltingly said, 'Hello Tommy,' his head wobbling on the end of his neck like a coconut wobbles at the fair ground before it falls off its perch.

He gestured for me to sit. I looked around at all the faces staring and smiling at me. They looked so young. The first one put his hand on his chest and said 'Khan.'

I didn't understand. Khan, does that mean welcome in their language? I touched my chest and answered 'Hello'. They all laughed as if this was the greatest joke they had ever heard.

The first Indian shook his head. Pointing to himself, he said 'Khan' again. Then he pointed to the boy next to him, and said 'Haled', then the next 'Reza', then Yusof, then Ali and finally 'Khan' again. Each one bowed his head slightly and touched his hand to his chest above his heart.

I understood now. I touched my hand on my shirt and said 'Richard.' They all laughed. A few of them tried to say my name. 'Lickat' or 'Rokat' were the closest they got to it. It sounded like they were trying to bring up this huge glob of phlegm from the back of their throats.

Then the first Indian pointed to the hookah that lay in the middle of the groundsheets. He picked up the end of the pipe and handed it to me.

I looked at the brass end, thought what the hell, you only live once, put the pipe in my mouth and blew. The water bubbled and all the Indians collapsed in childish giggles.

After he'd finished wiping the tears from his eyes with an oversized khaki handkerchief, the first Indian, Khan, I think he was called, started making loud sucking noises, pushing his two cheeks together with his brown fingers. The others thought this was as funny as Charlie Chaplin.

Finally I got it. Suck don't blow.

This time I took the pipe in my mouth and took one long lunch-gasping suck. They all watched me with their white eyes. The hookah bubbled. I could feel the cool smoke entering my lungs.

Then it seemed like Joe Louis had punched me in the middle of the chest. I coughed up the smoke, almost coughing half my guts up in the process. My eyes were streaming, my face red, and it felt like half the regiment had been using my tongue as a parade ground.

All the other Indians were on the floor now, holding their sides as their laughter shook their tiny, thin bodies. All except Khan that is. He was looking at me as one would look at a child.

Take small breaths he was telling me in mime.

I know now flower, I thought.

Then there was a shout behind me 'What are you doing here?'

I jumped to my feet and stood at attention. The other Indians followed suit. Into my view came a round, fat face, dominated by a walrus mustache. I looked down at the shoulder. A captain.

'This is the Indian Army, my boy, off limits for the likes of you. So get back to your barracks now.'

He then barked out a long stream of orders in Indian. My new friends immediately began to clear up the tent. I saluted the pompous old fool and marched back the way I came. Not without one last look over my shoulder though.

Sure enough Khan was watching me. He gave me a little wave and a big, brilliant smile. I waved back. I'll always remember his smile. It was the same smile that I saw on a crumpled and torn body lying in a ditch in the West of the island. But that was much later, much, much later.

*

Michael O'Neill

104

I'm on my bed staring up at the green, green walls of the cell. Each man thinking of a prison, each man confirms a prison. I don't know where that thought came from. Probably the fault of the Christian Brothers.

It was bullshit though. There are four walls, a large, high ceiling and they enclose me, keeping me here, confining my spirit in its own private coffin.

Awake, awake, it's time for your wake. The chik chak in the corner laughing at me lying here. Lying here. Not telling the truth, not any more.

What are you laughing at ye wee spalpeen?

It ignored me. A juicy tic had crawled across the ceiling and like an upside down tank it waddled to gobble up its prey. Laughing at me lying here, lying here.

The bastard and their green monsters even get to you here. And I used to love the green, the wearing of the green, green shamrock pinned to your coat as you go off to Mass to be greeted by the soft hand of the priest squeezing your shoulder Hello.

Bastards.

They will not keep me down, not I, not Michael O'Neill, descended from the High King of Connacht, son of Culchilain, offspring of a stony field where the moss and lichens grow in rich, tropical confusion.

My ma, God rest her soul, used to take me on the knee and tell me of the days before the English, may god rot their brazen souls. Days when heroes ruled the land and men, true men, lived with honour and died with honour.

Honour our father who art in heaven, bellowed be thy name, bellowed be thy name.

If I could only sleep, I could dream my way out of here. But their walls shall not hold me.

I will be free.

And hadn't I just thought these words when your man, the lovely pale chik chak, suddenly up and decides to go out through the bars. 'I would too if it was so fucking easy,' said I to the departing chik chak.

'It is,' he answered, 'just follow me.'

I tried. The bars wouldn't move. It was then I realised I could be losing my mind. But no, I finally decided, I couldn't do that, not in an 8" by 10" cell anyway. Sure, it would be easy to find.

'A terrible beauty is born. For fuck's sake, the eejits wouldn't know beauty if it came and bit them on the arse.'

The chik chak laughed again as it devoured another poor defenceless mosquito that had earlier been devouring me.

I searched the walls for them cracks that lay between the bricks and mortar. Errol Flynn had done the same in Captain Blood, rallying the men to arms, fleeing the prison, escaping on the pride of the fleet to ravish the Spanish Main.

But there were no cracks. There were no bricks and there was even less mortar. Just the solid wall of plaster-covered concrete, painted the kind of green the heathen English believed reminded them of home. A sickly pale colour that turned everything it touched sickly pale.

Sometimes I lie here and think about the old man I had killed on the long road to Damascus or Changi as it was signposted. It all seems like fate had decreed it. Him on his cart with his stupid cow on the road at the right time in that awful place. And me, me just being me.

They had me up in front of Major Brown when I came back.

'O'Neill, these are very serious charges Serjeant Shelley has laid before me.'

He was one of the better officers was Major Brown. At least, he seemed to care about what he did even when he was putting someone in the Glass House.

'Gross insubordination and dereliction of duty,' he read my charge sheet in his judicious voice, 'these are very serious charges O'Neill. And then there was the unfortunate incident on the road.' He paused for a moment as if looking for the exact words. 'A most regrettable incident indeed.'

He turned towards Serjeant Shelley and something passed between the two of them, I think. But you can never be sure with the bloody English or the bloody Army.

He put down the papers and looked straight at me. 'We are at war now, Private O'Neill, and we are expected to act differently when we are at war. You will serve one month loss of liberty and be docked your pay for this period.'

Nothing about the poor wee old man and his poor white cow of course. Just another casualty of war. But it was fate he should die then, as I will die someday soon. God only knows when though.

'I will be free,' I shouted again at the chik chak. And prayed sleep would rescue my soul.

*

Reg Dwyer

Block 15, Tanglin Barracks, Singapore
10th November, 1939
My darling wife,

No, the answer is No. I'm really firm on this. Once you let the kids out of your sight, you'll never see them again.

It's all well and good the Government saying Tommy and Evelyn should be sent off to the countryside for their own safety but who is going to feed them? Who is going to clothe them? What about their schooling? Tommy is doing well in that school in Stockport and we should leave him there.

After all, it's only the Government that thinks the Germans are going to bomb. It's not happened much so far, has it?

So my answer is No. You put your foot down and tell those interfering buggers from the Ministry of whatever, to piss off. They're not having our kids. If we have to send them anywhere it should be to your Auntie Doris in Glossop. I know you think she doesn't want them but if you explain the situation and twist her arm I'm sure she'll give in.

Enough of that. Life has pretty much returned to normal here in Singapore. It's as if the War didn't really exist. People are still eating and drinking as much as they want. You'll hate me telling you this, what with rationing and everything in Stockport, but here I can buy as much meat, as many eggs and all the flour and sugar I need. A lot of it comes from Australia. Every day I see advertisements in the newspaper for Cold Storage offering fresh lamb, tender beef, succulent chicken and even bloody Venison. Pardon my French.

It must be hard for you and the kids living there in Stockport. But keep your chin up, dear. It'll all be over soon, trust me. The French and the B.E.F. will soon teach Mr. Smarty Pants a thing or two.

Now for the news. I've sent out your Christmas presents for this year. With a bit of luck, you'll get them before Christmas this time. But you can never tell, what with the war and everything.

For Evelyn, I bought this lovely silk Chinese Dress called a Cheong Sam. All the Chinese girls wear one. It has a high collar, these tiny studs across one shoulder and a slit at the side so the girls can walk elegantly. I hope she likes it. I've got it a couple of sizes too big so she can grow into it.

You told me Tommy loves art at school so I've sent him a Chinese brush set. They use them to write a letter like we use a pen. They write in a strange way and their characters have all these strokes and boxes. I can't read any of it all. Doesn't seem to matter though, everybody we deal with understands English, even the taxi drivers. Even if it's not like proper English like in Manchester. He can use these brushes for his art lessons. They'll be great with a bit of watercolour.

Now for you, I've got a special present. I'm not going to tell you what it is until you get it. It's going to be a big surprise. Just for you.

Anyway, got to go now. I'm on guard duty this evening. I've agreed to do it for a mate of mine called Teale. He's got to go into town. I don't mind doing the duty though. It helps pass the time. It can get so boring out here.

I miss you and the kids all the time.

Your husband,

Reg

Censored by Lt. Whitehead

108

Chapter 13

Eddie Longhurst

I thought it would all change. Once war had broken out, we would become one unit, all committed to fighting and killing and winning.

But it hasn't. They are still out there doing their Saturday shopping in Robinsons. Or sitting at the long bar at Raffles, knocking back their bleeding cocktails. Or riding their cars to the races. Or making fucking money.

I saw a large fat man last week, dressed in the typical planter's outfit of white suit and straw panama hat on Stamford Road. He was going off to some Tiffin club or other. Anyway, he had just got off his ride and was arguing with the rickshaw johnny. I heard his voice getting louder and louder.

'Don't try to cheat me, my man. It's only ten cents from the train station to here.'

The stupid rickshaw twat just stood still with his hand out. 'No Tuan, you agreed twenty-five cents,' and then in a more pleading tone, 'remember?'

'Whatever, here's ten cents and that's all you're getting.' He threw the money at him and strode past me into his club. As he walked past he turned and said directly to me, 'They will try to get away with anything these days. Got to keep them in their place.'

He looked down at the rickshaw johnny scrabbling on the floor at his feet for the small silver coin. 'Damn wogs will try anything on.'

I could see a sheen of sweat on his round face. His tongue crept out and he licked his thin mustache. Then he realised he was talking to a soldier, looked at his watch, barked a quick, 'I'm late, blast the man,' and strode through the wooden doors of the club.

I watched him go. I wanted to knock the living daylights out of him then. To knock the sweat off his face. To cover that tongue, that mouth, those lips, that mustache with blood and bile and snot. Not for the rickshaw man, not for anything really. Just because him and thousands like him existed. And me and thousands like me didn't.

The bastards here don't care. Oh, they read their *Straits Times* and tut-tut over the news and the war. But life carries on as if nothing is fucking happening anywhere else in the world.

Even the army is the same. I expected more training and what have you for when we have to fight against the krauts. We're a regular battalion after all, not one of those reservist outfits, full of fat shopkeepers and clerks and draymen.

But no, we're stuck here in bloody Singapore still spending most of our time sleeping or farting or getting drunk or shagging or knocking some wee ball into an even smaller wee hole.

Fuck 'em all. I'm gonna be ready when we're called. I'm doing extra training now with Shelley most afternoons. He's a true professional, a real Empire soldier, not like those other daft twats.

We'll both be ready when we are called. That's all I care about – to be ready. Those kraut cunts won't know what's hit them when Eddie gets there.

I look up and see the dumpy shape of a large Catalina flying overhead. For god's sake, there are still people coming for holidays here. Only last week, myself and Serjeant Shelley had to provide the honour guard for some daft twat out from London. I don't even know the fucker's name.

We spent the whole morning ironing our best shirts, blacking our boots, polishing our rifles, rubbing Blanco into our webbing. I even had to steal a clean pair of socks from O'Neill's locker. Well, he wasn't going to be needing them where he was anyway.

Six hours of this shite we had. Then Major Tudor comes round to inspect us. Walked up and down the line four times the fat bastard did.

'Some lint there, corporal, remove it.'

'Call those boots shined private? Serjeant Shelley you should be ashamed.'

'There is a spot on your belt private. Blanco it all again.'

On and on it went. Finally, at four o'clock we were bussed out to the airport at Kallang and marched onto the tarmac. A plane slowly came into view. It circled past the control tower, out across the sea, and turned back to land in front of us. As it did so, two daft pillocks from the RAF rolled a huge red carpet onto the tarmac and then had to roll it up again as the plane stopped ten feet from their mangy bit of rug. Daft buggers, didn't have the sense to at least wait until the plane had stopped first.

From the look on their officer's face, they will be on fatigues for the rest of the year.

Finally they got it right and the door opened, a small step ladder unfolded and in the door of the aircraft appeared a woman. Not a bad looker, I'd give her one. She stepped back as she suddenly felt the full blast of 95 degrees of heat and 100% humidity.

Welcome to Singapore, love.

Then I heard Lt. Whitehead, 'Attenshun!' The whole platoon snapped to it like one group. That's what bloody years of training does for you.

'Present arms!' That was Lt. Whitehead again, almost sounding soldierly for once. We all brought our Lee Enfields up to the present position. Beautifully done, even if I do say so myself.

Out came the woman followed by a small dapper man and two brass, medal ribbons gleaming on their uniforms. Without looking at us, the group strode directly to the large waiting limousine, climbed in and were whisked away.

It must have taken all of ten seconds from the moment the door opened to the time the car pulled away. We were left standing there like a bacon sandwich at a Jewish wedding. Finally, Serjeant Shelley it was who gave the order, 'At ease.'

At ease. It's like the whole fuckin' place is 'at ease'. Bastards, all of them.

Bastards.

*

Reg Dwyer
Block 15, Tanglin Barracks, Singapore
5th January, 1940
Dear Marjorie,

I was extremely disappointed when I read your last letter. It arrived just before Christmas and, I can tell you, it spoilt Christmas for me.

How could you let the kids to be taken away from us? Those bloody do-gooders from the Ministry don't know nothing. We don't know what sort of family they could be put with. Country folk, they can be a bit strange at the best of times. You didn't even know where the kids were going. Tommy and Evelyn have only been in the country once before, they won't know what to do. I can't tell you how much your news upset me. Proper spoilt my Christmas it did.

But that's not all. You also told me David Endersby had finally got his hands on my allotment. He's been wanting that bit of land for the last ten years. Why didn't you stop him? I know the Government is pushing for every available bit of land to be used to grow food but bloody Endersby isn't going to grow food on it, he's going to grow Marrows.

I know him and his tricks. He wants my allotment so he can win the top Marrow contest at the Stockport and District Flower Show in September. Now you've let him have it. I'll never be able to hold my head high in Stockport again, Marjorie. This news upset me more than anything else.

Ask our Harry to get it back from him. All he has to do is put a few potatoes in. They'll grow without any help from him. Even he couldn't destroy a potato patch.

So all through Christmas and New Year, I've been worrying about you and the kids and the allotment. I feel so helpless out here. There's nothing I can do and all the news I get from you is always seven weeks out of date. You'd think the army could deliver letters quicker than seven weeks, wouldn't you?

But no, they can't. Bloody laziness that's all it is. Sheer bone idle laziness.

Anyway, I've got to go now. I'm doing guard duty again for O'Neill. He gives me a few bob for doing it for him. It all helps, especially when I've sent you and the kids presents.

Did you like the special one I got for you?

Your husband,

Reg

Censored by Lt. Whitehead

*

Richard Longhurst

'I hate this fuckin' patrolling.' It was Larkin speaking and, as usual, he was moaning. 'Look, nobody will see us here, let's stop for a fag.'

We were at the far end of the football pitch at the top of the camp. From here to the camp's perimeter fence was 100 yards of thick overgrown jungle.

'I hate going through there. It's full of fuckin' snakes and shit.'

He placed his Lee Enfield down, resting it against one of the rusting white goalposts. 'You having one Lanky?'

I looked over my shoulder checking nobody was about.

'Jesus, fresh bleedin' air,' said Larkin exhaling a long draught of blue smoke. 'There's nothing better than a fag first thing in the morning.'

Myself, Larkin and Reg had been on night guard duty. Most of it involved sitting in the guard room drinking cups of tea, checking late arrivals and standing like a dozy pillock out in the rain. We took it in turns to do the long stroll around the perimeter to check the wire. It's not like we're expecting to be attacked mind you. But some of the locals occasionally sneak in to pinch the stores.

We caught one about two months ago. Not me mind you, but one of the other patrols. Got a right kicking he did. No use in handing them over to the police so we administered Manchester justice. When you're being kicked in the head by fifteen beefy lads shouting 'Don't fuckin' try it on with us mate,' you soon get the message you're not wanted.

Poor bugger though, he looked a right mess when they threw him out of the camp.

'I hate these fuckin' dawn patrols. The grass is wet, you're wet and the fuckin' jungle is spooky as hell. All those fuckin' sounds give me the heebie-jeebies.'

I kept quiet. No point in arguing with Larkin. He was one of those men who was going to tell you his story whether you wanted to listen to it or not. And even if you disagreed with him, he pretended not to hear, carrying on his own one-sided conversation with not a care in the world.

'Fuckin' jungle. Fuckin' heat. I hate this fuckin' place. Give me Accrington any day. A warm pint, a nice meat pie and peas, and a mucky tart for afters. That's all anybody needs to keep him happy.'

I still kept quiet, silently dragging on my fag. The truth was I liked Singapore. I liked its smell and its dirt, and its noisy, crowded streets. I liked that nobody here had a past, they only had a future. I liked the jungle in the morning when the black and white birds were singing, their tails erect like a guardsman on parade. But most of all, I liked that it wasn't bleedin' Manchester. But I weren't going to tell him that. Silly chough wouldn't understand anyway.

'Come on Tommy,' I said, throwing away my fag. 'Let's get this over with so we can go back and have a cup of char.'

I picked up my rifle and slung it across my shoulder. Larkin hesitated behind me, drawing the last dying breath of smoke from his cigarette and reluctantly pushing up the heavy weight of his rifle on to his shoulder.

We slouched off through one of the jungle paths leading to the sentry post at the far south-western corner of the camp. I was leading of course. Larkin behind me, muttering to himself.

We'd been walking only for a few minutes when I heard a loud snap on my left. I held up my hand to signal Larkin to stop. He didn't of course, clattering into my back with a loud grumble.

'What d'ye fuckin' stop for?'

'Shush.'

'What?'

'Shut the fuck up!'

We both stood there in the middle of the jungle, listening. The early morning light was peeking down through the canopy of the trees, creating visible rays that one could almost feel. It was like my last day in York at the Minster. The light pouring in through the Rose Window and me standing there. Alone, at the centre of the universe.

Again, we heard a rustling on the left. But it was further away now.

'It's only a fuckin' dog.'

'Shush, listen.'

'I don't want to get bitten by no fuckin' rabid dog. Not here anyway. Not in fuckin' Singapore. Remember Ted Hunt.'

'But he died of malaria.'

'Same fuckin' thing isn't it? Just another one of those tropical diseases that eats you up from the inside without you knowing nowt about it.'

I motioned for him to follow me off the path into the jungle. I stepped high, avoiding the trailing vines and creepers snaking along the floor. Larkin reluctantly followed me, immediately tripping over a large, carbuncled root.

'Fuckin' Nora, what was that?'

'Shut up. It's only a root. Remember to lift your feet.'

'I'll lift my feet up your arse Lanky. That's what I'll do!'

'Shut up and follow me,' I whispered, but why I bothered God only knows. A deaf and dumb beggar would've been able to hear us with his eyes closed.

I hunkered down and crept through the jungle, keeping as low as I could. Whatever it was had stopped now about fifty yards to the left of us. It was making a snuffling sound like a pig.

'Think it's a wild pig,' I said to Larkin.

'What? One of those fuckin' things with big teeth sticking out of his fuckin' nose? I'm out of here!' He started to go back until I grabbed him by the arm.

'Hold on, we've got to find out what it is.'

'You fuckin' find out. It hasn't done me any fuckin' harm. Live and let live, that's my motto.'

'Larkin, you're a squaddie in the army, how can you have a motto like live and let live?'

'I just do, alright.'

'Come on, we'll go a bit further.'

Again I crept forward and again Larkin followed me reluctantly, muttering constantly in a broad Manchester grumble that sounded like an old train going across points.

Whatever it was, it was directly in front of us now, behind a large rain tree. The birds had stopped singing. The crickets, grasshoppers, frogs and other unwanted creatures that for some God-awful reason God had decided to create, had also fallen silent.

The only sounds were the thing rustling leaves up in front and Larkin's incessant grumbling. I raised my rifle to my shoulder and shouted 'Come out with your hands up.'

My voice echoed through the silence. I had shouted so loudly it was as if I had spoken through a megaphone.

The thing ahead stopped moving.

'Oh yeah, wild pigs are really gonna fucking understand. We'll see one in a minute walking on his hind legs with his hooves up in the air. Bright fuckin' call, Lanky.'

The thing started moving toward us now. 'Larkin, I think it's going to charge.'

I stood my ground. 'Stop or I fire.'

Then we saw it. It was dressed in a loose flowing khaki and knee high boots. But it was the face that was all wrong. It didn't have one. There was a blackness without features, hair or anything recognisably human.

'Jesus fuckin' Christ,' said Larkin eloquently. Then it spoke.

'It's alright chaps, it's only me.'

'Only me,' I thought. You've given me the fright of my life and all you can say is 'It's only me.'

'Who are you and what are you doing here?' It continued to walk towards us. Even Larkin had his rifle to his shoulder now.

It lifted its hands to where its head should have been and slowly peeled back its black skin, throwing it behind him like a veil.

We saw a chubby little face, round cheeks, a cherubic nose, small, bright eyes and thin, rather emaciated lips. The lips were wrong for the face. It was as if whoever had made him had decided they were the one part of his body that was to be devoid of any fat.

Then the thin lips moved and I heard the words again. 'It's only me chaps, Mr. Owens.'

Neither myself nor Larkin lowered our rifles. I was the one who spoke, of course, Larkin being unable to co-ordinate thinking and talking. Thinking and moaning he could handle. But thinking and saying something intelligible was always beyond him.

'Don't you know this is a Military Camp and you are trespassing.'

'Oh, that's alright, Colonel Holmes has given me permission.' He walked towards us now, moving clumsily through the undergrowth.

For the first time I noticed a large, clear glass jar in his left hand and a bag-like piece of muslin at the end of a long cane of bamboo in his right.

'Lovely morning isn't it chaps. Had a wonderful night. Omiza herois Prout, Achrosis spurca Swinhoe and Ourapterryx claretta Holloway were prowling but they didn't get away from me.'

He held up the large glass jar. Inside I could see a large mass of dead bodies, with a few others still beating their wings in the last throes of death.

'You mean to say you spent the whole night here sir,' I asked.

He nodded, 'It's the only way to catch the beauties.'

'Rather you than me, mate,' said Larkin sourly.

'I'm sure I agree, private,' Owens responded in a slightly more testy tone. He opened the lid of the jar to let me look. 'Lovely things aren't they?'

I looked inside. There were all sizes, shapes, and colours of moths. One was about three inches across with beautifully sculpted swallow-tail wings, each scale a graduation of brown that completed a wonderfully fragile living being. It lazily beat its wings, the feathery antennae slowly smelling the fresh air. I watched as the wings stopped beating and froze in mid stroke. The moth lay there surrounded by the bodies of the others.

'Yes sir. Like tiny breaths given a life. One minute they are here, the next gone.'

Owen looked at me with a strange intensity. 'Yes, that's it. Their beauty is in their transience. How perceptive of you.'

'Gives me the fucking heebie-jeebies. Pardon my French, sir.'

Owen paid as much attention to Larkin as he would to an elephant's fart in a typhoon. He turned to me. 'That's very well put, soldier. What's your name, private?'

'Longhurst R sir, 9253420.'

'No, what's your name, not your army name.'

I was puzzled for a moment. Name, what name? I thought. 'Oh name, yes sir. Richard sir.'

'Mine's Owens, but everybody calls me Owens.' He waited for a reaction. 'That was a joke, dear boy.' I smiled. Larkin, of course, missed it all.

'Can you read?' I nodded. 'And write?'

'Quite well,' I answered. It was one of the first things I was proud of about myself. My writing I mean. I loved the feeling of the ink on the paper, the proportion of the letters, the smoothness of ideas flowing from the nib.

'Good,' he said. 'I'm looking for an assistant to help with the catalogue of my tiny treasures. Would you be interested Richard?'

I thought for a short while. Why bloody not? At least it might be more interesting than lying in the barracks staring at the fan whirring noisily over my head. Or listening to Larkin's consistent whining. Or being strangled by Terry Teale's peculiar ability to fart a mixture of gases that had once been used on the Somme.

'I think I would sir. But I don't know what the army would say.'

'Oh, don't worry, I'll talk to Harry. Colonel Holmes, I mean. I'm sure it will be alright.' He smiled in that peculiar way he had of ending a sentence, a smile of finality. 'Good, that's all settled. I'll be in touch when I next go out. Butterfly it will be, on Bukit Timah Hill. Should be jolly good fun.'

His shoulders dropped and for a moment he looked like a little old man, warily searching for his stick he believed had been stolen by a mischievous schoolboy.

'Right, must be off before my treasures go off.' He turned and stumbled back into the jungle, stopping once as if he had remembered something. 'Don't forget your quinine. The bugs can be tiresome at times.' A slow wave of the hand, a last look and he vanished into the green.

'What was all that fuckin' about Lanky?'

'Don't know really. Looks like I could be doing something new.' Before he could ask me any more stupid questions, I started walking off toward the sentry post.

'I suppose we should report it, shouldn't we?'

'Oh yes, we'll report it. Just in case. First rule of the army, Tommy, cover your arse. And what's the second rule of the army?'

'Cover your arse,' he answered as the birds began singing and the jungle crunched beneath our feet.

'Fuckin' army is totally fucked,' were Tommy's parting words.

And for once, I couldn't agree more.

*

Reg Dwyer

Here we are out again at the Pussy Cat club. O'Neill has stood me a drink, as I'm broke. Usual story, I spent so much money sending the presents back to Margie and the kids, I've got nothing left for myself. Still got to pay a few of the lads back and all. Never mind, I'll soon make it up, what with me and the dhobiwallahs and our little arrangement. I feel like a boss more than a soldier. Imagine that, me, Reg Dwyer, a boss. They even call me sir sometimes. I think it's when they want to get paid. I quite enjoy it though, being a sir. Better than touching my knuckle to my forehead, like back in Stockport.

'Hurry up Reg, get it down your neck. You can't nurse that bloody Tiger all night.' It was Eddie speaking. I quickly swallowed a few mouthfuls to keep him happy. Wouldn't want to get on the wrong side of Corporal Eddie Longhurst, Not when I want his extra stripe.

Nearly got us all banned last week, did Eddie. One minute he was fine, laughing and joking with his arm round a lovely little lass. Then the next, he was up and over the table, kicking hell out of some Loyal. I don't know what happened. He told us later the lad had been looking at his girl. Well, we all do that, don't we? But Eddie took it the wrong way. Anyway, the mama-san had to come in and sort it all out. Gave us a free round of drinks didn't she? The poor Loyal had to leave though. Eddie weren't having him drinking anywhere near us.

Sometime during the fracas, the girl left. I don't know where she went but she didn't come back. Right canny looking girl she were too. Wouldn't mind a bit of that, if you catch my drift. Eddie didn't care though. He soon had his arm around another girl. Any port in a storm, that's Eddie. And with him, there's always a storm brewing somewhere.

Anyway, tonight there's just the four of us. Me, Eddie, Teale, and O'Neill. O'Neill's got his court case next week. Silly chough, caught trying to nick cars outside Raffles. I would have thought he were smarter. Just goes to show you, there's nowt as queer as folk, as my mum used to say.

More Tigers have been put on our table, the empties taken away. The mama-san has clapped her hands and the girls have appeared from the back. I see the lovely girl Eddie was with last week, and she comes over to sit next to me.

I quickly glance across to Eddie. He's already feeling up the girl on his knee. It looks like he's forgotten about the one next to me.

'Would you like to dance, Tommy?' she asked me.

'It's Reg. Reg Dwyer, not Tommy.'

'Okay, you want to dance, Rag?'

She took me by the hand, and led me onto the small dance floor in front of the stage. The radio was playing a lovely slow tune by Joe Loss I think. I was really surprised when she leant in to me and pressed her body against mine.

And by surprised, I mean really surprised. I've never seen John Thomas react so quickly. She knew straight away of course.

'You very upright soldier. A very hard man,' she said looking down at John Thomas. Even I could see him straining at the leash of khaki.

'Sorry,' I mumbled.

'Don't be sorry. Be happy. You strong man.'

She pulled me closer and we swayed together to the music.

'What's your name?'

'Me? You want to know my name?'

I nodded. She looked surprised.

'It's Grace in English.'

I was about to tell her it was also the name of my baby when I stopped. I don't know why. I just did.

'You want to come upstairs?' Her eyes indicated the second floor where the rooms lay.

'I've got no money, broke right now.'

'Never mind. You owe me. Not too much, just five dollars for me and one dollar for room.'

'I don't know.'

'Aiyah men, never know anything!' she said and grabbed me by the hand, leading me upstairs.

I could have resisted of course. I was much stronger and bigger than her. She was just a slip of a girl, really. But I didn't. I didn't want to, I guess.

Afterwards, when we had finished and she was buttoning up the side of her cheongsam, I asked her where she was going. All she answered was 'Back to work Tommy.'

At that moment, even though I was with her, I never felt lonelier in my life.

Chapter 14

Michael O'Neill

The canteen was empty for a change. Just myself and Richard sitting there, enjoying a mug of thick strong tea. We had both taken to drinking it like the local people; a dollop of sweet condensed milk floating on top and a couple of spoons of sugar. Really sweet it was, but refreshing, especially on hot days like today, when the sun would melt the smile off a badger's arse.

I'd been out of the Glass House for a while now, but lying there in my green cell all alone had given me time to think. Stupid English eejits think they are punishing Michael O'Neill with their solitary and their jails. Don't they realise it's the place where I grow stronger?

'I don't know what I'm doing here either.' This was Richard, mumbling away to himself as he always does. Sure, the man could talk for Ireland. I think he must have a wee drop of Irish blood in him the way he goes on. Either that or he's kissed the Blarney Stone somewhere.

'My brother loves all this.' He gestured at the canteen around us. But I knew he meant the army and its bloody rituals and its life. 'He wouldn't give it up for the world. Whereas me, I'd get shot of it tomorrow if I could. Sometimes I wish I could be more like you. Not caring what they think or what you do.'

It was then I decided to tell him. 'I'm off I am.'

He looked at me strangely, not really believing what I was saying. 'I'm off,' I repeated. 'I can't soldier it anymore so I'm going to take a ride on Shanks' pony.'

He looked at me like he didn't understand.

'You know, the No 11 bus, me gams, these things with boots on the end.'

I watched his face as he finally understood what I meant. 'Maybe head up to Kuala Lumpur. Hide out for a while until they stop looking. My little girl said she would help. Remember the one from the Pussy Cat club? Wee Eileen?'

He nodded. 'If they catch you...,'

'Sure they won't catch Michael O'Neill. I've the legs of a rabbit.'

He laughed. 'So they won't find hide nor hare of you,' he punned. Clever little bastard that he was.

'That's right. I'm on my bike. This lot are so fucking stupid, they couldn't find a pint at Guinness.'

'When you going?'

I touched the side of my nose. 'Ach, don't you worry yourself. When I'm ready. When I'm ready.'

We both took large gulps of our sweet tea. Richard stared off into the distance. He then whispered softly, 'I wish I could be you. Just be free. Do what I want, when I want. Just be me.'

'You can, Richard me lad, it's all up to you.'

He looked like he had awoken from a dream. That maybe he had said something aloud he should have kept to himself.

He shook his head and stubbed his fag out in the ashtray on the Naafi table. 'We'd better get back,' says he, 'Shelley will be looking for us. If he finds us here, we're on a charge.'

'Yes, better keep the bastard as sweet as this tea. At least for now anyway.' I thought for a moment. 'Want to come with me?' I asked him.

Richard raised his eyes from his glass and then dropped them back down again. 'Don't think I can. Sorry.'

'No worries. I'll be better on my own. Michael O'Neill is always better on his own.'

I got up and started walking out of the door. I turned back and Richard was still sitting there, lost in his own world.

'Come on Richard,' I said softly, 'Mother Shelley is waiting.'

*

Richard Longhurst

It was outside the Indian temple in Tank Road we first saw them. A long row of them going back into the distance, garlanded on either side by cheering rows of supporters, family and friends.

There were soldiers amongst these supporters. Indian soldiers mind you, no white men. I think myself and Owens were the only white men there. The drab olive green of the soldiers' khakis contrasted strongly with the bright greens, yellows, golds and browns of the saris, the simple white of the men, the nakedness of the priests and the gaudy white-washed blues, pinks and turquoise of the temple itself.

My eyes hurt from the colours.

The beating of the drums was getting louder and louder. And then, the first one passed in front of myself and Owens. He was a rather short, thin man wearing nothing but bright orange pantaloons. His bare feet dancing gaily through the rubbish-strewn street.

But what he was carrying made him different. Or rather I should say, how he was carrying it. Above his head was a large pagoda-like structure, swathed in peacock feathers. The pagoda sat on the small Indian's shoulder. Its base was covered in leather to prevent the metal chafing his skin.

From the outstretched arms of the pagoda ran thin strips of what looked like piano wire, which were attached to the man's skin by vicious hooks. Hooks that pulled and stretched his skin like a fisherman pulls the jaw of a fish before removing the hook embedded in its jaw.

There were eight of these hooks on his chest and eight on his back. These were complemented on the chest by a row of large limes hanging from the skin by even larger fish hooks. To add to the symmetry of it all, two more limes hung down from each thigh so that every time he moved their jostling reminded him of their presence.

His face was even more decorated. His tongue was struck straight out at me by a cross of pointed skewers, one of which impaled the tongue vertically whilst the other was pushed through both cheeks. The strange thing was, that even though I would see the skewers piercing his flesh, there was not a drop of blood.

And despite all the piercing and hooks and pagodas and limes, there was one place from which I couldn't take my eyes.

His eyes.

They were wild, white and lost in some world of their own. A heaven where there was no poverty, no hunger, no scrambling for money, no grubbiness. A heaven of simple, unadorned purity.

As if on cue, he suddenly stopped moving forward, the drummers increased their beat and he did a little circle of joy like a strange Asian dance around a non-existent maypole. His supporters clapped, his eyes smiled, his friends laughed. His drummers beat on.

Owens did his usual cough before speaking. 'They're devotees of Lord Muragam. Rather strange really. They ask this Indian God to grant their wish and promise, in return, they will carry these kavadi as penance on

Thaipusam, his festival. He must have been a very generous God this year. There are a lot of his devotees here.'

I looked down the avenue of spectators. There was a long line of peacock feathers, palanquins, pagodas, brass milk jugs, drum beaters, dancers and attendants walking toward me.

With each step of the devotee, I could see the pagodas sway like drunken soldiers coming out from the whorehouses of Lavender Street after a long and particularly liquid night.

'This will go on all day, you know. They've been preparing themselves for ages; ritual cleansing, prayers, all that sort of tosh.'

'But there's no blood.'

'Yes, strange, it's like they are all in a trance, unable to bleed.'

'Or maybe their God is protecting them.'

'Well, that's what they believe. But, as white men Richard, we have to maintain certain standards. These Indians may believe in all this mumbo-jumbo but we should take it with a pinch of salt. A jolly pretty day out though, don't you think?'

'Mumbo-jumbo? Like believing Mary was a virgin? And the water turns into wine during the Mass? And we're eating God's body when we take the sacrament? Stuff like that, do you mean?'

'Really Richard. It's not the same at all, dear boy. After all, these are Indians. You can't equate their arcane rituals with the sacraments of the holy church. I'm shocked you could say such a thing. It's...it's...it's blasphemy.'

For once, Owens did indeed look shocked. The small, reddened cheeks were puffing out, the wisps of white hair he ceremonially combed across his balding red pate waved in the breeze and his mouth flapped like a dying fish gasping for air.

'I...I...knew this was a mistake, bringing you here. You haven't been out here long enough yet. You have to realise these people need us to save them from themselves. I mean, can you imagine some Indian fakir walking through the streets of Chelmsford with a skewer through his cheeks? No, our job is to bring them the benefits of our civilisation – duty, honour, service, justice, the law. If they want to hang on to their colourful pageantry then so be it. But we mustn't be seduced by the East. We must tame it, control it. Remember that, Richard. Remember it.'

He wiped his sweating brow with a large, floral handkerchief. I could see the sweat seeping through the armpits of his white linen jacket adding another layer of stain to the shelter of tide marks lying there. 'I need to sit down.' he said. 'Let's go to Robinson's Café for a rather large Sundae. It will be my treat.'

*

Eddie Longhurst

Our Richard's off with the fairies again. Don't get me wrong, I don't think he's turning queer or anything. I'd kick his head in if he did anyway.

But he's started going off on his own into the city. I don't know what the fuck he does there but he comes back with a daft look on his face like he's been spending all day on the Tiger. But I smell his breath and it's as dry as a donkey's dick.

I've tried to get him out with me, training or playing football. He's not a bad winger despite being built like a long streak of piss. But he's not interested. 'I'm tired Eddie,' or 'You go off Eddie and I'll join you later,' or 'I've hurt my leg Eddie.'

One day I'd had enough of this shit and dragged off his bunk on to the floor. He lay there, not moving, not getting up. What could I do? I gave him a kick in the ribs and stormed out of our block.

I saw him afterwards. He sidled up to me as I was sat in the Naafi.

'Give us a fag.'

'Get your own.'

'I've smoked all of mine. Give us one of your Capstans.'

I took out the packet and flung it at him. He opened it, took one out, tapped it twice on the table and lit it up. 'You know you shouldn't be smoking these if you're a sportsman, don't you?'

'What the fuck do you mean?' I snapped back at him, 'a fag won't do anyone any harm. I mean it's just bleedin' tobacco, aint it?'

He carried on smoking, exhaling one long blast of smoke up into the air where it caught the sunlight through the fanlights.

'I read smoking is bad for you, messes up the lungs.'

'I read somewhere reading is bad for you. Messes up the fuckin' head.' I leant over and tapped him in the noggin. 'Too much fuckin' shit up here, that's your problem, Richard. Too much shit for brains.'

He took another long suck on the Capstan and stared down at the wooden table. It took a while before he spoke. 'I'm not like you Eddie.'

'Too fuckin' right, you ain't. But if you were like me, you'd be able to get along a lot easier.'

He stayed silent.

I thought it was about time I took a softer approach to him. More like an elder brother. 'You've got to get your fuckin' life in order Richard. No more mooning off to town for half a day. Tuck in. Be a mate. Be one of us. The Tads are a great outfit. Just be one of us.'

He nodded as if he was thinking about it. Then suddenly a big smile came over his face, 'Let's go off to The Lady Bar tonight, hey?'

'That's more like it. Time those tarts had a seeing to from some real men, not some bastard pansies from the RASC. Get some real wood in them for a change.'

'Here's to that,' he said, picking up his tea cup and draining the dregs.

Thank fuck. He's back to being a mate again.

And a brother. My little brother.

*

Reg Dwyer
Block 15, Tanglin Barracks, Singapore
17th May, 1940
Dear Marjorie,
I'm sorry I haven't written to you for such a long time.

You see I couldn't face writing this letter. I went to see Colonel Holmes at the beginning of March. He told me the bad news. Apparently, the War Office has a new policy in February. No new married quarters are to be given out and no families brought out to any overseas postings for the rest of the War. Colonel Holmes explained it was because of the dangers of German U-boat attacks on our Shipping. The War Office, he said, were worried about the effect on morale if soldiers' families were torpedoed en route to joining their spouses.

I tried to explain I had applied over a year ago and it was the army's fault we hadn't been reunited earlier. What with the change of CO and Major Tudor's reluctance to bring up the subject to him.

But he said there was nothing to be done because of the new War Office policy.

End of story.

So that's it, Margie. I don't know what to do now. You and the kids will never be able to join me here while this War is on. I think the only thing to do is to try to get a posting back to England so I can be with you, it's my only way out.

Lord, I pray every night I can see you and Tommy and Evelyn and young Grace. I pray and pray and pray. But it doesn't seem to do much good. Not anymore.

Your husband

Reg

Censored by Lt. Whitehead

*

Richard Longhurst

'That's it chaps, look mean and nasty.'

We were standing up to our waists in this stream while this pillock from the War Office set his camera up on the bank.

'Now, advance toward me down the stream. No. No. No. John, you there, third from the back.'

'Me sir?'

'Yes, you sir.' Of course it was Larkin he was referring to. 'Your eye line is straight ahead toward the enemy.'

'But there ain't no enemy.'

'You know that, I know that. But the British public hasn't got a clue, alright? So look straight ahead.'

'Yes, sir.'

'You know, Major Tudor. The shot lacks something. I don't know what it is. Michael, I say, Michael.'

A young puppy of a lieutenant came bounding up. 'Yes, Horace what is it?'

'They need to be more menacing, Michael. See to it.'

'Menacing? Right Horace.'

Michael, Lieutenant-what's-his-name, ran back to his shelter under the rain tree. He grabbed a bag and ran back to us. 'You can come out of the water now.'

Shelley, myself, O'Neill and Larkin stepped out onto the bank.

Lieutenant Michael jumped back in horror. 'Your leg.' He pointed at Shelley.

There was a large black leech sitting above Shelley's knee calmly sucking his blood. Shelley took his knife, dug the point under its mouth, and levered it off.

'Oh, you are a brave man,' said the lieutenant. 'I'll make you look very fierce. Trust me, Michael knows exactly what he's doing.'

He reached into his bag and produced a dark brown compact. He dabbed a powder puff into it and started dabbing Shelley's face.

It was now Shelley's turn to recoil. 'You're not putting any bloody make up on me.'

'It's just blusher. It'll give you lovely cheekbones and highlights for the camera. Think of it as camouflage paint.'

O'Neill stepped forward and said, 'Let him do it to me, sarge. Then you can see how it looks.'

'Who's a brave boy then? I always did have liking for the Irish.'

'You've met Errol Flynn?'

'Worked with him in Northampton Rep. Terrible play, all jolly hockey sticks and "what's for tea, Vicar?" Errol was wonderful though, bit of a naughty boy, if you know what I mean.' Here he touched the side of his nose and winked. 'He looks a bit like you. He's an Aussie of course, but not many people know. Tries to keep it hush hush, as if anything is ever secret where we come from. Same eyes though. Wonderful eyes our Errol, and a magic you-know-what.'

'What?' asked Larkin.

'That's for me to know and you to find out,' the lieutenant winked, again.

Shelley blushed.

I smiled.

Larkin said 'What?'

O'Neill looked at himself in the mirror. 'Sure, a little more along the jaw line. I think.'

'Well, we are a pro, aren't we?' said Lieutenant Michael. 'Right, next one up, as the actress said to the Bishop.'

I looked at O'Neill. The brown stain underneath the eyes, along the cheek and shading the jaw line had given his face a fierce resolution, like he'd been up for three days and was ready to fight anybody who dared to challenge him.

I stepped forward. Lieutenant Michael started dabbing my face gently. 'Now keep still, this won't hurt a bit.' It was strange hearing this officer chat to me like I was one of his mates.

'It's always the little prick that hurts the most.' He giggled out loud. 'Well, that's what they say, isn't it private...?'

'Longhurst, sir.'

'Well, Longhurst, you might not scare the enemy but you sure scare the hell out of me.' He pushed me away to arm's length and looked me up and down like a knackerman looks at a horse. 'God, I'm a genius. I can make a pig's ear look like a silk purse.'

I took this as a compliment.

'Hurry up, Michael, we haven't got all day.'

'Ready Horace, keep your shirt on. It's not easy working in this heat, you know. My brushes are all sticky.'

He quickly dabbed Larkin and Shelley's faces. 'Remember to look fierce, my little tigers.'

'Right back in the water, chaps. Now remember you're out on patrol in the jungle looking for the enemy who's lying in wait for you around the bend.'

'If we knew where he was, we wouldn't need to patrol, would we sir?' Of course this was Larkin.

'Pretend you don't know they are there, soldier.'

'Yes sir.'

'Right, when I say 'action', walk toward the camera scanning the jungle for the enemy. Remember, they're going to see this back at home so put on your fiercest face.'

The other lieutenant looked through the camera. 'I love the look, but could you give that Serjeant more. He looks a bit white compared to the rest.'

Lieutenant Michael signaled to Shelley who suffered the immense loss of dignity, having make-up applied to his manly features.

'They're going to love you down the Serjeants' mess tonight, Serjeant Shelley. You'll be more popular than Dorothy Lamour.'

'Shut the fuck up, O'Neill. Or else you're on a charge.'

'Yes, Serjeant, just a joke, Serjeant.'

'You three mention this to anyone and you're all on a charge.'

'Yes, Serjeant. We mean no, Serjeant,' all three of us answered in chorus.

'There, Van Gogh couldn't have done better,' said our lieutenant, eyeing his handiwork.

'Those rifles look a little weak, major.'

'They're the regulation issue Lee Enfields. If you want it more manly, you could try a Thompson sub-machine gun. We've just been delivered a crate of those. But nobody knows how to use them yet.'

'Oh, a Tommy gun? Like in the movies?'

'I think so.'

'That would be perfect.'

The major turned round to Captain Moriarty. 'Go back to the QM and get a couple of Thompsons will you. Tell him it's for the shooting.'

'Shooting what sir?'

'Shooting the film, you ass. Hurry up, we haven't got all day.'

'Yes sir.'

Moriarty ran off back to the main road about 50 yards from where we were filming.

We were supposed to be in the deepest, darkest, depths of the Malaysian jungle. But we were off Holland Road about a mile away from the camp. Dramatic license, the director called it. 'The magic of film'.

Just another bloody lie is what I thought. Just more propaganda about our brave troops, ever vigilant in their fight against the unseen enemy.

I'd seen exactly the same thing myself last week down at the Capitol. Myself and Reg had gone to see *The Four Feathers*. Of course, they had the Pathe news before the features like they always do.

There was this poncey announcer rambling on about the brave Empire soldiers defending the oppressed citizens of the world. This voice ran against footage of some poor buggers charging up a sand dune with fixed bayonets. They looked really bored and tired.

The worst was yet to come. The announcer proudly shouted: 'Take that, Fritz,' as we watched a Jerry bomber crashing in flames at night in the desert.

Even I could see it was fake and I'm no expert. To me it looked nothing like a bomber. It was one of those parachute flares they'd taught us to use at the deployment camp in Changi.

Captain Moriarty came running back with two Thompsons under his arm.

He handed one to Shelley and O'Neill grabbed the other.

'Lovely, lovely,' said the captain/director.

O'Neill took his Tommy gun and chattering away with his mouth, proceeded to execute all the surrounding ferns and palm trees.

'No. No firing. Remember you are a very vigilant patrol. Ready. Roll cameras, Action.'

He waved his arm and we moved forward through the water, looking aggressively to right and left.

There was a loud splash behind.

'Cut!' I heard the captain shout.

I turned round to see Larkin resurface, spitting water out of his mouth. 'My foot. It got all tangled in some roots. Nearly had me leg off.'

'Okay, return to Position A, people.'

'What?'

'Go back to where you started,' the other lieutenant explained wearily.

'Right you are sir,' answered Shelley.

'Did I look fierce enough, sir?' said O'Neill.

'You were perfect. In fact, could you swap positions with the Serjeant? That's right, you can lead. Now we'll put the man who fell over right at the back bringing up the rear.'

We all changed positions in the stream.

At this point, Major Tudor leaned forward. 'But that's not correct, captain. You see we wouldn't have a private leading a patrol. That's the Serjeant's job. That's the whole point of being a Serjeant.'

'Right you are major. But the Irishman looks really fierce out in front. He really looks the part. Any ideas?'

Major Tudor shook his head.

The captain seemed to think for a moment. 'Silly me, it's so simple.' He looked for the Lieutenant. 'Michael, Michael, we need your sewing fingers, dear.'

I could see Major Tudor visibly wincing at one officer calling another 'dear'.

The captain said something to the lieutenant, who ran back to the rain tree, reappearing seconds later with a pair of scissors, needle and thread.

'Right you are Michael, cut the stripes off him and put them on that one.' He pointed from Shelley to O'Neill.

Shelley's face dropped. O'Neill beamed.

'But, but , but ....sir?' Shelley protested to Major Tudor.

'You heard the captain, Serjeant.'

'Don't worry, this won't hurt a bit,' said Lieutenant Michaels.

'That's what they always say, remember?'

'Oh aren't we the clever one? I'm going to have to watch myself with you.'

The lieutenant started to cut away Shelley's stripes. His face was getting redder and redder. All the shit he had put up with to get those bloody things and now they were being taken away from him by some nancy boy officer. And, even worse, they were going to bloody O'Neill of all people.

'Does this mean they'll be giving me more money, Serjeant?'

'Don't say a word more O'Neill or you're on a charge.'

O'Neill looked down at his arm as the lieutenant was sewing the stripes on. 'Sure I think I could get used to these very easily. Don't you think they go with my eyes Lanky?'

I had more sense than to answer.

'There, you are, all finished, Serjeant.' The lieutenant twisted his head right and left, admiring his handiwork. 'Fit for a queen.'

O'Neill swaggered around the troop, proudly displaying his new stripes

'Right, positions everyone. Remember, think fierce. You're warriors of the King.'

'Warriors of the King – that's a new one,' said Larkin.

'Right. Ready. Camera. Action.' We waded through the jungle waters off Holland Road, our Tommy guns at the ready and our make-up already beginning to drip down our faces.

'And cut. Print that. Perfect boys. Now we'll go to the next set up which I believe is a bayonet charge, isn't it, Major Tudor?'

'That's right.'

'Good, Michael. Oh, Michael…,'

The captain/director walked off to talk with his lieutenant.

O'Neill turned to me. 'I think I've finally found out what I want to do with the rest of my life, Richard. Watch out, Errol Flynn - Michael O'Neill is coming.'

*

Reg Dwyer

Lord, how I wish it would rain.

A long drizzle like we used to get in Stockport when the day started a sort of raunchy grey and stayed that way until it gradually faded to black.

Here, I just melt. Not like in the Sinai when we were there. Jesus it was hot, as the Lord himself probably knows having spent forty days out there himself like. But you never felt wasted. It was sort of welcoming really. A sort of heat that cleared the soul and the mind and the body.

Here though, it's a heat that sucks you dry, like a straw emptying a glass. You feel tired, irritated, drained all the time.

I mean I just stick my head out of the barracks and walk across the parade ground. By the time I get to the canteen on the other side, I'm already soaking wet, dripping from the head to toe.

The locals understand how to handle it though. They get up really early, then break at 11.00 until 4.00, after that they might consider going back to work again.

Even the officers seem to have got it all worked out. We occasionally see them in the mornings but after noon they vanish back to their rooms or their houses for a long nap.

Except the stupid ones though and we seem to have our fair share of those. Them we see every afternoon on the golf course chasing a small, round white ball into a hole. They never seem to catch it though.

It's us poor squaddies who really suffer. We're marching or working or training or shooting, or doing some other damn fool army thing all day long.

We're lucky having Serjeant Shelley. We usually do all the exercise stuff in the morning when it's cool, leaving the other chores till the afternoon. Some of the other guys have lost so much weight even their mothers wouldn't recognise them.

But the heat's not the only problem we face. Malaria is the big worry. Sometimes I hear the doctors warning the Serjeants not to go too heavy with the training in the jungle in case we all come down with the disease.

We're all supposed to take these quinine tablets every day but I can't be bothered with mine. They taste sour – like dried rat droppings – not that I've ever eaten dried rat droppings you understand, but that's what they taste like, I'm sure.

And, of course, there's always the odd case of the runs especially after a night out on the piss. I think it must be the ice or something those bastard bar owners put in the beer because afterwards you're shitting through the eye of a needle for the next week.

I never eat the local food. Some of the lads have tried it like Lanky, and they say it's very tasty. But I always think my stomach's been brought up to understand bread, potatoes, meat and lots of veggies. It doesn't matter where you live, this is real grub. If it were good enough for my dad and his dad before him, then it's good enough for yours truly.

And there's the usual squaddie sickies. On Monday mornings, the doctors have a long line of walking wounded who have been pissing razor blades.

You can see them line up outside the office, all with that peculiar shyness and embarrassment. The doc couldn't give a toss though. He gets them to take their shorts down, whips back the old foreskin and whoopee yessiree we have another red, weeping bell end.

Some of the men lay bets on how many cases of clap the doc will see that morning. Three orderly serjeants run the sweepstakes.

I got really close once. I guessed 38. The answer was 37. If I'd have known I were so close, I'd have gone out and got the clap myself. You don't turn down $100 for nowt.

The doc knows nothing though. If you ask me, he's a bit doolally. He's got a routine he follows with each man:

'Where did you get it?'

The doc is a mite deaf so he usually says, 'Speak up man, don't whisper.' This has the effect of broadcasting whatever disease the poor soul has right across the parade ground and on towards the officers' quarters.

'From a girl sir.'

'I know that you bloody fool, which bar?'

'The Lady Bar sir.'

'What was her name?'

'Can't remember sir.'

'Put another don't know down for the Lady Bar, Serjeant. That's the twelfth this week.'

'Yes sir.'

'And you, wear a condom next time Briggs.'

'Yes sir.'

'Treat him Serjeant.'

'Yes sir.'

The usual questions, the even more usual answers. I've been lucky though, I always choose my girls carefully. One time, I got caught though and had to join the Monday queue.

'Oh, this is interesting Serjeant. Come and look.'

The orderly came and stared at my red, blotched willy, tightly grasped by the doc. 'Very interesting sir, we haven't had one of them for a while. Lovely bit of balinitis.'

'What is it? What's wrong?' I asked, fearing the worst. They ignored me. 'See the red lesion here, and here and beneath the head.'

He wrenched my poor willy round to show the short-sighted bloody orderly. 'Yes, sir, quite an advanced case really.' The doc looked at me. 'How long have you had this?'

'About two weeks sir. Er sir...?' I asked as he grabbed a magnifying glass from his table and examined my now enormous bell end under his glass.

'Yes, what is it man? Can't you see I'm busy?'

'Er sir, is it serious? This bally what's it?'

'Of course, it's serious man. All disease is serious.'

'Oh. Will I... will I...,'

'Out with it man.'

'Will I be able to use it again?'

'Use it? Use it? Of course, you bloody will. It's only a fungus man. Spot of cream at the end will soon sort it out, won't it Serjeant?'

'Yes sir.'

'But a word in your ear.' I leaned forward. 'Don't put John Thomas into that particular hole again, understand. It's not the cleanest place on earth.'

'Yes sir, quite understand sir, won't happen again sir...it's the wife sir...she's...,'

'Next.'

The Serjeant led me away to a dressing station. Behind me I could hear the doc barking, 'Don't just stand there man, drop them quickly, I haven't got all day,' followed by 'Whazzat? Speak up man, you don't need to whisper. Syphilis is it? Well, I'll be the judge of that. You're right man, well done, well spotted, we've got a lovely little suppurating sore oozing from there, haven't we? Very pretty.'

'Oi, did you hear what I had to say?'

It was the orderly Serjeant shouting in my ear. 'Slap this cream on your dick twice a day. Stay away from the tarts for at least two weeks and try not to give it the old J. Arthur alright?'

'Yes Serjeant,' I whispered, taking my ointment. Not a very pleasant time. Good job Margie won't find out though. That would have been the end of me. We would never have had marital relations ever again. Not that Margie was awfully keen on them in the first place. But, regular as clock work, every Sunday morning, Margie would wake up early and say, 'You can do it now, if you want.'

I used to love my Sunday mornings. Occasionally there was even a smile on Margie's face too. But I was never certain whether it was because of the relations, or because it was over and done with. It didn't bother me though. I'd had me oats and she always cooked a magic breakfast afterwards.

Nothing beats a sausage, bacon, egg, tomatoes, mushroom and a fried slice after you've had your oats. Except possibly more oats, but I wasn't going to get that, was I? Not with Margie anyway.

I don't know how I got into all this. It must be the heat getting to me.

Should write to Margie now. It's been a while.

*

Richard Longhurst

'Can you get away on the weekend if I give you enough notice?'

'Sometimes, I've got guard duty but I'm sure someone will do it for me. Reg is always looking for money. Why?'

Owens pushed back his glasses with his chubby index finger. I could see the line across his nose where they had sat. A strange little crease, connected to the flare of his nostrils, dividing his nose into two. He looked like an unnaturally thriving squirrel.

'Tiger,' he said pushing the glasses back to the bridge of his nose again. He had a strange glint in his eye, 'We're going after Tiger. There's been some killings up near Kota Tinggi. So, with a bit of luck, we'll be hunting one soon.'

He bent over the delicate black and white body of Parenticopus desertii and gently picked it up in his tweezers, wafting it in front of his face to remove the last gasps of formaldehyde.

'Such a pretty smell, I always think, don't you?'

'How do you tell the difference between a moth and a butterfly?'

Owens continued emptying his bottle of its dead butterflies onto the cream-coloured blotting paper.

Sunlight streamed through the windows, picking up the distorted breaths of formaldehyde as they rose from the bodies. It was as if their spirits were leaving the corpses to join the rest of their species out there in the jungle.

I was about to repeat my question when Owens pushed his thick spectacles back onto the bridge of his nose. 'Humph,' he began as he always did by clearing his throat of whatever obstacle or imaginary obstacle may or may not have been there.

I noticed the dirty grey ring lying around the top of his dog collar. A growing, climbing film of dirt that seemed to emanate from his body as if it were escaping from the confines of his cloth.

'Humph,' he repeated again, 'it's simple, dear boy, look at the head.' He pointed to one of the butterflies on the blotter. 'See, the long thin antenna has a tiny rounded knob at its end. Now with moths...,' he pushed forward what looked to me like another butterfly, 'the antennas are usually feathery but they can come in many different shapes. Remember, long, thin with a knob on the end equals butterfly. Anything else and it's pretty safe calling it a moth.'

'So it's not the colour, then.'

'No, dear boy, moths can be colourful as well. See this one, Syntonis Huebnarii, a lovely fellow. The orange and yellow rings around his abdomen are very dashing. And contrasted with the speckled black and white wings, well you have a veritable Beau Brummel of the moth world. I caught him drinking his fill on a Mile-a-minute plant. Lovely little fellow isn't he?'

Owens held the moth up to within three inches of my eyes. I could smell the biting stench of the formaldehyde oozing from its body.

'Right, let's start sorting this lot out. You write while I give our friends the once over. Ready?'

I nodded and pushed up the fountain pen with its aquamarine ink. He gently pushed the small pile of butterflies to separate the lifeless bodies.

'Now what do we have here? Humph, looks like Précis Orithia. That's P-R-E-C-I-S; second word O-R-I-T-H-I-A. Very sweet little thing, The English name is Blue Pansy.'

I looked at it. It was about one inch in length with six orange and black eyes on a field of dark green grey. 'But it's not blue,' I said, looking down immediately to cover my embarrassment at the stupidity of the comment.

'That's right, dear boy, it isn't. Just ours not to reason why. Maybe whoever discovered it was colour blind. He may have had a rather perverted sense of humour. Perhaps he may have loved the colour blue, God alone knows, dear boy.' Here he looked up toward the ceiling as if to ask forgiveness for taking the Lord's name half in vain. 'Ours not to reason why. Humph, let's get on otherwise we'll never finish before we lose the light.'

He cleared his throat again, picked up a pocket magnifying glass and confirmed his classification. 'Lovely chap, lovely chap, definitely Catopsilia Pomona.'

As he spelt out the Latin name, I wrote it out on a small white card in capitals, followed by the English name, Lemon Fragrant, in this case, in lower case exactly half an inch below it. In the top right-hand corner I wrote the date and time 20/09/40, 5:30. The weather; always the same either hot and humid, or wet and humid. At the bottom I wrote any notes he wanted to record; their habitat, how many were feeding, and the quality of the soil. Whatever came to mind.

Each butterfly was catalogued and then laid out on the cream-coloured blotting paper. By the time we had finished we had 23 tiny bodies all neatly filed in a row, like soldiers on parade.

Now, came the most important part of the day.

Owens rose from his seat and leaned over the blotting paper, God-like. 'Who is going to join the collection? Humph, are any of you boys right?' he said to the files of dead butterflies.

He paused, pushed his glasses back on his nose. He grasped his thin bottom lip between his thumb and forefinger, pushing it forward to form a spout. 'What do you think, Richard?'

'Sorry?'

'What do you think? Who should join my little collection?'

He'd never asked me before. Why ask me now? I don't know. My eyes flitted across the glass cases facing to the wall. Like a butterfly, my gaze stopped at one, fluttered to another, hovered over a third before returning to the first.

'Well, Richard?'

I got up and assumed the same pose as him, looking close at the butterflies from above. I took the magnifying glass. The butterflies suddenly became four times larger. Now, I could see each individual scale, each beautiful colour. I could see where the red of an eye became the yellow of a wing. And how the scales had beautiful graduations of blues, yellows, blacks, reds, magentas. There wasn't one colour but a thousand on each wing. A flying palette of colour beneath my glass.

I slowly examined each dead body. Owens waited patiently. He didn't say anything; he didn't help me in any way. All I could hear was the rasp at the end of each of his shallow breaths, as rhythmic as the ticking of a clock.

'I think I would keep the striped Albatross, the Blue Pansy and the Lemon Fragrant.' I looked at him for approval.

'Very good, very good, but don't forget Paraticopsis delesertii, a lovely specimen of the Malayan Zebra. Quite, quite marvelous, dear boy.'

He separated the four we had chosen and swept the rest into the bin at the side of the desk.

I looked at the lovely bodies, lying there dead and broken.

'Come along dear boy, it's time for a drink. I'll mount those later.'

I followed him out of the study, taking one last look at the bin before closing the door.

*

Eddie Longhurst

'Right then, you lot, attention.'

We all sprang to attention and lined up in our best parade ground fashion, except our boots were sinking into the sand of the beach.

'At ease men. My name is Captain McLaverty of the Royal Engineers. This morning we're going to start to build the beach defences for this sector of the island. My Serjeant, Serjeant Trimble here, will show you what to do. If you have any questions just ask him. Right then, Serjeant Trimble, carry on.'

Serjeant Trimble watched as his officer slipped his swagger stick under his arm and stumbled through the sand bank to the main road and his car.

'Right then lads, we're going to make some offshore beach defences starting from here, and going down to the end of the beach.' He pointed towards the far western end of the beach, where it met a headland on its way to the city. He avoided the majority of the Eastern side of beach, which went toward Changi.

Of course one of the lads had to speak, and of course it had to be Larkin.

'But what about the other half of the beach, Serjeant. Isn't that going to be defended?'

'Not yet lad. We don't have permission to work on that half of the beach. The civil government is still negotiating with the landowner.'

'Enough questions. Just listen, right.' That was Shelley shutting the idiot up.

'Right, we'll divide you into two. 13 Platoon are to start chopping down the coconut trees behind us to clear a field of fire. 14 Platoon are to drag the trees here and start sawing them into fifteen-foot lengths. Is that clear? Right away you go, then lads, step lively.'

'You heard the Serjeant, get on with it. Tools are in the trucks back at the road.'

Building fucking beach defences, would you fucking believe it? Don't get me wrong, I love the army. But we should be training to fight and kill people, not building fucking shore defences. Not when there's thousands of bloody coolies on the island, dying for a day's work.

Jesus, I've never chopped a tree down in my life. But here I was axe in hand, attacking the first one I saw.

'Hey, take it easy Eddie. We want to drag this out. If we work too quickly, they'll have us doing this for the rest of our bloody tour.'

That was Larkin, looking for a skive as usual. Well, fuck him.

So I went faster, swinging the axe over my head and bringing it down hard on the wood of the coconut tree.

I imagined I was an executioner bringing the axe down on the neck of a prisoner, seeing the head fall in one clean blow, watching the body topple forward, hearing the gush of blood from the severed arteries, the roar of the watching crowd.

But the coconut tree was tougher than a man's head. Each axe blow merely sent a few splinters flying, hardly disturbing the wood.

'This axe is blunt as your dick, Larkin.' The sweat was already pouring off me. I put the axe down and removed my shirt. Fuck dressing properly in heat like this. The others followed suit, carefully folding their Khaki shirts and laying them down neatly in a pile in the shade.

I spat on my hands. No fucking coconut tree was going to defeat me.

I lifted the axe high and brought it down. Again. And again. And again. A few splinters spat off each time as the axe started to bite into the wood.

It were going to be a while but we'd do it.

Tree by tree, we'd do it.

Chapter 15

Michael O'Neill

I was marched in by the Provost Marshal, a shite with a toothbrush mustache and a broom handle stuck up his arse. Major Brown was sitting behind his desk, a few papers neatly arranged in front of him, the rest of the desk empty.

'Atten-shun!' the little shite shouted. I gave them my best impression of a soldier. It wasn't very good. It never was.

Major Brown shuffled his papers before gradually lifting his eyes to register my presence. 'Private O'Neill,' he sighed.

'Yes sir?' I answered.

'Quiet in the presence of an officer.' The shite leaned in closer to me. I could smell his breath close to my face. A rotten smell that only comes from a mouth full of rotten teeth. 'Don't speak until asked to do so by the adjutant.'

I thought it was time to wind the wee bastard up. 'Yes, Serjeant.'

'Silence, you piece of Irish shit,' he shouted close to my ear. Once again, I caught the full force of something rotten in my nostrils, like the aroma of a dead cow after it's been lain in the summer sun for a couple of days.

Major Brown waved his arm. The Provost Marshal backed off slightly. I could still feel his eyes boring into the side of my head though. I could still smell the rotten mouth. I was still aware of the thug in him waiting to give me a beating.

'Private O'Neill, you are charged with being absent without leave on the nights of August 12th and 13th. How do you plead?'

'Not guilty sir.'

Major Brown lifted his eyebrow slightly and sighed once more.

'Were you or were you not in the camp for those two nights?'

I thought for a moment. 'No I wasn't sir.'

He put down his papers. 'Did you have permission to leave the camp?'

'I did not, sir.'

He seemed happy with the answer. A smile crept across his face like a lover's hand creeps across to touch the breasts of his mistress. 'Then

Private O'Neill, you were absent without leave. Do you have anything to say for yourself?'

I thought for a moment about telling him about it all. About spending the night with Eileen. For the first time since I'd left feeling free and happy and me again. Well, feeling her actually. But this eejit wouldn't understand. The morning after, I'd changed into some lovely civvie clothes she had bought for me. Bless her simple heart. We'd both gone to the Railway Station to get a ticket to Kuala Lumpur. She had given me an address of her cousin who I could stay with when I got there.

We walked into the hall of the Railway Station with its pictures of Malaya on the walls. I was stepping out like a dandy horse at a gypsy fair, so happy was I. She was going to join me next week as soon as the mama-san would let her get away. In the meantime, I was looking forward to a whole week's galloping with the fillies of Kuala Lumpur. Well, you can't expect a man to keep all his happiness for just one woman can you?

We walked up to the ticket station, her hanging off my arm like we were married and me pretending to be this big shot planter down to see his tottie for the weekend. I don't know what it was that gave us away. But as soon as we asked for the tickets, the clerk looked at us both strangely and asked us to wait. He went into the back room and came back with two of the biggest fecking Redcaps I'd ever seen.

'Right, let's be having you,' said the Serjeant.

'I'm sorry sir. What is the matter?' I bluffed using the best English voice I could muster. How it hurt my throat to use those foul vowels. But needs and circumstances must.

The Serjeant laughed to himself. 'You know Alf,' he said to the big thug standing next to him. 'Would you Adam and Eve it. These stupid wankers think they are the first to try this little caper. You've got to admit, this one is at least a bit cool about it.

'I'm sorry sir, what is the matter?' He aped my English accent. Then the mood changed. 'Come along sonny, we wouldn't want any trouble here, would we? I mean Alf here would, but I don't think you'd enjoy it too much. Alf isn't known for his patience, are you Alf?'

The big thug grunted something in reply. I didn't know what it was nor did I care. The Serjeant took my arm. I looked across at my wee girl standing there and she looked so beautiful at that moment. So beautiful.

'Do you have anything to say for yourself?' The major repeated, slightly louder this time. I was back in his office, facing him behind his desk, the sickly green walls and the Provost's stare drilling into my left ear.

'I just can't soldier the army any more sir.'

'Private O'Neill, this is the second time you have been up before me. I thought you would have learnt your lesson before but it seems I was wrong. Right, Provost Marshal, take him away. Three months in the Glass House should give him time to ponder the error of his ways.'

'Atten-shun!' shouted the Provost Marshal. I was marched out of the office. Three months. At least I would be on my own for a while, away from all this. There are always blessings in every cloud my ma used to say.

She didn't find many blessings though. Until she went to church. They were always waiting for her there.

*

Eddie Longhurst

Well it's the semi-final and for once Harrington is playing a blinder. I've had bugger all to do really. Pick up a couple of through balls and caught a few crosses. That's all really. It's been a doddle. The Royal Artillery have been playing like carthorses. Big fucking country yokels they are. Slow and stupid if you know what I mean. More used to pulling howitzers than chasing after a ball.

But we haven't scored yet. Liddle missed a sitter before half time. The cross came in, landed at his feet; he controlled it, just six yards out, the net open wide in front of him, easier to score than to miss. And the stupid bugger goes and puts it over the top doesn't he? Stupid Wanker.

Since then, we've had two or three more chances and put them all wide. Not one of our days. Hold on, a long ball from their centre-half. More of a punt really. Harrington has got it about ten yards out from our penalty area. Then the bloody donkey slips and in nips their centre forward. One on one. Come on Eddie lad, out to him, narrow the angles, break the fucker's leg if he tries to go past you.

But the bastard can see what's on my mind. As I'm coming out, he chips the ball over my head. I'm stood there like a fucking tree while the bastard thing soars over my head, into the back of the net.

Fuck.

Harrington walks past me with his head down. 'What the fuck d'ye think you were doing?' I ask him. No answer. 'Jesus H. Christ, get rid of the fucking ball next time. Look at that tosser.' I nodded towards where the centre forward was being congratulated by his carthorse mates. 'Break the fucker's leg. I'm not having him take the piss out of me.'

Well, to Harrington's honour he did exactly that, or near enough anyway. Straight from the kick off, the Gunners hoof the ball up to their centre forward again. Harrington, smart bastard that he is, lets him bring it down on his chest then wham. Harrington dives in and nearly cuts the bugger in two. The centre forward goes down like he's been pole axed. The ref, Serjeant Major Collins from the Gordons, blows his whistle for a foul, gives Harrington a telling off but no booking. Meanwhile the centre forward is limping off, supported by two of his mates.

Last we'll see of him. Good riddance to bad rubbish.

'Well done Jimmy,' I shout to Harrington and give him the thumbs up. Now they are down to ten men. Only about eight minutes to go.

'Come on you Tads,' I shout to gee them on. It seems to work because no sooner as I start shouting than Tommy Brown ghosts past their fullback, gets to the byline and chips over a lovely ball. Liddle, for once in his bloody life, rises like a trout and nods it home.

1-1.

We're up for it. Then I know we're going to win. It's a matter of time. You see, there's always a point in a football match when the tide of the game changes. The heads of the opposition go down. The match flows toward their goal. Football is just about creating that unstoppable tide where the opposition gets swamped, and stop believing in themselves. You've got to keep up the pressure though. Keep your boot on their throat. Don't relax. Push your body, yourself, and your team to the end.

Liddle's got it again on the left. He shoots. The keeper touches it around the post for a corner. I see the ref looking at his watch. He looks over at his two linesmen and gets the signal for the end of time from them. I can see him thinking, 'Shall I end it now?'

So then I go and do it. I start running from my goal line up to the opposing penalty area. I can see a smile on the ref's face. Brown was going to take the corner. But he waits and steps back two paces, giving me time to come up. The Gunners haven't got a clue what to do.

I raise my arm in the air. Come on Brownie, right on my noggin. You can do it lad.

He knows what I'm thinking. He starts his run forward and hits the ball. Before I can even start to jump it soars over my head. But Harrington's behind me. He jumps up with one of the Gunners. The ball hits them both and somehow lands at my feet.

I seemed to look at it for ages before acting. Then I swing my leg and the ball flies high. High into the back of the bloody net that is. I started to run back to the centre spot, all the other Tads trying to catch up with me to congratulate me. I could hear the Tads on the sidelines cheering.

Fuck it made me hard.

The Gunners are complaining to the ref. 'A goalie can't do that, ref!' And 'It's not allowed, ref.'

Serjeant Major Collins though was cool as a rabid dog. 'It's a goal. Kick off!'

I was racing back to my own goal by now. The lads were keen as mustard, ready to hack down anything looking vaguely like a Gunner. But there was no need. As soon as they kicked off, the ref blew for full time.

We're through to the final. I drank myself silly on this game for the next week. All the Tads bought me drinks in the canteen and down at The Lady Bar.

Made a name for myself, didn't I? The goalie who scored the winner.

*

Michael O'Neill

They look after you really well in here. I know it's supposed to be a punishment being in the lock-up but, for me, it's a great break from all the old shite the army puts you through.

No more smelly feet except my own.

No more grousing from twenty-odd evil throated squaddies.

No more hairy backsides farting the night away.

No more marching up and down like toy soldiers.

No more serjeants screaming blue murder.

No more sad nights down the Naafi with poor Reg spending hours whining about missing his wife.

None of that in here, thank God and all the blessed saints. That eejit of an adjutant thought he was locking me up, but he was really setting me free. Sure the old body's stuck inside four green walls but the mind is a free as an eagle above the mountains of the Mourne.

And I don't even have to spend time with the miscreants in the rest of the prison. A little bad behaviour on my part – throwing a plate of food against one of the warders in this case – and I'm soon on a charge, given time in solitary.

Lord, I love being alone. I'm never solitary in solitary if you get my drift.

Better to be away from all the rest of the shites. Jesus, there's a man there who got a year for theft. The problem was he stole from the offering box in the church. You know, the wee box where you stick your threepences before lighting a candle to the blessed Virgin and saying a few prayers.

I asked him why he had done it. All he could say was 'the Tiger made him do it.' I thought your man was as mad as a box of spanners till he took time to explain to my slow mind. He had been out drinking with a few others from the Royal Artillery and they had run out of the pennies, as you do. One of them had the bright idea of going down the church and seeing if the Lord was going to be generous. They had done it before and it seemed the easiest place in the world to pick up a few more coins for a few more Tigers.

They took off their boots at the door. 'Well you 'ave to pay some respec' dun you?' he explained in the whine that went for a voice in London. Two of them crept into the crypt whilst their pal kept a look out on the door.

They were jimmying open the lock on the offering box when in walks this full colonel and the wee priest with the bald head. All he heard was 'What are you doing there, my man?' And he stood as still as a rake with his hands stuck in the till, or the offering box in this case. His mate was far smarter. He knocked over one of the tall candle stands towards the priest and the colonel and took to his heels.

'I only stood there, didn't I ? Like a bleeding flagpole I was, me hands stuck in the box looking like a dozy bugger.'

'So you was done for theft, was it?' says I.

'Nah,' says he, 'they did me for damage to church property. To wit, breaking a lock on a box. I didn't actually nick anything see.'

'A year for a lock? That's precious.'

'Next time, I'll just nick the box. Then they won't be able to do me for nowt.'

With companions like these, you can see why I prefer being in solitary.

Here, I get my meals delivered by a friendly screw. A slice of bread and porridge in the morning with a brew of tea. A stew or something like that for dinner, again with a thick slice of bread. Then for tea they usually try to surprise me with something tasty.

'Here you are Michael, here's a bit of cheese.'

'I hope you don't mind Michael, but we only got this rind of bacon and potatoes for you tonight.'

'A nice side of cabbage for your tea, Michael. How many sugars would you be wanting in your pot of Darjeeling?'

See what I mean. It's always the same screws and all you have to do is turn on the Irish rover side of the charm and they are eating out of your man's sticky palms.

That's why I love being here. Gives me time to have a wee think.

The only time I really feel alone is when I'm with other people.

*

Reg Dwyer

Block 15, Tanglin Barracks, Singapore
October 20th, 1940
My dearest Margie,

I do hope you and the kids are well. It is all the same out here. Nothing really changes very much even though we are at war. We all read the papers and listen to the news. It doesn't sound too good from France now but don't worry your little head, I'm sure we'll push the krauts back like we did in the First War. It could mean more trench warfare though. So I'm happy I'm out here rather than over there, if you see what I mean.

Remember how your Uncle Dennis came back from Ypres. Coughing his guts out every night he was. And still coughing ten years later. Poor bugger. I know it's wrong to say but I'm glad he passed away finally. He had been in too much pain for a long, long time.

As I said, nothing really changes here at all. It's like the war didn't really exist. You would be shocked at what some of the young ladies get up to here, Margie, wearing their thin silk dresses and flirting with the officers. It's nothing short of shameful.

I've put on a bit of muscle recently too. We've been building these defences   along

XXXXXXXXXXXXXXXXXXXXXXXXXXXXXXXXXXXXXXXXXXXXXX
XXXXXXXXXXXXXXXXXXXXXXXXXXXXXXXXXXXXXXXXXXXXXX
XXXXXXXXXXXXXXXXXXXXXXXXXXXXXXXXXXXXXXXXXXXXXX
XXXXXXXXXXXXXXXXXXXXXXXXXXXXXXXXXXXXXXXXXXXXXX
XXXXXXXXXXXXXXXXXXXXX. It ain't half-tiring, slogging away in the sun. You'd think they would hire some coolies to do the work for us. But no they don't. Instead, it's us Tads who have to grin and bear it.

We've got the Cup Final next week. Us against the Loyal's. Eddie's still in goal for us and playing a blinder. But they've got this ex-professional centre-half who used to play for Blackpool. It should be a great game. I'll let you know how we get on in my next letter.

It's great the allotment's finally sorted out and you're getting some vegetables from it. Dig for Victory like they say. Just like we have been doing on the East Coast.

Anyway time to go dearest heart. Give all the kids a big hug from me. And give yourself a special one too.

Your husband,

Reg,

Censored By Lt L Whitehead.

*

Richard Longhurst

'It's nice to see you Richard. Glad you could get away at a time like this.'

'No problem, Mr. Owens. We still get time off.'

'Come on and say hello to our visitors before we start work.'

Owens walked upstairs to his cavernous front room. His house was in the middle of Adam Park, at No. 20. In front of the house a long lawn stretched down to a bamboo-covered valley. An unused tennis court was on the left and behind it lay a small city of outhouses and servants' quarters.

The stairs led straight onto the living room. A fan whirled overhead and beneath it sat four English women gently sipping tea, while a Malay servant danced attendance.

'Oh hello Richard, good to see you again.' Mrs. Owen got up and came over to greet me. I quickly wiped my hands on my shorts which is really difficult when you're carrying a topee in one of them.

'Richard, meet Margaret Lawson, Elspeth Little and Theresa Cunningham. We've all been friends for years. Richard is the young man who's been helping my husband with his work, aren't you Richard?'

'Well, I try Mrs. Owens,' I said immediately, feeling a hot blush descend on my ears.

I looked at the assembled ladies. They all wore a uniform of flowery dresses, elegant high heels, hair tied into a bun at the back and far too much make-up. Each one had the whitest alabaster skin, like the small figurines you win at the fair.

It was Margaret Lawson who spoke first. 'Which Regiment are you with Richard?'

'The Manchesters, mam, since 1936.'

Theresa Cunningham suddenly became animated. 'Oh you must know Bumble Tudor. Such a dear boy and terribly, terribly funny. You know, yesterday afternoon, we were taking tea at Raffles and Bumble was there, frightfully the worse for wear. But he's awfully charming even when he's a little tipsy, isn't he Margaret?'

Mrs. Lawson ignored her. 'Do you know Bumble?' the other one asked me.

'Yes, mam, I know Major Tudor.'

She seemed to relax. 'Well, that's good, we have mutual friends.' She seemed to think for a moment, 'Actually Richard, we're heading to Raffles later for a drink. Would you care to join us? We're bound to meet Major Tudor there.'

'I'm afraid I can't mam.'

'Oh please do, Richard,' said Mrs. Lawson. 'It'll be so much fun.'

'I'm afraid I can't mam.'

'Geoffrey, how long will your awful cataloguing take?'

Mr. Owens appeared at the door of his study. 'What was that, Margaret?'

'How long will your awful butterflies be this time?'

'Oh, we only have a few to look at. 'Bout an hour I expect.'

'There, Richard,' said Mrs. Lawson, 'we can go an hour from now. I'm sure we could show you a good time. Got to do our bit for our brave soldiers, haven't we?'

'I'm afraid I can't mam.'

'Now you're being tiresome, Richard.'

'It's not that mam, enlisted men aren't allowed in Raffles.'

I smiled the smile of the truly innocent. It was met by a cold frostiness as if we had been suddenly transported to the Arctic. It was Theresa Cunningham who spoke. 'But you said you know Bumble Tudor?'

'I do mam. He's my company commander. I'm just a regular squaddie, a private.'

The four women stared at me. It was Margaret Lawson who recovered first. She slowly raised her China cup to those red, red lips and sipped her China tea, little finger as erect as a rifle bolt.

She turned to Mrs. Owens. 'Monica, you must tell me about your tennis party on Saturday.'

'Oh, it's going to be so exciting Margaret. I've invited some Australian officers.'

And I was left standing there, my topee in my hand, the fan whirring overhead, my face getting redder and redder and redder as these women ignored me, pretending I no longer existed.

It was Mr. Owens who rescued me and led me to the study to begin the cataloguing. As he was closing the door, I heard the unmistakably cold tone of Mrs. Owens. 'Geoffrey, we have to talk later.'

'Yes m'dear,' was the reply.

I blushed again.

*

Eddie Longhurst

It was always going to be a brilliant day. Most of the lads had been given time off by the colonel to attend the match. Most of them did too, all except my fucking brother. I mean, this is one of the most important days of my life. How many times can you say you played in a Cup Final? Even if it is a poxy army tournament in poxy Singapore. But does Richard bother to turn up? Does he fuck.

Well. fuck him.

But I must say the army has done us proud. We're playing in a real stadium on Jalan Besar in Little India. There's even a fucking band playing before the game. Marching up and down like toy soldiers, playing oompah oompah music.

In the stands, the terraces are filling up with men from the Manchesters and from the Loyals. They are kept well separate of course. We wouldn't want too much trouble, not on a day like today. The NCOs make sure everything is in order. The stupid bleeders can kick two shades of shit out of each other in the bars later tonight but at the ground, it's all going to be sweetness and light and British fair play.

All this bollocks because the two colonels are also watching from the stands. Not in the terraces mind. Couldn't have a proper colonel standing for the whole game. No, they sit in the Director's box on the half-way line. Worst place to see anything if you ask me. Too far away from the pitch and not behind one of the goals.

Who gives a toss anyway?

There are even real dressing rooms. We are there getting ready now. I'm pulling on my green goalkeeper's shirt and rolling down the collar so it looks neat. I can see Harrington is going through his usual ritual. He ties his laces three times on each foot and then blesses his right foot like a priest. He sees me watching him and smiles.

'Got to get everything right,' he says. 'Last time, I were in too much of a hurry and fucked up the whole game, givin' away two penalties.'

'Just a normal game for you then Harrington.' I turned my back on him. Mustn't let him see me do exactly the same thing. It wouldn't be right for the bastard to know. I pull on my socks, always the left before the right. Then the boots. This time it's right before left. Finally I pull on my shorts. Always leave the shorts to last I do. I don't know why. But once you've hit on a winning formula, you can't change it. You never know what will happen if you do.

I open my bag and pull out the liniment and start to rub it into my thigh muscles. Now I used this stuff in England to keep my legs warm and dry in the middle of those winter games. No bloody use in hot, sweaty Singapore, you might think. But I find it keeps the sweat in, otherwise I would be soaking in less than five minutes on the pitch. It stinks like buggery mind but who cares as long it works and feels right.

Then I begin my routine. Ten jumping jacks, twenty press ups, ten knee bends, all finished off with two minutes running on the spot, lifting my knees as high as I can. I do an extra minute of the running because it's a final. Well, you have to be sure, don't you?

'You're going to be knackered before you start Eddie.' This was fucking Liddle, the cocky little bastard centre forward.

'Look after yourself, Liddle, and don't miss another fucking sitter like you did against the Gunners.' That shut his cocky little mouth shut. Nobody takes a pop at me.

The referee came into the dressing room. 'This is a final lads. Let's play fair and square. May the best team win.' I recognized him as the vicar of St George's. Jesus, we've got a fucking god squadder as a ref. Trust the bleeding army.

The black widow gave a patronising smile and went off to the Loyals' dressing room to mouth exactly the same sermon. He must have been practising the same shit for years.

It's two minutes to four now. We begin to file out of the dressing room into the tunnel. I see the Loyals are already there and waiting.

The ref blows his whistle and we run on the pitch. As I step out of the tunnel, I hear the roar from the crowd.

'Get into them Tads.'

'Up the Loyals.'

'Step up Manchesters.'

I run out onto the pitch and head towards the right-hand goal. I always go there first. One time both of us goalkeepers headed the same way. I put a sprint on and got there first.

'I always go for this goal,' the other goalie whined at me.

'Fuck off, I were here first.' And fuck off he did. We won 6-0 that day, so I always go this way whether they want me to or not.

I'm in the goal now. Just fielding a few shots from Liddle and Brown. Got to get a good feel for the ball early on. It's always right to catch it and throw it out again, letting it nestle in your arms, hugging it close to your chest like you would a tart. Well, not like a tart actually, closer than that. Much closer.

Brown centers a few from the left and I move smartly out to catch them. Liddle tries a shot from near the edge of the area but scuffs it and the ball rolls into the corner of the net.

'They all count.'

Fuck him and fuck his mother, the cocky cunt. I feel like breaking his leg except it's before the kick off and I don't think it's a good idea. I'll get the little shit later though. You just wait and see.

The ref has called our captain, Dave Spenmoor, to the centre with the captain of the Loyals. He used to play for Blackpool people are telling me. 'What the fuck's he doing as a soldier then?' Nobody could answer. Nobody knows why anybody joined up.

And the ref blows his whistle and we've started. I see their captain on the ball. He's a good mover, dancing round a tackle from Swannel as if he weren't there. He passes out to the right. In comes the cross and I see it early. 'Mine,' I shout so loud even that deaf bastard Harrington can hear me.

Of course, the stupid fucker goes for it anyway. Luckily, Tommy Brown clears it before it reaches either of us.

'Keep you fucking ears open Harrington.'

The ref whistles and stops the game. He strides over to me and says, 'There'll be no swearing on my pitch.'

I open my mouth and think about giving him a right mouthful but instead I just say, 'Yes ref, sorry ref.'

Well there's a time to be humble and there's a time to kick someone's teeth in, isn't there?

The match restarts and their captain has the ball again. Another neat swerve like Stanley Matthews and he's shooting. I go down to my right but the ball creeps beneath me and into the back of the net.

1-0.

1 fucking 0.

Their fucking squaddies go wild like the stupid twatheads they are. All the Loyals run to congratulate each other and then run back towards their own goal. I pick myself up slowly and take the long, slow walk to the back of my net to pick up the ball. Don't let anybody tell you any differently, the longest, loneliest walk in the world is a goalie going to pick up the ball from the back of his net.

Their squaddies are still chanting and singing like fucking cannibals before a feast. Bastards.

'Come on Manchesters,' I shout to try to get them going. The lads look like they have bottled it though. I don't hear anything in reply.

We kick off. The ball goes up to Liddle with his back to goal. He tries to do some sort of fancy turn but treads on the ball and their centre half steps in to take it away from him as he lies on the ground.

'For Fuck's sake Liddle, get it right.' I see the ref looking at me again and waving his finger. Jesus, mate, there are no saints on the football pitch, unless you play for Southampton.

The rest of the half went past in a blur. Their captain was bossing the midfield and shots were coming in from all over the place. I made one good save from their tricky winger, going down sharply to my right to smother a curler from just outside the box. I tried to get the lads going but we were being slaughtered.

The ref blew his whistle for half time and we trooped off. Their supporters were singing and cheering. Ours were quiet. Now it's not often a crowd from Manchester is quiet, but this day they were. Silent as a Manchester copper on the take.

We're back in the dressing room drinking a cup of hot, sweet tea and Serjeant O'Connor is speaking. 'Ye've got to be tighter on them. Ye're giving them too much space. Harrington, push up the line, let's crowd them. That captain is killing us.'

'I'll sort the little fucker out, you wait and see.'

O'Connor stopped talking and looked at me. He gave a nod of his head. We were on. About fucking time, too.

The ref started the second half and we did what O'Connor had told us. Harrington pushed up and the midfield ran harder, closing in much quicker on the Loyals. It didn't do too much good though. They simply moved the ball quicker. Every time their captain got it, he simply played it out wide to one of their wingers. We were constantly having to turn as their wingers ran into the space behind our full backs. A cross came in and I reached round to turn it away for a corner.

Their winger ran across to take it. Our defenders man-marked all their men in the box. I saw their captain making his way forward.

'Come on, my beauty,' I whispered to myself.

Their winger swung his foot and across came a perfect corner. Their captain ran forward to meet it. I rushed out from my goal line and jumped high to push it clear. My fist came up and hit the ball just as their captain jumped high to head it goal-wards.

I hit the ball and let the arc of my fist carry forward to connect with the side of their fucking captain's head. You should have seen him. He collapsed in a heap at my feet. Out cold he was. Best punch of my fucking life.

'Did you see that ref?' Their centre half rushed for me. I stood up to him. No fucker is going to push me around. Harrington stepped between us.

'Ref, he nearly killed him.'

The ref was there looking at the captain who was still out cold in the centre of the penalty box.

The ref had a quick glance at me and at their centre half, working out which one of us was worth supporting. 'Accident, could have happened to anyone.' He whistled and waved for the stretcher to come on.

It took three minutes before their captain even knew where he was. Best punch I ever threw.

Of course, I went over to him and apologised. I mean, you have to play the game, don't you?

We didn't see much of their captain for the rest of the match. He sort of wandered around the centre of midfield, not doing much and not really knowing where the fuck he was.

It didn't help us though. Liddle missed two other sitters and I was fucking glad when the ref finally blew for full time.

1-0.

1-0.

1-0.

The chants from the Loyals' terrace went on and on, through the cup ceremony and into the bars that night.

We had fucking lost.

Best punch I ever threw though. So even though we lost, I won.

I always win, me. I said it was going to be a brilliant day.

*

Reg Dwyer
Block 15, Tanglin Barracks, Singapore
December 12th, 1940
My dearest wife,
This is the third Christmas I've been away from you and Tommy and Evelyn.

It seems for the rest of the year I can forget about it, burying myself in XXXXXXXXXXXXXXXXXXXXXXXXXXXXXXXXXXXXXXXXXXXXXXXXXX XXXXXXXXXXXXXXXwhich is all we seem to do these days.

But come Christmas it always seems to hit me hard. I'm sorry to be writing to you like this. I know it doesn't help you or the children but all I can say is I miss you all so much.

I've been reading about the bombing. It seems to be getting much worse lately. I hope you're not getting hit too badly.

Mr. Turner seems to be an awfully good chap letting you use his Anderson shelter. It must be terrible sitting there below ground as the bombs are failing all around.

How is our Harry doing? He's finally joined up, hasn't he? I knew he'd join the Manchesters as well. He couldn't find a better regiment or a better bunch of lads.

Remember I told you about the lad who got arrested for trying to go back to England. O'Neill his name was. Well, I went to see him in the Glasshouse. Proper strange he was. If you ask me, he's gone off his rocker a bit. That's what prison can do to you. Rather him than me though.

But he'll be alright once he gets out, you mark my words. He's a good lad, O'Neill, but a bad penny if you know what I mean.

Anyway, I've got to sign off now love. I'm sorry I won't be able to send you or the kids any present this year. I hope you understand. But I'm a bit broke and the cost of sending them is more than it costs to buy them. It all seems a bit stupid to me. When I come home, I'll bring lots with me. I hope you can explain it all to Tommy and Evelyn and little Grace. I'd love to see them all now and give them all a big hug from their dad. But I can't because I'm so far away.

Your husband,

Reg

Censored by Lt. L. Whitehead.

Chapter 16

Michael O'Neill

I've always hated Christmas.

As a kid, you're supposed to love it. The food and the presents and the singing and the Mass. But there was none of that in our house. For us, it was always a time when our ma went into mourning.

A couple of days before Christmas me ma would go into a sort of shell as the darkness crept over her, crawling into bed and hiding there for a week or so.

Me and my brothers were used to it of course. We went about our business as if nothing had happened; cleaning the house, feeding the chickens, checking that the old sow was still happy. The neighbours looked in of course.

'Happy Christmas there, Mrs. O'Neill. Sure it's a lovely bright morning to be lying in your bed on a day like this.'

There was never any answer from me ma. She just lay there, staring at the walls. They would always leave something when they came. A pail of milk fresh from the cow, a loaf of bread, a wrap of tea. There was only so much they could spare. Christmas dinner was always a cup of tea and a slice of toast for us and then a run up the mountain to see what the other kids had got.

We all knew why Ma fell under the shadow at Christmas. It was the time she received the telegram from America.

I was eleven at the time, and lying here, on this green bunk surrounded by green walls, the memory of it still covers me like a shroud.

In our part of the old sod, telegrams were as rare as Christmas feasts. It arrived in the post office in Ballyhaunis and was carried along the roads in a special delivery by Patt Murphy on his bike. He made a special trip did Patt, his thin legs pushing hard on the pedals, the bell ringing to clear the way even when there was no one there.

Me ma saw him leave his bike down on the dirt road and clamber over the wall to walk across our field. She went outside, wiping her hands on her apron and adjusting her hair. She was always very keen on appearances was me ma. I was in the yard clearing the muck from the old sow. I looked up as Patt slowly got closer to our croft. When he was about ten feet away, he took off his cap and handed her a small brown envelope. He didn't say anything, just stood there, his other hand hanging by his side, tugging at the corduroy of his trousers.

Me ma wiped her hands again and reached for the envelope. Nothing was said between them. I think me Ma knew what was there but she didn't want to know. She took the envelope and nodded at Patt. His hand tugged at his trouser again.

'Ye have to open it,' he said not looking at her, 'In case there's a reply.'

Me ma nodded once more. She took the small brown envelope and carefully worked her thumb under the edge of the flap. She took out the thin onion paper, unfolded it and read what it said. She folded it again, placing it carefully back into the envelope.

'There is no reply,' she said.

And she walked into the house, leaving Patt standing there in the yard, his worn fingers tugging at the worn corduroy of his trousers.

'I think you'd better look to your ma. I'll talk to the neighbours,' he said looking at me.

I put down the broom and walked into the house. The only sound I could hear was the ticking of the clock above the mantlepiece. In the grate the turf had nearly burnt out. I took a few more turves and placed them carefully on top of the embers. Above the mantelpiece, a picture of me ma and me da on their wedding day stood proud.

The envelope lay on the kitchen table beside the jug of milk. I walked over and with the same care as me ma, I opened the envelope. Inside was a telegram, the first we had ever received. I folded back the thin paper.

PATRICK O'NEILL DEAD STOP. WILL BURY HERE STOP. RIP.STOP.

AUNT NORA.

So that was it, seven words that killed me ma.

She never really recovered. Oh she was good enough; looking after me and my brothers, cooking us dinner, making sure we went to school, but something, some spark of life, left her that day before Christmas.

It never came back.

*

Eddie Longhurst

159

I'm the youngest corporal so I've been given the job to organise the annual Christmas dinner for the men. One of those traditions defining the regiment, uniting the men and the NCOs and all that tosh.

If I screw it up that's the end of my career. I'll probably end up as Corporal Shithouse, the NCO in charge of the crappers. If I do well, then bob's your uncle. Or your cousin or whatever it is.

So I've been planning this for the last three weeks. 'Remember the 6 Ps' Serjeant Major Whatmough had said, 'Proper Planning Prevents Piss Poor Performance'. So get your thinking cap on lad. Here's the file from last year. I'm sure you'll do a great job.'

He marched off across the parade ground. This was a great chance to shine. What with the CO, Colonel Holmes, turning up as well as 800 men and all the NCOs.

I've realised I haven't told you what makes this Christmas dinner different. Well, it's the only time in the year the NCOs serve the men. We're the waiters, the barmen and the butt of all the jokes, while the men sit there downing ale and eating their bloody turkey.

I opened the file. The first thing that hit me was the list of food required:
- 200 turkeys
- 1,500 lbs potatoes
- 200lbs Brussels sprouts
- 1,000 gallons gravy
- 600lbs Christmas puddings
- 100lbs rum butter
- 50 gallons custard
- 6,000 mince pies
- 800 gallons beer

800 gallons of fucking beer? 200 turkeys? 6,000 bleedin' mince pies? Where am I going to find all these just three weeks before Christmas?

So I did what you always do when faced with crisis in the army. I formed a committee.

There was Serjeant Williams from the cookhouse. Serjeant Truitt from the QM office. Sergeant Hanlon and Corporal Bullock from HQ Company and of course, yours truly.

I handed Williams the list. He took his fag out of his mouth, whistled a long blue plume of smoke and said, 'Nah, no problem. The rum butter's a bit difficult. But I'll nick the rum from the officers' mess. They'll never notice.'

'You can do 6,000 mince pies?'

'Yeah, easy, bit of mince, bit of pie, stick it in the oven and there it is. Wouldn't touch 'em myself but the squaddies love 'em. Reminds them of their mothers' shit cooking at home probably.'

'But will we be able to eat 'em,' I asked. He looked at me the way cooks have always looked at soldiers. I took it as a yes.

'Now decorations. Can I leave it to you Jim to make sure the dining hall is decked out in all its Christmas finery?'

'Do I have any money Eddie?'

Good question I thought. But here Serjeant Hanlon stepped in smartly, 'I'm sure I can scrape up a $100 from the Welfare fund. It's the Officers' fund but they'll never miss it. And what do they need with welfare anyway.'

'We'll make the place look like Santa's whorehouse.'

'A few decorations will be fine, Jim. Don't want to make it look like a knocking shop, do we?' I stared at him to make sure he got the message. 'Now Bob, we've got the usual NCO's parade with the pipes and drums before the dinner. Can I leave you to organise that? Most of the NCOs will need their drill smartened up, especially with the CO watching. You know what a stickler he is for sharp drill.'

'Right up my street, Eddie. I'll have the buggers looking like the Coldstream Guards in no time.'

'Well done. Any questions? Good, let's meet next week to check how we're doing. Let's say Monday at 2pm. Alright?'

They nodded, making a note in their books. I got up to leave when Taffy Williams spoke, 'And what are you doing, Eddie?'

'Supervising you buggers, aren't I? It's a hard job but someone's got to do it.' That shut him up. Bolshie bastard. I'll have to watch him. If the food's bad, I'll never hear the last of it.

Well, to cut a long story short, the night went off very well.

The march past was as sharp as a row of knives. Even the CO commented that it 'was as fine a body of men as he had ever seen in the regiment.'

The canteen looked like it could have been back in Manchester, except there were duck feathers instead of snow, Chinese lanterns replaced the usual Christmas bells, and a small tropical tree with large dark green leaves stood in the corner where the Christmas tree should have been. Serjeant Truitt dressed himself as Santa Claus in a long Chinese gown and a kapok beard, handing out hats, whistles, blowers and crackers to the men.

'Does your turkey want stuffing Santa?'

'I want a better woman this year Santa. Last year's has already split.'

'Where's your fuckin' reindeer?'

'I think the bugger came on a rickshaw this year.'

And on it went, the men taking a year's worth of revenge on the NCOs who served them. Even the food was vaguely edible. The turkey looked like turkey, the sprouts were green and the carrots were amazingly orange.

Only the rum butter looked strange. A dark grey splodge next to the Christmas cake. But the men ate it anyway once they had been told it contained a case of rum. Most even had the cheek to ask for seconds.

Then, of course, some idiot had to spoil it.

Everything was going so well. The men were getting gloriously pissed. The serjeants were singing carols. The beer was flowing nicely. And the colonel was beaming. 'Best party we've ever had in Singapore, Longhurst. Well done indeed.'

Then an idiot from the radio room walked in and announced, 'They've bombed Manchester.'

That was the end. You can't enjoy a party on Christmas Eve when news like that comes in. Gradually, the men began to drift away. The spirit was gone. The CO took his cue and simply left with a quiet, 'Well done.'

I'll wring the bastard's neck. He should have kept his bleeding mouth shut. Now I'll forever be the corporal who organised a fuckin' party the night Manchester was bombed.

Bastards.

Bastards.

Bastards.

*

Richard Longhurst

Nobody spoke. Nobody laughed. Nobody even breathed. We all sat there waiting. The news, delivered in such haste at the Christmas dinner, had thrown a shroud over all our celebrations.

By now, we should have all been down in The Lady Bar or the Black Cat on Lavender Road, trying to work out where we would be getting our end away.

Or, at least, the others would, I'd be sitting there, watching everything, slowly letting the Tiger seep into my brain.

Not tonight though. Not this Christmas. *The Straits Times* had reported it in gory detail. 'Go on Richard, read it out,' someone had pushed me. So I did but I wish I hadn't.

'Heaviest German Night raid on Manchester,' I read out loud, projecting my voice as Mrs. Trante had taught me at school so long ago, 'Widespread fires were brought under control by morning.'

'Speak up Lanky.' This was Reg Dwyer. He'd moved from his bunk to be closer to me. I could see the rest of the barracks, looking up and listening now, their faces outlined against the white walls of Block 15.

Overhead the fans whirred noisily.

I took a deep breath and plunged on. 'Manchester had its longest and severest air raid last night. After many hours of blitz, a pall of smoke hung over the city this morning.'

'So what's new, hey, a pall of smoke hangs over the place every bleedin' morning,' said Larkin, looking around for agreement.

Only Eddie answered him. 'For once, shut the fuck up Larkin.' He turned to me, 'Keep on reading Richard.'

I could feel their eyes on me as I found my place in the middle of the paper. 'The raid started shortly after dark when enemy raiders apparently approaching the city from the south, spread fanwise over a wide area and adopted the familiar tactics of flare dropping, followed by incendiary bombs. Wave after wave of planes roared over the city every few minutes.'

'When was this, Lanky?' asked Teale.

I looked at the top of the article. 'It's dated London, December 23rd, so I guess the raid must have happened on the night of the 22nd.'

'Jesus H. Christ, five days ago? Margie will have been doing the last of the Christmas shopping for the kids. She always leaves it until the last few days before buying stuff in case the kids change their minds. You know what it's like, children and all. Never know what they want. Not that we have much to give them mind you, but you try your best.' Suddenly Reg stopped, realising he was rambling on.

'But there was nothing on the radio about the raid. Nothing.'

'What do you fuckin' expect Larkin, the real news from the BBC?' Eddie threw his boot against the far wall of our hut. 'Carry on Richard.'

'The whole resources of the city's fire brigade services were at their posts ready for dealing with the outbreaks.' Shocking English this. Whoever wrote it should be shot.' I looked up. There was a sea of anxious faces looking at me. The last thing they cared about was the quality of the reporter's English. I quickly found my place in the paper again, before my face began to redden.

'Later high explosives and incendiaries dealt death to people and destruction to property. The number of casualties is not yet estimated. This morning most of the fires were under control.'

'I hope Margie and the kids are alright.' This was said softly and quietly by Reg, 'They said the bombers came in from the South. Stockport's in the South...,'

'I hope me mam isn't hurt. She hates doctors does me mam. Can't stand them. When she had me, she didn't bother with a doctor. She'd had eight already, see, knew exactly what was going to happen. Plenty of practice like.' Larkin chuckled his little laugh. Nobody else joined in. Even the fans above our heads had gone silent.

'Carry on Richard.' This was Eddie again.

'Two enemy bombers were destroyed last night during the raid says an Air Ministry and Ministry of Home Security communiqué.'

'Good, got the bastards back.'

'Shut the fuck up Larkin,' snarled Eddie. 'Hasn't it occurred to you they've already told us there were waves of bombers. We only managed to shoot down two. Only fuckin' two.' He gave Larkin a long, lingering look of disdain before curtly nodding at me to continue.

My eyes danced across the page, looking for the right sentence, 'Full reports of casualties are not yet available but it is known a number of people were killed and many others injured.'

I could feel all the eyes on me now. There must have been near forty people crowded round my bunk.

Now they were all silent. As silent as death. All of them with mothers, fathers, wives, children, brothers, sisters and lovers in Manchester. Imagining the bombs raining down, the flickering roar of the explosion, the explosive light of the fires, the sirens of the fire engines and the silence of death.

'Well, go on.'

'That's it. The rest of the report deals with a few bombs in Merseyside and the East Midlands. Even Parliament was bombed last night. Nothing else about Manchester though. Nothing.'

'A-ten-shion!' someone shouted. Immediately forty bodies snapped rigid like tin soldiers. I threw the paper down on the bed and jumped to attention.

'Stand easy lads, stand easy.' It was Regimental Serjeant Major Whatmough who spoke.

The RSM was an old Tad who'd been decorated for heading a charge against a machine gun on the Somme. The regiment had lost 400 men, killed or wounded out of 700 who had left the trenches that morning. Whole units, whole families, whole streets of Manchester were wiped out. Not RSM Whatmough though. Legend has it the bastard was so hard the bullets bounced off him. And looking at him, I believed it.

As the lads ran to stand in front of their beds, he strode purposefully to the centre of the barracks. In a voice used over many parade grounds in the countless different outposts of the Empire, he announced to all the lost souls of Block 15, 'Men of the Manchesters, you know about the raid on our fair city just before this Christmas…,'

He spoke like some biblical prophet, his voice deep, profound and leaving no opportunity for argument, no opening for questions, no possibility of error.

'….Unfortunately in war, in this war against the evil that has invaded our German brethren, there will be casualties and victims.'

It was then he produced two brown envelopes from behind his clipboard. We all knew what they were. Every soul was praying he wasn't going to receive one. A mass whispered prayer of 'Let it not be me. Let it not be me.'

RSM Whatmough looked down at his clipboard and I knew it was going to be me before he even read my name. 'Private Richard Longhurst 3253418.'

I took one step forward from my bunk. 'Sir.'

He marched up to me, stiff as a pole, clipped mustache greased and edged perfectly. Holding the brown envelope in front of me he said, 'I'm sorry son.'

I took it and held it in my hand, feeling its crisp brownness like a knife designed to stab you through the heart with a few cutting sentences.

He walked away from me and once again looked at his clipboard. Everyone was staring at the one remaining brown envelope in his hand.

They all seemed to take a collective breath and, as one began praying once again, 'Let it not be me.'

RSM Whatmough looked down to check the number once more, before commanding 'Corporal Edward Longhurst 3253420.'

There was a vast sigh of relief. Only Eddie remained stiffly at attention, stepping forward with a crisp 'Sir.'

And, once again, the death march was repeated, followed by the simple, discomforting words. 'I'm sorry son.'

RSM Whatmough then strode out of Block 15, leaving a vast emptiness where he had once been. I looked over at Eddie. His eyes met mine and for once I knew I was the stronger of the two of us.

I opened the telegram: 'The Home Office regrets to inform you of the death of your mother, Agnes Elizabeth Longhurst nee Smith. STOP. And of your step-father, Eric Bates, in an air raid in Manchester on the night of the 22nd December. STOP. Please accept our heartfelt condolences. STOP.

I looked up from the telegram to see Eddie had also finished reading.

'Good riddance to bad rubbish,' was all he said.

It was then I lost it completely.

I suddenly launched myself at him, trying to beat his mouth bloody with my fists. But before I knew it, I was on my back with him on top of me strangling the life out of my throat. All I could feel were his hands tightening their grip on my Adam's apple.

Then I lost consciousness.

*

Reg Dwyer

It was terrible news the bombing of Manchester. I was hoping and praying Margie and the kids were safe. The paper seemed to say all the destruction was around the docks. Rough area that, full of rough pubs and even rougher people. I wouldn't let Margie or the kids go anywhere near there.

Richard were reading *The Straits Times* to us. He often does that. Has a lovely reading voice does Richard, makes the words come alive as he tells us what's happening, makes it all very dramatic.

Then in strode RSM Whatmough. Of course, we all snapped to attention. A right stickler for the rank is Whatmough. Then I saw what he had in his hands. I prayed for it not to be Margie or any of the kids. Just give me this one chance, this little hope, and I won't go down to The Lady Bar or the Pussy Cat any more. Just one chance. I crossed my fingers as they hung at attention down the seam of my trousers, hoping Whatmough didn't notice.

He read out the names on the telegrams and you could feel the whole room letting out a sigh of relief. All except for Lanky and Eddie though. They both opened the telegrams and read the contents. I bet it was the usual 'Her Majesty regrets to inform you...,' Always the same, has been for years, even during the first war.

Eddie said something then. I don't know what it was. But suddenly, Lanky were all over him like. Hitting and hitting, trying to knock his block off. At first, Eddie didn't react. He just seemed to lie there and take it all, hardly moving to dodge the blows. Then he lost it. Lanky didn't have a chance. He was soon on his back with Eddie pummelling two shades of shit out of him. Then Eddie started to strangle Lanky. I mean it wasn't just grabbing him round the throat. This was a right strangle, trying to choke all the breath out him.

It was Larkin who stepped forward first and tried to pull Eddie off. But Eddie, he's a strong bugger. Larkin called for help. 'Come youse lot of tits, get him off. He's going to choke the death out of him.'

Teale and Mytholmroyd jumped forward and managed to get Eddie's hands off Lanky's windpipe. Lanky was really out of it by now. He sort of lay there not making a sound or anything, his eyes closed and his head on the floor. I thought Eddie had killed him for a moment. Then I heard him cough and his head rose slowly from the ground, gasping for air.

The lads had dragged Eddie off by now. He stood there panting for a while, his hands on his knees like he'd played a really hard game of football.

Then he shook himself free from Teale, Mytholmroyd and Larkin and strode out of the barracks, without looking back.

It was Lanky who had the last word though. He rose up on his elbow and still gasping for breath, he sort of whispered hoarsely to his brother's back.

'Fuck off, you're not my brother.'

Eddie stopped at the door. I thought he was going to come back and give Lanky another pasting for a minute. Then he walked out.

*

Michael O'Neill

Sometimes, I think about the man I killed.

Not often mind, but when I'm here listening to the footsteps of the screws on the walkway outside, the demented coughs of the TB-addled old man on Landing Two and the clanging of iron gates being opened and closed, sometimes, just sometimes, he appears in my thoughts.

He's not real of course. Just a figment of my imagination. He's there and he's not there. A flash of white cloth, a loud whack on the lorry, a tumble of limbs. But what's always there is his fear. A quick flash of frightened eyes before the impact.

Jesus, those eyes scare me. That old monk, with his chewed, tobacco-stained fingernails had been right. I was going to stoke the fires of hell one day.

Perhaps he had known I would kill someone. The joke is if somebody, an officer, had said 'Kill that man' two seconds before I hit him with the truck then everything would have been allowed in the eyes of God. Or so they say. I would have been obeying an order, and the old heathen monk would have clapped his hands at the thought.

But nobody did give an order. It was just me. On my own.

I have wondered if I could have avoided him. Pulled to the left and swerved off the road. A thought even crossed my mind that I pressed my foot on the pedal a little harder before I hit him.

I'm not sure. Memory does play its tricks.

But I do know it doesn't really matter. It was all pre-ordained, like me da dying in America and me being in the army and the old man and his cow dying.

Nothing could be done to stop any of it.

Nothing could have been done to stop any of it.

Nothing can be done to stop any of it.

When I get out of here, and they will come for me soon. I know what I have to do. It's written down.

Somewhere.

*

Eddie Longhurst

I remember the day we both decided to leave, Richard and me. It was summer, June or maybe July. God, it'd been hot. The cobbles outside our house were boiling and I still can see the old coalman's hoss, a soapy lather covering its collar, its head down around to knees and its tongue sticking out as if it were licking the road. Bloody thing dropped dead soon after in Arkle Street. Shame really, it were a lovely hoss with a red brown skin flecked with strands of gold.

When we were young we used to feed it. It didn't matter what really; a few carrots, toffee, bits of paper. It ate everything with its shiny yellow teeth. Shame it died but that's life, eh.

Anyway, the sun was melting everything. I'd been at work, Mam was out, she didn't say where. There was only bastard Bates and Richard in the house when I got back.

He was sitting in front of the empty fire as if warming himself there. But it wasn't lit. He took in long drags of his Capstan. He'd hold the cigarette with the lit end facing his palm and sort of sucked the last drags of smoke from its glow. As he did so, the end lit up to highlight his hands.

I would always see the deep lines of the palms, the roughness of the skin, and the line of dirt lying beneath his nails. He'd scrub his hands every day with the soap we got from the Tat Man but he could never get rid of the dirt. It was always there. Like a scar beneath the fingernail.

I remember getting home. Richard was sat at the table reading some book or other, Bates was perched over the empty fire. His jaw was set tight. He stared into the empty fire grate. He sucked on the end of his cigarette and threw it into the dead fire.

I watched the glowing fag end land amongst the ashes. Finally, he turned to me, 'Get us a gill of beer.'

'Fuck off, I've just got home. I'm not going out again.'

He didn't answer me but turned back to stare again into the ashes.

169

Without moving his head he said softly, 'Richard, go down to pub and get me a gill of beer.'

Richard carried on reading. I don't know if he heard or was simply pretending not to hear.

Bates didn't look at him. He carried on staring at the place where the fire should have been.

'Richard, get me the gill of beer.' The voice was louder now, more insistent. But again, Richard didn't reply, hearing or not hearing, it didn't matter.

I was now aware of a silence filled with sound. The clock ticking. The cat deliciously licking its paws. The rustles of a page being turned on the book in Richard's hands.

Then suddenly Bates was out of his chair and Richard lay on the ground. He was kicking and punching and hacking. I saw Richard's head jerk back. His teeth clenched. The boot hitting his face again and again and again.

And then it was over. The door was slammed outside and the room was silent again. Richard lay on the floor, not moving, not saying anything.

I stood there. He looked up at me. I'll always remember his eyes and the way his head twisted to see me and the appeal in his eyes for the help I couldn't give.

The clock ticked on. The cat had vanished. Richard's breathing came in long gasps. And I stood there, weeping.

Nobody ever made me cry again though, I made sure of that, didn't I?

Chapter 17

Michael O'Neill

'Sure, your angel of Connemara is home again.' I announced my arrival to the sleeping bodies of 13 Platoon in the turgid air of Block 15 on the green fields of Tanglin Camp in the colony of the King Emperor, George VI.

There were a few replies:

'Fuck off O'Neill.'

'Shut the fuck up O'Neill.'

'Welcome back O'Neill.' The last was my friend Tommy Larkin, who was the only one to greet me in the manner befitting of the conquering hero I was.

It was a sleepy afternoon in the barracks. Nothing had changed all the time I had been gone, 'away for a while,' as the English say. I wasn't away, I was inside, in jail, doing time.

'How was it?' Again, this was Larkin who looked at me with his mouth open wide as he polished his boots. He liked polishing boots did Larkin. 'Helps me relax,' he would say. 'There's nothing like a clean boot to relax with.'

'It was fine. Three meals a day and a better class of inmate than most prisons hereabouts,' I answered.

I could see Larkin was itching to ask more questions but I quickly stopped him with 'Where's my bunk now? I don't want to go and upset Lord God Alshitey Eddie Longhurst again, now do I?'

'Take any of those. They're all free at the moment. Some of the guys have been transferred.'

I slung my pack down on the bunk. The springs creaked in the usual army way. Nothing had changed.

I looked around the hut. The fans were still whirring overhead. The bunks were still laid out in two rows with lockers in between. There was still a large brown box at the end of each bunk. And still sleeping squaddies occupied the squeaking beds.

Larkin was sitting on his bunk surrounded by the accoutrements of brightly polished boots – cloths, polish, two different types of brush and a bowl of warm water. In front of him was one boot, sitting all on its lonely own in the middle of the bed. One of his hands was shoved into the other boot like a vet shoves his arm into the arse of a cow. Larkin wasn't helping his boot to give birth though.

He looked down at the already shiny boot, hawked a large splegm of gob and spat on the toe. He started polishing away like a fiddler scraping a lively reel.

There were no dancers, just the sleeping bodies of 13 Platoon.

'I likes a nice shiny boot, I does,' said Larkin to nobody in particular.

I was home but it wasn't home anymore. Not for Michael O'Neill. I felt a sudden surge of emotion like a wave coming up from my guts and lodging in my throat. I hadn't cried since I was eleven and I wasn't going to let these spalpeens see my tears now.

I mumbled something to Larkin and stepped out into the fresh air, gulping in great acres of air, forcing the tears back into the wells behind my eyes.

I was home again.

*

Reg Dwyer
Block 15, Tanglin Barracks, Singapore
5th February, 1941
Dearest Margie,
Got your letter last week. I'm so happy Tommy is finally settling in at school. You have to tell him to stand up for himself. Ask Uncle Ronnie to give him a few boxing lessons so he can give those bullies as good as he gets.

Manchester sounds like it's getting a bit of a pasting from the Jerries. I was so worried about you and the kids when I read in the paper about the raid before Christmas. Two of the lads lost their mother in the raid. Sad really, but I know they will get over it. But you should remember to rush down to the Anderson Shelter as soon as the siren sounds. Don't let the kids play on the street either. You've got to be able to get them into the shelter.

The other thing you could do, and before I write this Margie, don't bite my head off, is to send them to their Auntie in Glossop until the bombing has finished. I know we've talked about this before but I want you to think about it now again.

I couldn't bear it Margie if anything happened to you and the kids whilst I'm stuck out in Singapore.

Anyway, life goes on here. The days are as boring as ever. We spend most of the day sitting in the barracks. A few of the lads, me included, have taken to napping for a few hours in the afternoon. Nobody seems to mind. I think they all put it down to the heat.

Occasionally, we might do some firearms training or go on an exercise but that's a rare event, and even then the M.O. seems to complain we are all risking malaria.

The war seems so far away from here. Of course, we can read about what's happening in England but it seems not to be real. Here, nobody seems to worry. They go about their lives as they always have done.

A few of the lads wanted to go back to England and fight but the CO soon put them right. We're a regular regiment, he said, our duty is to obey the orders of our commanders. Good man the CO, a 'Tad' through and through, been with the regiment for years. He's always firm but fair.

Sorry for going on about the army. Sometimes I wish I'd never joined up. I've been away from you and the kids for nearly three years now. I miss you so much my heart is breaking.

Got to stop writing now, give my love to the kids.

Your husband

Reg

PS: Mr. Brown seems a nice bloke, digging a shelter for you. Tell him we'll have a pint in the Jockey together when I get back to Stockport.

*

Richard Longhurst

I don't know how we ended up there. It was probably Eddie who suggested it. Or perhaps Teale or even Larkin.

There was a Japanese brothel off Middle Road. At first, the mama-san wasn't going to let us in but the five of us pushed our way past her.

We'd been out drinking in the Green Cat Club in Anson Road. Reg had grabbed hold of the mike as he always does when he's half-cut and launched into a fairly acceptable version of *Somewhere over the Rainbow*. Obviously he didn't look anything like Judy Garland. Truth is, he didn't sound like her much either.

But the song decided us. 'We've got to do something different tonight. Another night dancing at Beauty World or on Lavender Road is going to make me sick as a dog,' said Eddie.

Then someone said, 'Let's go to a Japanese whorehouse.' And I remember it wasn't Eddie or Teale. It was me who said it. Me.

Next minute we were all in a taxi and Eddie's saying to the driver, 'Japanese girls, you savvy, Japanese girls'

The driver just nodded, bored with the job and also scared the mood in the taxi might suddenly turn violent. One minute he's nice, polite, friendly. Next, he's shoved a broken glass in your face. That's our Eddie. A little unpredictable.

The taxi driver dropped us off outside this shophouse in one of the alleys behind Middle Road. From the window hung a large paper lantern with bright red Japanese writing. It swayed slowly in the breeze. A little flicker of light and a soft, gentle swing in the night.

A light to attract the moths. Or in this case, five lads from the nether regions of Manchester.

Eddie rapped on the door. It was opened by a middle-aged woman wrapped in a grey housecoat. I think they call it a kimono.

She saw us and her face dropped. She tried to close the door but Eddie was too quick for her. He stuck his size ten Army boot in the door to stop it closing and leaning against it, forced it open.

She stepped back and then she did the strangest thing.

She bowed.

A long, deep bow that left her eyes looking straight down at the ground. As each of us entered, she sang what sounded like a song in Japanese.

'Now, that's what I called a welcome,' said Eddie.

I looked at the room. It was bare. A small table with a vase sat in the corner. On the left against the wall was a long, low platform. A few paintings highlighted the white walls and, on the right, the one stranger in the whole room: a German piano.

Teale immediately went over and sat at the piano, idly playing with the keys.

The mama-san gestured for us to sit on the low platform. From nowhere came two young girls, one of whom carried warm, rolled-up towels.

She kneeled down in front of me and handed me one. It was hot. I thanked her and wiped my sweating face in its soft heat.

Then still kneeling, she moved along to Eddie and gave him another towel.

'Hey, is this for wiping your dick?' shouted Eddie. The others collapsed in fits of laughter. The girl merely kneeled in front of us, her eyes averted, concentrating on some far off place on the floor.

The mama-san said something to her. She shuffled across on her knees giving a towel to Reg and one to Ray before rocking back on her heels, rising and waddling out of the room.

The other girl had been kneeling quietly on my right all through this. She hadn't said a word. Her eyes met mine for an instant just once. I smiled. For a second, I saw her eyes light up and then they remembered themselves, drifting off to an invisible spot in the distance.

Then she moved.

Even though she was only three feet away from me, she rocked back on her heels, rose, took two tiny steps, then kneeled down again directly in front of me.

I waited for her to do something.

She waited for me to do I know not what.

Then the mama-san spoke again.

Now the girl leant forward and slowly began unlacing my boots. First the right then the left. She removed both my boots and placed them neatly beside the platform.

I smiled at her. She didn't look at me or even register my presence. Her whole body, her whole being, concentrated on the task in hand.

Next, she kneeled down in front of Reg, repeating the process. As she removed his boots, I could smell the sour sweet tang of his feet. But she betrayed no emotion as the aroma filled the room.

'Hey, I can get used to this. I should teach Margie how to do it when I come home from work.'

Next, she moved along to Eddie. He had a strange look in his eyes. A look I'd seen on Eddie's face many times before. Usually, it meant trouble.

This time it meant sex. As she removed his boots, he leaned forward and pinched her small breasts through the cloth of her kimono.

She didn't react, pretended nothing had happened, and levered off the boot from Eddie's foot.

He reached out and took the small breast in his hand again. She didn't flinch or look at him.

He laughed. 'This one's up for it. Lovely little pair of tits she has.'

She placed both boots next to the platform, bowed and moved on to Ray. He was so out of it he was lying flat on the platform snoring. Nonetheless, she removed his boots. I hope he can put them back on himself in the state he's in.

When she'd finished, she bowed once more at the sleeping Ray, rose and shuffled away from us into a dark doorway on the left. Teale was still playing the piano, oblivious to everything happening around him.

The mama-san clapped her hands. Six small girls came through a curtain on the left. They walked slowly, their kimonos trailing the ground. One by one they halted in front of us, forming a line abreast.

'Not a bad little parade,' said Eddie.

Mama-san then held her arm up with the five fingers of her hand extended. She spoke in Japanese.

'What the fuck's she saying?'

'I don't know, I don't speak their fucking language do I, you soft prat.'

But I knew, somehow I knew. 'She says it's five dollars per girl.'

The others looked at me. I took out my wallet, searched for a five-dollar note and handed it to the mama-san. She bowed in front of me, taking the five dollars with both hands and softly trilling a sweet thank you in Japanese.

'Oh well, in for a penny in for a pound, or a bloody Straits Dollar,' said Eddie, giving her his money.

'Do you think Japanese girls are horizontal?' said Reg.

'Well, now's the chance to find out mate. Put your money where your dick is.'

Slowly, reluctantly, Reg took out his wallet and counted five single notes carefully. He handed them to the mama-san saying, 'This better be bloody worth it. Margie'll kill me if she finds out.'

The girls had been standing there all the time, not looking at us, their eyes focused on the floor. It was Eddie who made the first move. He stood up, walked to the end of the line and pointed at a small, rather plump Japanese girl in a bright green kimono.

Without raising her eyes from the floor, she turned and walked through the beaded curtain. 'Well, I think I'm in. See you later tosspots.' Eddie himself vanished through the curtain.

'Time is sex,' said Reg, wasting neither. He walked along the line, selected the smallest girl of all, and he too then vanished upstairs.

Next to me on the platform, Ray snored gently. Teale had stopped playing the piano now. He sat there, staring into mid-air, barely conscious of where he was through his fug of alcohol.

The mama-san spoke to me, gesturing that I should choose. None of the girls looked at me. I couldn't look at them either. The mama-san spoke again. I shook my head. 'Another time, maybe,' I said.

She spoke to me once more, a long trill of Japanese. I gestured with hands, 'No, it's okay, I'll stay here.'

Without looking at me, she spoke to the girl in the middle of the line who wore a brilliant pink kimono, elegantly decorated with large green flowers.

The girl stepped forward and shuffled across in front of me. She bowed once and took my arm, speaking softly as she did so.

I let myself be taken. I was powerless to do anything else. Well, I like to believe I was powerless but the truth is I wanted her. It was when she spoke to me that I knew. The voice was so soft, so gentle. I could have bathed in its quiet tones.

I felt like a sixteen-year-old again. She took me through the beaded curtain, down a long corridor to a room on the right-hand side. She opened the door and stepped back, waiting for me to enter.

She wasn't beautiful by any means. Her hair was pulled back from her head to reveal a high forehead, her nose was squat and short, her lips small and painted in the most extravagant cupid's bow. She reminded me of a country girl from Lancashire; warm, welcoming, homely.

I entered the room. It was obviously hers. A hand painted photograph of her lay on the bedside table. She was smiling gaily at the camera, a wax umbrella twirling behind her head.

The bed itself was small and low, covered in the whitest of white sheets. In the corner was a stand-alone cupboard in which I could see a few colourful dresses hanging. She turned off the main light and lit a candle beside her bed. The light flickered, giving her face an eerie, unreal quality.

For a moment, I was afraid. She seemed to know this for she took my hand and led me toward the bed. She gestured for me to stand still and then she slowly began unbuttoning my khaki shirt.

Time had stopped. My breath had stopped. The candle flickered on.

She placed my shirt carefully on a hook behind the door, I stood watching her all the time, transfixed by the simplicity of her movements. Then she unbuttoned my belt, pulling it slowly out from the loops and laying it on her table.

She never spoke once, never even seemed to breathe. Everything was done slowly and carefully, with not a word spoken.

She knelt down in front of me now, removing my oversized army shorts gracefully, without saying a word. She gestured for me to lie on the bed. I did, my clumsiness only emphasised by her elegance.

I lay there while she walked to the door. I could hear the key turn in the lock and the next minute she was beside me.

I felt the soft skin of her shoulder. She took my hand and placed it on her small breast. I felt its round softness, capped by the different, red texture of her nipple. As I stroked her, the nipple hardened beneath my fingers, an erect Mount Fuji.

I kissed her shoulder and slowly moved over her body until I found the erect little nipple. Its hardness filled my mouth. Her body moved beneath me. Her hands wrapped around my back, her head thrown back revealing a long, elegant neck.

And then the next thing I knew I was inside her. The slow, rhythmic movements drawing me in deeper and deeper. I was lost inside her. I could hear myself breathing. Hear myself kissing her. Hear myself give small grunts of pleasure. But it wasn't really me. It wasn't really Richard Longhurst, it was someone else. Someone I didn't recognise.

Then it was over in a few juddering jerks of the knees, a final thrust of the pelvis, a swoon of the head down to her shoulder. I lay beside her, her nipple tickling my lips. And we both lay silent, not speaking, both dreaming of the past, present and the future.

I must have fallen asleep. I felt someone pinching my arm. I didn't know who it was at first.

I opened my eyes and saw her round face smiling down at me. Soft, gentle face once again. I reached out and touched her breast through her thin kimono.

She didn't take my hand away, she just smiled like my mother used to smile when I was a child. Then, she said something in Japanese to me. I shook my head, understanding nothing.

She took the hand that was stroking her breast and pointed to my watch. It was time to go. I stretched, and sat up in bed.

From somewhere she produced another hot towel and gently bathed the sweat from my body. I shall never forget the way her small, dark hands caressed the angles of my white body. She seemed to bathe every crease, every wrinkle in the softest, most gentle warmth.

Then, she got up and held my khaki shirt out for me. I slipped both arms in and she began to fasten my buttons. I tried to kiss her but she simply turned her face away from mine.

She fetched my shorts, socks and belt, helping me to dress as she earlier had helped me to undress.

Then, she did something strange. She took a coin and holding it between her index finger and thumb, gestured that she wanted me to give her another. I dug deep in my pockets and found 10¢. Then she led me to a large glass jar in the corner. I looked into it. It was three-quarters full of coins from every country in the world. I could see Norwegian Krone, German Marks, Chinese dollars, Japanese Yen, Thai baht, Indian rupees and a mint of other coins.

There must have been nearly 2,000 coins in the glass jar.

She held my hand and together we dropped my coin in with all the rest. It made a loud *ching* as it landed, rolled and came to rest next to a Vietnamese Anna.

She smiled at me, bowed and said something in Japanese.

I looked down at the coin-filled jar and realised these were her lovers. Every single coin represented a remembrance of her lovers. From every corner of the world came a coin from every man she had slept with.

I couldn't look at her again. I couldn't feel or understand her sadness. A sadness she kept in the corner of the room in a large glass jar.

I walked straight out of the room, leaving her standing beside her coins, I couldn't look back.

The lads were waiting for me downstairs. 'Trust fucking Richard to take his fucking time about fucking,' said Eddie. 'Mine was a right dirty bitch. Bit of a fighter too.' Eddie proudly showed the red scratch marks extending from beside his ear to below his neck. 'But after a little talking to, she gave us no more trouble.'

'How was yours Lanky?'

'Fine,' was all I could say. They couldn't, wouldn't, understand I'd left something of me behind in that small, candle-lit bedroom.

'Let's get these buggers and piss off back to camp before we get into trouble.' Eddie took hold of Ray and Reg slung Teale's arm over his shoulder. I opened the door, the two soldiers, with their walking wounded, shuffled outside into the warm, humid air.

I took one last look over my shoulder. She was there behind the beaded curtain looking straight at me. My eyes went down to the floor and I hurried out leaving her behind.

'Well, we've fucked the Japs, what's left then Richard?' Eddie asked me.

I didn't answer.

There seemed no point anymore.

No point.

*

Reg Dwyer
Block 15, Tanglin Barracks, Singapore
16th March 1941
Dear Marjorie,
I received a letter from home today.

It was signed from 'a friend'. It said you were carrying on with Mr. Brown every night. It said you stayed in his shelter and when all-clear was sounded, you went back to his house.

He should be ashamed of himself taking advantage of a woman when her husband's been posted overseas. If I ever see him, I'll kill him. You tell him that.

And, as for you Marjorie, you should know better, a woman of your age with three kids.

Think of me, all alone out here, defending the Empire and I can't even trust my wife back home in Manchester.

Anyway, I've written to our Harry to get a few mates together from the regiment and give your fancy man a good sorting out.

If he doesn't leave you alone, then I'll have to come back myself.

Please think of the kids Marjorie. For their sake, give up this man.

I'm willing to forgive you. I'm not saying I'll forget, but I am willing to forgive.

Think of our kids.

Your devoted husband

Reg

Censored by Lt. L. Whitehead

*

Reg Dwyer

''Permission to speak, sir.'

Major Tudor looked up from his papers and eyed me over his glasses. He had a bored look on his face that said I was disturbing his important work with my request. I saw his important work was a crossword.

'At ease, corporal.'

'Yes sir.'

'What is it?'

'Well, it's like this, sir; I have a personal problem which means I have to go back to England, sir.'

'We all have personal problems but that doesn't mean we all have to go back to England to solve them, does it, corporal?'

'No sir. But I can't solve mine here sir. I need to go back to England.'

Major Tudor sighed and took off his glasses. He rubbed his eyes and refocused them on the desk in front of him.

'We have an important job to do, defending the Empire, defending the Singapore Fortress. We can't have all the soldiers up and going when they feel like it, can we?'

'Well, no sir,' I agreed reluctantly.

'Well, there you are, corporal.' He put his glasses back on and returned to his papers. I stood there refusing to move.

'But sir, it's a personal problem. A marital problem.'

He leant back in his cane chair obviously wanting me to continue. But I didn't want to wash my dirty linen in public.

'Well continue, corporal.'

'It's the wife sir, she …,'

'Seeing another man?'

'Yes, sir.'

'Well, these things happen in any marriage particularly when the man and wife are separated.'

'Has it happened to your marriage, sir?' I looked him straight in the eye. He looked away.

'Well, no, it hasn't. Helena is here with me in Singapore.'

'There you are sir. If I can see my Marjorie. I'm sure it will all be sorted out. For the sake of the kids, sir.'

He looked down at his papers and began shuffling them nervously. He refused to look at me when he spoke.

'There are no compassionate leaves allowed at present.'

'But sir ...,'

'Permission denied.'

'But sir ...,'

'I said permission denied, corporal.'

'I don't think you understand the situation.'

He looked down at his papers once more and said, 'Escort this man from my office, Serjeant Shelley.'

'But sir...,'

'Interview over, Shelley.'

'You heard the officer, Dwyer. Permission is denied.'

I stared at the balding head of Major Tudor, his shiny head bent over his paper like some balding monk.

'Attention. About turn.'

I couldn't force myself to salute. It was as if the backbone had been sucked from my body.

I walked out of the office a dead man.

Suddenly, I felt Shelley's arm around my shoulder. 'Don't worry Reg, It'll all be sorted. You'll see. It'll be sorted.'

*

Michael O'Neill

The trial was a farce.

There was this eejit sat up on a high chair, wearing a wig and a black gown. Now let me tell you, there's nothing so stupid as a man with a rug on his head. And this was a moth-eaten old thing that looked as though it had been nibbled by a pack of rabid sheep.

Your man had one of those high-pitched woman voices. Every time he got angry, which, for some reason, was often with me, his voice would break.

Every time I looked at him all I could think of was the old cock my mum used to keep to service the chickens. At 4 o'clock every morning, the old bastard would get on top of the chicken hut and tell the world who he was. Of course, his voice broke half-way through his crow like this old judge in front of me.

Anyway I was standing there, behind the bars. There was the usual row of eejits in front of me. They'd even appointed Lieutenant Whitehead to defend me.

Why? God only knows. But I wasn't sure what was going to happen.

The first witness they called was Inspector Travis, the stupid slag who'd arrested me.

Jesus, Mary and Joseph, he was thick. I had to break into nearly four cars before he grabbed hold of me. And it was only when I smashed a mirror in the last one outside the Raffles Hotel, he finally took me down to Beach Road jail.

Anyway, he stood in the witness box, wearing his suit and tie, and sweating like a pig.

'I was proceeding down Beach Road past the Alhambra Theatre when I saw the accused...,'

He was interrupted by the other old shite in a wig who was leading the prosecution. 'Do you see the man standing in this court?'

Of course he does you stupid eejit. It's me. Haven't I spent the last two weeks in the jail? Of course he sees me here. Hasn't he been interviewing me every day?

'Yes.'

'Could you point out the accused for the judge?'

Why for feck's sake? Is the old dotard stupid, blind and drunk? Can't he see I'm standing in the dock, surrounded by three hairy coppers?

'It's him,' said Inspector Travis, pointing at you-know-who.

I pointed at my heart with my hand and mouthed 'me?' as innocently as I could. Well, you've got to have a bit of a craic with the poor eejits, don't you? Otherwise, what's the point?

The old drunkard woke up immediately. 'The prisoner will not make any untoward movement while he is in the dock.' Then his voice broke. 'This is a court of law and the prisoner will give it all the respect it deserves, is that clear?'

'Yes, your honour,' says I, 'I'll give the court all the respect it deserves.' The stupid old fart seemed to be happy with my answer. Shows you how thick he was.

The inspector continued. 'I was proceeding down Beach Road past the Alhambra Theatre when I espied the accused loitering with intent in front of the cars parked thereto.'

I didn't understand this gibberish but the judge seemed to love it, scribbling away in his book without looking up.

'I watched the accused try the handle of two different cars before giving up and...,'

'By 'try the handle' do you mean attempt to enter a car that wasn't his?' asked the judge.

Jesus, talk about leading a cow to water and helping her drink. I looked down at Whitehead and expected him to interrupt but the eejit sat there cleaning his nails.

'Yes M'Lud, that's exactly what I meant.'

'Please continue, inspector,' said the old fart. I could imagine him bringing out the square of black cloth, planting it on his head and smiling as he pronounced the sentence of death.

'Yes M'Lud, thank you. I then followed the accused to Raffles Hotel where he proceeded to attempt to force an entry into two more cars with the purpose of purloining them. Finally, frustrated in his attempts, he picked up a rock and smashed the side window of an Austin 10, registration number S7438. It was then I made my arrest of the accused, taking him to Beach Road police station at 6:42pm.'

'Thank you inspector. A very timely intervention, I'm sure,' said the old fart with the wig.

'Thank you M'Lud,' answered Travis, preening himself like some Christmas turkey waiting to be stuffed.

'Any cross-examination, Lieutenant Whitehead?'

'No, your honour.' Finally, my defender had spoken. Didn't help me much though did it.

'Now, Lieutenant Whitehead, are you going to call any witness for the defence?'

'No, your honour.'

'Noooo?' The old fart's voice rose like a whore faking her orgasm. 'Then why is your, he stumbled over the word, '....your client....pleading not guilty?'

'He so pleaded against my advice and that of his other lawyers, your honour.'

Oh thank you, thank you. Why don't you just hang, draw and quarter me right now. Or starve me to death like you did to my poor countrymen during the famine. You can only trust an Englishman so far as you can throw up on him, and that's God's honest truth.

'Why, pray, are we wasting the courts' time on a case against which there is no defence?'

Well done, me old cock, there's the rub isn't it?

'Well my lord, the army believes the defendant is trying to work his ticket.'

'Work his ticket? What on earth do you mean?'

'To get a discharge from the army, your honour, before he has served his time.'

'But surely that would be a dishonourable discharge?'

'Yes, your honour, but we believe the defendant doesn't really care.'

Whitehead shrugged his shoulders. The judge looked outraged, his face getting redder and redder beneath his moth-eaten rug by the second.

Me? I was shocked. How did Whitehead know what I was up to? It must have been Shelley who told him. I'll hang for him one day.

'Michael Patrick O'Neill, you have been shown to be a man of dubious character and even more dubious honour. Do you have anything to say before I pass sentence?'

I thought whether I should play with the old fart or tell the truth. For once in my life, the latter won out. I don't know what came over me.

'If I be pleasing your honour, your worship, I can't soldier the battalion.'

Then I shut up. They obviously expected more because they kept silent, waiting for me to continue.

Eventually though, the old fart gave up, simply shrugging his shoulders which set both his gown and his wig askew.

'Well, if that's all you have to say then I'm afraid the full force of the law will be faced by you. We, the peaceful citizens of our Empire Colony, have become somewhat fed up with the bad behaviour of those who have been sent to protect us. You are not the first soldier that has been before me in recent times for violating the laws of Singapore. Oftentimes, I think that we have more criminals in the army than we have soldiers.' He then looked around making sure everybody laughed at his little joke. I could see the reporter from *The Straits Times* scribbling away in his notebook.

He paused, taking a sip of water from the glass in front of him, obviously enjoying the torture of the moment.

'Particularly at times like these when the Empire is fighting for its life against the forces of Evil, we need every soldier to stand up and be counted.' He took a long gulp of water from the glass in front of him. 'I sentence you to six month's imprisonment on the charge of attempting to steal cars, with a further three month's imprisonment for wilful damage of property. Both sentences to be served concurrently. After serving your sentence you will be handed back to the Regimental authorities to be dealt with as they see fit. Take the prisoner down.'

What a load of bollix. I even tried a little wheedling, as you do.

'But my Lord, I've got a terrible bad chest. Them prison walls will make me wheeze like a steamroller.'

The judge nodded and then leaned over to his clerk. They whispered to each other, both nodding at the outcome.

'Then the sentence I pass will be six months without remission and with hard labour. The fresh air will do your chest good,, Private O'Neill. It may also help you, and the rest of your regiment, to see the error of your ways. Take him away.'

I felt this light touch on my elbow. Well, it wasn't exactly how I planned it but at least I was out of the fecking army for a while.

The grip on my elbow grew tighter now.

And, as I was led below, the only thing I could think of was this was another fine mess you've gotten me into, Michael O'Neill.

Chapter 18

Richard Longhurst

'It's all lies.'

Reg suddenly ran into the barracks brandishing this piece of paper high in the air.

'It's all lies, Eddie, it's not true. All lies, Lanky. It's all lies.'

'Reg, calm down, what's all lies?' I said, looking up from my *Birds of South East Asia* book.

'The affair. Marjorie and him. It's not true. See.' He threw the piece of paper down on my bunk. 'Read it.'

I picked it up and read out loud. 'Reg, how could you believe those lies. Stop. Nothing going on. Stop. Always, loyal to you. Stop. I'm your wife. Stop. Always your wife. Stop. Remember till death us do part. Stop. How could you think so badly of me. Stop. Tommy, Evelyn, Grace send love. Stop.'

'It's all lies, Lanky. But I thought she was having an affair you see. It all added up. She kept mentioning how kind this Mr. Brown had been in her letters. Then she doesn't write as often as she used to. But the final nail in the coffin was when I got a letter from a neighbour telling me Marjorie was having it away with this bloke. But it must have been my imagination. I see that now. And the neighbour has always hated Marjorie, interfering old bitch she is. I'll do her right good and proper when I get home.'

'So what are you doing to do now?'

'Do? Nothing. Maybe get drunk down at the Black Cat to celebrate.'

'I hate to tell you this Reg but I think your wife is a bit upset. She thinks you're accusing her of having an affair with someone.'

'Well I did.'

'Don't you think you should apologise?'

'I suppose so…I'll write her a letter right now.'

'But it will take six to eight weeks to get to England, Reg. A telegram would be better.'

'You're right, Lanky. You're right.' Reg felt his pockets. 'But telegrams cost money. I've only got…" He counted all the coins from his pocket one by one. 'I've only got $2.53. Payday is still two weeks away. What am I to do?'

'Well, you have been blowing a lot down at the Black Cat on that girl you keep seeing,' said Larkin, not looking up from his *Picture Post*.

I don't know what came over Reg. One minute he was on his bed, the next he had hold of Larkin and was beating him around his head. 'Don't you ever talk about Desiree like that, get it,' he said. 'Get it?'

Larkin nodded weakly.

Reg let him go and sat back on the bunk. His hands went to his head. He sat there cradling his head and rocking back and forth, back and forth.

Larkin had recovered now. He sat up, rubbed his neck and moved away from the bunk. 'You're fucking mad you, Dwyer, fucking mad,' were his last words as he stepped out of the barracks.

Reg looked up at me. 'What am I going to do, Lanky?'

'I could lend you the money for the telegram, Reg. I'm a bit flush at the minute.'

'Would you, Lanky, I'd be ever so grateful. And I promise I won't see Desiree again.'

'You don't have to promise me, Reg.'

'No, I don't. I'm promising her really.'

I handed him the ten dollars I had in my pockets.

'That's far too much Lanky.'

'Better to be safe than sorry, Reg. You never know how much they charge these days.'

He looked down at the money, staring at the notes lying in his big tanned hands.

'What am I going to say?'

'Just tell her the truth.'

'But I'm not good at that. I know what I want to say but the words always let me down. Like they're there, but they're not the ones I would have chosen, if I had a choice. D'ye get what I mean?'

'No.'

'You write it for me, Lanky. You're good at that sort of stuff. Words and all.'

'It's a telegram Reg. It's not bloody literature.'

'I know. But come on, do it as a favour.'

I grabbed a pen off my locker. The sooner I get this over with the better. 'Alright, what do you want to say?'

'I want to tell her I'm sorry. I jumped to the wrong conclusions and I miss her terribly.'

'What's her name again?'

'Marjorie.'

'Darling Marjorie.'

'No, I call her Margie.'

'Alright, Darling Margie. Stop. I'm sorry. Stop. I've been a fool. Stop.'

'Yes, that's good. I have been a fool.'

'Please forgive me. Stop. I miss you. Stop. I love you. Stop.'

'We never say that.'

'What?'

'I love you. It's not us. Not me and Margie.'

'Don't you think you should Reg, just this once?'

'We never did, never, even when we were courting.'

'Well, do you love her, Reg?'

'What sort of question is that, Lanky? I married her, didn't I?'

'Well, do you love her?'

Reg looked down at the piece of paper lying in his hands. Without looking up he answered, 'I suppose I do.'

'This is the time to tell her, Reg.'

'I suppose it is. Yes. Go on.'

'I miss you. Stop. I love you. Stop. Till death do us part. Stop.'

'I like that bit. It's in her telegram.'

'How do you want to sign off?'

'Oh, I usually put your husband.'

'How about 'your one and only Reg'?'

'Great. Magic. I knew you could do it, Lanky. You have a way with them words.'

He read what I'd written. I watched his lips move as he read each and every word. I watched as he stopped at the sentence, 'I love you.' He thought for a while and I could see him deciding to say it.

He folded the paper neatly into four and started running out of the door.

'I'll send it right now. With a bit of luck, she'll get it tomorrow.'

He turned back at the door. 'Thanks, Lanky. I won't forget this.'

And before I could say anything, he was gone.

*

Michael O'Neill

I'm lying here.

Now that doesn't mean I'm telling fibs or anything like that, even though I have told a few in my time. Even now, I can still feel the edge of the ruler as the old bastard monk, with his brown-stained fingers from the Sweet Aftons and the hangman's cord knotted around his waist, brought it down on my fingers. Jesus, the pain still stings.

And then there was his smile, the old bastard was enjoying himself. 'Michael O'Neill,' he would say, 'you are lying to me once again. God knows where you will end up but I'm sure the divil is stoking the fires waiting for you.'

Funny thing is, the old bastard was right.

The Judge decided the short, sharp shock of time in the Glasshouse, under the benevolent care of some certified nutcases, would make me see sense, and understand how kind and loving and wonderful the bloody army was. 'I sentence you to six months without remission,' the old spalpeen had boomed from his chair high above me.

Well, here I am, lying in one of His Majesty's beds.

I soon got out of the hard labour bit. Yet another spot of disobedience earned me a month in solitary. When will they ever learn I like being here, it's the people I can't stand. At least I'm on my own again, no longer surrounded by the fools who actually got caught for something they did wrong.

Now tell me this, how is it possible to be caught for anything? The police are eejits, they couldn't catch a cold. The only criminals that get caught are those so stupid the police have no choice but to arrest them.

'What do you plead?'

'Criminal stupidity my Lord.'

'Sentenced to a lifetime of being put in four walls, fed three times a day and the joy of utter boredom. Next case.'

What a load of bollix. At least I wanted to be nabbed. Jesus, it took me four goes before the eejit finally had the sense to put me inside.

So inside I am. All cosy and green-walled, bathing here in my memories. Because that's what the bastards can't touch.

They can march you up and down like King Billy. They can beat you down every day of every month of every year. They can make you jump at the sound of a voice or the swish of a swagger stick. But they can't get at your memories.

I remember who I am. And who I will be.

*

Richard Longhurst

The car was waiting at the main gates of the Botanical Gardens. Owens was already there loading his haversack into the boot. I saw the stocks of the three guns wrapped in coarse muslin at the back.

'Welcome, dear boy, this is Mohammed Jaafar, he'll drive us to Kota Tinggi.'

'Salaam Malai kum, tuan.' The old Malay man touched his stomach, his heart and his lips as he spoke. He ended his welcome with a nod of the head. I thought it was tremendously dignified, bestowing a status upon me I didn't normally receive as a run-of-the-mill squaddie. But strangely, it bestowed even more status and more dignity on him.

'I thought we were going to Lim Chu Kang. Kota Tinggi is in Johore, isn't it?'

Owens nodded. Jaafar ignored my question and went to the front seat of the Austin 4.

'But I can't leave the island. I need permission. In case there's a drill.'

'Don't worry.' Owens moved to the front passenger seat, opened the door and got in, shouting 'Hurry up, dear boy, we haven't got all day. Tigers don't wait for everyone, you know.'

I stood there, hobbled by indecision. Fuck it, I thought. The most they'll give me is ten days confined to barracks. Fuck it. Fuck them.

I got in the back seat. Owens had a peculiar smile in his face. 'Good to see you could join us. We're in luck; our tiger has taken another tapper this morning on the Bukit Palai Estate at Masai. We've got the bugger, he doesn't know it yet, but we've got him.'

Jaafar started the engine, ran back to the driver's seat and jumped in. He crashed the gears making a grating sound of metal on metal, and swung the car into a wide U-turn. At Farrer Road, he signaled left and turned right.

'Is he alright to drive?' I asked

191

'Jaafar,' Owens patted the old Malay man on the shoulder, 'Jaafar has done more trips with me than you have had hot dinners, dear boy. I won't be driven by anyone else.'

At Bukit Timah Road, we turned left and headed for the Causeway.

'Now, dear boy, I see you're dressed in your normal Army Fatigues.'

I looked down at my green shirt, shorts, my knee-length socks and heavy boots. 'It's the uniform,' I said pathetically. 'Humph.' Owens cleared his throat. 'Not much good in the jungle, I'm afraid. You'll be drenched with sweat in five minutes and those ridiculous boots will be covered in mud. Walking in them is going to be next to impossible. I've brought some clothes for you, dear boy, and at least you won't be filthy when you return to camp. Mustn't get you into trouble with our officers, must we?'

I nodded. No answer was required. I was to do as I was told.

'Now, you've been taking your quinine?' I nodded again, 'Good. When we get to Bukit Palai Estate make sure you cover your body, face and hands with this.' He handed me a small medicine bottle full to the brim with a dark green oily liquid. I pulled out the stopper and immediately jerked my head back and away from the foul smelling reek that hit my nostrils and battered my nose.

'Don't worry, dear boy, it smells foul but it works a treat. I think the Malays make it from coconut oil, ginger and assorted strange herbs. The mozzies hate it though. And even better for us, the tiger won't be able to smell you from miles away. Because with this you'll smell like the jungle.'

'Rotting plants, decaying wood, mulching leaves, you mean.'

'Exactly, dear boy, I call this stuff, Eau de Decay. A rather pungent perfume but guaranteed to keep mosquitoes, blow flies and all girls looking for husbands away from you.'

I sat back in the car and looked out of the window. Bukit Timah hill passed by on the right, the small fire station with its horse drawn fire truck guarding the tropics against the remote possibility of spontaneous combustion. The sun was getting higher and its rays burnt through the windscreen, magnifying their warmth on my leg. I wound down the window. In rushed a zephyr of warm air, drenched with humidity.

We passed a sleepy hamlet of human habitation, a car repair workshop, the Ford Factory, its large sign dominating the road. Its size dominating everything around it.

Jaafar drove on in silence. I lit a Craven A, letting the hot smoke ease down my throat.

We were on the Causeway now. On the right I could see the cranes and wharves of the new Naval Base. A few funnels lay at anchor there, guarding Singapore from the encroachments of the real world outside.

On the left, I looked across at Johore, dominated as it was by the tower of the Sultan's palace, looking down on everything, all knowing and all powerful.

We drove through the perfunctory border into the State of Johore. I was in Malaya now. Away from the army, away from my brother, away from the endless repetitive monotony of life in barracks. I felt the wind rush through my hair as I stuck my head out of the window.

'Careful, dear boy, you don't want to lose your head.'

I moved back into the car, stretching out along the seat. Johore and its endless long line of rubber trees raced past outside. I couldn't care, I was free at last.

I felt a hand on my shoulder, 'Wake up dear boy, we have arrived.'

I opened my eyes and pushed my legs out of the open door. '*Aaraghump*,' I stretched.

'I totally agree, but you'd better get changed rather quickly. The warden is concerned we get a move on this morning.'

Owens had changed. He was wearing a long-sleeved shirt with the sleeves buttoned tightly around his wrists, loose green trousers with a drawstring waist and drawstring bottom, and on his feet were light, ankle-high canvas shoes.

He handed me a similar set of clothes. 'Hurry up and get changed, we haven't got all day.' I took the clothes and looked around for a changing cubicle. There was nothing but trees everywhere. Trees that looked as though God had taken an immense rake and combed them exactly into position. They stretched out in long straight lines over the hill, their branches and leaves curved upward toward each forming a long, semi-lit tunnel.

And, as if by chance, each tree had a single red tin cup attached to its trunk. It was almost like a long line of penitents holding their cups out for alms.

'Do hurry up, dear boy.'

'Where do I change?'

'Behind the car if you're bashful, but do hurry up.'

I took the clothes Owens had given me and ran to the rear of the car. The boot was open and I could see the knapsacks and guns were gone.

Quickly, I stripped off my khaki shirt and singlet, unlaced the boots, and peeled off the already stinking army socks. After a quick look over the top of the boot, I peeled off my long army shorts and folded them neatly over the rest of my gear.

'Don't forget this, dear boy.' Owens was holding out the dark, green oil to me. I watched him look down at my clumsy feet and move up my body until his eyes rested on my shoulders. 'Would you like me to put some on your back for you?'

'No, it's alright, I'll do it myself.' I took the oil from him. The cork came out with a gentle tug and, trying not to breathe, I began rubbing the foul smelling gloop all over my body.

'Have it your own way then. But do hurry up dear boy, everyone else is ready to go.' With that final admonition for more speed, he turned away from me sharply and walked to the edge of the forest.

It was there I noticed two new Malays I had never seen before.

One was minute. He was no taller than Owens' chest. He wore only the flimsiest of white vests, the baggiest shorts I'd never seen and nothing on his feet. Next to him, talking to Owens, was another Malay chap. He was thin almost to the point of emaciation with a thick, very dark mustache dominating an even darker face. He seemed to speak only monosyllabic grunts with Owens asking long, complicated questions in Malay but receiving only the shortest grunt for an answer.

I pulled on the shorts, fastening both the neck and the sleeves, and slipped my feet into the canvas shoes. I noticed for the first time the soles were covered in smooth, quiet pliable rubber. The canvas had been hand stitched to the rubber with a stout, fibrous cord. They were the most comfortable shoes I had ever worn. It was like laying another thick layer of skin between one's feet and the ground. But I was still able to feel the earth - its texture, temperature and terrain. How did Owen know my size? The man never ceased to amaze me.

I pulled on the trousers, tucked in the shirt and tightened the drawstring. I did the same at each leg, tying the drawstring so it wrapped tightly around the boot.

Proud of myself, I walked toward the group and announced, 'Ready.'

'About bloody time, too. The body lies about half a mile that way.' He pointed up the hill, 'Ali here hasn't disturbed it yet. The tiger will return later for the rest of his kill.'

He turned to Ali and produced a long, soft garble of words, receiving merely a grunt in reply.

'Ali says the tiger will return soon, so let's get a move on.'

Ali and his small, darker companion promptly sat down at the side of the road. From his bag, he produced an old copy of *The Strait Times*, and four bundles of what looked like dried leaves.

He looked up at myself and Owens and said one word, 'Makan.'

That seemed to explain everything. I found the sleeves of my shirt being tugged by Owens and I was gently pulled down to sit crossed-leg on the other side of the newspaper.

'Ali says it's time to eat, dear boy. We're going to be in the jungle for a long time.'

Ali was by now untying the knots of raffia that kept the bundles of each of the individual oteh packets together. I could see that the leaves were folded one over the other like some green leaved chocolate box. He unfolded them and instantly steam rose from within, followed by the mouth-watering aromas of cooked food.

I suddenly realised how hungry I was. I looked into the first packet and saw cooked rice with chicken, covered in a reddish-brown sauce.

'Belacan, dear boy, avoid it unless you like spicy food. Usually, it doesn't go at all well with the English stomach. Not that they ever cook it with an English stomach. Not often anyway, usually it's chicken.'

Ali had opened the other two parcels. The first contained an assortment of vegetables but nothing I recognised. Owens, however, seemed to know them all.

'Okra, lady fingers to you, dear boy. Sambal kangkong. Again, avoid it if you can't eat hot stuff. Fried Brinjals. This is a treat.'

The third packet continued a dark brown almost desiccated meat on top of which lay a few even more desiccated onions. 'Beef Rendang, delicious cooked in coconut milk, Ali's wife has excelled herself.'

The final packet lay next to it. For once, I didn't need a translation of the recipe from Owens, inside lay four fried eggs, their yolks gleaming yellow against the dark greenish brown of the oteh. On top of each egg was a tiny white spot of fertilization. Some poor chicken had given her child's life for my stomach.

Ali now came back from the forest carrying four large leaves. He placed them in front of each of us. For a few seconds, he looked down and mumbled a few words in Malay.

Owens prayed in his own way, 'For what we are about to receive may the lord make us truly thankful.' A moment's silence followed by, 'Well get stuck in, dear boy, we don't have much time.'

I watched as Owens took a small scoop of rice with his right hand. Placing it on the centre of his leaf, he reached over and added a few pieces of oily purple brinjal. Then he seemed to play with the food like a child plays with mashed potato, making roads, airplanes, and houses. Finally, when the whole mixture of rice, brinjal and sauce had formed a ball slightly larger than a golf ball, he picked it up in the thumb and first three fingers of his right hand, cocked his head back, opened his mouth, and slowly pushed it in like a dockside crane lowering a palette of cargo deep into the hold of a ship.

I watched him chew, his cheeks becoming even fatter with each slow mastication.

'Hwy doh, dere aiting?' he said

I didn't understand a word. He held up his hand and concentrated on chewing. Swallowing with difficulty, he repeated, 'Hurry up, they're waiting.'

I looked at Ali and the little pygmy. They were both watching me, waiting with a quiet politeness I found extraordinary.

'Oh sorry!' I looked down at the food. 'Er…Mr. Owens, how do you eat fried egg with your fingers?'

'With difficulty, dear boy, with difficulty.'

Helpful as ever, I thought. Well, here goes. I picked up a large lump of rice and deposited it in the middle of my leaf. I looked again at the food and decided safety was the better part of valour. I leant over and picked up the smallest of the fried eggs. I was about to tear it apart with both my hands when Owens leant over.

'Remember only use your right hand, we wouldn't want Ali here and his friend to think we are savages. Got to keep up appearances. Using your left hand in front of Malay is equivalent to farting at the dinner table. Frightfully bad manners. Could create an awful stink.'

I put my left hand behind my back, hooking it into the loop of my trousers to ensure it never tried to help eat my food of its own volition.

The egg stared at me with its single, unblinking yellow eye at the centre of which was a single white dot.

I stared back at it.

The table, or what passed for a table in the middle of the jungle, was silent.

I noticed at the top of *The Straits Times* that Derby had beaten Everton 2 – 1 to go top of the table in England. Funny though, the article was headed 'Home results'. Home? I looked around me at the lush jungle, inhaled the earthy aromas of decay and looked down at the living green plates in front of me and thought this was about as far from 'Home' as anyone could get.

But the egg still looked at me and the others still waited.

Taking my courage in my right hand, I plunged my fingers like a dagger into the heart of the egg. The yellow yolk oozed out over the rice. I pulled back, separated the egg into two equal halves. I repeated this again, creating two quarters out of the egg half. The rest was easy. Mixing the quartered egg with the now moist, yolky, rice. Repeating Owens' cargo delivery using my right hand as a crane.

I was fortunate, the rice was deposited securely in the back of my gullet. It tasted warm, yolky and strangely sweet.

'Well done, dear boy, you've got most of it in the right place. However...,' He pointed to a large smear of egg and rice on the front of my shirt just below the point of my collar. It looked like a giant pigeon had shat on my chest.

'Sorry, sorry...I'll clean it off.'

'It doesn't matter. Finish eating first.'

Ali and his friend were now quickly devouring the food. Moving with quiet elegance, they scooped up the vegetables, broke off pieces of meat, separated slices of egg, added a spot of red sauce and flicked this ball of all the known food groups into their waiting mouths.

Nobody talked. The only sounds were the magpie-robins singing for domination in the jungle like a whole chorus of Gracie Fields, orchestrated with the soft sounds of food being mixed with saliva and swallowed.

I tried some of the brinjal, it tasted like eggplant. 'That's because it is, dear boy,' Owens told me later. Finally, I plucked up enough courage to eat a piece of the chicken with the belacan. I wish I hadn't. I couldn't taste the chili, I couldn't taste the belacan and what was worse, I couldn't taste my mouth. I sucked in air across my burning lips. I tried smacking them together to cover them in saliva but it felt like two pieces of rubber had somehow got trapped at the entrance to my mouth.

Owens handed me the water bottle. 'Welcome to the wonderful world of belacan, dear boy. It kills all known living brain cells. What it does to the stomach I shudder to think. But Ali and his friend love every lip-smacking, tonsil-torturing moment of their meal. Me? I've lived here so long I've started to love it. Can't eat a meal without it now. It's like HP sauce to me, only twice as tasty and three times more fun.'

I drank more water. It seemed to have no effect. Ali gave me a packet filled with white crystals.

'You're honoured dear boy, Ali obviously likes you.'

'What is it?'

'Oh don't worry, put some on your tongue and lips. It'll help take the heat away.'

I dabbed my finger into the small brown paper packet of crystals. Gingerly, I took my crystal-crusted finger and put it to my tongue. Almost instantly, the heat disappeared to be replaced by an intensely sweet taste that lingered and lingered and lingered.

Smacking my lips, I asked 'What is it?'

'Sugar, dear boy, only sugar. But Ali doesn't have much, so give it back and say thank you.'

I handed the packet back with both hands and, as I had been taught by Owens, whispered 'Terima kasih, Ali.'

He smiled, took his packet and carefully rewrapped it before placing it securely in one of the small pockets of the knapsack.

The food was finished now. Ali was wiping his mouth and hand with a small cloth he kept in his bag. The little pygmy was off in the jungle doing whatever little pygmies do in the jungle after they have eaten, while Owens was wiping my shirt front with some grass he had found.

'A right mucky pup, you are, aren't you?' For the first time I heard a strong Yorkshire twang in Owens' voice. He told us he'd been born in Leeds but his accent, and the way he moved and talked, were those of the south.

'Right, let's get the guns and finally get started.'

Owens handed me one of the shotguns which I immediately hoisted over my right shoulder in the classic position that the regimental Serjeant major had spent hours and countless thousands of swear words teaching us.

'No, no, no, dear boy, carry it low, across the crook of your arm. Otherwise rain, humidity and all the other denizens of the forest will make a deliciously warm home in that barrel of yours. You'll come to fire it and, boom, no more Private Longhurst.'

'Oh right, no problem.' I cradled the barrel across my chest, letting it nestle in the crook of my arm.

'Perfect, now let us depart. Ali smells our tiger up ahead.'

The pygmy led the way into the rubber plantation moving with a grace and speed, ignoring all the creepers, tree roots, ferns and grasping plants that covered the ground. Owens followed about five yards behind, carefully stepping in the exact tracks of our pygmy. I stumbled after him, constantly discovering every grasping root, every clinging vine, all carefully placed to snatch at my ankles or trip up my tracking boots.

'Do lift your feet; you're not walking down Pall Mall.'

'I've never walked down Pall Mall.'

'Well, wherever it is you do walk in that dreary Manchester of yours. Lift them up so they clear the ground cover. Look at Ali.'

I turned around and saw Ali about ten yards behind us. His movements were as graceful as a ballet dancer and as lithe and dangerous as Dixie Dean. He lifted his shoeless feet high and placed them gently down, one step ahead of him. I heard no sound of breaking twigs, no crunch of decaying timber. Nothing except my own breathing.

Ali was beside me now, pointing forward with his hand and grunting, 'Tuan.'

I moved forward, desperately trying to imitate the nimbleness of Ali. I'm afraid it wasn't a success. At least, though, I did make less noise and the journey became noticeably less tiring.

Still the rubber trees stretched endlessly onwards, their slender trunks covered in the various fungus shades of green, grey, brown and black. A white band, like an ancient Saxon armlet, twisting around the trunk, to disappear into the ever open mouth of the red tin cup.

'See, fresh tapping, sap's still running.' I followed his pointing finger to the tree. I could see the flow of thick white liquid as it traveled down the white scar and dripped into the cup. Malaya's lifeblood, oozing out of the tree into a small red container.

The plantation was growing darker now. The sun no longer freckled its way through the tops of the trees. The arch of rubber had grown thicker, forming a tunnel like officers do at a friend's wedding.

We walked on in silence. Even the magpie-robins had decided they didn't want this territory, the plantation could keep it.

The pygmy raised his hand suddenly. I stopped, conscious only of my breathing. I felt a drop of sweat ooze out of my pores above the eyebrow, run down the side of my eye, picking up pace and liquid to drip off the end of my chin on to the already sodden shirt.

The pygmy moved forward slowly. I looked across at Owens. He motioned for me to stay absolutely still.

I did, even though the thick, coarse, lallang itched at my knees, trying to pierce my trousers and threaten the soft white skin beneath.

More sweat decided it wanted to escape from the confines of my body. I was melting, slowly, in this far-off place that will never, no matter what Rupert Brooke says, be a corner of England.

The pygmy was now about forty yards away. I could just make his dark body out moving through the grey twilight of the plantation. I heard a whistle and Ali moved myself and Owens forward.

'We're in luck, dear boy; it seems the body is still there.'

I moved forward cautiously. Lift your feet. Lift your feet. Place them down carefully. Well done, now next one. Good. Next. Next. Next.

Then the smell hit me. A sweet, cloying, decay smell like no other in the forest. Almost perfume-like, it clung to the nostrils, smothering them in its aroma.

I shook my head. The smell remained. I walked forward to where the pygmy and Ali were standing. At Ali's feet lay another thin leg, peering out from a dirty pair of canvas shorts. A large red ant crawled across the knee and disappeared into the leg of the shorts.

I followed its path. A thin white singlet covering an emaciated chest, the ridge of ribs slipping out from the top of the vest. A bony white neck with a prominent, protruding Adam's apple. An unshaven jaw, spotted with black dots of hair. An open mouth, teeth exposed in a grimace with the left front one missing so I could gaze into the hollow blackness within. The eyes were still open, set back in the thin white face and mounted on the high, sharp cheekbones.

The old Chinese tapper lay on his back amongst the rubber trees. The forest that had claimed his life for many years, had finally claimed his life for good.

The pygmy said something in Malay. He picked up a red-knobbed lump and brought it to us. As he walked closer, I began to make out the outlines of a thumb, then fingers, then nails. I saw the little hairs above the middle joint. The thick black line of dirt beneath the nails.

I looked down at the body. At the shoulder where an arm should have been, lay nothing but a dark black emptiness.

Ali moved forward to the old tapper. The blackness surprised by his sudden movement, raised itself and hovered above the body. It hung there for a few moments before hunger and the maddening smell of fresh blood attracted it gradually back to its feast. There it swarmed for a while, savouring the delicious smell, before it reformed itself and returned to the red gash to feed.

'The tiger's taken the arm and shoulder. He'll be back though. Couldn't resist a delicious treat like this.'

I looked down at the body, or what used to be the body of the Chinese tapper. 'Shouldn't you say a few words over him. Maybe bury him.'

'Not now, dear boy, we've work to do.'

Suddenly Ali became voluble, and then I understood he was giving orders. The pygmy ran off into the jungle and Owens turned to me, 'We're to build a hide. Over there, downwind.'

I could feel no wind. 'What about him?' I pointed to the tapper's body, lying on its back amongst the roots of the tree.

'Don't worry about him, he's 'armless.' He laughed a hearty, one-of-the-boys laughs. I stared back at him, not knowing what to say, how to feel.

'Don't worry, dear boy, only a little joke. We can't help him now. He's the tiger's. Come on, let's build the hide.'

He walked over to the next row of rubber trees. 'Look for the thick, strong creepers, while I cut some of the branches.'

He took a long, curved parang from his knapsack. Like a horticulturalist selecting roses, he chose the branches he wanted and lopped them off with one, clean swipe.

Meanwhile, Ali was doing exactly the same. Chopping branches about four feet in length, sharpening one end and hammering them into the ground close to the tapper's body. Gradually, as more branches were added, the trap fanned out from the body in a V-shape for about fifteen feet. The body, lying at the foot of the rubber tree, formed the apex.

'Come along, dear boy, we haven't got all day.' Owens was hammering his sharpened branches into the ground on one side of the tree, binding them together to form a small semi-circle about five feet across. My creepers were then interwoven between the branches like the old reed fencing the tattle man would occasionally sell back in Manchester. When this was finished the hide was covered in foul smelling leaves the pygmy brought from somewhere. God knows where he got them. Hell possibly.

I watched as Ali mounted two of the guns at the ends of the legs of the trap. He checked their registration point on the old Chinese tapper, ensuring that the one on the left was sited fractionally ahead of the one on the right. From his knapsack he removed a thin length of piano wire. This he ran across the centre of the trap forming a bar exactly where the guns were sited. He stretched it tight around the trunk of another branch and attached it to the trigger of the gun.

Then he repeated the process again with the other shotgun; stretching the wire tight, running it around the branch and back to the trigger.

He looked at his handiwork and seemed satisfied.

He tested the tension of the first gun. Then, he ran his fingers along the trip wire, feeling every inch of the way to the second gun.

Owens shouted something at Ali in Malay. He seemed annoyed at the interruption, merely grunting an even more abrupt grunt in reply.

'We're ready now. All we do is wait.'

Ali ran back to the first gun and released the safety catch. He did the same with the second gun. One last look to see everything was all right and he ran to join us in our hide.

Here, we lay and waited. I could smell the pygmy's body next to mine. A sweet, cloying smell like a brewery hung over him. Owens lay on the other side of me. His breath came in short pants and like me, he was drowning in sweat. Ali was on the outside closest to the trap. His lean body taut like the trap he had created. His eyes watching for the slightest movement. His ears listening for sounds nobody else could hear.

'It's going to be a long wait,' Owens whispered without moving his lips, his eyes straining out into the shadowy twilight of the forest.

I lay on my back and stared up through the canopy. Up there, somewhere, the sun shone down, projecting like a Lloyds light all over the world. Except Manchester of course. There it would be still dark. A city enjoying the cold hand of winter, where light only penetrated with a steely reluctance.

I remembered the joke my father told me about Manchester, 'Look lad,' he said, 'if ye can see Pennines, it's going to rain, and if tha' can't see them, then it's already raining.'

Other memories came washing in. His return from work, me sitting on the windowsill, my mouth filled with a beautiful sweetness as he offered me another toffee. And the day he died. Another grey day, hiding under the kitchen table with my brother, playing some strange game only we understood. Above, adults speaking in whispers, me not understanding the words only hearing the sounds, but feeling the pity in these voices. All I could see were the long skirts of the women, some wearing dark stockings, others bare-legged, their veins tracing blue arterial roads down their legs.

And later, hiding under my mother's skirts. The damp warmth, the soft pleasant scratch of shin against my cheek, the sweet smells that lay all about me. Like the jungle. Just like the jungle.

I wiped an ant from my face. Owens lay beside me gently snoring. The pygmy sat, or rather squatted down on his calves; unmovable, silent, still.

Ali watched. His eyes constantly roaming the jungle, looking for the movement, the noise, the smell revealing the presence of our prey.

I lay my head down again, letting the dreams and the smells of the garden of memories permeate my body. It was good to travel back to those long gone days, relive every second, review the theatre of my memories, revisiting each one again and again, hoping to see one more detail that may have been missed, to hear a word that may have been forgotten, to see it all once more.

Ants crawled over my legs and face. They burrowed into my ears, exploring the dark, labyrinthine tunnels lying within.

I lay still.

Then I sensed a stiffening in Ali's body. The pygmy opened his eyes.

Slowly, I lifted myself up. Ali looked across at me, his eyes shouting out for silence, ordering stillness.

I held my body stiff, twisting my head to peer through the cracks in the leaves and cross-hatched creepers.

Nothing.

The forest looked as it had always looked. The lallang grew. The trees reached up toward the light. The ants like small, dedicated cleaners scoured the floor for succulent tidbits.

Ali slowly reached for his gun. Our one remaining protection against the tiger, red in tooth and claw. Only one gun. Jesus, if he went for us and not for the Chinaman. The thought made me jerk my hand, a leaf rustled beneath it.

Ali looked at me with eyes that had all the malevolence of a kris. I sensed movement outside. The slight lift of a head, a sniffing of the air, a pause in mid step. A paw raised waiting to fall.

Our tiger was at the entrance to the trap, immobile, still. Its whole body tensed. Now I could see it, yet before it had been invisible, silent, and deadly.

It looked at the dead tapper, but it smelt the presence of something else. Should it go forward and eat or not?

I watched its terrible indecision. It just waited, and looked and sniffed the air.

Ali was slowly raising the shotgun to his shoulder. The tiger, its body orange and black velvet still, absorbing all light, the one movement being the tail with its white spot, slowly moving from side to side as if it had a life of its own.

It took one step forward, as if to test the ground. Nothing happened. It took another step, smelling the blood of the dead tapper, tasting the soft flesh in its mouth, enjoying the crunch of bone, savouring the sweetness of the marrow. It took another step forward, then another.

Both shotguns went off, one after the other, the two loud bangs, deafening the silence.

The tiger seemed to jump up in the air, as if scared by the strange bang. Instantly forgetting the feast waiting for him, it turned tail and ran back, past the red tin cups, past the long lines of rubber trees standing guard, into the darkest twilight of the forest.

Owens, as startled as the tiger, sat up quickly.

'What's up, what's happenin'?' The Yorkshire accent appeared again.

Ali and the pygmy were already running toward the trap.

'The tiger, it came exactly like Ali said it would.'

I got to my feet and immediately tripped up over one of the tree roots. Scrambling to my feet again, I joined Ali and the pygmy at the opening to the trap.

They were both speaking in Malay, the longest, most profound speech I'd ever heard either of them say.

Owens joined us. 'They say the tiger's wounded. He won't go far.'

Then I noticed four spots of blood on the ground at Ali's feet. Such little blood for such a strong beast. I looked across at the tapper. The open eyes staring right at me, accusing me of leaving him there.

Ali removed both shotguns from their place on the top of the trap. He checked the barrels and reloaded them from his pockets.

Already, the pygmy was following the trail of thick, red, wine-dark blood. His eyes on the ground, his steps deliberate but eager, like a bloodhound on heat.

Ali handed one gun to me and the other to Owens, keeping his own for himself. He then said a few last words to Owens, following the pygmy as he did so.

'He says, we're not to shoot until he gives the order. The tiger is hurt but still dangerous. Soon he will turn on those who prey on him.' Owens looked at me, 'Isn't this exciting, dear boy.'

I took one last look at the tapper, propped up against the tree. Or should I say, he took one last good look at me.

Then, catching up with Ali and Owens, I plunged deeper into the twilight with them.

All around us was still as we picked our way through the forest. The birds had flown the coop. The magpie-robins had vanished. Even the cicadas, their ever-present scratching providing the rhythm of the forest, had packed up their instruments and decided today was a day of rest. On this day, the tiger would be killed and they would lay unmolested, unharmed in their nooks and crannies.

We plunged deeper into the forest. Now, the rubber trees were not as evenly spaced as before. It seemed like God had got bored with his work and decided to be more haphazard. Now, there were other trees fighting for life in the darkness. The lallang grass was longer, clinging and scratching like a jealous wife.

I gripped the stock of my shotgun. The sweat of my hands sliding across the polished wood. A river of sweat dropped off my chin, down on to the polished gun metal, formed round drops on the surface of the gun oil and slid immediately to the ground. The salt of the earth to be.

Nobody spoke. Even Owens kept silent as he inched forward, eyes scanning the dense forest, unable to see the wood for the trees.

Suddenly, the pygmy raised his hand. We all stopped, crouched, my muscles shouting out in pain. The pygmy squatted down and seemed to peer through the dense green as if he were looking through a telescope at some far-off beauty undressing before an open window.

He said a few words in Malay.

'It's over there, beneath the bush,' translated Owens in a whisper. He pointed but I could see nothing.

Then, I glimpsed a slight movement. A chest going up and down as air inflated and deflated the lungs. A white underbelly, ribs like corrugated iron stretched tight across the skin.

And then the strange sound. A loose, uneven bubbling, breathing like a pan of water on a rolling boil.

Ali crept slowly forward, his shotgun at the ready, his body tense, the muscles of his legs stretched tightly across the teak brown skin, watching everything, eyes darting here, there and everywhere.

Gradually, carefully, he neared our prey. The tiger smelt him. Its nostrils flared. It tried to raise its large head but gave up. A sound like a throttled roar emerged from its throat. The head sank even further into the ground. The breathing stopped.

Ali crept forward slowly, keeping the shotgun pointing down at the tiger.

About six feet away from it. He squatted down and looked into its eyes.

Dead. Dead eyes glazed over already with a film of glaucoma. Never to see its prey again.

Ali called us forward. I stepped in front of Owens. As carefully, and as cautiously as Ali, I advanced toward the tiger, stopping only to stand next to the squatting Ali.

I looked down and was filled with an immense sadness.

The tiger no longer breathed. It no longer padded the jungle trails. It no longer haunted the night. It no longer preyed. Its God had forsaken it.

Ali slowly crept towards it and opened the jaws. The tongue flopped out between the four large canine teeth. A flood of dark blood oozed from the tongue, dripping gently on to the forest floor. Already, the ants were there, sensing a feast for their nest.

Ali spoke to Owens in Malay. He turned to me, 'See the teeth. Ali thinks this is an old male. He's lost half of his teeth. Can't hunt any more. Humans are easier prey. He developed a taste for man. Shame really, magnificent beast.'

Owens seemed to think for a while. I thought he was going to deliver a eulogy over the dead tiger. Instead, he spoke very softly.

"Tiger, Tiger, burning bright
In the forest of the night
What immortal hand or eye
Could frame thy fearful symmetry."

Owen delivered the poem over the dead tiger as he would a sermon over a dead accountant or merchant. But now ashes to ashes were replaced by Blake. The effect though was the same.

'Frightful poet, terrible Christian and a bit of a charlatan if you ask me. But Blake certainly caught the character of the tiger, didn't he? Water, dear boy?'

Owens handed me his flask. Now I realised how dry my mouth was. I unscrewed the top and drank greedily.

'Hold on there, save some for me.'

'Sorry, sorry, it tasted good.'

'Always does after a kill, dear boy, always does.'

Ali gave a few orders to the pygmy who ran back the way we came.

'The villagers will celebrate tonight. This one's killed two women in the last month. The tapper must have been careless.'

'What's going to happen to him?'

'Oh, Ali will sort it all out. They can come and collect the body now. We'll never find the arm through.'

'No, no I meant the tiger. What's going to happen to him?'

'Oh, he's one of Ali's perks. He'll skin him. Sell the pelt to some ignorant planter who'll dine out for years on the stories of the day he shot a tiger. The gall bladder and the bones, he'll sell to the Chinese. Use them as medicine you know. The meat will be for his family. Nothing's wasted, you know. Our *Tiger, Tiger, burning bright* will continue to shine long after he's dead.'

Ali covered the tiger's body with layers of large leaves, reverently laying one overlapping the other.

'It's time to go home, dear boy.'

We returned the way we came. None of us spoke. Above us the sun had slipped to tree level, suggesting the coming of night.

A night the tiger would never see again.

I don't remember much about the drive back to the camp. Neither myself nor Owens spoke much. I just stared out of the window, not seeing anything really.

But I knew something had changed inside me. I didn't feel like Private Richard Longhurst 9253418 anymore. I don't know what I did feel like but I wasn't him. I had become someone else. Not fully formed yet.

Not yet.

Chapter 19

Michael O'Neill

Up in the corner I can see a memory.

Beneath the bed another one lies lurking. Next to the washstand there's another. They are all around me these memories. It's like I'm living in the past here in my cell. The Brits have jailed me in my past. It's a lovely place to hide.

Sometimes I can't control where I go to on the sleigh of memory. It's like the runners are stuck in the old ruts of the past.

I can't really remember me da. I try. I try really hard. But he's always out of reach, not quite there.

I remember him coming home from the fields one day and greeting me as he came through the door. Picking me up from the sideboard and hugging me close. I say I remember but I don't really. What I remember is the feeling that day. The feeling of warmth, of being loved. I remember the smell of him: the hay and the earth and the sweat and the roughness of his skin.

But I can't remember what he looks like at all. The memory is gone, who knows where.

I also remember the day he left. I was eight then. Me da had been one of those who had fought for a United Ireland. Always a bit of a dreamer, he was. Joining the IRA in East Mayo, cutting the roads, burning the barracks, hiding from the English. When the treaty was signed, he joined all his other pals and carried on fighting. But this time he was fighting the Irish. They lost and he ended up in Kildare prison with a lot of the same pals.

I talked with one of them once. Tom Carney was his name. I wanted to fill in the gaps about me da. Me ma never talked about him of course.

As Tom said, 'Your da was a man with a few stars in his eyes. He was brought up on the milk of an Ireland free and fair. For him, fighting was as natural as mowing hay.'

Here Tom lowered his voice. 'But we had no chance of winning and we both ended up in jail with all the rest of the men. You were born by now of course. Your ma had married your da in the brief bit of peace between us fighting the English and us fighting Dublin. She had you all on her own. Alone there on the farm, you popped into the world as bright as a button. Now, your da came home in 1924 but he wasn't the same. I think it was leaving here that changed him.'

Tom looked out across the field of potatoes and cabbages lying outside our house. 'He couldn't see the point of here anymore. And there were no jobs then for old IRA men with nothing to show for the years of fighting the Brits except wheezing chests.'

I understood then. Somehow, fragments of conversations between me ma and me da, overheard as I lay between the sheets with my brother, came back to me.

'There's nothing here for me...,'

'America is the place to go. I can make some money and then send for you and the kids...,'

'I've got to go...,'

'Please let me go.'

And so he went. One bright April morning, I remember the cart coming for him. He had packed a suitcase borrowed from Mick Kilkenny with his two shirts, his rosary, an old pair of boots, a spare pair of trousers and an overcoat Tom Carney had found for him. He put on his best clothes and said, 'I'd best be off.'

He picked up me first and said, 'Michael, look after your mother while I'm gone, there's a good man.'

Then he picked up my brother James and said exactly the same thing. Then he looked at me ma and started to move toward her but he stopped.

'I'll be off then,' he said.

Picking up his case, he strode across the field to the waiting cart.

'Da, Da,' me and my brother shouted as we ran after him. He stopped and turned towards us. I reached into my pocket and gave him the penny I had been saving since Christmas.

'It's for you, for America,' I said like the stupid wee child I was.

He smiled, I'll always remember that smile, took the penny, picked up his case and climbed up to sit on the front seat of the cart.

The driver clicked his mouth and the horse trotted on. He slowly pulled away from us, never looking back.

I turned and saw me ma standing there in the yard. Her arms crossed over her belly. I think she already knew she was going to have Sean then.

It was the last thing he ever gave her.

*

Eddie Longhurst

'Desiree. Desiree!'

It was Reg, pissed as a newt, shouting up at the window of the girl. She must have brought him back here behind Lavender St after they left the Pussy Cat Club. Now he's here again, his voice roaring like a bull with its bollocks caught on a fence.

'Desiree! Desiree! Come on down, ah want to see ye.'

'Shut up, Reg, you'll wake the dead.'

It was Larkin speaking. Somehow me and him had chased after Reg when he left the club. When I say chased, I really mean stumbled because that's what he did. It was like he had one idea in his mind and he was going to do it.

I've never seen such a look in all my bleeding puff. I'll give Reg this. Where there's a bit of hole to be had, Reg will be up it like a frog up a pump.

Myself and Larkin did try mind you. But Reg is a lot stronger than he looks. A right little British bulldog the man is.

'Listen Reg,' says I in my best Shelley voice. You know the one – hard but with a touch of understanding. 'She's not there, Reg. She's probably at The Lady Bar. Let's go looking for her there.'

Reg stared at me with the glassy eyes of a drunk. You can always see when they are trying really hard to focus but can't make it somehow. The brain is too full of the beer to handle something incredibly difficult like focussing the old eyes.

He swayed a little closer to me. 'I shud ca. Just a proz.'

'What's that, Reg? I can't hear you.'

He moved even closer and drunkenly placed his hand on my shoulder. I knocked it away. I'm having nobody touch me like that even if he is a mate. He leant in even closer. I could see him really concentrating on what he was going to say.

'I said, I shouldn't care.' His mouth moved around the letters like one of the old brewery horses munching on a bag of oats. 'Just a prozzie.'

With those words, he shuffled back against the wall of the shophouse and started crying. Big, breath-heaving sobs came from him. He slid down the wall and sat there.

'Pull yourself together Reg. Come on, be a man.' I pulled him back to his feet and pushed him against the wall. I can't stand it when men go like this. No point in it. He was going to get a kicking soon unless he watched himself. I'm having no bleeding pansies in my outfit.

I slapped him a couple of times to bring him to his senses. It seemed to work because his eyes became suddenly clearer and he stopped swaying.

And then, in a voice as clear as a graveyard, he said, 'I want go home. I want to go home to Margie and the kids and Stockport and my family and the Trams and United and Belle Vue and Sunday lunches and the pub and my vegetables.'

His voice trailed off. Myself and Larkin looked at each other. The next minute we hear him snoring. The bugger had fallen asleep on the six-foot way outside the shophouse.

'Come on, let's get him back to camp. We're not going to hear any more from this nightingale tonight.' I heaved him on to my shoulders and started walking down the street. Bound to find a fuckin' taxi somewhere in this shite hole of a city.

*

Richard Longhurst

My heart isn't in it any more. Oh sure, I go through the motions. I wear their uniform. I do guard duty. I salute them and say 'Yes sir, three bags full, sir, anything you say, sir.' But my heart, my soul isn't in it anymore.

I'm just an empty squaddie.. A ghost in a khaki uniform. The only time I'm really alive is when I'm with Owens or when I go into town to walk around on my own.

Last week, I walked along the Singapore River, past Andersen Bridge and the godowns lining the waterway.

All around me was the hustle and bustle of activity. Rubber being loaded. Planks of wood being stacked. Bales of cotton being shifted. Machinery whirring. And always, the sound of bare feet against the pavement.

Somehow, I've come to love the smell of the river. Its sharp odours of dying fish, old durian, human waste and above all, the smell of money. You can see the fat Taipans in their white suits sweating as they tell the wrinkled coolies what to do.

I love to see them sweat.

I walked down the river, alone as usual, nobody paying me any attention at all, when I came across this crowd of people.

I pushed to the front and, at its centre, was an old, blind man. He was talking in a quiet almost whispering voice, the sounds going up and down as he played with the melody of his story.

In his right hand, he held a hollow bamboo tube which he could occasionally bang on the pavement to emphasise some important point or to signal a change in character.

I didn't understand a word he said, but I could follow his story and be entranced by the sound of his voice. It was like music without lyrics, without a melody, and without any chorus.

I looked around at the assembled faces. The children were sat at the storyteller's feet, the men stood with their arms folded, straining to hear every word, leaning forward, afraid to miss a sentence.

Occasionally, the crowd would laugh out loud. The storyteller must have told a joke or passed a witty remark. I never understood. I wasn't supposed to understand.

After about ten minutes, a young boy came around holding a red tin up. He jingled it in front of the watchers' faces, hoping to shame them into giving some money.

Most gave something. Some walked off before he got to them, their meanness ensuring they didn't hear the rest of the story.

Then, he passed in front of me, waving his cup in my face. I thought about waving him on. But then, I realised my entertainment had been watching the old man, looking at the crowd, seeing the smiles on their faces.

I dug into the pockets of my shorts and brought out two ten cents which I dropped into the boy's cup.

'Thank you, guv' nor,' he said with a broad London accent.

'Where did you learn English?' I asked him.

He shrugged his shoulders, not understanding a word I had said to him.

I looked into his face as he shook his cup at another listener.

The blind storyteller continued telling his story. I didn't understand a word. And yet somehow, that afternoon, I felt I understood everything.

*

Reg Dwyer
Block 15, Tanglin Barracks, Singapore

23 August, 1941

Dear Marjorie,

Well, I've been here nearly three years now. Three years away from you and Tommy and Evelyn and baby Grace. I've never seen baby Grace. I bet she's not even a baby anymore!!

I miss you all so much. You know, they say the army is one big family but it's not really. I'm not knocking my pals like Lanky, Larkin, Teale, O'Neill and even Eddie, but they are not a family. They can't give you love when you need it or let you cry on their shoulder or give you a big hug and tell you to cheer up.

Anyway, enough of me going on, it doesn't help me or you. Life goes on here in much the same way as it always does. There's a lot more troops here now but everywhere else, everything carries on. It's because Singapore produces all the war stuff England needs to carry the fight to the Germans. That's what Larkin says anyway. I'm not sure if he knows nowt though.

But you should see some of the carrying on. People drinking and dancing like there was no tomorrow. Nothing is rationed here. You can go down to Cold Storage and buy anything you want. Beef, eggs, chicken even whiskey are all on the shelves. Not that I go down there and buy anything mind you, me being broke most of the time. But sometimes, it's good to wander around and look at everything.

It must be hard for you in Stockport what with the rationing and the bombing. That butcher seems a real so and so to you now. Shame as he was so kind before, not giving you an extra bit of pork when you wanted it. Why did he change all of a sudden? I hope our Harry hasn't put the kibosh on it.

Time to go now dear heart. One last message before I sign off.

I love you and the kids. There I've said it. But I think you've always known it haven't you Margie?

Best regards

Reg

Censored by Lt. L. Whitehead

*

Richard Longhurst

It was Larkin who started it all of course. We were all lying as you do in our bunks one Sunday afternoon. I was reading *War and Peace*,

214

wondering when I would eventually get to the end of the bloody thing. Reg was doing Eddie's uniform for him. He's a lovely ironer is Reg. He's even put the dhobiwallahs out of business. Always after a few extra bob is our Reg. Eddie is still on his bed, staring at the ceiling. He's been in a strange mood for the last few days, I wonder what's eating him. Larkin was polishing his boots. Spitting and rubbing. Spitting some more and rubbing some more.

I watched him over the top of my book as he suddenly stopped and said, 'Let's go down to Happy World. We haven't been there for ages.'

Teale, always the dancer, piped up, 'I could give number 23 a spin. Got a lovely pair of legs on the dance floor she has.'

Reg whined, 'But I'm broke lads. We don't get paid until next Friday.'

I needed to get them out of here. 'Don't worry Reg, I'll lend you something.'

Eddie was silent.

'So we're off then?' asked Larkin, looking in Eddie's direction.

He took his time, enjoying the decision for the evening, enjoying making the others wait. Finally, he swung his legs off his bunk and slipped his feet into his shiny boots (courtesy of Reg). 'Time we got ourselves ready lads. Time for the 4Fs. Time for a bit of fun.' He looked at his watch, 'Time to get a fucking move on,' he shouted.

There was a scurry of activity in the hut. Larkin and Teale rushing around like blue-arsed flies, Eddie getting himself ready slowly and meticulously as usual. Me, I lay on my bed, watching them all.

Reg's shadow loomed between myself and the light. 'You're sure you're okay to lend me a few dollars, Lanky?'

'No worries, Reg, I'm not going so it's alright.'

'Not going? But you have to come. Who's going to look after me?'

'You'll do fine Reg.'

'But you know me and the tarts, Lanky…,'

'What's that?' Eddie joined Reg to loom over my bed. 'My little brother isn't coming when all his mates are going out on the town?' He turned to the rest of the hut and shouted, 'Hear that lads? Richard isn't coming out to play tonight. Too good for his mates is Mister-High-and-Mighty Richard Longhurst.'

He snatched the book lying across my chest. 'War and fucking Peace. I'll give you War and fucking Peace.' He flung the book to the far end of the hut where it slammed into the wall, dropping down as dead as a corpse to the floor.

I looked at it lying there. And then I looked back at Eddie standing over me, a smug smile on his face. 'Good riddance to bad rubbish,' he said with the same smile playing across his lips.

I could feel the anger welling up in me. It sort of started as a tightness in my chest, surging upwards to a clench of the jaw. The next thing I was on top of Eddie, my legs straddling his chest, hitting down with all the force I could.

He threw his arms up to protect himself but I could feel my punches hitting the top of his head. God, it was a glorious feeling as I sat there and hit and hit and hit and hit.

One moment I was punching him, one after the other, the next I had stopped. I don't know why. It was like all the anger and bitterness and hatred had suddenly left me. I sat there on top of him, seeing his arms cover his head from the blows no longer raining down on him.

Then I felt a knee in my back and I was flying toward the door. Eddie quickly got to his feet. He had blood streaming down his face from a cut to his left eye. He wiped it away with his hand, looking at the smear of red across his fingers and palm.

'So you want another round, do you? Come on my little brother…' He raised his fists and crouched down into a boxer's stance. 'Come on, come on.' He prowled around me as I lay on the floor like a tiger circling his prey. 'Come on, come on…,'

I got slowly to my feet, feeling the redness of my knuckles, and looked around. Larkin was standing open mouthed. Teale had a wide grin on his face, enjoying the blood sport. Mytholmroyd was pretending this wasn't happening. Only Reg said anything, 'Come on, lads, time to go down to Happy World. Time to be happy, hey?'

Eddie kept on staring at me, circling me with his crabby boxer's shuffle.

I saw the book lying there across the barracks. Its white pages kissing the dirty wooden floor. Its spine broken, bent awkwardly backwards. Its white cover hanging loose like a shroud.

I launched myself at Eddie, trying to get on top of him again. But he was ready for me this time. I caught the edge of his tunic but he was on my right side now. I felt the fist hit the top of my head but there was no pain. See, you bastard, you can't hurt me anymore. I know there were more punches coming in but I didn't feel anything. I held on to his tunic as he hit me. Grabbing and holding on. More punches thumped into my body now. I heard the air leaving my lungs and it felt as if my throat had suddenly lost the power to swallow air. Then another punch on the top of my head and I was falling backwards.

I saw Eddie's face, the blood still streaming down from above his eye. I saw Reg with his mouth open. I saw the fan turning slowly as it disturbed the hot afternoon air. I could see the motes of dust, speckling in the light as they floated around looking for somewhere to land.

And then I was on my back, on the floor.

Reg told me later I was out for about ten minutes. They dragged Eddie away from me – it took five of them to do it. Reg lifted me on my bed, put a cold compress on my forehead and then they all went to Happy World, leaving me lying there.

I could understand why they went of course. Better to get Eddie out of the barracks in case he decided to finish me. At least, that was Reg's thinking. They even had another fight that night. Well, Eddie did. He took on five of the Indian jagas guarding the place. He ended up getting beaten badly and they carried him back to the barracks.

Now both of us are lying here. But, it's over for me. The army, Eddie and all the rest of the bullshit can go fuck themselves.

Chapter 20

Eddie Longhurst

We ain't family no more.

The only family I have is the army. They are the ones who look after me. They are the ones who I care about. They are the ones who care about me. They say blood's thicker than water, but I think it's a load of bollocks. Blood's just blood. It's red and sticky and if you cut yourself you bleed.

That's all. That's all the fuck it is.

I'd always known me and Richard were different. I mean, for fuck's sake, we even look different. He's tall and thin and I'm short and chunky. How can we be real brothers? My mam never said owt of course but she dropped a few hints now and then about seeing some office fella when da was away before the cancer got him.

It was him lying there on his bunk, reading his fucking book and looking so smug. Fucking books, who need fucking books? Burn the fucking lot of them. Take a couple of mattresses, douse them with petrol and then lay all the fucking books in Singapore on top of them. A box of Swan Vestas and bob's your uncle. Just a pile of ash and a lot of black smoke is all they are.

No more words. No more reading. No more education. Who needs all that fucking shite?

He had a good go at me though, I'll give him that. Nearly gave me a pasting did Richard. But he's a soft shit, he had his chance and should have taken it. I would have done.

When I'm on top banging hell out of some tosser, I don't let up till he's fucked up. No point in being kind about it. You don't want the bastard coming back for seconds, do you? If you don't give him a real kicking, he's going to think you're soft like Richard and come back for more. But if you really hurt him, and I mean really hurt him, he's going to think twice about having a second go, isn't he. It's the law of the fucking jungle.

I was so worked up, I even had a go at those Indian jagas. A bit stupid I know. But I gave as good as I got and there's at least one of them who won't be giving his misses a seeing to for the next couple of weeks. Reg and his shiny boots worked a treat. I have to take it easy for the next few days though, the body's a bit fucked. All part of the game, isn't it? You give a few and you take a few. You just hope you give more than you take.

Richard's ignoring me now. Not looking at me, not speaking to me. He'll come round though, he always does. And if he doesn't, who gives a fuck.

Not me. Never me.

*

Reg Dwyer
Block 15, Tanglin Barracks, Singapore
October 30, 1941
My Margie,
I don't know what to say right now but it looks like the war is coming to us. According to The Straits Times, the Japs are getting closer to the Empire. But don't worry, me and the lads will see those little blighters off. Some of the other regiments
XXXXXXXXXXXXXXXXXXXXXXXXXXXXXXXXXXXXXXXXXXXXXXX
XXXXXXXXXXXXXXXXXXXXXXXXXXXXXXXXXXXXXXXXXXXXXXX
XXXXXXXXXXXXXXXXXXXXX.But those newspaper Johnnies are always war mongering. I'm sure it's not going to happen at all. More likely, we'll be transferred homeXXXXXXXXXXXXXXXXXXXXXXXXXXXXXXXXXXXXXXXXXXXXXX
XXXXXXXXXXXXXXXXXXXX At least, if we go there I could be close to you and the kids.
.XXXXXXXXXXXXXXXXXXXXXXXXXXXXXXXXXXXXXXXXXXXXXX
XXXXXXXXXXXXXXXXXXXXXXXXXXXXXXXXXXXXXXXXXXXXXXX
XXXXXXXXXXXXXXXXXXXXXXXXXXXXXXXXXXXXXXXXXXXXXXX
XXXXXXXXXXXXXXXXXXXXXXXXXXXXXXXXXXXXXXXXXXXXXXX
XXXXXXXXXXXXXXXXXXXXXXXXXXXXXXXXXXXXXXXXXXXXXXX
XXXXXXXXXXXXXXXXXXXXXXXXXXXXXXXXXXXXXXXXXXXXXXX
XXXXXXXXXXXXXXXXXXXXXXXXXXXXXXXXXXXXXXXXXXXXXXX
. So there you have it. Fine men the Aussies and so healthy. Maybe we should think about moving there when this war is over. It would be a great place for the kids to grow up and the weather is much better than soggy old Stockport.

And don't you worry your little head about me, if it all comes to fighting, which I don't think it will, there ain't no flies on Reginald Dwyer. I know how to keep my head down and out of trouble. I've already sorted out a new job for myself. I'm to be batman for XXXXXXXXX. A batman is a sort of personal servant. It's a really cushy number and I don't mind doing it. Funny though, how you said I was such a messy bugger, pardon my French. Now here I am clearing and tidying up after an officer. The army really is a funny place.

Give my love to the kids and give yourself a specially big hug. You know how much I miss you.

Your husband,

Reg

PS. Dig for Victory. Is that the excuse David Endersby said when he took over the allotment? Tell him I'll dig him for Victory when I get back. And make sure he at least gives you something from it.

Censored by Major R. Tudor.

*

Eddie Longhurst

I've made it. Finally fuckin' made it.

Major Tudor called me into his office this morning before he went off for his tiffin and his nap. I thought I was for the high jump. Maybe word had got back to him of my little set-to with Richard. There are so many fucking tittle tattles in this place, all trying to worm their way in to the good books of the officers.

I was preparing my excuses as myself and Shelley marched over to the command building. 'Stress brought about by heat' popped into my mind. Or 'it was nothing sir, an argument between brothers.'

Nah, that wouldn't wash. He would simply say 'A non-commissioned officer should never use violence against an enlisted man' in that fruity voice of his and I would lose my stripes.

Bastard.

We passed in front of the command building. A few of the officers were enjoying their golf on the small course next to Holland Road. I can't see the point myself. Chasing a wee ball round a field. I mean it's not even exercise, is it? You wouldn't get me wasting my fuckin' time.

Then I had it. 'It was more than I could bear, sir, when he attacked the good name of the regiment.' That was it. Perfect. The old fool couldn't argue any more. He couldn't put me on a charge for defending the regiment. All I'd get was a little slap on the wrist and told not to do it again, naughty boy.

Shelley knocked on the door of Tudor's office. We heard a shuffling of papers and the scraping of a chair followed by 'Enter' delivered in the same old voice.

We marched sharply in, snapped a stiff salute and stood at attention. Tudor loved all that bollocks. A proper stickler for the 'correct' way of doing things was our major. I'm sure he lay in bed at night with the missus instructing her on the proper way to fuck.

I saw his missus once at one of the regiment's garden parties for officers and NCOs. Arse like the back end of a Salford bus she had, all squashed into a brown, stretched dress. It looked like a sack of spuds with a head and two legs.

Rather him than me. Rather fuckin' him than me.

'At ease, men,' he drawled, pretending to scan the papers in front of him.

We both did the correct army at ease; legs spread by eleven inches, arms crossed left over right behind the back, eyes looking slightly up. Of course, this isn't 'at ease' at all. It's just a different form of attention. If I really wanted to be at ease I would sit in the armchair in the corner with my legs stretched out smoking a fag. I looked across there and knew what Tudor had been doing before we marched in.

'Listen up both of you,' he spoke directly into his papers, never looking up at myself or at Shelley. 'We've been sending some men back to Blighty to help form new Manchester battalions there.'

My heart jumped. This was it. Myself and Shelley were going back to England to do some real fighting. About bloody time too. Finally, the army was doing something sensible. Thank fuck for that.

'The colonel suggested you two should be in the next party going back, leaving on...,' he reached over to another page and scanned it with his finger. I watched his lips move as he read the dates. '...leaving on Wednesday, no, the 8th November, a Thursday, isn't it?'

For the first time, he looked up at both of us and gave a hesitant smile. I couldn't see much of his lips or teeth beneath the mustache, but I think it was a smile anyway. Not that I saw Major Tudor smile much. Come to think of it, I didn't ever see much of him.

'Anyway, it doesn't matter because I've put the kibosh on it. I'm sure you are both glad to hear it. You two are much too valuable to me here, helping me run the show. Plus the Japs are getting a mite frisky at the moment. God knows what the little men might do.' He tugged at his mustache, stroking the hair from the outside end of his lips to the point beneath his nose and then pinching the lip.

'Permission to speak, sir?' This was Shelley at his most formal. 'We'd like to do some real fighting, sir, not stuck out here in Singapore, sir.'

'I'm sure you would, Serjeant, however, as I have said, you are far too valuable to me here at the moment. And if like me, you had spent your formative years in the trenches, you would know the best thing to do with war is avoid it.' Again, he stroked his mustache. 'No, I've called you here because the men going back to Blighty have left us short of a few NCOs, damn inconsiderate of them, so Shelley here has been recommending you get promoted to Lance Serjeant, Longhurst.

I glanced across at Shelley. He was still staring eyes front at the green wall. 'Thank you sir, I won't let you down.'

'I'm sure you won't, Lance Serjeant.' He looked across at Shelley. 'Serjeant Shelley here has assured me, haven't you, Serjeant?'

Shelley continued to stare at the green wall in front of him.

He touched the paper in front of him with his index finger. 'It says here you have a brother in 13 Platoon. Damn awkward dealing with family members. Don't I know it, Ethel's uncles have been a constant source of trouble to me for years.' He suddenly shivered as if a thousand squaddies had just marched down his spine, 'can't have that, can we? We'll transfer your brother to HQ company. They need some new bodies there.' He paused for a moment and looked up at both of us for the second time.

I could feel Shelley wanted to speak, to try one more time to get back to England, but he didn't.

'Well, jolly good. That's all. Dismiss.'

We saluted smartly once more, turned and marched out of the green-walled office.

I was serjeant at last. About bloody time too.

*

Richard Longhurst

They moved me to Headquarters Company. I wasn't surprised when the orders came through. After the fight with Eddie, nothing was ever

222

going to be the same again. The next morning, Reg took me down to the duty nurse and told her I had fallen into a drain. I almost believed him myself, so convincing was Reg.

I'm not sure she did though. But she was Army too and it's always best not to ask too many questions. You never knew what you had to do with the answers. That was the army way. If you knew nothing, you didn't have to do nothing.

And nobody got reprimanded for doing nothing.

She patched me up and ordered me to spend two days in the camp infirmary. I had a quiet time there – clean sheets, hot food and none of the barrack smells of sweaty feet and rotting underwear. Two days of peace and quiet and rest. Reg came and brought me some books.

'I thought you would be needing these. Can't make head nor tail of them myself. But I brought a couple from your locker. I hope you like them. You had so many in there I didn't know which to choose.'

I looked down at the books. One of them was the copy of *War and Peace* Eddie had thrown against the wall. The spine had been bound and strengthened with sticky tape and the pages which had fallen out were stuck back inside. I saw they weren't in the right order but it didn't matter. 'Thanks Reg, they're great.'

'Larkin sent these.' From behind his back, he produced the biggest bunch of grapes I had ever seen. 'He nicked them from Cold Storage, the other day. They were a bigger bunch but you know Larkin, couldn't resist trying a few, just for sweetness like.'

'Thanks Reg, and thank Larkin for me.' I was going to say 'Thank Tommy for me,' but it didn't feel right. Nobody called him 'Tommy'. I'm sure even his mother knew him as 'Larkin'.

'The nurse tells me you're getting out in a couple of days.' Reg paused here and I could see him thinking, trying to form the words in his head before he formed them with his mouth. 'It'll be good to have you back but don't keep it up…,'

'Keep what up, Reg?'

'You know, it…the thing with you and Eddie. It's not worth it.'

I kept silent.

'Well, I've got to go now. We're off to see *Four Feathers* at the Capitol. It's got air-conditioning, so you don't sweat as much see, even if the film is real hot stuff.'

'Bye Reg, I'll see you soon.'

The transfer orders were waiting for me when I got back to Block 15. Off to HQ company. I'll miss the lads though.

Life is a bit of a doddle here. We get bits of paper in, shuffle them about and send them out again. The Serjeant, Hanlon was his name, was an old army regular who was nearing the end of a successful career doing nothing.

'Keep your head down here lad. Cover your arse and make sure all the officers get their tea and toast in the morning. If anything is marked urgent, you put it here, we'll get round to it eventually. If it's marked secret, you bring it to me so I can take a quick shufti and decide whether it's worth passing on. And, never, never, give anybody anything after 3 o'clock. Always put it here, so they can deal with it the following morning. All clear?'

I nodded.

'Good. You look a bright lad. We've got a nice cushy number here so don't fuck it up. Anything, you don't understand, pass to me, ok?'

I nodded again.

'Right, there's your desk. Get yourself a cup of tea and park your bum. Nothing will come in till 11 o'clock so you can relax till then. I'm off down the Naafi so hold the fort till I get back. If anybody asks, I'm checking stores, ok? None of them ever want to go down there. See you around eleven.'

I got myself a tea and some biscuits, custard creams, only the best for our Lords and Masters, sat down at my desk and took out *War and Peace*. At least, I would have plenty of time to read now.

BOOK THREE

Chapter 21

Reg Dwyer

Block 15, Tanglin Barracks, Singapore

9th December, 1941

My dearest Margie,

Well, dear, it looks like the war has finally started now. Last night,
xxxxxxxxxxxxxxxxxxxxxxxxxxxxxxxxxxxxxxxxxxxxxxxxxxxxxxxxxxxxxxxxxx
XXXXXXXXXXXXXX Anyway, I'll look after myself, don't you worry.
There ain't no flies on Reg Dwyer.

How are Tommy, Evelyn and young Grace? Give them all a big hug
from me. I know what you mean when you say they can be a handful but
remember Margie, you're only a kid once. And what with the war and
all, we want to make sure they grow up well, don't we? So don't be too
strict with them, for my sake, please.

Obviously, I can't tell you what's happening or where we're going, the
censors will have a fit, but I'm sure the generals know what they are
doing and soon we'll push the little Japs all the way to Japland.

You told me Bert Henderson had finally joined up. About bloody time
too. He'd been skiving off down the pub whilst the rest of us have been
out here defending the Empire. Pity about his wife being pregnant
though. Women need a man around at times like this. I remember how
much you needed me to fetch and carry for you. And when you wanted
black pudding one Sunday night, well, do you know how difficult it was
to get it?

This is a short letter now. We've got to go. Say hello to Mr. Brown the
butcher for me and say thank you for the bit of lamb he got for you and
the kids. I'm sure they enjoyed their day out to Blackpool with him. He
does seem a really nice man.

Got to go now. I miss you Margie. And I miss the kids. Give everyone a
big hug for me.

Your one and only,

Reg

Censored by Lt. Whitehead.

*

Michael O'Neill

Well, the lad is back. After a short stay at his Majesty's pleasure, I have returned. But why His Majesty could give a two penny toss about me staying in one of his guesthouses is a wonder to me. Keeps the old bugger happy I guess.

None of the others understand. I think Richard guesses but I'm not certain. I might let him know one day, seeing as how we're together all the time. I probably will have to tell him about my mission. He might get in the way or hold me back in some manner. So I'll have to tell him that I will.

They came to me in the gaol they did. Two of them, both officers, both dressed like real officers, none of them part-time soldiers you see poncing into Raffles.

'O'Neill,' they said, 'O'Neill, your country needs you.'

'Ireland,' I said, 'what does Ireland need from me?'

'No, no, no, not Ireland, England, your home. You're a soldier of the King, remember, an Empire soldier.' I kept quiet. You learn a lot at his Majesty's pleasure and one of the things you learn is to keep quiet when the spalpeens talk to you about being a soldier of the fecking King.

'Now, O'Neill, you can either be a hero and save the Empire or you can sit and rot in here for the rest of your God-given days.'

I still kept quiet.

'Do you understand what he's saying to you?' the taller, older one interrupted.

They want me to be a hero. At last, somebody recognises me for who I am. They want me to save the Empire. At last they realise I'm the only one who can do it. I've always known it but at last they've admitted it. Hollywood will have to wait, I've to be a hero first. And anyway, it's always best to go to Hollywood with a few medals on your chest. Adds to the authenticity, sure it does.

'I'll be happy to save the Empire,' says I.

Your man jumps us and claps me on the back saying, 'Good man, good man.'

'But after I've saved the Empire, I'll have to go to Hollywood to teach that fellow Errol Flynn how to act. Is it a deal?'

The older one's mustache quivered and he went bright red but it was the younger one who spoke. 'We'll talk about that later. Now you should return to your unit Private O'Neill.'

I snapped to attention and gave him my best salute.

'Good man, good man,' the younger captain said leaving my cell.

'Yes sir, you can count on me to save the Empire.'

'Good man, good man,' he said knocking on the cell next door. But he won't get anywhere with that fool. Sure he's mad he is. As mad as yesterday.

*

Reg Dwyer

I met some Aussies last night. A right bunch of lads they were. Full of themselves and how they were going to give the Japs a roasting.

'Have another coldie, mate.'

'Sure Gary, pale ale for me.'

Even the names are different: Paul, Gary, Bruce, Slimo, Whitey, Goggles. I met them down at the Handle Bar on Anson Road. Me and Larkin had gone there to get away from the camp and all the lazy buggers moping around.

Also, there might have been a chance of seeing Desiree. I know what you're going to say before you say it. I'm a soft bugger for getting mixed up with her. Daft as a brush she is. But I can't help myself. Margie's miles away and despite what the others say, Desiree is a really sweet girl beneath it all. And I heard on the grapevine she's not seeing the bloke from the Loyals anymore.

But she wasn't there. The mama-san said she'd just left. Story of my life really. Just missing out on something.

We were sitting at the bar, me and Larkin, when the Aussies strolled in. He'd been yakking on as he always does and I'd been pretending to listen as you do. The Aussie said 'Excuse me, mate,' and tapped me on the shoulder, 'but do you know where a feller can get a fuck around here?'

Bruce his name was and he'd been stuck on a ship sailing round Australia for the last three weeks.

'I could shag a sheep right now. Don't suppose you know where I could find one, mate.'

Of course I didn't know anything about sheep but I gave him a quick tour of Singapore: Lavender Street and Beauty World and Stamford Road and Queen's Road and Middle Road and the Chinese places on Bukit Pasoh and the Japanese whorehouses around Middle Road. Not forgetting Anson Road of course. How could I forget Anson Road and dear little Desiree?

'Hang on mate, hang on. I just want to shag one Sheila not a whole fucking army of them.'

'Alright then, I'd head down to The Lady Bar on Lavender Street if I was you. It's always full of nice girls.'

'But not too nice, hey. Do you fancy a coldie, mate?'

I like these Aussies, they don't mess you around like other people. They're straightforward, direct sort of blokes.

Lord, we drank a few that night and then went off to the Club. Desiree wasn't there either so I just got drunk.

I miss Desiree.

I miss Margie.

I miss my kids.

I miss home.

*

Richard Longhurst

I was sitting, having a cigarette with O'Neill when we heard the news.

'The bastards have sunk The Repulse and The Prince of Wales.' It was Larkin doing his impression of a headless chicken as usual.

'Bollocks ye gobshite, they couldn't have done.'

'Heard it myself on the radio.'

'Fuck off, it's just Jap propaganda.'

But it wasn't, it was true. We found out later from the paper. 'Over 2,000 naval survivors – official,' said the headline. It was only when we read more did we learn the two ships had been sunk.

'Jaysus,' said O'Neill, 'sure didn't we only watch your men sail out a few days ago with their flags flying, the sailors cheering and those big guns pointing toward the sky.'

The article said the ships had been sunk yesterday somewhere off Malaya.

'The bastards don't even know where the fucking ships were sunk,' shouted Larkin.

'No, Larkin, it's put like that so as not to reveal the position to the enemy.'

'But don't the enemy know where they are? After all, they have just sunk the bloody things.'

It was never worth arguing with Larkin. So I carried on reading *The Straits Times*. Maybe I could find out what had happened.

'Jaysus, though, it's a bad day. And don't you be reading that poxy rag. Wasn't it there that we heard the Japs were so blind they couldn't even fly. Mind you, those ships were so big even a squinty-eyed Jap could hardly miss them. You know, back home in Ireland we had this feller as blind as a Englishman called Desmond McCartney. Couldn't see a thing, kept tripping up all the time, covered in bruises from head to toe your man was. But you put a shotgun in his hands and he was a changed feller. Always be able to get a few rabbits or pigeons for the pot. Never missed he didn't. Never missed a shot. And when the fair came around, Jaysus, didn't he go on and win every fucking teddy bear, goldfish and picture of the Virgin Mary the poor gyppos had.'

I let O'Neill ramble on to himself, occasionally nodding my head or grunting with approval. The article still lay in my hands. Two ships dead in the water. What was going to happen to us now?

*

Eddie Longhurst

Looking out over the bloody sea again. Water every fucking where. The waves coming in one by one by one by one. On and on and on.

No more barracks now. No more canteen. No more film shows. No more beer. No more drills. This is it. This is real. This is what we are paid to do. This is what we are meant to do. Everybody is up for it.

It was another bloody mess moving us out here. You would think the army had learnt its lesson over the years. But not a bit of it. There wasn't any transport as usual so we stole a truck from the engineers. Gave it back of course. Major Tudor was in a right blue funk when he found out.

'It's just not cricket, Shelley.'

'But sir, we needed to move the men, the lights and the generators out to the beach. How were we going to do it without transport?'

'Find a way, Serjeant. That's your job. But don't steal other units' equipment.'

'They weren't using it, sir. And anyway, we didn't steal it, just borrowed it. The keys were even in the ignition...,'

'Whatever, Serjeant. Now their CO has complained to our CO and he needs me to write a complete explanation before 4 pm this afternoon. It means I shall have to miss the bridge game at Colonel Devlin's. What a bother.'

Shelley shrugged his shoulders like he does. He had found a way to get us out here. With all the Vickers and the Lloyd lights and the generators and the ammo and the grub and even a few bottles of Scotch to keep us warm on the long nights looking out at the sea. That's Shelley for you. Always does his job.

The other serjeants haven't been as lucky though. Yesterday, their mess was bombed out at Changi. Poor bleeders were just sitting down to a hot lunch in the tent when along comes this Jap bomber and blows the fucking lot of them up.

Two or three died I think. Our first casualties. Our first blood spilt.

The lads thought some fifth columnist had signaled the Japs to show them where the mess tent was. After all, it had just been put up a few days ago. But I told them that was a load of bollocks. Those serjeants, their time was up. Nothing you could do about it.

So, we sit here in our pillbox, looking out across the wire at the waves.

The beach we had spent preparing for the last two years stretched in front of us. We've got the fields of fire calibrated. The range of the guns is set at 400 yards. We've got enough ammo for the Vickers to last us into the next century. Even the Lloyd light and its fucking generator is working.

All we need now is the Japs. We know they are out there. It seems strange to me that here we are staring out at the open sea when the Japs are behind us in Malaya. But mine is not to reason why. The brass must know what they're doing.

I hope the Japs come here.

I sometimes dream of my finger pressing hard on the Vickers feeling the recoil of the machine gun through my shoulders. Hearing the chatter of the bullets. Smelling the rich, loving scent of the cordite. Seeing the Jap bodies fall at my feet like wheat mown in summer.

RSM Whatmough talked to us once about the Great War. 'It were beautiful boy, these long lines of Germans advancing toward us. Me at my Maxim, waiting, waiting, waiting, and then it began. And you know, it wasn't really me behind that gun but some avenging angel scything through their bodies, doing the Lord's work. They went down never to rise again, like our boys had done on the first day of the Somme. That was a day for the regiment. 800 went out and only 150 returned. Proud day, men, a proud day.'

I want to feel that power, that pride.

I hope the Japanese come today.

Please let them come.

Please.

*

Richard Longhurst

It's strange how dead bodies don't look like people.

I know they were once full of lusts, tears, love, hate and despair. Now they are twisted rags of clothes, discarded like some child's doll.

The ARP men had formed long lines to remove the piles of debris engulfing the shop house. Searching for life, finding only more dead bodies. A young child here. A broken woman there.

Overhead, the sirens wailed yet again, heralding another bombing raid. The ARP wardens simply stood still for a few seconds, gazing up into the sky, shielding their eyes from the sun. Then it was back to work again, searching for the still living, listening for breath, fighting for life.

I lit another cigarette and leant back on the open door of the three-tonner. We were at the corner of Middle Road, where, before the war, (how strange to think of a time before the war), we had gone shopping, all of us, searching for bargains in the Japanese shophouses lining the road.

Now, the ARP searched for life in the same intense manner we had once burrowed deep into the oddments bins for cheap socks and shirts.

I can't remember a time before war. That was another life, a lazy, past life. War is the only thing existing now. The terrible beauty of war.

And beautiful it is too. Just as the wings of a butterfly are beautiful, with the sharp colours blended into each other by the hand of some unknown god. So this war has its colours, its sounds, its smells created by the unknown hand of some man far above us in his flying machine.

I sat there, smoking my cigarette as the roasting smell of flesh, cordite and wood barbecuing together assaulted my nostrils. I could see six once-people laid out before me. An old couple who will age no more. Two young children who will cry no more. A man and his wife holding hands in death, her dress obscenely torn.

An ARP warden came over and looked at the young couple. Slowly, he covered her face with his jacket. Then he walked away again to rejoin the line

I see O'Neill gliding in on my left eating a sandwich. 'There's nothing to be done here, Richard my lad. It's time we were off to win this war,' he said between mouthfuls of bread and egg.

I just looked at him.

*

Reg Dwyer

'I think we'll listen to Frenesi now, Dwyer.'

'Yes, sir.' I picked up Artie Shaw and his Orchestra and laid him down in the turntable. I worked the handle until the speed was right and lowered the needle.

Instantly, the tent filled with the clarinets and trumpets of the man himself.

Major Tudor was sat in his armchair drinking tea. Of course, he was wearing his tin hat but other than that it was exactly like any other deployment at Changi.

The fact that the Japs had invaded Malaysia; we could hear the bombers going over in tight formations of 18 or 27 planes, and we were supposed to be in a state of war, never seemed to affect us here.

Even when one of the bombers blew up the Serjeants' mess in Changi, we didn't change what we did much. Major Tudor ordered more camouflage netting for his position but that was about it.

I'd landed this cushy number as batman and runner for Major Tudor to the forward defences on the beaches. But as the radio wasn't working again, we had to rely on written messages from the regiment to know what was going on.

Major Tudor didn't seem to mind though. 'Jolly decent cup of tea, Dwyer.'

'Thank you, sir.'

'You'd better be off and check the posts. Tell everyone to sit tight until we get orders.'

'Yes sir.'

I stepped out into a beautiful Singapore day. In the distance, I heard the screams of children and the raucous crows of their scrawny chickens from a village of Malay huts.

I ran off in the direction of the beach posts. I did take this running job seriously you see, even though after a hundred yards .

I was huffing and puffing and sweating worse than an old steam train.

But as long as Major Tudor was watching I thought I had better keep it up. As soon as I got out of sight I'd stop for a smoke.

Don't want to hurry too much. It wouldn't be right.

*

Eddie Longhurst

Thank fucking Christ. At last, I'm actually going to be doing something.

Yesterday, Serjeant Shelley came to the platoon asking for volunteers to escort trucks up to Malaysia.

I know you're not supposed to volunteer for anything in the army but I stepped forward and I was followed by Teale.

'That's the spirit,' was all Shelley said, but I could see he were right chuffed. It meant he could go straight back to Major Tudor and say we had all the men we needed and more.

I can't stand sitting here, watching the sea and waiting for the coconuts to drop. I mean if I don't see another coconut tree for the rest of my life it will be far too soon.

We did have some fun yesterday though. One of the villagers' cows strayed into the camp. We threw a few stones at it to make it run away but the gormless bugger stood there looking at us, batting its long lashes like Anne Sheridan.

Then I remembered our first deployment after O'Neill had killed that man. So I picked up a rifle and shot it right between the eyes. Dropped like a fucking stone it did. And there were hardly any blood just a lovely little .303 hole in the white hair.

Shelley nearly had kittens though. He wanted to know who did it. Of course, nobody shopped me, there's a code in the regiment we all live by. Shelley didn't even expect anybody to squeal but he had to ask the question, didn't he? Just to cover his own arse. Shelley knows how to play the game, he knows the rules.

Anyway, when he'd finished getting no answers, we still had the problem of a load of cow to get rid of. Shelley were magic. 'Take it to the cookhouse,' he said, 'bout time we had a bit of steak.'

So me, Larkin, Teale and Mytholmroyd threw it in the back of one of the three-tonners and took it to Serjeant Flynn.

'What am I supposed to fucking do with this?' he said.

It was Larkin who answered, 'You could try cooking it.'

'But we don't ever touch fresh meat. It all comes in cans.'

'Well, here's your chance,' says I.

'I suppose I could get Sampson to cut it up. He used to be a tanner in Burnley.'

'Tanner? What's that got to do with anything?' said Larkin.

I looked at him and he got the message really quickly. 'Where will we put it?' I asked our cook.

'Oh dump it on the ground next to the spuds. She'll be alright there.'

'Oh yeah, Serjeant Shelley says can you make sure 13 Platoon gets the best steaks. After all we did find it.'

'Sure, tell him to send someone to pick them up this afternoon.' Then I could see a thought go *whirr* in his brain. A thought coming from years of covering his arse and cooking the books. 'One minute, how did this thing die?'

'Tripped up and hit its stupid head, didn't it?'

He nodded his head. The answer had passed his test. He could deny all knowledge of how it died while still enjoying a nice piece of liver for his tea. 'See you this afternoon.' He wiped his hands on his grubby apron, stuck a new fag in his mouth and went back to reconstituting his eggs.

We all grabbed hold of a leg and heaved the cow onto the ground, where it lay dead and forgotten, save by a few thousand flies.

Of course, the owner came looking for it later. We were just finishing the steaks. Best fucking piece of meat I'd ever tasted in my life. Well, at least since the last time we deployed here when the war started. There's something about a good bit of meat and the fresh air. No wonder cowboys in the movies are always eating them. Makes sense now.

This old Malay man walked into camp, shouting, 'Fauziah, Fauziah.' He came over to our platoon and taking off his little hat, asked us, 'Tuan, have you seen a cow? A white cow with horns. She's called Fauziah.'

We all shook our heads, a look of complete innocence on our faces. I cut up my steak and putting a big chunk in my mouth said, 'Yes, I saw a cow down on the beach near the barbed wire.'

I was chewing all the time mind you. The others were pissing themselves.

'Thank you, tuan,' the old man said, hurrying off to the beach in search of Fauziah. Silly chough.

Lovely bit of meat though Fauziah was, a lovely bit of prime steak.

Chapter 22

Richard Longhurst

All the regiment's radios have packed in again. We've known all about this since the first exercise in 1939. Bloody things are useless in this climate. I think the heat and humidity affects the valves so the only sound we hear is static. Not very useful when you're trying to tell HQ we've seen a whole formation of Jap bombers heading straight for the city.

Anyway, the adjutant heard on the grapevine there were some replacement sets available so he told me and O'Neill to get our arses up to Yishun quickly and get those bloody radios before the rest of the army hears about it.

Well, we were too late. We'd driven from Tanglin up past Adam Park and on to Thomson Road. Of course, we'd kept our eyes peeled for any Jap bombers or fighters prowling about. But that day they seemed to be having the afternoon off. Maybe it was the Emperor's birthday or Japanese Christmas or whatever.

O'Neill, of course, was whistling some Irish reel or jig. Around his neck, he wore a purple silk scarf he'd bought at the market. I asked him what it was for but his eyes glazed over and he answered, 'It's for the mission. To help the mission.'

I thought it was something to do with the church. 'Well, don't let the RSM see it or you'll be on a charge.'

'That's ok, it's for the mission,' he repeated and gave me this outrageous wink as if I knew exactly what he was on about.

Silly Irish Mick. You can never tell what he'll do next. Anyway, we were coming down Thomson Road, getting close to the camp when we saw a long line of three-tonners queuing up outside the gates.

'Jaysus, it looks like half the fucking army is after them there radios.'

'We'd better join the queue. Let me off here and I'll go and see what's happening.' I jumped down from the running board of the three-tonner and ran to the front of the camp.

There were about five drivers arguing with this supply Serjeant.

'I know but orders is orders.'

'But don't be a silly prick, man. We're here now and you've got the radios right?'

'Right, but the orders says we can only start issuing them at 0900 hours tomorrow.'

'Get the wee radge to change his fucking mind.' This came from a small Gordon Highlander wearing a kilt.

'Listen chief, if a don't get the radios ma sergeant gonna chop ma balls off.' This was from another Scot to my left. Singapore was full of Jocks now, each one of them eager to prove he was the biggest little swinging dick in the army.

'Orders is orders. Come back at 0900 hours tomorrow.'

'Ooh, away fech yourself.'

It was then we first heard the sound. A drone of an engine, and then another, and another, getting louder and louder. All of us looked up at the sky, searching for the source of the noise.

It was the Scot who spotted them, first.

'Jesus fuck, the bastards are ganging up for a run.'

I looked to where he was pointing. Three small Japanese planes were banking round about a mile away. I could see the round red circles against white painted on the green of their wings. I even imagined I could see the small grinning eyes behind the goggles of the pilot.

Then they flattened out and came straight at us. 'Bastards, shouted the Jock on my left.

I started to run back towards O'Neill and the truck. All around me I could hear shouts and screams as men dived for cover or fought to get out of the comfortable seats of their trucks and into the comforting safety of the ditch.

I ran like I had never run before. I heard the sound of bullets exploding around me.

A scream. A shout. A truck exploding. And then the whine of the engine as a plane passed over me. It almost felt as if I could reach out and touch its undercarriage.

Then more bullets exploding on the ground in front of me. I saw a ditch to my right and dived in there, burying myself deeper, deeper, deeper into the mud.

The two other planes passed over my head. I waited for the crump of the exploding bombs. I waited, waited, waited.

Nothing.

I looked up over the top of the ditch. Seven or eight bodies lay back on the road to the camp gate. I could see the small Gordon Highlander lying in the middle of the road motionless. The supply serjeant was still guarding the gate but now he lay against the wire, his left leg, a tangled mass of bone, sinew and blood, stretched awkwardly beneath him.

I looked down the long line of trucks. One or two were burning, the rest were deserted, their doors thrown open.

The Jap planes were banking round again, coming in for another run.

Then I saw him. He was as cool as an eccles cake. Sitting on the roof of his three-tonner, rifle at his shoulder, aiming at the oncoming Jap planes.

'O'Neill, get the fuck out of there,' I shouted.

He ignored me.

I looked back at the Jap planes. The first one was firing now, its bullets throwing up plumes of dirt to my left .

I looked back at O'Neill. He was calmly working the bolt of his rifle, aiming and then firing. The Jap planes still came on, for some reason, concentrating their fire on the seated O'Neill.

He never flinched. He calmly aimed and fired his Lee Enfield.

Now I know you're not going to believe this. But I watched O'Neill aim and fire at the first Jap plane as it dived towards him. I could see the small explosions of its bullets marching straight at him. And then they stopped. I looked up at the Jap plane. It was past O'Neill now, a plume of black, oily smoke oozing from beneath its wings. A change of note from the engine. It coughed, spluttered and died.

There was a long whine and it hit the ground with a thunderous crash in the middle of the camp. A loud explosion erupted into a fireball soaring high into the sky.

The strong stench of gasoline.

A sweet, sickly smell that will always remind me of death. And then meat burning, and more gasoline, and then a roaring, consuming sound sucking in all the air around it.

I watched as the last two Jap planes flew off into the sun. I don't know why they left, they just did.

I climbed out of my ditch, mud clinging to my uniform, and walked back to where O'Neill was still sitting on top of our three-tonner.

Now the chances of a .303 bringing down a plane flying at over 200 miles per hour are virtually non-existent.

I know it. The army knows it. Every pilot knows it.

Yet, I believe O'Neill shot down the Jap plane that day. I don't know how he did it but he did. When I got back to him he was calmly wiping his face with his purple silk scarf.

'I'm on a mission,' he announced, 'they've asked me to save the Empire.'

I thought he was joking.

But he didn't smile at all. He wiped his face with his scarf and said, 'Sure, there'll be no problem getting the radios now.'

And there wasn't.

*

Eddie Longhurst

What a fucking shambles. Nobody knew where anybody was anymore. We kept getting the same answer, 'Up ahead, up ahead.'

We were carrying a load of anti-tank rifles for the Argylls at Kampar, wherever that is. We weren't given any ammo though, it was following us later.

What good is an anti-tank rifle without ammo?. So myself, Teale and Shelley nicked a few boxes for the Jocks. At least they'll have something to throw at the Japs.

We hadn't gone far into Malaya when we came across a couple of roadblocks. And there was this fucking stupid customs inspector, still in his poncey uniform, asking for our fucking papers.

'What do you mean, you want our papers?' said Shelley.

'Well, this is a state customs post. You have to produce your papers and a customs declaration form when you cross from one state to another,' said our dickhead.

I couldn't believe my ears. Neither could Shelley. 'We're at war. We're in uniform. What more do you fucking want?'

'There's no need to use such language with me, Serjeant. I'm only doing my job.'

'But there's a war. The Japs are up ahead fighting our boys.'

'I am quite aware of that, Serjeant. But civil regulations are clear on this point. All papers must be produced and a customs declaration signed.'

'But we don't have any papers.'

'You're in the army right?'

I wonder what gave him that bleeding idea, seeing as we were in a green three-tonner and all of us were wearing uniform.

'Then your pay books will do. You've all got those, right?'

Again, we nodded and handed them over. He looked through them carefully before handing them back with a polite, 'Thank you Serjeant Shelley, Private Teale and Lance Serjeant Longhurst. Now, if you'll just complete this customs declaration Serjeant Shelley, you can be on your way.'

He produced a form from behind his clipboard, slowly extracting it from the bindings holding it in place.

'Now Serjeant Shelley, are you carrying any livestock, botanical specimens, agricultural produce?'

'We're in the fucking Army not a bleeding sod buster.'

The customs inspector looked at Shelley and then rolled his eyes in exasperation. 'The quicker we fill the form, the quicker you can be on your way. Look, you're creating a traffic jam behind you.'

We looked back at a long line of army lorries, all stopped by the road block. A broad London accent from the truck behind us rang out. 'Getta fackin' move on, mate.'

The customs inspector turned back to look at us again with an I-told-you-so look.

'Now shall we continue?'

Shelley nodded.

'Are you carrying any firearms, explosives, guns or materials that may endanger his Highness' subjects, or realm?'

'We're in the army, of course we are.'

'I'll put that down as a yes. Now, I have to ask you what you are carrying, but I must warn you it's against the Official Secrets Act for you to tell me what's in this truck.'

Shelley let out a long sigh. 'Let me get this right. You have to ask me but I'm not allowed to tell you?'

'That's right.'

'So what do I do?'

'You say I'm not at liberty to reveal that information under the Official Secrets Act of 1923.' He then waved his hand, encouraging Shelley to speak.

From behind us, we heard two loud honks and an even louder, 'Hurry it fucking up, mate.'

Again, the customs inspector waved his hand in the air to encourage Shelley to speak. Finally he got the message, 'I am not at liberty to…,'

' …reveal that information,' encouraged the inspector.

'…reveal that information,' parroted Shelley.

'…under the Official Secrets Act of 1923.'

'And I now declare you man and wife,' said Teale.

Both Shelley and the customs inspector glared at him.

'Now, if you'll sign here…. And here…. And here…. And finally here…You can be on your way.'

Shelley signed his life away with a fierce scribble of the pen.

'Thank you Serjeant Shelley. Give the Japs one for me.' He signaled for a Malay corporal to lift the barrier. Shelley simply muttered under his breath as Teale put the three-tonner into gear with a loud crash of machinery and accelerated slowly down the tree-lined road.

Behind us the next truck rolled forward to take its place beside the road block. Ahead lay the war and the Argylls.

*

Reg Dwyer

Spit and polish. Spit and fucking polish. If I have to do his webbing one more time, I'll…I don't know what I'll do, but I won't be happy that's for sure.

At least, we're back in camp now. After Serjeant Shelley, Eddie Longhurst and Mike Teale left, the brass put another company out on the beach watching the sea. I was never more happy to see a barracks again, I'll tell you.

The lads seem to be taking a bit of a beating in Malaysia. The papers are full of strategic retreats and well-organised withdrawals. Me, I'm no soldier and I couldn't tell the difference between a right flank and wet fart but even I know if you're retreating, you're not winning the battle, whatever they might say at HQ.

The local news is next to useless. We find out everything in the nine o'clock news from London. That's how I heard about the sinking of *The*

Repulse and *The Prince of Wales*. This stuck-up bloke with a toffee-nosed accent just announced it like he was telling me Tommy Dorsey was about to play 'Boogie Woogie'.

I can imagine him sitting there in London, dressed in his tuxedo looking like a well-fed penguin, telling us here in Singapore about the sinking of two big ships.

And how did the bloody Japs sink the bloody things? They were supposed to be the most modern boats afloat. I remember going drinking with a tar from *The Repulse*. Proud of his ship he were. Proud of his guns and her speed, and her sleek lines. 'A race horse with tiger's teeth,' he called her.

Well, now she's well and truly nobbled. I hope he's alive though. Good man, from Dukinfield. Don't know what he was doing in the navy. Dukinfield's miles from the sea. Poor bugger probably had never even seen the sea before he signed up. Except at Blackpool on Wakes Week maybe. Hope he's alive.

But I'm here polishing my little heart out, staring up into the rafters of our barracks. I can hear the snores of the other lads around me. I can smell that peculiar barracks odour of sweaty men, sodden socks and stale farts.

And, worst of all, I'm suddenly afraid I'll never see Margie or the kids again. I couldn't bear it.

*

Eddie Longhurst
I could get sick of this.

The RCT driver sits there, smoking fag after fag, never saying a word. Shelley is asleep beside me, his head slowly nodding forward onto his chest, then he lifts it up, snuffles a few times and settles back into his old position. But two minutes later, it nods forward and the whole fuckin' waste of time begins again.

Behind me, Teale is snoring in the back of the cab. That twat could sleep for England.

I'm smoking a Black Cat and looking out at the endless green surrounding the road. It stretches away into the distance, an endless sea of green.

There's another crash of gears. We're crawling uphill now, slowly winding up to the top of the crest.

I don't know where the fuck we are. I know we're in Malaya but that's about it. The last sign I saw was about ten miles back saying Ipoh was eight miles away. Strange about the signs though. I thought we were supposed to remove them to confuse the enemy. But they're still up, pointing the way, wherever it is.

Me and Teale wanted to give it up and leave the stuff by the side of the road but Shelley would have none of it.

'Our job is to deliver these anti-tanks. The Argylls need them and we're not going to let them down.' He stuck his chin out and his bottom lip crept up above the top one. I knew there was no point in arguing, so we went on.

We hadn't seen any other squaddies for at least half an hour. Sure, we'd been passed by trucks, motorcycles and ambulances heading south but nobody seemed to be going the way we were.

The last lot we'd seen were a bunch of wogs sitting by the side of the road. They were a sorry looking bunch. They didn't even look up as we passed, just sat together in their group talking. Teale stopped to check we were on the right road. They didn't answer. Just ignored him completely.

So we drove on, heading north to look for some Jocks in the middle of the jungle. Like looking for a lost needle in a tropical haystack.

I'll be glad when I get back to Singapore.

Fuck this for a game of soldiers.

*

Richard Longhurst

Another trip up to HQ on Fort Canning. I'm climbing up the hill now and I can feel my lungs fit to burst.

I mean, it's not that high up but it's still a bit of a climb. It must be the cigarettes, I suppose. Working with O'Neill means I've been smoking more than usual. It's not that he smokes. On the contrary, the only time he does is when he has a few pints. It's that he makes me want to smoke. An almost unquenchable need that leads me to light one after another after another like an Indian chief with a lot to say.

It's his sheer unpredictability that makes me feel so nervous. One moment he is as lucid as a milkman, the next he's rambling on about the mission, Errol Flynn and stardom. And by stardom I don't mean the celebrities one hears about in Hollywood but the twinkling things in the sky.

He has become obsessed with sleeping out in the open at night. Or in his case, not sleeping, but simply staring at the sky, watching the stars with those emerald green eyes of his.

Everyone in the barracks thought he'd gone doolally when he got out of the Glasshouse the first time.

'Does that to some people,' said Larkin. 'Take my Uncle Ronnie.'

'No thanks.'

'Just shut up for a moment and you might learn something, you. Anyway, as I was saying, my Uncle Ronnie went inside once...,'

'What for?'

'He got caught with something that fell off the back of a lorry in the docks.'

'What was it?'

'Half a ton of oranges, I think. Poor bugger couldn't find anywhere to put them so he started selling them from his lorry. Silly tosser, forgot where he was one day and pitched outside a cop shop. Anyway, it was only after he'd sold most of them to the rozzers that they started wondering where he'd got them. Always was a bit of fruitcake our Uncle Ronnie.'

'Runs in the family, right Larkin?'

'Shut your mouth you and listen. Now, as I was sayin', our Uncle Ronnie got shut up inside Strangeways for two years.'

'Some bloody strange ways in Strangeways Hotel.'

'True enough, true enough. He came out a changed man.'

'What do you mean?'

'Let's just say, he came out a changed man.'

'Come on Larkin, you can't leave it at that. What happened?' That was me, winding Larkin up as usual. He took the bait.

'Well, something must have happened. I don't know what. But he came home and he wasn't interested in the wife.'

'You mean he...,'

'Yeah, started wearing women's skirts, stockings, suspenders, high heels, all that sort of stuff. Prison made our Uncle Ronnie a changed man.'

The barracks was quiet as everyone digested Larkin's story. Then Dobson, the new recruit from England, spoke again.

'But what's that got to do with O'Neill?'

'Nothing really,' answered Larkin, 'O'Neill's a fuckin' nutter. Now our Uncle Ronnie had class. Finally ran off with a sailor from Ark Royal he did. Lovely legs in a pair of stockings mind you.' Larkin looked wistful. 'When he remembered to shave of course.'

I was turning right now, walking past the main building to get to the Battle Box in the rear. I'd been here before delivering messages. HQ company had the task of guarding the bloody thing and I saw Tommy Halford and Wesley Crawford standing smartly to attention, stiff as pokers in the hot afternoon sun.

'How do?' I said to Halford.

'Oh, you're back again Lanky,' he answered. 'You'd better be quick, there's a bit of a flap on.'

Just then a whole pride of colonels walked out from the dark entrance. Halford, Crawford and myself snapped to attention and I whipped out my smartest salute at the assorted array of brass hats and red tabs.

They ignored me.

One rabbit-like man brought up the rear. A small caterpillar of a mustache, a sharp angular nose, jug handle ears and small smiling mouth all led down to the absence of a chin. His uniform was sweat soaked, damp with long hours of tedious discussions and debates.

He walked straight past me on his own, his eyes darting from wall to wall, soldier to soldier. Finally, he remembered to return my salute and did so with a casual tip of his swagger stick on his topee.

It was only the commander of the Allied Forces, Lieutenant General Arthur Percival, waiting for his car. His shoulders were slumped, his body sagged. Only his eyes jerked around, constantly watching, constantly looking for something that obviously wasn't there.

The staff car arrived and like an old man, he climbed into the back, alone.

'Was that who I think it was?'

'Yeah, our Lord and Master.'

'Does he always look so shattered?'

'Sometimes he looks worse. I don't think it's going well Lanky, not well at all.'

I left Halford and walked down the slope and underground, through the blast doors of the Battle Box.

A row of electric lights guided my way for about fifty yards before I reached another blast door. Another Tad checked my ID and opened the door. A wind of stale air, even staler sweat and the indescribable smell of fear rushed out at me and grabbed my throat.

I gagged. And then gagged again.

'Get a bloody move on, so I can close the door.'

I stepped inside holding my breath. On my left the constant jingle of phones and operators sang like a chorus from some ancient opera. I walked straight on. I needed the brigade major who was attached to the general commanding the Singapore Garrison. First left, second right, second left.

I'd passed an open Op room. A group of WAAFs were moving tiny wooden boats across the top of a map of Singapore.

'27 bandits at 13000 feet,' she intoned in a peculiarly mechanical voice into the microphone. Then she listened. 'No, no, no Tengah. 27 bandits at 13000 feet heading East South East. Repeat East South East.'

Around her, people shouted into other microphones, phones rang, men swore, officers ran in with more messages.

In the corner, two men lay sleeping on miniature camp beds. They looked peaceful, their faces blessed with a sort of innocence that only comes from sheer exhaustion.

I found Major Davies and handed him the message. He took it without looking up, saying a curt 'Thank you.'

I left the way I had come. Dodging the runners in the corridors, ignoring the smells of rotten food, stepping over the sleeping bodies in the entrance and out into the bright, bright light of a beautifully sunny Singapore day.

It felt like I had been let out of prison.

*

Eddie Longhurst

'We never even delivered the anti-tank guns. Brought the fuckers back with us to Singapore. I were all for dumping the bastards at the side of the road but Shelley wouldn't have it. He said we were accountable for these guns and in the army once you'd signed for something, you were accountable until some other poor bugger signed for them.'

'So you brought 'em back.'

'Yeah, they're in the store now.' At first the QM didn't want them but Shelley convinced him. Stupid bugger should know better than to cross Shelley.'

'But did you see any action?'

'What? Like fighting you mean?'

'Yeah, you know fighting, hand-to-hand combat,' said Larkin.

Eddie scowled. 'Nah. We heard the guns in the distance. Looked like some poor bastards were getting a right kicking. The closer we got to the front the only thing we saw were Jap planes. It got so bad we could only travel at night towards the end. Then, we were driving without lights, hoping we didn't hit anything.'

'So you didn't see any Japs then?'

'Not a sight. Lots of knackered Tommies. We were looking for the Argylls. Never found them though. Everyone said they were up ahead. So we kept on driving through these retreating squaddies. We saw the Leicesters. They took a right pounding in North Malaya. We thought we'd only met a company of them. Shelley asked one Lance Jack where the rest of the battalion was. 'This is it, mate,' was the answer he got. Can't have been more than 100 of the poor buggers left.'

'Blimey,' said Larkin.

I took a long, hard drag on my fag. 'Then we met this Indian officer. I mean he wasn't an Indian but an officer who was in an Indian regiment. Anyway, the stupid fucker had lost it completely. He was waving his pistol in the air and shouting at us to go back, there were thousands of Japs up ahead and we had to go back. The bastard were shitting it real bad. I couldn't see any of his Indians anywhere. They'd already done a runner I think. Shelley was all for ignoring the bastard and going on. But this officer he points his pistol straight at Shelley. I'll always remember the hammer going back and clicking and then he says, 'Turn back now, Serjeant.'

'Just turn back now, Serjeant?'

Eddie nodded. 'Didn't Shelley thump him or nothing?' said Larkin.

'Listen dickhead, you don't thump nobody with a fucking great Webley pointed straight at your head. So we turned back.'

I took another long drag of the fag. 'We kept going. Nobody stopped us. We parked in the jungle by day and drove at night to avoid the Jap planes. Now we're back.'

A swallow of beer, another long suck on my fag. 'You know mates, it's a fucking shambles out there. The only ones who seem to know what they are doing are the Aussies.'

'Yeah, the Aussies will teach them a lesson.'

Another swallow of beer to empty the glass, a final long hard drag of my fag. 'Whose fucking round is it?'

*

Reg Dwyer

Block 15, Tanglin Barracks, Singapore
29th January,1942
My darling wife,

Well, love, it's a new year and I hope you're having a merry time. I heard the Jerries aren't bombing Manchester as heavily as before. You'll be able to get a good night's sleep at last.

Well, it looks like we could finally be doing some fighting soon. Yesterday xxxxx xxxxx xxxxx xxxxxx xxxxx xxxxx xxxxxx. But I'm not scared. The xxxxx xxxxxx xxxxxx xxxxxxxx xxxxxxx xxxxxxx xxxxxx xxxxxx xxxxxx xxxxxxxx.

I can't say much though. You know what the censors are like. I don't want to send you a letter with nothing but black lines in it, do I?

I was sorry to hear about our Ethel's boyfriend. He only joined up six months ago. To be killed so quickly in the desert. Isn't a good way to go. It must be hot and dry there. Maybe, he'll end up like that Egyptian mummy we saw in Manchester Museum with the kids. Do you remember?

Lord, that seems so long ago. Like it was another lifetime away. Sometimes, I try to remember what you and the kids look like. There are times it comes easy to me, but at others, I can't focus on your face. It's like a picture you've left out in the sun. It fades over time.

Sorry to be so maudlin, but I don't think there isn't a minute when I don't think about you and the kids. Don't get me wrong. I'm proud to be in the regiment and an Empire soldier but I know I'd be better if you were around. I wish you could have come out here to join us.

Tell Tommy to study hard at school. He's the man of the family now and he has to be strong while I'm away.

Running out of space now, love. You know what these wartime letters are like. When you get round to saying what you want, you run out of space.

But I know I don't have to tell you how I feel, you know already. You've always known.

Your husband,

Reg

Censored by Major R. Tudor.

Chapter 23

Richard Longhurst

'Sure, are you going to lie in your pit on a fine sunny day like this with the Nips aching to kill you?'

It was O'Neill. He was standing over my bed, still with the purple silk scarf tied around his neck.

'Your man knows we have a mission to do and Serjeant Hanlon isn't going to be too happy at your continued absence from this war. After all, it is the only one we've got at the moment.'

I opened my eyes and acknowledged his presence with a flicker of my lips. 'Water' emerged from deep in my sandpapered throat.

'Is it water you're after? Well, General O'Neill is happy to oblige.'

Soon a tumbler of the coolest, clearest spring water is balanced precariously on my lips. I swallow in a long, sweet gulp and it glides down cooling every inch of my body.

I let my head fall back on the pillow and stare up at the ceiling. No sweats. No pain. No chills. No fever.

'Now, get your arse out of pit because if you don't, a certain serjeant is going to commit murder. Unfortunately, even in time of war this murder will not be licensed by His Majesty's Government. It always amazes me the commandment says 'Thou shalt not kill', but we men have always been able to add a few exceptions to this simple instruction. Thou shalt not kill unless the person is of another religion. Thou shalt not kill unless it has been sanctioned by a higher authority. Thou shalt not kill unless it is the duly ordained revenge of the law. Thou shalt not kill unless one has been paid to do so by His Majesty's Government. Thou shalt not...,'

O'Neill continued with his monologue as I concentrated on the task of getting up. First move one leg, then the next. Well done, now swing them over the bed and raise the body to a sitting position at the same time. Made it.

I lay at the edge of my bed. I shouldn't have gone drinking last night. Don't know why I did it, and then to end up at the Lady Bar was really stupid.

'....sure, wasn't so difficult now was it?'

'Fuck off, O'Neill.'

'Ah, another display of that dazzling Manchester wit and repartee. My sainted mother would be turning over in her grave at the dazzling elegance of it all.'

'Fuck off, O'Neill and pass over my shirt.'

He reached over and threw the sweat-stained khaki to me.

With difficulty I pulled it on, seeing it settle around my shoulders like a shroud. This was followed by my shorts, socks, boots and belt. I was beginning to feel more alive by the second.

Then another pain hit me in the stomach. Hunger. Jesus, I hadn't eaten for a day.

'Jesus, O'Neill, I'm…,'

From somewhere he produced two immense, butter soaked egg sandwiches. 'You can get these down your neck as we drive.'

I grabbed hold of them and began tearing at the first like a tiger ripping into the body of a fat planter.

'Where are we going?' I asked between soft cotton wool mouthfuls of egg and white bread.

'On up to B Company at the Causeway. We've to take some shit up to the poor bastards. We've to keep our heads down though. The Japs are wasting their venom on the island, spitting shells like a cobra spits poison.'

Suddenly it struck me. Other than his non-government issue purple silk scarf, O'Neill was the most normal I'd seen him in ages. 'What's happened?'

'Oh, the siege has started young Richard. Hadn't you heard? The Japs pushed the Argylls back onto the island yesterday when you were on your wee thirsty bender. They crossed the Causeway with a lone piper playing 'Scotland the Brave'. Aye and that's what the poor bastards have been if these two eyes of mine tell me the truth.'

'No, I mean with you. You seem to be almost well…you know…,'

'Sane?'

'Well no, I didn't mean that…,'

'I think you did, young Richard. Don't worry, it's only a temporary respite. I'll be back to normal soon.' He looked across at me with a glint of humour in his eyes, and an impish smile on his face. He looked nothing less than a six foot tall leprechaun dressed in khaki.

I climbed into the three-tonner and he ground the gears into action.

'Haven't you learnt to drive this thing yet?'

'Sure, it's more fun to hear the clash of metal. Tells me the engine is actually working. It's sort of like a wail of metal banshees, the sound of the shidhe, the war cry of Culchulain all rolled into one.'

'Just drive the fucking truck,' I said already needing another cigarette.

I must be back to normal too. O'Neill was getting on my nerves.

*

Reg Dwyer

Block 15, Tanglin Barracks, Singapore

February 5th, 1942

My loving wife,

Well, this would be my last letter to you for a while my dear. The Japs have reached Singapore but the Fortress is looking strong at the moment.

All the lads are saying this will be another Mafeking. If it is, I'm sure the Manchesters will be at the centre of it just as we were then.

I couldn't say everything I wanted to in my last letter. But Margie, you are my heart, my soul, my everything. Without you, I have no life, no being. You make me complete.

Before I met you, I always felt lost, somehow, never completely knowing what I was doing, or why I was doing it.

I always loved you Margie. I may not have been the best husband to you and the kids but I always loved you.

I wanted to tell you in case something happened to me.

You don't know how hard this is for me to write. I've never been able to express my emotions very well. Perhaps it was my dad dying so young. It meant that we could never say what we really meant in my family. It all went unsaid until it was too late.

That's why I've written this letter to you Margie.

To say what I've always wanted to you but never been able to find the words.

I've always loved you Margie. And I always will.

Your loving husband

Reg

PS I've given this letter to one of the Naafi girls who is being taken off the Island. Write to me and let me know you got it, ok?

*

Richard Longhurst

'Right, Longhurst, you and O'Neill take this message down to the Australian HQ. You are to hand it to General Bennett or his chief of staff personally. Nobody else. Do you hear?'

'Yes, sir,' we both chorused.

He handed us a brown envelope rather than the usual white message form.

'Get a move on and then get back here.'

'Sir, you haven't told us where they are.'

'Oh right, yes.' As he reddened and his glasses slipped down his nose, 'You'll find them somewhere between the Bukit Timah and Clementi Roads. But watch out, there are reports of Jap snipers in the area.'

He stared at O'Neill.

'What's that around your neck?'

'It's silk, sir. Purple silk. For the mission.'

All he said was 'hmm' and looked down at his mess of papers. Around him new messages were arriving constantly, phones were ringing, men were running. Above a fan droned noisily on, hardly stirring the thick muggy air.

He looked up again, seeming not to recognise us both, or even remember why we were there. 'Well, get a move on.'

'Yes sir.' We both saluted him in a smart, soldierly way and turned to walk out of his dank office, out of the Battle Box and into the bright sunlight of a beautiful February day.

We could smell the burning oil in the air. Below us on Fort Canning Park, an anti-aircraft gun was angrily banging up at the sky, aiming at nothing in particular. Columns of smoke drifted across the sky. The largest came from the north in the direction of the Naval Base.

'See, your man knew I needed the purple for protection. He knows all about it. He's been informed. Didn't question me, did he? That shows you, sure it does.'

I refused to answer O'Neill. There was no point. He would merely launch into another tirade about God, Hollywood, stardom and the nature of death. Right now, it was the last thing I wanted to hear.

The engine coughed into life. The gears connected and we were off down the hill.

'We'll go down Bras Basah and Selegie and get onto Bukit Timah. Maybe we should stop off for a pint at the Union Jack club on the way.'

'No, O'Neill you heard the major. This one is urgent. Let's get it to the Australians and piss off back here, before we got the shit kicked out of us.'

O'Neill put his foot to the floor and accelerated down Fort Canning Rise. Neither of us seemed in a mood to talk, we just sat there, O'Neill concentrating on avoiding the debris lining the streets.

I watched as the Singapore I knew disintegrated before my eyes.

Of course, all the shops were closed now. Nothing was for sale in a city where once money could buy anything.

On every street corner, there was evidence of war; discarded cars, bombed out homes, dead bundles of rags lying in the streets. Once people, now they were just crumpled bodies.

O'Neill kept his eyes on the road, his smile never leaving his lips. There weren't many other vehicles on the road anymore. Everybody but us had the sense to keep under shelter.

In the distance, we could hear the constant thump of artillery. It came from the direction we were going.

We were on Bukit Timah Road, the canal to our right. O'Neill suddenly started humming. It was Elgar again. The stirring melody contrasting with the oily grind of the engine.

Suddenly there was a barricade in front of us manned by Australian soldiers. The sergeant, a thin wiry man with a deep tanned face and the sharpest nose I'd ever seen, ambled up to us, his Tommy gun pointing carelessly in our direction.

'Where you going mates?'

'To the Australian HQ at Bukit Timah Road.'

He turned back to the five or six Australians who accompanied him. Some were armed, some not. Some had their tunics open to the waist; some weren't wearing tunics at all.

All were dirty, tired and had a wildness about them that contrasted sharply with the uniforms of myself and O'Neill.

'This pom says he's going to see Gordon Bennett.' The others laughed. He turned back to me. 'Can you give us a lift, mate.'

'Sure,' I said. 'Jump in the back. We're heading straight up there.'

He shook his head. 'No mate, you got us wrong, we want a lift to the Docks, back there.'

As he lifted his hand off the Tommy gun to point to the Docks, O'Neill stamped his foot on the accelerator.

The truck surged forward, forcing the Aussie sergeant to dive out of the way.

The other Aussies were surprised by O'Neill and stood open-mouthed as we raced past.

'What the...,' I blurted out, turning in my seat to look over my shoulder. I watched as the Aussie sergeant raised his Thompson. I saw the red flames erupt from its spout. I didn't hear or see the bullets. It was all lost in the mad roar of the engine. My head was thrown backwards as O'Neill accelerated away.

'Sure those boys had wildness in their eyes, didn't they?' he said.

Then he smiled, and I saw once again the same look as after he had killed the old Indian.

A smile of pure elation, pure joy. He was enjoying this. Enjoying the thrill and the excitement and the madness of it all.

I gripped the seat tighter, crushing my hands against the metal supports. Oh Lord, keep me safe from harm.

Again, O'Neill started humming "Nimrod".

I closed my ears to the madness, to the war, to everything. It wasn't me anymore. I could understand nothing.

*

Eddie Longhurst

I'm looking out across the sand to the point where the waves greet the shore. The wind is blowing through trees, their trunks creaking as they sway before its strength. And still we are here staring out at the fucking waves.

Down on the beach and at the edge of the water, the bamboo poles we spent hours making, are still guarding the beach.

One or two have already fallen over, so the whole exercise was a waste of fucking time. If the Japs ever came here, they would be through that lot like a dose of Epsom salts.

How much sweat and graft did we put in? All under the gaze of that useless engineer Serjeant. If I ever see him down the Naafi, I'll give him a right chinning. Time for the Manchester kiss right between the eyes.

I'm soaked with sweat of course. As is Teale and Larkin with me. Even our Vickers is hot and we haven't even fired it. You could fry an egg on the barrel.

You know in the three years we've been here, I've never actually fired this fucking gun. It's just like new, fresh out of its crate, the oil from the factory coating its levers, the stamped letters of its makers as clear as tram tracks on the side of the barrel.

I'd love to fire it. To feel its jerk and stutter. To watch the long belt of 303 bullets vanish into the machine, to emerge hot and deadly out of the spout. To watch them hit home and lines of charging Japs fall under the hot lead.

Teale coughed in his sleep. Both him and Larkin are napping in the bottom of our position. No point in us all standing watch in this heat. May as well get some shuteye. The waves still roll in onto the beach. And I'm still here waiting, same as I've waited for the last three years.

*

Richard Longhurst

'I wouldn't go any further if I were you mate.'

'Trouble?'

'Aye, you could say that. Half the bleedin' Jap Army's coming down the road.'

'D'ye not know where I can find the Aussies?'

'They've vanished mate. Pulled back a day ago. Somewhere off Reformatory Road.'

'Thanks, Sarge.'

O'Neill pulled left on to Reformatory Road and started to climb the hill.

'What are we going to do now?'

'Sure I'm banjaxed. There doesn't seem to be a lot of Aussies round here.' He looked to either side of the empty road. 'There doesn't seem to be a useful lot of anything happening here.'

It was then the truck decided it had had enough of the war.

We had reached the summit of a small rise in the road when we heard a *phut-phutter-plut* from the engine.

Then silence.

'Come on now, don't do this to Uncle Michael.'

I ran out with the starter rod, eyes darting here and there, wary of any waiting Japs.

Quickly I shoved the starter into its hole. Shit, wrong end. I looked around again, certain that hidden eyes were watching, waiting to line me up in the sights of a sniper rifle.

'Will you be getting a move on, Richard. There's a war going on, don't you know.'

I turned the starting handle twice. The engine coughed into life, coughed twice more and died.

'Shit. Shit. Shit.'

Once again, I gripped the starting handle, swinging it viciously with all my strength. Once, then again and again and again.

Nothing.

'Can't you get it started, O'Neill?'

'I'm not a miracle worker. Not with trucks anyway.'

O'Neill jumped out of the cab and came round to the front of the lorry. He lifted the engine cover and was immediately swallowed up by an aggressive cloud of steam.

He jumped back holding his face. 'Holy Mother of Jaysus…,'

The steam had cleared and we could see a long stream of boiling water pouring from the engine.

O'Neill walked to the front of the cab. 'Sure, there's the problem.' He pointed to a neat round hole in the radiator. 'The Aussie who shot at us, he killed the truck.'

'We'd better get out of here then. Before the Japs come.'

'Now, don't you be getting nervous on me, young Richard. We still have to do our duty and deliver the orders to the Aussies. So let's get our packs and we'll be off.'

'But…wouldn't it be better to go back to town?'

'Don't be an eejit. It was difficult enough getting here never mind getting back. Our job is to deliver these orders and that's what we're going to do.' He swung his pack over his shoulders and picked up his Lee Enfield from the cab. 'Are you coming then Richard?'

I looked back towards the City. Then back at O'Neill. He seemed to have a charmed life. And I didn't want to be on my own. Not out here. Not anymore. Never on my own. I picked up my own pack and rifle and joined him.

'Good man. Did I ever tell you it's my mission to save Singapore? Yes, God told me. He said, 'Michael, my boy, you're the only one who can do it.' And then he promised me I would become a star, as long as I saved Singapore. So this is our job, Richard, we're going to save Singapore.'

Then, he started humming his bloody Elgar again. The sound of our boots scraping on the road providing coarse counterpoints to the melody.

I wondered what the hell I was doing, walking along this deserted road, with a madman, bent on saving Singapore.

I looked at him, striding out as if he didn't have a care in the world. It was like he was out for a Sunday afternoon walk, a little stroll to see the beach and plantations of Singapore.

Maybe the purple scarf does protect him. We certainly haven't seen any Japs or any sign of fighting all the time we've been on the road.

We walked on. Me trying desperately to keep up with him.

A chicken, resplendent in his coat of black and red, crowed noisily from a bush beside the road, disturbed by O'Neill's rendition of Nimrod.

'It's a lovely day for a stroll, Richard, a beautiful sunny Singapore day.'

And then all hell let loose. It began with a single shell landing about 100 yards away. Then another. Then another.

Then the earth dissolved into a mass of heaving, churning soil, reaching up to the blue, blue sky.

The barrage was creeping forward now, coming straight toward us.

I felt my shoulders being roughly grabbed. O'Neill was pushing me into a roadside culvert, 'Keep your head down.'

I did as I was told.

I always did as I was told.

The road dissolved into nothing. The air was alive with the explosions of shells, the roar of the earth, a volcano of soil, the harsh strangle of cordite.

I buried myself deeper into the culvert, hiding from the noise just as a child I had hidden in a cupboard to escape my father's drunken rages.

'Where are ye? Ye wee bastard, I'll find ye.' I could hear him limping outside my hiding place. His wooden leg alternatively walking across the floor and the carpet. The harsh crack of wood on wood contrasted with a softer thump of the wood on the carpet.

And then silence.

I could hear him breathing, followed by a soft, whispered 'Where are ye?'

I knew better than to answer. He was cunning when drunk. Too cunning for me. I lay in my small cupboard beneath the stairs, surrounded by mouldy smells of old boots and damp newspapers; the decay of lives.

A lump of road landed on my back forcing me even deeper into the culvert. I glanced up at O'Neill. His head was up above the edge, casually looking at the explosions around us.

The barrage was moving forward now. There were fewer and fewer explosions on the road. O'Neill stepped out of the culvert, brushing the dust and earth from his uniform.

I unfolded my cramped body. The place where the rock struck, a soft bruise. I winced as I touched it.

Suddenly, we were surrounded by running men. Indian soldiers with their turbans all askew. An officer, his head bloodied, his major's crown glistening on his shoulder, tripped and fell. Quickly he picked himself up again and plunged into the jungle on the other side of the road.

O'Neill put his body in the way of one of the runners, holding him in his strong arms. The man was young. A face devoid of knowledge, empty of sun, full of fear. His eyes wild, darting here and there. He struggled in O'Neill's arms. He looked exactly like the young soldier I met from the Hyderabads, in another life and half an age ago.

'What's happening, man? Tell me, what's happening.'

The soldier simply struggled on, desperately trying to escape from O'Neill, escape from whatever terror lay back there.

O'Neill punched him. Not hard, mind you, a little tap to the jaw around the chin strap. The man was still, staring still at O'Neill.

'Tell me what happened?'

'Crossing the valley, out in the open, the shells landing right amongst us, hundreds dead, thousands.'

He wrenched himself free from O'Neill and staggered off into the jungle at the side of the road. Running to he knew not where.

O'Neill turned to me, 'We better get out of here, Johnnie Jap will be along very soon.'

I got up out of the culvert and went to follow the major, the soldier and the others into the jungle.

'No. This way Richard.'

'But all the others have gone through here.'

'That's why we'll go down the road. We'll make quicker time and the Jap artillery is bound to follow those running men.'

As he spoke, a single plane flew overhead.

We both jumped back into the culvert, waiting for the bombs to land around us.

They didn't.

Instead, we heard a loud whine followed by three even louder bangs in the jungle where the man had gone.

'Let's be going now. Before your bad men arrive.'

He strode off down the road.

I followed. What else was I to do?

*

Eddie Longhurst

The waves are still flowing onto the beach past our shore defences.

Every single minute of every single hour of every single day, they come toward me. I keep looking out, staring at the fucking great sea.

Sometimes, when I'm looking too hard, I start to see shapes forming in the waves. One time, I was sure I could see something dark and black approaching us.

'Get yourselves ready lads, here they come,' I shouted at Teale and Larkin. Teale jumped up straight away. Larkin just lay there. I gave him a sharp kick in his fucking back. I moved behind the Vickers raising the sight and checking the belt of ammo.

'What's up? Wha'?'

'Get yourself fucking up, Larkin, they're here.'

'Who's here? Wha's here?'

Teale was next to me now, staring at the sea.

'I can't see anything Eddie. It's just sea...look.'

I got up from behind the Vickers and stared across the ocean. Nothing there. Fucking nothing there except sea and fucking waves.

Nothing.

'I'm sure there was something there.'

'You must have been dreaming, Eddie.'

I stared at Larkin forcing him to look down and mumble something beneath his breath.

'You take this watch Larkin. No more fucking kip for you.'

We've been out here for a while now, still in our bunkers waiting for the attack. Four hours off and four hours on. Watching the waves come into the shore every minute of every hour of every day.

When was it going to end?

*

Richard Longhurst

We didn't have far to walk. After the shelling and the plane, it all went quiet again. Just another sunny day in Singapore.

The only difference was the bodies. There were six of them, all lying beside the road. Sorry, that's not true. Four were lying; the other two were sitting upright, as if quietly chatting whilst their mates took a nap.

They were new to Singapore as well. None of them had the tell-tale tanned faces and arms, with the brown V defining the neck. They were all a pasty white; fresh meat for the grinder.

Even stranger, none of them was marked in any way. There were no missing limbs. No charred remains. No gashes. No blood. No bullet holes.

Just six dead lads sitting and lying beside the side of the road, like it was the most normal thing in the world to do.

'They're dead,' said O'Neill.

'They look like they are sleeping.'

'Well, if they are, it's going to be a long, long night of dreaming.'

'Shall we bury them?'

'Nah, they're not going to thank us and we don't have the time. We could be digging here for the next ten hours. We could be still digging when the Japs come.' He looked past me and down the road. 'No, that's where we have to go. Over there.' He pointed to a small ridge overlooking the land.

'Are the Aussies there?'

He walked towards the bodies and didn't answer me.

'I'll say a few words for them. Richard.'

Then, he made a sign of the cross and began to speak in Latin. 'In nominee patria et spiritu sancti ...,'

He bowed his head and was lost to the world.

The men lay there, staring at the sky, not saying a word, not breathing, not alive any more. ·

'Amen.' He lifted his head and put his helmet back on. 'Well, we'd better be moving on. We need to reach the ridge before dark.'

I put my helmet back on my head, slung my rifle over my shoulder and followed him.

I took one last look at the men resting beside the road.

They just looked like they had stopped for a few moments to have a cup of tea and a bite to eat.

But I knew they were as dead as my mam and dad.

*

Reg Dwyer

'What did you bloody say?'

Shelley and Eddie were both staring right at me, putting the fear of God into my soul.

'It's ....orders,' I stammered.

'Orders from who?'

'F-f-from Major Tudor.'

'You mean to say after two years of building these bloody pillboxes, stringing out this fucking wire and erecting those bleeding boat traps we're going to pack up and go. Here you are slant eyes. Have this fucking beach, we don't want it?'

I nodded. It seemed the only thing to do.

Eddie turned to Serjeant Shelley. 'Two years of fucking work. Two years sweating my bollocks off on this beach for fuck all.'

'Let me read it.'

I handed him the form. He knew it well. Army Form C2136, large, pads of 100, requisitioned from the quartermaster at intervals of not more than three months.

He passed over the In and Out lines with their times for the signals. He saw Major Tudor's neat block capitals written, as always, in aquamarine ink from his beloved Parker pen. He read his own name with his rank missing of course.

Down past the message instructions with its bold number four, indicating there were four copies of this order, across the security classification, in this case, secret, and on to the originator's number, which in Tudor's case was 05, a number of which he was very proud.

'Near the top of the classification, Dwyer. Promotion soon, you wait and see.' Tudor said the same thing every time he gave me a message.

'Yes sir,' I always answered, 'I'm sure you'll get what you deserve soon, sir.'

He always enjoyed that response. He felt he deserved so much.

And me?

Well, I just wanted to keep my cushy number, didn't I? I would have licked the floor clean with my tongue to stay close to the home comforts of the mess rather than out on the beaches, staring at the bloody sea.

But then the bastard kicked me in the teeth.

'Oh and Dwyer.'

'Yes, sir.'

'Tomorrow, you can rejoin 13 Platoon. I won't be needing you anymore. Bent will take over your duties.'

I stood there, mouth opening like a goldfish gasping for water.

'Get a move on, man. We haven't got all day.'

I saluted and walked slowly over to Shelley's position, making sure I stopped off for a fag on the way.

Sod them all. Sod them fucking all. Pardon my French.

Shelley had taken a long time to read the message, as if he were reluctant to understand his orders. Then finally he read them out loud, stumbling over the words. 'Strategic Withdrawal to new positions. 'D' Company to cover withdrawal at Tampines / Tanah Merah Besar junction on Changi Road. Withdrawal to begin 0400 hrs ,13th February. All company commanders and CSMs to report to Company HQ at 2130hrs, 12th February for briefing.'

He looked down and saw Major Tudor's scrawled signature along the bottom of the order.

'That's it, then,' said Eddie, 'that's fucking it. We're pulling out leaving this bastard beach behind.'

He kicked the concrete wall of the pillbox, again and again and again. Shelley watched, not doing anything to stop him, letting the fury spend itself on three tons of grey concrete.

'You'd better get on, Dwyer. Tell Major Tudor. I'll report to HQ at 2130 hrs.'

'Yes, Serjeant, tomorrow I'm to report back to 13 Platoon.'

'Lost your cushy number, have you Dwyer?'

I looked down at the floor of the pillbox. A pile of sea shells lay in the corner, put there like a child had collected them after a long stroll down the beach in Blackpool.

'Oh, Reg, don't mention anything you've heard here. This is between us. It's not for their ears.'

'Yes, Serjeant. I mean no, Serjeant. Well...you know what I mean,Serjeant.'

'I know, Reg. You'd better get back now.'

'Yes. Serjeant.'

Perhaps it was Eddie's outburst or maybe it was hearing the orders. Or just because Shelley suddenly called me Reg. But whatever it was, I did something which surprised even me.

I asked Shelley a question.

'We're losing, aren't we?'

He looked down at his freshly polished boots and wiped away an imaginary piece of dirt lying on the surface. Then he looked up at me. The late afternoon sun streaming in through the firing slit of the pillbox caught his face, dividing it into two. A light half where the mouth was and a dark side, behind which lay his eyes.

It was the mouth I saw move. 'I don't know Reg. I don't know any more. But we're going to fight. That's what we're here to do. Fight.'

Eddie had lifted his head now and was looking at Shelley like a child watches his father.

'You'd better get on now, Dwyer.'

'Yes, Serjeant.'

'Oh, and Reg...,'

I turned back towards him. 'Yes, Serjeant?'

'Tomorrow, you'll be joining 13 Platoon again under Eddie here.'

'Yes, Serjeant.'

*

Eddie Longhurst

Strip the Vickers down. Done it thousands of times before. Easy. Teale can carry the tripod. Larkin the ammo. Me, I'll take the heavy weight of the barrel.

I smell the gun oil on my fingers. It's like after you've been with a girl, forced your finger inside of her, again and again. Felt her struggle against your probing, pleasure and pain all at one.

I smell my hand and fingers again. Gun oil, pussy juice, same fucking difference really.

I really lost it back there in front of Shelley and Reg.

Shelley took me aside and told me not to show it so much. Not to show the anger. But me, I can never control it. It's like there's someone else there running my head. I can't see nothing except the anger. I'm wearing these angry blinkers like a fucking racehorse but I'm not running anywhere except to kick someone's head in.

The beach is still there. The waves are still rolling in. The coconut palms are still swaying like the girls down at the Lady Bar.

'Hurry up, Eddie, truck's waiting.' It was Larkin, fucking idiot.

I look through the slit at the beach again. I always expected to see the Japs charging across there and me mowing them down, one by one, with the Vickers. The smell of cordite in the air mixed with the fear of death.

But I've never even fired the bloody thing. Not in anger. Not in joy. Not even in practice.

'Come on Eddie, they're ready to go.'

It was Teale this time. Larkin was too shit scared to come back again. I don't blame him. I wouldn't.

'All right, hold your bloody horses. I'm coming.'

I hoisted the barrel of the Vickers on my shoulder and stepped out of the pillbox. It was quiet on the beach. Only the sounds of the waves caressing the shore, something they have always done.

Something they always will do.

We're gone though. The Manchesters I mean. Two years we've spent on these beaches; changing them, fighting them, attacking them.

Now, we're going.

And I don't think the beach cares.

Nobody cares.

*

Richard Longhurst

'Get your head down.'

O'Neill pushed me further back behind the wall. I looked over the top. Curiosity always one of my weak points. 'Curiosity will be the death of you,' my mam always said to me.

I never believed people could die of curiosity. Until today, that is. Now I know they do.

Myself and O'Neill looked across to the other side of the crossroads. The sign said Pasir Panjang village. It was no more than a few houses lazily camped beside the road, their attap roofs bleached by the sun.

On the slope overlooking the road, we could see soldiers in their dugouts. They overlooked the road we had used, but for some reason, they hadn't seen us.

Occasionally, a man would run down from the top of the hill to one of the dugouts. Stay for a while, and then run back up the hill again.

Some of the slit trenches were still being made, their occupants only waist deep, bending over every few moments and re-appearing with a spade-full of red earth.

A glimpse of a brown, sunburnt face. A shock of white teeth. The green of a tunic.

'Looks like the Japs got here,' I whispered to O'Neill.

'Sometimes Richard, you and the rest of your heathen English never cease to amaze me with your stupidity.' He looked to the heavens for patience. 'Tell me why would your Japanese soldiers have a white officer giving out the orders?'

I kept quiet.

'Sure, it's as plain as the nose on your face. These are the Malays. Remember, little fellows. We saw them at the King's Birthday parade.'

I shook my head.

'For a clever man, Richard Longhurst, you're an awful eejit.'

I looked over the wall again. And sure enough they were dressed in British uniform and they did have the look of those Malay soldiers.

'Well,' O'Neill continued, 'Our only problem is to avoid them shooting the blazes out of us.'

He looked around him and saw a long bamboo pole. The sort the Chinese use to hang out their washing. I always thought it was so funny to see these bamboo poles hanging from the open windows wearing white shirts.

O'Neill was tying his purple scarf around the top of the bamboo.

'Come on, Richard, let's hope those buggers are only half as nervous as you.'

He hopped over the wall and into the open, carrying the bamboo pole in front of him. The purple scarf streamed out from the top of the pole in the late evening breeze.

I jumped out and ran to catch up with him. It felt like my first holy communion at Church. All of us lads following the priest and the head altar boy with his purple banner.

Except this time there was only me. And I was following O'Neill. And there was no banners, only a purple silk scarf.

God save my soul.

They didn't notice us at first. We got past the crossroads and were climbing the slope before they turned toward us.

Instantly, we heard the bolts of rifles *click, clack* as a bullet was put up the spout.

'It's alright, lads,' shouted O'Neill, 'Sure it's only me himself.'

A pair of white eyes, surrounded by a round brown face and topped with a tin helmet looked out at us warily, his rifle never moving from O'Neill's chest.

He was joined by a subaltern.

We stopped.

They looked at us.

We looked at them.

Finally, the corporal shouted across at us, 'What regiment?'

'The Manchesters.'

He nodded once and ran up the hill. Myself and O'Neil moved forward to follow him. Three other rifles appeared from the dugout. And again, we heard the *click clack* of the bolts as they slid into place.

'I think that means we stay here,' whispered O'Neill, 'but I wish the buggers would get a move on, my feet are killing me.'

Our corporal arrived back with another short Malay man who looked less than sixteen years old. On his shoulders wore the pips of a lieutenant.

O'Neill immediately saluted. 'Private O'Neill 9563433, reporting for duty sir.'

What? Reporting for duty? We're not reporting for duty. We're trying to find the bloody Australians. And if we can't find them, we're heading straight back to bloody HQ. Out of habit, I followed O'Neill's salute.

'What are you chaps doing here?' The lieutenant spoke in a precise, clipped, yet friendly English accent. 'You're miles away from your regiment.'

'Delivering orders to the Australian HQ sir. But we couldn't find them and then the truck broke down.'

'Hm, my corporal says you're from the Manchesters.'

'That's right sir.'

'You're in luck. Captain Davies is seconded from them to us. You'll find him over the ridge. My corporal will show you the way.'

He stepped aside to let us past.

We had only walked a few paces when O'Neill stopped and turned, 'Good luck tomorrow, sir.'

A smile lit up the face of the young Malay lieutenant. 'Tomorrow? Oh, you mean with the Japanese?' He looked back down the hill at the road along which we had walked. 'Luck has nothing to do with tomorrow, private. Whatever happens, happens. Insh allah.'

For the first time that day, I saw O'Neill smile, 'That's it sir. That's it exactly.'

We both walked up the hill following the small corporal, walking directly into the setting sun.

Chapter 24

Eddie Longhurst

'Come on, we're pulling back.'

'But we've only just fucking got here.'

'Don't piss about. We've got to pull back to the Perseverance Estate, closer to the city.'

We were retreating again without seeing sight nor sound of the Japs. Retreating without firing a shot, without even getting a smell of the enemy.

I hoisted the Vickers on my shoulder once more, its hot metal warmed by the sun, melted comfortably into my body.

Teale grabbed the tripod. Larkin a belt of the Ammo. We carried them to our three-tonner, parked out in the open road.

In the distance, an old Malay man walked behind a small plantation of papaya trees. He hitched his sarong up and began to piss into the ditch.

I turned away and mounted the truck, dragging Teale up behind me.

No point in getting upset. Shelley's right. We're just squaddies. We take orders and do what we're told., End of story.

The old Malay man had finished pissing now. He squatted down at the edge of the ditch and lit a cigarette, watching us pack up and leave the crossroads.

As our truck drove away, I looked back at him sitting there, calmly smoking, no sign of emotion on his face, as the Empire soldiers finally left behind part of the Empire.

He was still smoking as we drove around the corner and out of sight.

*

Richard Longhurst

We lay in the dugout waiting.

Captain Davies had remembered O'Neill but not me. 'Aren't you the chap who was involved in the little fracas some time ago?'

O'Neill nodded.

'Well, it's good to have you back. We're expecting a big Japanese push tomorrow. Are you two staying with us or moving on?'

It was O'Neill who answered. 'Sure, we'll be staying here, if it's allowed by your honour?'

'Good, jolly good. Well, I'll put you with 'A' company under Lieutenant Adnan.' He pointed to the map. 'The Japs are here at The Gap. They will probably come down Buona Vista Road.'

'The road of the beautiful view.'

'Yes, that's right. I didn't know you spoke Spanish, O'Neill.'

'I don't sir. It seems the right name.'

'I suppose it does. Strange though to find a Spanish road here in Singapore, what?'

Captain Davies was a tall, cheerful man with tortoise-shell glasses and a bushy ginger mustache that clashed awfully with his brown hair. His teeth stained yellow by tobacco, his voice a deep, melodious hum as if he were lecturing about fine art rather than war.

'Well, get yourself something to eat and then report to Lieutenant Adnan.'

We ate. Rice, some vegetables, a little chicken, the heavy red sauce.

O'Neill hated it. For me, it brought back memories of a hot, humid day sitting beside the rubber plantation with Owens. A memory a year and half an age away, as if it had happened to some other person not me.

Luckily, we didn't have to dig our own slit trench, it had been already done for us. A tiny Malay corporal gave us the range marks for our rifles. 100 yards to the tree. 200 to the road. 250 to the crossroads.

Then, we'd ducked down behind the sandbags and listened and waited. Around us, the sounds of the tropical night were everywhere. The cicadas constantly humming their rattling songs of love. The soft chirrup of a night jar. The distant crump of artillery.

And myself and O'Neill, lying in our trench, smoking not talking, not even breathing really. We both had nothing to say any more to each other. I was there with him, that's all that mattered.

Above us, the stars. Below us, the earth.

And us two, suspended in between, waiting for tomorrow.

*

Eddie Longhurst

We're setting up the fuckin' Vickers again. By now the lads can do it in their sleep. First dig a platform about ten feet square and four feet deep. Then start at the bottom with the two walls of sandbags placed to the front and to the left-hand side. Build both walls to exactly four feet in height and insert the corrugated iron on top of each wall. Then continue building for another two feet, making sure we have an aperture in the front and left-hand walls of exactly one foot. Then the ammo boxes are placed exactly two paces behind the firing position, perpendicular to the left-hand sandbags. Finally, the Vickers' base is placed on the firing platform and the barrel attached to the base. The men stand back and look at me.

I take out my tape measure and height of the walls first and the size of the firing aperture.

'Only three foot nine inches. Take it apart and start again. I want the firing position at exactly four feet.'

'But Sarge…,' Teale moaned.

'Fuckin' do it, Teale.'

I looked over the top of the sandbags. We were in at the Eastern edge of the city at the junction of McPherson and Paya Lebar Road. In front was nothing but lallang grass and an old quarry with a disused railway. To our right the road stretched on toward the coast and the Chinese Swimming Club. On the left, was a few deserted godowns.

I couldn't see any Japs. But the truth is I had never seen any Japs, not since this bloody war started.

Major Tudor came down to our position, followed in his wake by Lt. Whitehead.

He took out his measuring tape and began to lay it across the top of the position.

'I'm getting them to rebuild it sir, it's not right.'

'Damn bad show Serjeant…,'

'Longhurst, sir.' Whitehead helped him out.

He looked at Whitehead like he was a piece of chewing gum on the end of his shiny brogues. 'Yes, Longhurst, do it again, and do it properly this time. We can't let standards down at a time like this. Not in The Manchesters we don't.'

He scanned the horizon. 'What's to our right Whitehead?'

'It's supposed to be the Gharwalis sir, but we haven't seen any of them yet. Our flank is open as far as I can see sir.'

'Send someone out to check where they are, will you? I'm sure they are over there somewhere, otherwise HQ would have told us they weren't. Stands to reason, doesn't it?'

'Yes sir, but suppose...,'

'But me no buts Whitehead. Time to head back for a spot of luncheon. Carry on Serjeant ...,'

'Longhurst, sir.'

Again the long stare from Major Tudor. He hitched up his Sam Browne, adjusting it so the well-oiled leather rested on the top of his stomach.

'Get this sorted, serjeant. Standards, remember standards. We're the Manchesters, not some bloody territorials.'

*

Richard Longhurst

We heard the Japs before we saw them. It was about half an hour before dawn. Captain Davies had visited our post, checking we were comfortable. Lt. Adnan was there with us and another Malay private who never said a word. O'Neill tried to get him to talk of course, but he stared out down the hill towards Reformatory Road.

Davies had just left when we heard this almighty crash of whistles and cymbals and God knows what. Lt. Adnan told us to keep our heads down. We couldn't hear where the sound was coming from. In the early hours of the morning it seemed to be all around us.

In front, at the side, behind us.

'O'Neill, they are behind us, we're surrounded.' I must admit I was scared shitless now, gripping my Lee Enfield so tightly my knuckles stood white against the dark grain of the wood.

It was Lt. Adnan who answered. 'They are going to attack soon, get ready.'

O'Neill was next to me, whistling something between his teeth and a half smug smile on his face. I listened to him. It was 'It's a long way to Tipperary'. But he whistled it so slowly it had become a lullaby, not a march.

Suddenly, it went very quiet. And with the silence, I was aware of the smells of the earth. Deep, dank, dark smells of thick forest loam. I buried myself even deeper into the smell.

Then O'Neill started whistling again. A comforting sound that fought the silence.

I stared out down the hill but still could see nothing.

Lt Adnan was walking down the line of slit trenches now. 'Siapa tidal,' he whispered as he came to each of the small holes. Then he got to us, 'Steady, they are coming soon.'

O'Neill nodded, even he was quiet now.

Then, over on the left, I head a quiet *pop* like one of the potato guns they used to sell at Hyde Fair. A soft, whistling noise, gentle as a child's toy.

Lt Adnan jumped into our trench. 'Mortars!'

The first explosion landed about fifty feet to our left, right in one of the trenches. We heard a loud scream followed by more silence. Then another soft *pop*. A mortar exploded, further back now, behind the lines.

It was followed by others, one after another, throwing up large clods of earth. Myself and Lt. Adnan crouched in the bottom of the trench covering our heads from the assaulting earth. O'Neill stood there, staring down the hill.

'They are coming, Lt. Adnan,' he said quietly.

Lt Adnan stood up and shouted, 'Commence firing, rapid fire…,'

His voice was swallowed by the bark of O'Neill's Lee Enfield. 'That's one of the wee bastards gone to see the Emperor.'

I heard the loud *crack* of the rifle again accompanied by the sharp tang of cordite.

'Missed the fecker, won't miss again. There he goes. Shuffle off this mortal coil, me old pal.'

I looked up at O'Neill from the bottom of the trench. He looked down at me. 'What are you doing down there, Richard? Nothing going on down there.'

Gently, he took my elbow and raised me up. 'Here you go, plenty of them to aim for. You can't miss. A bit like the Tinkers' shooting gallery at the August fair in Aghamore. Except they're firing back. You'd better grab hold of that,' he pointed to my Lee Enfield, 'can't stare your man to death, can you?'

I looked across at Lt. Adnan, he was firing down the hill with his Webley. I picked up my rifle and sighted it on one of the leading figures coming up the hill.

He seemed keener than the rest. Charging up with his mouth open wide. I couldn't hear what he was shouting but it didn't really matter. He was a little man, slightly plump with a uniform matted with sweat.

I fired and he continued to run up the hill.

I fired again. And again. And again.

He still ran up the hill.

I looked down at my rifle, checking everything was correct and then looked up again, but I couldn't see him anymore. There were Japs in front of us and more to the right. But I couldn't see my man anywhere.

Lt Adnan was staring over to the right where a large group of Japs were starting to flank us. He put his whistle to his mouth and blew a long, piercing shrill. 'Pull back, pull back...,'

O'Neill grabbed my arm. 'It's time we left, Richard, we're done here.'

He pushed me up and out of the trench. I could see the Malays moving up the hill, firing as they did. A mortar went off in the middle of a large group of them. A bang of smoke, a volcano of earth and then nothing.

O'Neill grabbed my arm and pulled me left. I tried to follow the rest of the Malays but he wouldn't let go.

'This way, it's better for you.'

I followed him. We ran to the left along the side of the hill. Behind me I could now hear more explosions and the steady *rat-tat-tat* of a machine gun. We scrambled around the side of the hill into a small gully.

Behind and above us, we could hear the sounds of fighting and shouting and guns and explosions and war.

*

Michael O'Neill

Well this is another fine mess you've got me into Michael O'Neill. You with your volunteering and your hand held high like some old flagstaff on top of a British fort.

I raised my fist to the skies and shouted, 'You old fecker, it's been Michael O'Neill you've been playing with, pulling his wings off like you would a fly.'

Over my shoulder, Richard was following behind me like a puppy dog. Good man Richard. He doesn't know what's coming though. He hasn't been let into the secret and he never will be.

Poor fecker.

Up ahead, our narrow gully has blended into the hillside and vanished. The only cover is from the grass and a few short bushes. We must have followed it all round the side of the hill. Behind me and to the left, I can still hear the sounds of firing. Not much now though. Just the occasional burp of the machine gun and the sharp *pop* of a rifle. I sit down in a small depression carved into the hillside.

'What are we going to do now, O'Neill?'

Funny how he never calls me Michael. None of them do. It's always O'Neill this and O'Neill that.

'Well, I think we've got to find a way out of this mess, Richard. But not to worry, where there's a will, there's a way as my old ma used to say.'

He slumped down beside me, keeping his head close to the earth. 'I wish I were you O'Neill. I know I've said this before but I really wish I do.'

He looked at me with those big frightened eyes, and for a moment, just a moment, I believed him.

'Now then Richard, if you were me, what would you do?'

He thought about it for a moment and then said, 'I'd probably make a mad run for it over there.' I followed his pointing finger to a gap in the next ridge.

'Sounds like a plan, Richard my young warrior. We'll head back to town and join up with the rest of the lads.'

Above a plane circled us. I can see the small red roundels on its wings. Not one of ours then. It's never one of ours.

'How are we going to get there?'

I pulled him closer and made sure he could see. 'There, to the left of the green painted oil tanks, that road leads in to town. If we move quickly enough, we'll get out of here before the Japs reform and push on.'

Above we heard the sounds of the machine gun, followed by a series of screams and shouts.

'Time to go I think Richard.'

*

Eddie Longhurst

'Signs of movement to our right sir.' I point out the small figures about 300 yards away. 'Shall I fire sir?'

'No, wait a moment, Serjeant, where are my bloody glasses?'

'You left them in the pillbox on the beach sir. You thought we'd only be gone a day or so.'

'Yes, yes Serjeant, I'll need to check with Major Tudor. They could be Gharwalis.'

'We haven't seen hide nor hair of them since we got here, sir.'

Lt Whitehead turned to Larkin. 'You man, go to Major Tudor and ask him if he would be so kind as to join us on the right flank.'

Larkin stood there, 'Me sir?'

'Yes, you...now...hurry...go.....' He shooed Larkin away like one shoos a child. Larkin grabbed his rifle and ran back towards HQ.

I looked over toward the right. 'It doesn't look good, sir. They are setting up some sort of position out there.'

After about half an hour, we were joined by Major Tudor.

'So what's going on here? That private was in an awful state, you should train them better, Whitehead.'

'Yes, sir, I will, but at the moment, we have a problem.' He turned and pointed to the Japs down the road.

The Major coughed. 'This better be good Whitehead, I still have to finish the reports for HQ.' He raised his field glasses to his eyes. 'But they are where the Garwhalis should be, on our right. Whitehead, where are the Garwhalis?'

'I don't know sir. We haven't seen them since we got here. And the patrol we sent out couldn't find them either.'

Major Tudor started to walk towards the Japs, thought better of it and rapidly walked back to the wall of sandbags. From there, he looked through his glasses again. 'We're going to have to retreat. Our position is compromised. Whitehead, organise a few men to clear the way for our lorries.'

'How should I do that, sir?'

'Simple man, do I have to think of everything? Fix bayonets and charge them, what else? Clear the little men away from here. I'll follow up with the lorries.'

'But it's an open road sir, wouldn't it be better to flank them over there?' Whitehead pointed to a track through the lallang grass leading behind the Jap position.

'You have your orders, Whitehead. Clear them away.'

Richard Longhurst

Myself and O'Neill crept round the back of the hill. Suddenly the hillside in front of us erupted in a curtain of orange flame. I smelt the greasy tang of burning petrol.

'The bastards have set the petrol tanks on fire,' I shouted at O'Neill.

'Our baptism of fire. Will we be up to it I wonder?'

He looked behind him. It had gone quiet on the top of the hill but we knew the Japs were back there. In front of us, there was nothing but flame. 'When in doubt go forward. That's what they always told us in training, Richard. When in doubt go forward.'

I looked again. About 60 yards in front of us, the nullah, a deep ditch really, was covered in flame. Obviously, the bloody RAOC men had opened up the valves and filled it with petrol from the oil tanks to stop the Jap advance.

Behind me I heard the soft *pop* and then a loud flash and bang. Mortars. They could have been from the Japs or from our side, but at that moment, I couldn't give a toss either way.

Another explosion landed much closer to us. Both myself and O'Neill buried ourselves in the earth. Then another and another. The last was so close we could feel the blast wash over us. A lump of metal whistled past my ear and buried itself in the hillside, thin wisps of smoke coming from the hole it had made.

The hole was in the perfect shape of a cross. They say there are no atheists in a foxhole but I think that's rubbish. There are no believers in a foxhole either. Only a bunch of men hoping they could live a little longer.

'Richard, we've got to cross that ditch through the fire.'

Another bomb landed, even closer now. We both clung to the hillside, our bodies drenched in earth from the blast.

'You go first, I'll follow.'

I looked at the flames, brighter, more orange now, as if consuming the earth itself. I could see the edges of the ditch. At least six feet across. My mind flashed back to all those years ago and the old bastard serjeant shouting in my face, 'You're never going to make it, Longhurst.'

Another mortar landed next to us.

'You've got to go now Richard.'

He pushed me away from the hillside towards the wall of flames. I looked back at him. His purple scarf was now a torn, sweat-gorged rag around his neck. He was waving his arms, forcing me forward. I turned toward the flame, white now in the centre with orange and red flashes at the edges. I could hear the crackle of the burning petrol and feel the searing heat.

I turned back to O'Neill. An arc of earth was just covering his body from another mortar.

I started to run toward the flames. Moving forward, one step after another, running forward. The heat coming closer. The reds and yellows and oranges throwing tongues of flame toward me. O'Neill was beside me now, running too, still with a smile playing across his lips.

I saw the edge of the ditch.

I saw the edge of the ditch.

I saw the edge of the ditch.

The next moment I felt a huge shove in my back and I was in the air. I don't know if I jumped or stumbled or heaved myself across but I went through the flames. I felt no heat, no burning, but there was a strange white light. A light that seemed to wrap around me, covering me.

I landed on the other side, tumbled on to my hands and knees, tearing what was left of my smoking uniform. I rolled over and over, putting out the flames on my khakis, rolling as far as I could from the flaming hell of the ditch.

I picked myself up and limped away from the flames. The only desire I had then was to get away, to get as far away as I could.

Around me, the grass covered hill sloped lazily up to a gentle summit. Here, there were no shells, no explosions, no sound.

It was as if I had been carried throughout the flames to another world.

I turned back. The flames still engulfed the hillside behind me, a wall of flame separating heaven from hell.

All my hair on one side was scorched. I moved my hand across my ear. It was crispy and charred but there was no pain. I guess that would come later.

I looked back into the flames, scanning the length of the orange curtain for O'Neill. I expected him to emerge gracefully from it, land on his feet and jog slowly up to me, saying, 'Well, that was a great craic, wasn't it Richard?'

But I didn't see him.

The flames seemed to be lessening in intensity now but still he didn't come. I thought I caught a glimpse of him for one moment. Something large had flared up in the centre of the flames. a spear of light and a dark shadow, but nothing emerged.

A terrible tiredness came over me and I sat down there in the middle of the hillside. Above me the sun had gone a very pale yellow.

I looked back at the flames and I could hear them now. Crackling, reaching for the sun, soaring in to the air only to vanish in one last gasp of heat.

And then for me came darkness.

Chapter 25

Eddie Longhurst

'Right Serjeant Longhurst, are the men ready?'

Lt. Whitehead was nervous; his left hand lined up with the seam of his trousers in regulation pattern but the index finger beat a constant tattoo on his leg.

I adjusted the chin strap of my helmet. '13 Platoon all present and correct, sir.' I looked across at the platoon: Teale, Larkin, Dawson, Rogers, Mytholmroyd, Dwyer and the rest were lined up like marathon runners at the start of a race.

'Fix bayonets men.' Lt. Whitehead whispered.

12 bayonets rasped out of twelve scabbards and I heard the locking sounds as they were fixed into place at the end of the Lee Enfields. Reg Dwyer was still messing about with his. I walked over and watched his hands shaking as he tried to attach the bayonet to its locking ring.

'Can't make it fit Eddie, maybe it's broken.'

'Bloody hell, Reg, here…,' I snatched the Lee Enfield and slotted the Bayonet into the ring. It snapped into place with an easy, satisfying click. I tossed it back to Reg who dropped it on the tarmac of the road.

All the others looked around as the rifle clattered to the ground.

'Quiet that man,' shouted Lt. Whitehead.

Reg bent down and retrieved his rifle. 'Sorry Eddie, sorry…,'

Lt Whitehead looked down at the line of men. 'Right then, when I blow my whistle at…,' he looked down at his watch, 'Exactly 1.30, we are going to take the position with a bayonet charge.' He pointed down the road about 200 yards away. 'It's time to chase the little men off, chaps.'

I followed his arm to where it pointed down the road. The Japs were in behind us. Not in force yet though, I hoped.

'Ready men. Steady men.' Lt. Whitehead raised the whistle to his lips. A drop of sweat dripped from my nose on to the road where it splashed and sizzled on the hot tarmac. So this is it, what you've waited and trained and wanted all your life to do. Here it fuckin' is.

'Men, I suggest we walk for the first 100 yards and then when I blow my whistle again we will charge. 12 Platoon will be laying down covering fire so the little blighters should be keeping their heads down.'

He sucked in a vast balloon of warm air and blew his whistle. Unholstering his Webley, he stuck it out in front of him and began to walk forward.

I followed, looking down the line to check all the others were walking too. They stretched out in a line across the road. Bayonets at the ready, walking forward like they were on the parade ground at Tanglin. Even bloody Larkin looked like a soldier right then.

God, was I proud of these men, my mates, my friends, my family.

Reg was beginning to fall back. 'Dwyer, keep up,' I shouted over the heads of the others. He doubled his pace and brought the line back to a lovely straight edge again.

Looks perfect, text book.

Another drop of sweat fell from my nose. I stared at the Jap position. There was no sign of movement yet. Nothing to show anybody was there at all. Maybe they had already gone while we were forming up?

I don't know and I didn't care.

The point was to be here, to be now, at this moment, advancing towards an enemy ready to kill them. I looked across at the wonderful straight line. The men's boots beat a beautiful rhythm on the tarmacked road.

I knew then this is what I'd been born to do.

*

Reg Dwyer

Lord protect me, this isn't why I joined the army. I only went into the recruitment office because there were no jobs and the kids had to be fed and clothed and schooled and Marjorie had said it would be a good idea and her brother had been in the army and loved it and we could leave Stockport and finally get out of the place.

Eddie was looking at me again. He knows I'm the weak link. I hope he won't shoot me. I read about them shooting people who didn't charge during the Great War. Eddie's staring at me, like I was nothing. I hear Lt. Whitehead talking but I don't hear the words. All the others start to pull their bayonets out. I reach for mine but it won't come out. It's stuck in the scabbard. I tug it harder and then harder and harder. It still won't come out.

God, it's hot. I wish this would end.

I look down and realise there was a tab holding the bayonet in place. I release the piece of khaki and grab the handle of the bayonet. God it feels cold. It's like the sun had never shone on it.

Never.

I tug the handle of the bayonet and it comes up in my hand. I hear the sound of the metal against the lining of the scabbard. Shivers run down my spine at the noise followed by a long trickle of sweat.

Marjorie, I miss you Marjorie. I wish you were here to hold my hand. Help me throughout this Marjorie. Help me do this as you helped me do everything else in my life.

My hand was shaking as I tried to fix the bayonet in its mounting. It wouldn't go in. It didn't fit. I pulled it away and looked at it again. Sweat dripped from my forehead onto my shirt front. I tried to force it to lock. It wouldn't go in again. I could see Eddie looking at me. He's coming over. I try to fit the bayonet in again. He's standing in front of me.

'Can't make it fit Eddie, maybe it's broken.'

'Bloody hell, Reg, here…,'

He snatched the rifle from me and took my bayonet. In one easy movement he slotted the Bayonet down the rifle and into its mounting ring. I heard it snap into place.

Suddenly the rifle was flying in the air towards me. I reached out my arms to catch it but it hit my forearms and tumbled to the ground. The sound echoed in my helmet. I saw all the others turn to look at the rifle as it clattered on the floor.

Lt. Whitehead shouted, 'Quiet that man.'

I bent down and picked up my rifle, 'Sorry Eddie, sorry…,'

He stared at me for a year and then went back to his position on the far right of the line. I looked across at the rest of the men. They were all looking straight ahead. I lifted the tip of my helmet where it had fallen forward and stood like them, hoping it looked right.

Lt Whitehead was saying something but I couldn't hear what it was. Down the road in front of me was nothing there except a few sandbags blocking the next junction.

Suddenly, Larkin on my right started moving forward. I looked and everybody else was doing the same thing.

I started walking holding the rifle in front of me. Lord it was heavy.

I'm sorry Marjorie. Sorry for you and the kids. Sorry for being who I am. Sorry for those girls in the clubs but you were so far away and I was so lonely. Sorry for not being with you. Sorry for you not being with me.

Maybe if I held back, the others would cop it when the firing started. I slowed my pace slightly, taking shorter steps. That way Larkin would be in front of me on the left and Teale on the right.

'Dwyer, keep up!'

It was Eddie's voice. I ran faster to come up to the same level as Larkin and Teale. I looked along the line. They were all staring straight ahead.

I turned my head to look at the end of the road. Perhaps the Japs had gone. Perhaps they had seen us forming up and decided it was time to scarper. Sense being better than valour or whatever the words are.

There was no movement there. But we were getting closer now.

*

Richard Longhurst

When I woke up I was cold, very cold. The sun was high in the sky but it could have been the next day for all I knew.

The flames were still burning in the ditch but less fiercely now. I could see through to the opposite hillside. I looked for O'Neill but there was nothing there. It was as if he had never existed.

There was no sign of the Japs either. All that remained were large holes in the earth where the mortars had landed.

And then I saw it lying on the ground, next to a small bush. It was on this side of the flames but God knows how it had got here.

It was torn and dirty and creased. A large smudge of oil blemished it on one end. But the purple was still bright and clear. I picked it up and tied it around my neck.

On my right, the ocean sparkled in the light. A few ships steamed away from shore, accompanied by smaller boats. A small flotilla heading out to sea. Above them swarmed a circle of planes, buzzing like wasps around a nest. One of the wasps broke away and dived down towards the flotilla. The largest ship suddenly zagged to the left and a large splash of sea drenched its side.

I stumbled down the gentle slope of the hill and reached a road on the other side going toward the city. Smoke rose lazily over the rooftops but there were no soldiers in sight.

I walked on down the road. On either side, old black and white houses flanked it, like some beautiful dream of peaceful suburbia. I expected to see a postman on his bike delivering letters, a milkman walking his horse on his rounds and the local bobby waxing his mustache as he ambled by on his beat.

I saw nothing.

As I got near to the city, the black and whites gave way to godowns and warehouses. Here, there were more signs of life and of death. A Sikh soldier draped lazily over a hedge, his stomach dripping towards the ground. The soles of his boots, brand new, the maker's mark still clear on the bottom, staring up at the sky.

Further on, an Austin abandoned beside the road, its back seats filled with opened and rifled suitcases. Next to it, the front door of a shophouse tilting drunkenly on its hinges. Inside I could hear a few voices amidst the wreckage.

I walked on and met a few more soldiers lying in the pavement, one of them was clutching an empty bottle of Johnnie Walker.

'G'Day mate.'

I ignored him.

He wobbled up to a sitting position, as if to stand, but thought better of it and fell back against the wall. 'A bloody good day mate...,' he mumbled to nobody in particular.

At the next crossroads, a black staff car turned the corner and screeched to a stop. The doors opened and out piled a group of staff officers, red tabs like warning signs on their shoulders. They checked all around them, before a grey-haired man stepped out, quickly adjusted his cap and tucked his swagger stick under his arm. He hustled his way into the docks. They ran after him without noticing me or anything else.

I walked on.

More abandoned cars, more wrecked shops, more looted suitcases, more corpses lying in the street. I passed a woman dressed all in black as if she had been preparing to mourn her own death. She stared at me saying nothing.

As I stared back at her, an officer on horseback rode up to me.

'You there, where's your rifle?'

'Don't know sir.'

'Where's your regiment?'

'Don't know sir.'

He looked me up and down and said more softly this time, 'Which regiment are you, son?'

It seemed such a long time ago, the regiment and being a soldier and marching and polishing and drinking and being together. 'It's the Manchester's sir…I think.'

'You think? They are concentrating over at the Canning Factory in Kallang. You should join them. The war's over now. We signed a truce. It's all over.'

He dug his heels into the side of the horse and galloped up the road the way I had come. I didn't have time to ask him where this factory was.

I guess it didn't matter.

Nothing mattered any more.

*

Eddie Longhurst

I hear the whistle blown by Lt. Whitehead and break into a jog. The others follow me, running with their packs banging against their backs. I look across at the line. It's more ragged now.

'Keep the line straight lads. Come up, Dwyer.'

I see Reg try to run faster but he's not really up to it. I look ahead to where the Japs are. Still nothing. To our left, I can hear the sound of firing. Who's it from? At the end of the road, tiny spurts of dust rise from the road. It's our covering fire.

I hope the stupid bastards stop soon or we'll all be killed. Stupid fuckers couldn't hit a whale from two yards. At least, it seems to be keeping the Jap heads down.

Up ahead, Lt. Whitehead is firing his Webley. God knows what he's doing. He's still miles away from the Japs and there's nothing to fire at. Then I see what the stupid fucker has been doing. There's a squad of Japs and they seem to be moving something off to the left into the lallang grass. They are pulling away. We've chased the fuckers off.

Lt Whitehead starts racing toward them, still firing the Webley. I look across at the men and scream at the top of my lungs, 'Charge! Get the Bastards!'

Teale screams like he was on the obstacle course and suddenly we are all running.

And then it all slows down.

I know I'm running as fast as I can go. I know Lt. Whitehead is racing away in front of me. I know the Webley is firing. I know the Japs are pulling out. But it's all slowed down and I'm moving as if swimming in clear treacle.

Lt. Whitehead falls down. I think he's just tripped up. Teale moves over to help him to his feet and he falls over too.

And then I'm aware there are other bullets hitting the road around their feet. Bullets coming from over on the left. I look up and see the Japs melting into the lallang. One minute they were there and the next minute they had vanished.

The lads are still running though. Larkin is helping Teale up and he goes down too.

I shout, 'The left, watch the left…' But nobody hears me. They just keep running towards the empty Jap position. Rogers has fallen now too. Nobody is helping him though.

I run on with the rest of them. More bullets hit the ground at my feet. Then I turn and I see Reg still running behind me. Good old Reg, always keeps going.

And then he starts to fall and I think he's been hit too, but no he keeps going and is running toward me again.

After three steps, he stops like he's run enough and can't run anymore. He just stops there, in the middle of the road. I shout to him to keep going toward the Jap sandbags but he doesn't move.

I watch as his knees sag and his body goes loose and he collapses to his right. He falls slowly to the ground and his left arm reaches up toward the sky. Then it falls to his side and he doesn't move any more.

'Fire into the lallang on the left. Jap machine gun there.' I know it's me shouting but it doesn't feel like my voice. It's someone else using my throat and my body. There's firing all around me now as each man blazes away.

I look back down the road the way we had come.

Lumps of khaki lay strewn across the road. I count them. Seven lumps.

I shout, 'Enough, enough…' The firing ceases and all goes quiet.

There's a fire in the lallang, blowing dark smoke across the road, drenching the bodies in its fog.

I see Teale and Larkin and Lt. Whitehead lying furthest away. None of them moving. A little group of three khaki shapes, pressed together like lumps of plasticine. Not three bodies but one.

I feel a sharp pinch and look down to see a red ant crawling across my skin. I pinch it between my forefingers and drop the dead carcass on the road.

I look up again. Four more bodies lay between the group that was Whitehead, Teale and Larkin and me. Closest is Reg, his arm still lying by his side.

I stumble over to him. He's staring up at the sky with the same daft look on his face he always had. A slight smile across his lips and a lock of hair sticking out from beneath his helmet.

Behind me I heard the revving of a lorry. A screech of brakes and the clang of boots.

'Get these men in the back of the lorry, Serjeant.' It was Major Tudor. He was looking everywhere, his eyes popping out of his head and his Webley waving around at the end of its lanyard.

'Serjeant, didn't you hear me? We have to get out of here before the Japs come back. It's not safe.'

I could see the round face and the brown, clipped mustache. I watched the lips moving but once again I couldn't hear what they were saying.

I was pushed to one side as two squaddies picked up Reg. One took the hands and the other the feet. They carried him to the back of the lorry and flung him in.

I found myself walking toward the lorry. I looked in the back and saw the mound of bodies all thrown together, inseparable.

I climbed up the step and sat in the back, the bodies at my feet.

Major Tudor stared at me, and I stared back, before looking away.

'Drive off man. Let's get out of here now. Move.'

The lorry slowly moved away down the road. I looked back to where we had begun our charge. It was empty. No soldiers. No Japs. No sign we had ever been there.

Just a road, somewhere in the East of Singapore.

*

Richard Longhurst

It seemed like I had been walking for years. Nobody stopped me, nobody even talked to me. I'd walked through town past the bombed-out buildings, past the drunken groups of Aussie soldiers, past the buses parked sideways across the street.

All I remembered were the smells. Smoke and fire and burning, all tinged with the pungent aroma of alcohol, like a pub in the morning before it's been cleaned.

I could see columns of black smoke coming from the river. They brought the different smell of burning tires from a rubbish dump.

I passed the cathedral and wondered if Owens was there. On the lawn outside, there were ambulances parked all over the place at strange angles, as if nobody cared any more.

I walked into the cathedral and saw soldiers lying across the tiled floor, some even piled next to the altar. Nurses were rushing around giving them water, tearing bandages, hands reddened with blood.

One came up to me, 'Can I help you soldier?'

She was an older woman, still looking fresh and clean in her uniform despite the chaos around her.

'Let me look at that head of yours. Burnt yourself, did you?'

She started to run her fingers across my ears. For the first time, I felt pain and pulled my head away.

'It's going to hurt but you'll live. Let me bandage it for you.'

She led me over to one of the cathedral's pews, pushed me down into it and started to clean my ear.

'It's all over now. The Japanese will be here soon. I'm glad it's finished. Too many boys have died. Too many mothers have lost sons. You'll be alright though. However, you will need a new haircut soon.' She talked as she worked. I felt the cool softness of a cream being smoothed across my ear and my head. Then she started to bandage me up, wrapping me quickly in some clean, white bandages.

'We've run out of tape so one of these will have to do I'm afraid.' She showed me a large baby's nappy pin and fixed it to the bandage around my head. She stepped back and admired her work.

'Rather fetching and manly, even if I do say so myself.'

'Nurse?'

'It's Matron actually.'

'Is Mr Owens here?'

'You mean the deacon?' She turned and looked over the throngs of patients and nurses and soldiers and beds. 'He's over there.'

Next to the pulpit, I could see Owens kneeling down with his head close to the ear of a soldier, whispering something. Then he knelt upright, looked down at the soldier, kissed his stole and bowed.

With a gentleness I'd never seen in Owens, he reached over and let his two fingers softly close the eyelids of the soldier. Once again, he bowed his head and I could see his lips moving in prayer.

'Do you know him? Shall I call him over?'

'No, not now.' My ear started to throb and I put my hand on it to try to make it stop.

'Don't do that.' She slapped my hand as one does with a child. Someone called her from the apse. 'I have to go. You sit here quietly. It's all over now.'

'One more thing. Do you know where the Manchester's are?'

'The Manchesters?' She turned to another orderly carrying water. 'Jim, the Manchesters, where are they?'

'Over near Kallang, I think.'

I nodded my thanks to her and she rushed off to treat another patient.

I got up, but immediately sat down again. Take it easy, take it slowly lad. I looked around the cathedral for a while, getting my breath back. The nurses were still rushing around, carrying bottles and blood and towels. The doctors were still quietly going about their work, examining the injured and the dying. Owens was still whispering his prayers to those who would listen.

I rested for a minute or so and got up again, stumbling out of the cathedral into the bright sunlight and the smell of cordite and burning rubber in the air.

*

Eddie Longhurst

'Pull yourself together.' Shelley was leaning in really close to me, snarling in my ear. 'Set an example, Lance Serjeant Longhurst.'

He pulled away from my head and stared down at me.

I was sitting with my back to one of the piers of the Canning Factory where the regiment was assembling.

'But…,'

'But, fucking what? Do you want to be like them?' He jerked his head towards the rest of the men who were sitting on the floor in groups, smoking and talking, their clothes disheveled, helmets and rifles thrown in the corner, a few had even fallen asleep, their heads resting on packing cases of tinned pineapple. 'You're better than them. You're a Serjeant. You're a Manchester Serjeant.'

'It's Larkin and Teale and Reg...,' As I said their names, I saw them falling, Reg's arm lifting toward the sky, Lt. Whitehead firing his Webley, Reg stopping. 'Why did he stop? Why did he stop?'

'Do you think you're the first one who's lost men?'

'But it was so stupid, we could have...,'

'War is stupid, or haven't you worked it out yet? It's not some fucking game you play because you want to be men.' He rapped me on the side of the head with his fist. 'We fought, we lost. But you falling to pieces isn't going to help this lot.' His voice softened. 'If we go to pieces now, we're all fucked. We've got to make them Manchesters again, not the fucking rabble they've become.'

I saw RSM Whatmough march up to us. He was dressed as if he had just come from a march past; uniform creased, boots shining, cap tilted to the right. 'You ready, Serjeant Shelley?'

'Yes, RSM.'

'What's he like?' He jerked his head towards me.

'Fine, RSM. Longhurst, is going to register all the stragglers as they come in, aren't you, Serjeant?'

I nodded my head.

'Tell him to tidy hisself up, Serjeant Shelley, can't have him looking like a tramp, can we Serjeant?'

'You heard the RSM, Longhurst. Get yourself looking like a Tad, then take over from Kelly.' He pointed to a stack of pineapple cases constructed to look like a desk. Behind it Kelly was interviewing all the squaddies who had been separated from their platoons.

'Right, it's time, Serjeant Shelley.'

Shelley leant forward and whispered in my ear, 'Remember who you are.'

I watched as they both pulled down their tunics, adjusted their caps and marched towards the groups of men sitting on the floor of the factory.

'Right, you shower of shit,' bellowed RSM Whatmough, 'let's be having you.'

For a moment, all the men looked up at Whatmough and did nothing.

'Lively, now, lively.'

Then they started to move. Getting up and forming themselves into lines. Shelley was going around and kicking those that were asleep.

'Wakey, wakey, tosspot. Time to get up.' He kicked one soldier hard in the ribs. The man sat up with a jerk and immediately began to slide out of his bunk before realising he was lying on cases of Pineapple chunks and falling to the floor.

'Let's be having you,' shouted Whatmough at the top of his lungs, 'Straighten up there. Button your collar, private. Where's your belt soldier? Well, go and fetch it man, I'm not having a slovenly soldier on one of my parades.'

I got up, fastened my buttons, pulled down my jacket and straightened my army issue shorts. I saw a fleck of blood on my boot. Was it Reg? Or Larkin? Or Teale? I didn't know.

'That's it, eyes forward, Attenshun.' It was Whatmough bellowing again like he was on the parade ground at York. Perhaps he was, in his own head.

I rubbed my boots on the back of my calves. I looked down again and the spot of blood wasn't there. Maybe it had never been there.

Shelley was right, I had to try to keep it together now. I pushed my shoulders back, stiffened my back and marched across to take over from Kelly.

*

Richard Longhurst

I don't know how I made it to the factory. I just kept walking towards Kallang Aerodrome, one foot in front of the other, one foot in front of the other.

Nobody stopped me, nobody even talked to me. There were plenty of squaddies around. Some were lying in the middle of Beach Road, fast asleep. Some were drinking, empty whiskey bottles making a glass fortress around them. Others were standing there, doing nothing, staring into space.

I seemed to be the only one going anywhere, even though I wasn't sure where I was going.

I met one captain close to the river. 'Sir, do you know where the Manchester's are?'

He had the hammer and anvil flashes of the ordinance corps on his shoulder. He looked right past me, out into the ocean. I thought he hadn't heard me.

'Sir, can you tell me where the Manchesters are?' I repeated.

He continued to stare out to sea. His eyes weren't focussed on anything though, just staring, lost.

I stumbled on.

As I said, I don't know how I got there. One minute I was walking near the Aerodrome and the next I was standing in front of a large poster with 'Del Monte Pineapples, Good for you every day!' Next to the can was a picture of a cherubic young English girl with red cheeks, a big smile and her hair dressed in pony tails. In her hands she held a bowl full of pineapple chunks, holding them out, offering them to me.

I looked past the sign and saw a long, flat warehouse with the Del Monte sign proudly displayed. I walked up the long drive leading to an open door. A few soldiers ran past me, in an immense hurry.

I got to the entrance and peered inside. Sitting behind a desk made out of cases of pineapple was my brother. He was staring down at a bunch of papers. I wanted to turn away, to run from here and him and the army and the regiment and the war, but my legs wouldn't move.

I knew what I had to do.

It was time to be somebody else, not sniveling Richard Longhurst anymore.

Time to be me.

I marched up to him as smartly as I could. Still he didn't look up.

'Private Michael O'Neill 9253418, reporting for duty, Serjeant.'

Slowly, his head came up and he looked at me for the first time. I don't know what was going on in his mind. His eyes were dull and lifeless. There was no recognition there, no sense of brotherhood.

I watched as he shrugged his shoulders and went back to his papers, shuffling them into some sort of order.

Finally, he found the one he wanted. He scanned down a list of names until he came to one and ticked it. 'Private O'Neill, reporting for duty?'

'Yes, Serjeant.'

'Go over there to the medical orderly and get your dressing checked, private. When you're finished report back to your platoon and await further orders.'

'Yes, Serjeant.'

He seemed to want to say more, to ask me a question, but he shrugged his shoulders and went back to shuffling his papers.

I took a deep breath and walked over to the medical clearing station.

I knew then I had changed. I wasn't the man I was before. It had been coming for a long time, but the war had finally made it happen.

I was a new man ready to face a new world.

Chapter 26

Michael O'Neill
May 1998

He felt the weight of the wreath in his hand. Such a pointless waste of flowers he thought. These men, these friends of his were too long gone to appreciate flowers. They had been lying here for so long, all alone in this foreign soil. Nobody had remembered them.

Even he had forgotten the details of their faces. What did Larkin look like? All he remembered was a pair of wire-rimmed glasses being pushed back onto the bridge of a nose.

He looked up at the sky. Where was God when these men needed him? Or anyone needed him?

No matter.

He hadn't believed in God since that day. Later, at the camps in Thailand, he knew there was no God, just men. Men who could love and hate, sometimes both at the same time. But that was the story of a different time and place. He wasn't ready to face that yet.

Not yet.

He walked along the line of the gravestones. Teale and Larkin, Lloyd and the new lad, Dobson. He had only been in Singapore for two months when he was killed. Lt. Whitehead was next, a nice bloke with the light stupidity that is a product of the better type of public school.

And then, next to him, lay Reg.

He looked down at the white headstone. Lance Corporal Reginald Dwyer 9253722 was inscribed on the memorial, above a large fleur de lys, the badge of the Manchester Regiment. Even in death he was always a Tad. At the bottom was a small afterthought. 'Always remembered by his wife and children.'

At least, somebody kept Reg alive somewhere. Maybe he had grandsons and grand-daughters now. Reg would never see them, never hold them in his arms, never write them letters.

He moved toward the last gravestone in the row. He bowed for a moment and just let his head rest on his chest. Slowly he leant forward and placed the wreath in front of the gravestone.

'Pte. Richard Longhurst 9253418.' He wondered who they had put here instead of him. Some poor bastard who hadn't got a name or a face. Another unknown soldier that was going to have a name whether he wanted one or not.

Another casualty of a war everybody but him had forgotten.

A sharp gust of wind blew from over the half-built racecourse. Suddenly the banging and hammering became louder, clearer.

He looked again at his name etched so clearly on the white stone and he knew Michael O'Neill would have been proud of him. He had lived his life, the one he talked and dreamed about. He had done what he wanted to do, become who he wanted to be, without fear or favour.

He stepped back from the line of graves and quietly whispered, 'I hope I did what was right. It was so long ago.'

And then the words came to him. Words he knew so well but had never really known until that moment. He lifted his head and spoke to all of them lying there:

'The weight of this sad time we must obey;
Speak what we feel, not what we ought to say.
The oldest hath borne most: we that are young
Shall never see so much, nor live so long.'

He took out the purple scarf, still grimy after all these years, tied it around his neck once more, pulled his jacket tight around his shrunken chest and walked slowly down the hill.

Michael O'Neill, the famous actor, didn't look back.

21817109R00174

Printed in Great Britain
by Amazon